MW01226218

Hidenor Hair

ÉVA ARROS

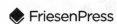 FriesenPress

Suite 300 - 990 Fort St
Victoria, BC, V8V 3K2
Canada

www.friesenpress.com

Copyright © 2021 by Éva Arros
First Edition — 2021

All rights reserved.

Original artwork by Éva Arros

No part of this publication may be reproduced in any form, or by any means, electronic or mechanical, including photocopying, recording, or any information browsing, storage, or retrieval system, without permission in writing from FriesenPress.

ISBN
978-1-5255-9602-5 (Hardcover)
978-1-5255-9601-8 (Paperback)
978-1-5255-9603-2 (eBook)

1. FICTION, LESBIAN

Distributed to the trade by The Ingram Book Company

Hide nor Hair

CHAPTER 1

On November 29, 2001, around nine-thirty in the evening, amidst fog and icy drizzle, I was suddenly transported into another dimension. In layman's terms, I died. I got hit by a truck as I crossed the street near the intersection of Sherbrooke and Saint-Laurent, in Montréal. I did not hear the truck coming, nor did I see it in my peripheral vision. I certainly did not smell it. There was no taste of blood in my mouth. I felt nothing at all. I do not remember anything about the instant of my death. This is probably a good thing, since I have always wanted to die without suffering.

There was no tunnel with a beacon of light waiting for me at the end. While I was still alive, I sometimes wondered if this tunnel really existed. I'm still left to wonder. Just because I did not experience it, I can't claim that the tunnel is a mere story invented to make the living feel better about dying. Everything is a mystery to me. I know even less than when I was alive. Now, even though I have been stripped of my physical body, my "I" has, in a way I can't explain, remained intact. I don't know how long this phenomenon will last, so I thought I better tell my story before it disappears into nothingness.

As remarkable and unfortunate as it was for me, my death made nary a dent in the big, global scheme of things. So, even though the act of dying is a relatively common, daily phenomenon on Earth, you can be assured that no one else but me dies in this particular story. Nothing is lost; nothing is created. This is the only law that I have retained from high-school physics. Everything moves, changes, decomposes, and recomposes constantly. But only from a time-based point of view. Otherwise, the present moment flutters eternally.

From my non-vantage point, I have yet to grasp the concept of eternity. I am suspended, yes, in some unexplainable way. I am existing in a non-existing sort of way, until the fire of my desire might sizzle enough to materialize me into the next illusion. Maybe.

Given the current exponential population growth on planet Earth, it is possible that there is a giant reincarnation sale going on. If so, it would seem to be the ideal opportunity for me to tempt my fate and get reproduced on the beautiful blue planet. I am not in a hurry. My time, if such a time exists, has not come yet. Earthly time, as I remember, was said to be accelerating. Many also said that the population explosion, the abuse of non-renewable natural resources, all fuelled by limitless, ruthless greed, was sweeping its inhabitants, two-, four-, or a thousand-legged, sentient or not, into the abyss of total annihilation. This is fertile ground to sweat one's bad karmas out. If such a thing as waiting exists, I'd rather hold out for a better offer or look for another planet.

When I am ready, if I ever will be, I see my planet of choice as interesting, providing lots of entertainment for the senses. Maybe we can even add more senses than the five or six there are on Earth. My planet will be populated with an ecologically balanced number of caring, sexy, and smart individuals with a healthy sense of humour. Homogeneous standards of beauty will not be important. Bring on the unusual, the diverse, the warty, hirsute, and the multicoloured, including iridescent!

✴ ✴ ✴

This story begins about six months before my physical death. It starts in early June 2001. I woke up alone. My girlfriend Julie had suddenly left the warmth of our conjugal bed, during the night or at the first light of dawn, I am not sure. All I know is that I woke up, reached over, and her side of the bed was cold. She must have taken every precaution for me not to have anticipated this feat of conjuring on her part. We had been together all the time, even when going to the toilet, sometimes. I am a very light sleeper, like a rabbit. Still, she somehow womanaged to slip away from under my embrace. She didn't even leave a note.

At the time, we had been living on a tiny island lost in the Salish Sea off the Canadian West Coast. Apparently, Julie had ceased to be happy. I only found out later that her dissatisfaction had nothing to do with me, really, or even with us. But at the time, I did not know this. I could not have known. Not yet. All I knew is that I was shattered. I got obsessed with trying to figure out what I might have done wrong. For a few agonizing days, I wandered around, racking my brain. I fed the animals and tended the garden like a zombie. I don't remember eating anything, even though I probably did. Or maybe I didn't eat at all. For sure I slept little, wandering at night like a mad ghost. I have very little recollection of those first few days. I was on automatic survival mode.

Meanwhile, the world got on without me. A man known as the "*Roi du tatouage,*" or "Tattoo King," was arrested for drunk-driving in Québec twice in the space of four hours, and in two different cars. Miss Kamasutra 2001 got elected in some hick town. The scandal of the flesh-eating bananas was running its course, and Milosevic was delivered in front of the La Haye Tribunal. Julie and I never read newspapers. Lost as we were on our island, we savages obviously didn't have cable either. Radio reception was sporadic at best. Some news items just have a way of being known without one's consent.

To make our isolation even more extreme, we often spoke French between ourselves. It was my first language. For Julie, it was mostly her second one, but she liked the challenge.

Julie could have gone anywhere. As far as I knew, if she had the money, she could even have gone to the moon. I took our ancient, dog-eared and shopworn world atlas down from the cobweb-decorated shelf. I blew the dust off and slowly flipped the pages, looking for ideas.

When I got to Japan, I remembered what she'd said one day, with her Anglophone accent—and I translate—"You know, Claire, we should go to … how you say 'Japan'?"

"*Japon.*"

"We have to go to the '*Japon.*'"

"Okay … but why Japan?"

"Dunno. To learn one other language? It is good for the brain."

"But Julie, beautiful Julie, Japanese is one of the hardest languages on earth to learn! It's up there with Hungarian. Why can't we go to Hungary, instead? I might even have some distant relatives there. And it's in Europe. The cultural shock would be less intense…"

3

"I have already been in Hungary. That was a long time ago, but it's done. I think the Japan is a good idea. You know, if you don't want to come, I can go with myself…"

I should have seen the red flag with this last sentence of hers. But at the time, innocent as I was, I reassured myself with the idea that, when the time came, we would go together anyway. Besides, we did not have the money yet.

Before she met me, Julie loved to project herself to unknown places. She told me she used to spin a globe with her eyes closed, point to a place, any place, open her eyes, pack her bags, and head out the next morning. She had hitchhiked all over South America with a girlfriend, working wherever they could. New Zealand and Australia were also on her must-see list. I love travelling too. Or rather, I would have loved to but never did for lack of funds. Julie could have given me a chance to see the world on a tiny budget. She knew how. But for some mysterious reason, she never mentioned wanting to go anywhere with me. Her idea about Japan had come out of the blue. That was one other reason I did not pay much attention then. Usually, she would say she was content to cocoon. I figured it must have been a mere stopover, a temporary rest in a comfortable love nest in between her wanderings.

Julie. She abhorred profoundly the slightest trace of femininity on her person. She used to say that nature had played a big joke on her and given her the wrong attributes, some I could have made much better use of than her. She had lots to be embarrassed by, according to her own standards. The natural pitch of her voice rang in a pearly mezzo-soprano. Her hands were delicate like a white-collar's, her throbbing throat was smooth like a swan's, and—oh glory! —her divine bosom floated like candy-floss. She had all the right curves in the right places. Oh my! Julie was the physical womanifestation of the Goddess herself in all her female glory! She hated it all.

My favourite of all her delicious attributes, if I had to choose only one, would incontestably be her full, soft breasts. They would have looked absolutely scrumptious resting in a satiny white bra, edged with crisp lace, from Bruges. In the summer, her round, sun-licked orbs reminded me of brown eggs that could nestle in a giant titanium-white Styrofoam egg carton. However, Julie never wore bras. Not for a second, not even in play. In all fairness, I have to admit that she didn't actually need a bra. She had no use for push-ups, or push-togethers, nor to have her heart crossed. Julie's orbs would hold their own, supported by her powerful pectoral muscles. Unfortunately for both Julie and I, as delicious as her breasts might have appeared to my venerating eyes, they were attached to her naked torso, not mine. Julie could simply not stand the fact that she had to drag her own orbs around wherever she was going. She hated her breasts so much that I had to get special permission to touch them. Some days, I never got to caress them at all.

I wish I had known at that time what I know now. Then she would have been free to pursue her illusive fantasy, as she set out to do, undisturbed. She could choose to spend her time only with people who completely understood her, who wouldn't ask any questions. And me, I could have stayed on my island, continuing to live my peaceful life with our gang of Girlz, Sam the Cat, Ralph the Pig, and our garden without a name. Everything. Alive! I had been living an idyllic life. I thought Julie and I were together in this idyll. Instead, we were merely leading parallel lives, me alone on my island of personal bliss, and Julie biding her time, charging her batteries, and waiting for the perfect opportunity to sever the ties that had held us precariously together.

Julie's leaving opened my Pandora's Box. All my treasures spilled out and spoiled into a steaming compost heap of questioning and unrest. I corrupted my own chance to enjoy complete happiness, ever. Even my own death, six months later, did not offer me deliverance from evil. My death ended up being a simple transition, just another anonymous door—another box. Death as absolute rest in peace? Certainly not. And it's not because I had led a particularly wicked life. I am not burning my sins off in the eternal flames of Hell. Nor am I fluttering, lyre in hand, waiting to be admitted into a white-clouded Heaven full of floating, happy souls. I am simply nowhere. I have a sense that where I am and am not has nothing to do with how I have lived my short life. If I had anything to bet with, I would put all my money on the idea that I would be "here," in the same "place," even if I had had an average life, living according to average standards of law-abiding straightness and conventional morality. It's entirely possible that I would be at this same non-place even if I had gone to Church every Sunday and holiday.

I haven't the faintest clue how to find peace and rest. Maybe this is why I am not ready to apply for a posting in this illusion created by desire, also paradoxically called life. Besides, even if I wanted to reincarnate, I have no idea how I am supposed to go about it. There is no guidebook for re-entry to Planet Earth, or any other planet in this no-time nowhere. There is no information booth, no toll-free number to call just to reach a well-meaning, badly paid waif pretending to be able to help me with her heavily-accented English all the way from some exotic tourist destination. I am suspended within an infinite sea of nothingness. On Earth, this may be called "The Waiting." Religious aficionados might call it" Limbo."

✴   ✴   ✴

After my zombie phase, following the initial shock of Julie's disappearance, I went through denial. I refused to accept any possibilities as to why she would have needed to leave. We had our little hand-made abode, the garden, the animals... We also had some excellent women friends living on the women's land nearby. They called themselves the Naiads. There was Calypso, sensuous, complex on the inside, and practical outside. Then there was Minerva, the gentle and sensitive artist-soul, and Diane the feisty Amazon, superbly robust. And funny! And all the other women of the Naiads' commune too, making up a core group, a covenant, of thirteen souls. To top it all off, there were the nomads too.

Every year, at the first signs of spring, the nomads would come to the Naiads' commune next door. They would arrive from the city in hordes, flutters, droves, gangs, and gaggles, riding the tree-frogs' mating songs. They would get brown all over in the golden fields throughout the summer, lounging, working, loving, and then leaving with the ripening of the first red arbutus berries. Julie and I knew the only *raison d'être* for the lovely nomadic visitors on the commune was for them to let their hair down. And they did it well, in their wild, delicious, and carefree way.

At first, I was very excited. I wanted to frolic with them in the golden fields too. Julie had been my first and only woman lover. I was curious.

Julie put every effort into discouraging me from gambolling with the enchanting nymphs. Maybe she was jealous. Maybe she was afraid one of us would fall under their fickle spell. I asked Julie one day why she did not want to partake in the summer festivities. She just shrugged her shoulders and said that those girls were mere ephemeral nymphs, like dragonflies. They would catch my fragile heart in springtime just to drop it in the deep, dark pond of depression come fall. Julie was probably right. Still, I longed to experience the sinking, the bittersweet descent into the dark, unfathomable depths where creatures who have never seen daylight live.

I did not act on my longing. I ended up joining Julie, reluctantly at first and then more decidedly, in denying myself the enchantment of basking in fresh Sapphic sorority. I soon came to realize it was probably better this way. It dawned on me that Julie had a good decade's worth of experience over me in seducing young damsels. She would be more adept than me in getting the attention of the best girls, leaving me with the remains of the day. She could easily have fallen in love herself and flown off with one of said damsels at the first sign of autumn, abandoning me to a lonely grey, wet island winter.

With giant sighs, I learned to discipline myself before I even gave my nostrils the chance to whiff the nomad's scent. I hardly ever went next door, especially in the summer. When I absolutely had to go, such as when I needed a cup of brown sugar, I made sure, at the risk of appearing rude, not to engage with any of the nomads. This didn't mean I could not look. And look I did and found them all absolutely delightful. Then at the very first signs of falling under their spell, I would run back home and engage in extreme physical activities. I would chop some wood. I would feverishly dig in the garden, whether it was called for or not. Sometimes, with sweat dripping into my eyes, I could still hear the mermaids' call drifting over the fence. On those times, I made myself move further away, all the way to the end of our garden. That area got weeded very well. I did this year after disciplined year until eventually the girls' seasonal, crystalline laughter mingled with the other echoes filling the air around me, such as the bark of the sea-lions and the eagles' mating calls.

Slowly and surely, Julie and I sank into a thick and deep codependency. We even shunned the older, settled Naiads, the ones safely tucked into a snug monogamous year-round relationship. At the time of Julie's leaving, we had not paid our neighbours a real visit for over four years. If I ran out of brown sugar, I learned to do without. Julie and I found a colourless comfort in the mere certainty that the commune's year-round regular inhabitants lived nearby. We knew that a simple telepathic call, or failing that, a resonating howl, would bring the entire fleet of thirteen regulars, plus any visitors, to our houselet. They would readily arrive armed to the gills with home-made musical instruments of all sorts wrapped with peals of belly laughter. They would bring scrumptious Goddess food. All we had to do is show interest of any kind. The Naiads were very eager, responsive women. It was in their womandate.

Julie and I had, in our isolation from the Naiads' and the rest of the world, made ourselves a perfect little love nest. Or so I thought at the time. We even enjoyed passionate sex, despite the well-known fact that after seven years of Sapphic bliss, we could have long exhausted all the possibilities of mutual discovery. Somehow, we had miraculously escaped boredom. We always found fresh delight in each other's treasures as we experienced them with a perennially virginal attitude. Our love grew in eternal springtime in our private Garden of Eden. We took our inspiration from Mother Nature's overflowing eccentricity womanifesting herself in physical form. We lived in symbiosis with our giant lilies, plump asparagus, and ever-bearing strawberries. We fertilized our beds year-round from the plenty of our own secretions, such as the sweat of our brows and the rich products of our composting toilets. To complete the cycle of life, we saved our heirloom seeds lovingly from year to luxuriant year.

The animals helped too, in their own animal way. We loved them enormously. They were part of us and us a part of them, albeit in a more platonic sort of way than our plants. The only exception to our communion, our live-and-let-flourish lifestyle, would have been the various pests. Especially the slugs. We womanifested our contradictory sentiments towards them by sending any and all that we ever found to their next reincarnation. We had to play Goddess and exert our right to choose. It was either the pests or the garden. The choice was obvious. For us, at least.

All our opulence would have proved itself insufficient for my dear Julie. At the time of her disappearance, I was ignorant about the true nature of her own dissatisfaction. All I knew was that the precarious balance of our idyllic life had depended on not one but two willing accomplices.

A mere few days after Julie's disappearance, I received a little package in the mail. There was no return address, just the sender's full name: Julie Amalia Rosenberg. I didn't know anyone else by that name. The postage stamp was from Japan. Is that really where she had gone? Somehow, I knew her well enough to guess that she would not reveal the answer to her whereabouts in such an obvious way. On the back side of the parcel, a single line of writing, hastily scrawled in her uneven hand with a thick red felt-tipped pen, warned me:

"Do not open before Christmas."

We were in June. Only Julie would do something like that to me, even though she was Jewish and her people—who I am told are still waiting for their own Messiah—obviously do not celebrate this Christian holiday. Consequently, we did not ever exchange presents on Christmas. To be fair, we did not celebrate Hanukkah either. We didn't even really observe Wiccan rituals. We made up our own, very personal, eclectic and haphazard brand of spirituality.

I was puzzled. I disregarded the warning in red pen and opened the package. Inside, wrapped in starry tissue paper, there was a small red Buddha molded in the kind of hard plastic that tries to imitate stone. I did not understand the meaning of the statue itself. Nor did I get why Julie would have sent me something, anything, in plastic. We avoided plastic objects like the plague. I was doubly disappointed. I don't know what I had been expecting exactly, but it was certainly some other, better clue that would have helped me find her, wherever she was.

I fumbled some more throughout the wrapping paper. I only found a note, also in red felt-tip pen, in Julie's same chicken-scratch scrawl,

"What did I tell you!?"

Julie knew me well. She knew that I would be too curious to wait until December to open the package. If she had been there with me when I opened the parcel, she would have said something like, "See, I told you not to open the package until Christmas. You have created your own disappointment. If you had really waited until Christmas, there would have been a better clue in there for you." That was the kind of logic I had to put up with, with Julie. She would also probably say that, since we create our own reality, it would be my very fear of not finding her that would prevent me from figuring out where she had gone. *Oy veh.*

I flung the plastic Buddha across the room. It did not give me the satisfaction of breaking. It just rolled under the bed. Our bed. I wondered if Julie chose a plastic statue just to prevent me from being able to break it in anger. Or did she actually choose the statue? I retrieved the paper wrapping that the Buddha had come from. I found nothing but layer upon soft layer of star-studded paper. I examined the postage stamp on the brown outer wrapping very carefully. The date-stamp was difficult to read. Fortunately, the few letters and numbers I could make out were printed in English

9

characters. It appeared that the package had been mailed in a place starting with "K." Kyoto? Kawasaki? Kumamoto? The month was the easiest to read. The package had unmistakably been sent in May. The fourteenth? Sixteenth? Eighteenth? I could not make it out, but definitely in May. Julie was still with me in May. Had she been planning her exit already? Did she contact a friend from Japan to send me the Buddha? Not to mention the notes and wrapping, which she would have had to send along to them first? I let out a resonant growl.

That night I dreamt that Julie and I were making love. She kept missing my clitoris. I got so enraged that I made myself wake up. I thought of taking things into my own hands. I reached down. There was nothing but an unfathomable abyss between my frozen thighs. Nothing and no one in the world can equal the exuberance of sensations that I have known with her. Julie. The mere sound of her name would evoke smooth nectar flowing over me until I would be entirely covered with its unctuousness. I had to find her.

★　★　★

I still had no idea why she had left, and so suddenly. I racked my brain. Silly me, the only idea I could come up with at the time was that her leaving might have had something to do with my having once said, a few days previously, that I needed some space. I don't even remember why I said that. Maybe at the time I simply needed to focus on writing a few pages in my journal or do yoga. Julie seemed to have taken my words too seriously. I thought she might have pounced on the occasion and left me with the luxury of being alone for a short while. I was wrong. She ended up giving me more than the hour or so of space per day I had casually asked for. She put the distance of a whole continent between us. In fact, she gave me space from her for the rest of my life, as short as it turned out to be.

I have to admit, in all fairness, that Julie and I had ended up, on our remote island, in a state of fusion much feared by commitment-phobes, past telepathy, past the physical limits of our bodies even. Over the course of seven years, we had become truly, codependently, and simply "one." We moved as one unit. We were always together. It would actually have been the ideal situation for us to take our extreme intimacy one step further and experiment with Tantra. Not the one where you're supposed to meditate only. I'm talking about the kind of Tantra where you get to have super, metaphysical sex. Julie and I did not take that step. I'm not entirely sure why. Goddess knows we tried everything else. All I knew is that there didn't seem to be any sex-related enlightenment in store for us in the grand scheme of things, if such a thing even exists. Our special union womanifested itself mostly with our simple isolation from the world as we knew it. The biggest advantage I could see to our reclusiveness was that we had womanaged to avoid the gossipy potlucks with the Naiads.

Since we took every care to avoid meeting fellow human beings of any gender, especially those who thought they knew us, we had to be as self-sufficient as possible. To this end, we gradually let go of worldly conveniences. We liberated ourselves from owning fossil-fuel-guzzling cars. If we absolutely had to go to town for things we could not make ourselves, or could not do without, we walked to the ferry at the end of our road. We walked on, walked off, then hitchhiked or took the bus to the second-nearest town. The closest town would have been easier to reach. We wanted to avoid, as much as possible, running into some fellow islanders out for a day on the town. We happily travelled the extra miles to the next town just to disappear in a crowd of strangers.

At home, we called all our time "free time." We had no bosses, deadlines, or obligations. We had complete say on how we enjoyed every minute of each day. Most of our free time was spent gardening, taking care of our animal friends, eating or preserving our harvest, smoking our home-grown, drinking home-made blackberry wine, and making love. The more we made love, the more we wanted to make love. Few activities had precedence over sex. It was not unusual for us to interrupt ourselves during a meal or from working in the garden for a roll in the hay. We were hooked on sex like sleep-deprived, googly-eyed addicts.

Julie and I were far from being lazy. A typical day would start like this: Sam the Cat would get us up at the first light of dawn. He would jump up on our bed, purring. The covers would get gently but persistently pulled off our heads. Julie and I would ignore him, stretch, yawn, and reach for each other to make love before we even rubbed the crust out of our eyes. Sam knew better than to try and participate. He would be content with thoroughly cleaning himself at the foot of our bed. Then when we were all done, we would all roll out of our love-nest.

We would feed Sam first, then the chickens. Ralph the Pig was the last animal, us excepted, to be fed. We wanted to devote our full attention to him. He was very special to us. We had saved Ralph from slaughter as a young suckling pig and adopted him. He was more than a friend to us. He was family. In the spring, summer, or fall, Julie and I would go to the pump and return to his pen with a basin full of fresh, cold water. As Ralph looked on, we would lather each other with home-made horsetail soap, standing in the mud. We would shiver, laughing, as we rinsed each other off. Then we would take turns cleaning Ralph with his own raspy brush. As soon as we were all done, Julie and I would run out of the pen, wipe our feet off on the grass, and skip back to the house, as Ralph would finish his own bath by rolling in the mud.

In the winter months, Julie and I would continue our waking-up ritual by lighting a fire inside our cabin, then opening the door and skipping, naked, over the cold, sometimes hoar-frosted grass to the pump. We would fill up a bucket with water and return with it to the cabin to heat it up on the stove. While the water was heating up, we would go back outside, still naked, to Ralphs' pen to brush him. Then we would leave him to do whatever he wanted while we ran inside the cabin to wash from the bucket and warm ourselves up in front of the roaring fire, often with more making love.

We had a huge shaggy carpet in front of the woodstove. It was made out of creamy white wool woven in long strands to resemble a bear-skin rug. The rug had even been fashioned into the shape of a sprawled-out polar bear, complete with a felted, childlike teddy bear head. Sam the Cat often joined us on the rug. In winter, it warmed us; in summer, it absorbed our profuse sweat. Of all the places we would make love at home, the shaggy rug in front of the fire was our favourite. We used it often, at any time of the day, in all seasons.

The idea of us making love on our fake bear-skin rug may conjure up some mainstream images of pornographic lesbian activity. I can proudly say that the picture we formed did not copy this vision. We were not show-girls. Most of our lovemaking gestures might be considered too slow, even boring to look at. All of the action was interior for us. Watching us make love, if we had been watched, might be compared to looking at a deep, deep dark and still pond for hours on end. There were no ducks swimming on the surface of our pond, no jumping fish, not even reeds swaying in the breeze around it. There was no sexy music to accompany us. Our small thoughtful caresses were not driven by any urgency. Our skin was in choice places puckered and wrinkled by too much sun and salty wind. We had pimples and moles, some with a hair growing out of them. Our tits and asses were slightly sagging and bound to get more so with time. Our legs and forearms were also covered with coarse hair. Julie was in fact quite a hirsute gal. She even had a clearly visible moustache under her nose. She did not trim her nose-hairs. We both perennially had what might be called bad haircuts. Our hands and feet were roughened with farm-work, our nails short, cracked, and often dirty. To each other, we were beautiful and always immensely desirable. I can only hope that the above description of our appearance might allow us our privacy from some eager pervert's fantasy world.

In our everyday lives, Julie and I tried to keep our ecological footprint as small as possible. We recycled absolutely everything, way before the practice became expected of households from so-called developed countries. Recycling takes extra time. Free time. We were not afraid to use as much of it as was needed. We tried not only to reuse our waste but also reduce our consumption. We encouraged plants with soft leaves to grow around the land, such as lamb's ears and mullein. Then we would sometimes use these in lieu of toilet paper. Other times we used small beakers filled with water as a makeshift manual bidet like they did (Julie told me) in India.

When we had our period, we used pads made of cut-up old t-shirts stuffed with bulrush or milkweed-fluff. After use, we composted the fluff and washed the cotton casing until it got threadbare, then composted it too. That was in the winter. In summer, we spent most of our days outside. We just walked around naked, occasionally wiping our thighs with flowers or leaves. At night, we slept on old towels. The washing and scrubbing ritual of our bloody cloths had the extra advantage of helping us sublimate the hormonal rage we each felt rising from the depth of our bellies every month. I loved witnessing that rage course through my body. It made me feel more alive, in an animal sort of way. I turned into a furry, growling, red monster out for the kill. My periods made me insatiably horny.

Julie experienced her own periods' rage in a different way. First of all, she hated her moons. No wonder, as hers often arrived with a day and a night of very bad cramps. On those days, she would stay in bed with a hot-water bottle on her belly, doing nothing but moaning. She certainly did not want to be touched in any way. I tried many times to convince her that the uterine contractions of orgasm and the subsequent release of oxytocin would alleviate her cramps. She just pushed me away every time. Fortunately for both of us, those bad days of pain and forced celibacy only lasted for thirty hours or so per month. Unfortunately, our periods had synchronized themselves over time. In this way, we were typical of communities of women living and working together in close quarters, such as in nunneries and factories. I think the phenomenon has something to do with pheromones present in sweat. In our case, this synchronicity was indeed very lamentable. It meant that while Julie laid there moaning, I was seething and gnashing my teeth. I saw red. I wanted to jump on Julie and bite her.

Nature had played a bad joke on us. I was sure of it. She made Julie unavailable at my best peak of horny rage. Sometimes I wished I had been another kind of animal. Like a Komodo lizard, for example. I had done some research on animal behaviour. The animal world is indeed very fascinating, especially the sexual aspects.

You see, this period-synchronicity phenomenon that a lot of humans seem to be experiencing is only prevalent in some animal communities. It is certainly not the case in all of them. If we had been Komodo lizards, for example, we would have taken turns ovulating. Komodo lizards are very interesting from a sexual-behaviour point of view. For one thing, they are parthenogenetic. This means they only have one gender. They can all lay eggs. Therefore, in the biology world, they are all considered female. Pairs of parthenogenetic lizards—the ones who have been observed in captivity at least—have been found to often synchronize their fertile periods to be at opposite poles. It is doubtful that this is a conscious choice on their part. It just seems to happen, like human females having their own periods synchronize.

Then something strange happens. The non-fertile captive Komodo lizard starts exhibiting a behaviour that is more typical of males from two-gendered species. Indeed, the non-ovulating of the two captive parthenogenetic lizards bats the other fertile lizard around, mounting her and biting her until she releases her eggs. In dual-sexed lizard pairs, this egg-releasing time is when the male fertilizes the eggs by releasing his milt over them. The eggs of parthenogenetic lizards are viable from the start. They do not require fertilizing. They eventually hatch into cute, perfect little clones of the mother. Parthenogenetic animals actually do not even need another of their kind to be anywhere near them in order for them to reproduce. This is why the aggressive behaviour of another lizard towards an egg-laying one is unnecessary for effective parthenogenetic reproduction. The main purpose for the aggressive mounting behaviour in captive parthenogenetic lizards seems to be purely accessory.

Maybe Julie and I would have fared better if we had synchronized our own cycles to match the captive Komodo lizards' pattern. This way, I could have expressed my blood-fuelled passion on a happy, ovulating, hot-to-trot Julie. And since I tended to feel creative and happy during my own ovulating times, I could easily have left Julie to her moaning in peace when her period came and go paint a Mona Lisa or something.

Julie and I were obviously not captive parthenogenetic lizards. By definition, we were indeed captives to the nature of our isolation, albeit by our own choice. We just did not master the art of cloning ourselves. Not that we would have necessarily wanted to. Some of the Naiads claimed that they were practicing this art. As far as I know, none has yet succeeded. They only got as far as experiencing the mainstream phenomenon of having their cycles synchronized. Julie and I were living far enough from them not to be included in their hormonal aura. We would content ourselves with proudly hanging our towels and t-shirt squares to dry on the clothesline like warning flags to whomever would have been foolish enough to think about paying us a visit.

Julie and I worked very hard at being as self-sufficient as we were. We grew most of our own food. We even cultivated our own grains, quinoa, buckwheat, and amaranth. We did not habitually use much flour, but if the fancy ever hit us, we ground small quantities of our grain into fine flour with a contraption copied from an ancient homesteading magazine. It involved the use of special stones activated with bicycle wheels. In the long winter evenings, we crafted jewellery with found objects. Then we would sell our artifacts to tourists the following summer at the local market. We used our humble seasonal income to pay for a few small luxury items we could not grow or harvest from the wild ourselves, such as shade-grown, fair-traded organic coffee and chocolate.

Another one of our luxuries consisted of watching movies. We had scored an old TV set and video player from the island's recycling dépôt and taken them the long way home on a wheelbarrow. The journey must have taken most of one day. Then, with the help of ingenious wiring, we plugged our system into an old marine battery that we would also transport on our trusted wheelbarrow to and from the local fire station where we charged it as necessary, for a small fee. Except for an annoying purple circle on the upper right-hand side of the TV screen and some deep scratches, the system worked well enough for us. Julie had brought into our relationship a carefully-selected collection of lesbian videos she had pirated from her numerous past lovers' libraries over her roaming years. On a special, carefully chosen, astrologically favourable night, we would watch one, two, or an orgy of these movies, sometimes recreating, live, our favourite love-making passages in front of the set on our fake bear-skin rug.

With all our hard work and light, environmentally sensitive lifestyle, we still sometimes found ourselves wanting. There were some essential services and more expensive objects that we desperately needed but simply could not afford to buy with our meagre income. Other than coffee and choco-late—easily paid for with our crafts—there were other items such as shoes, cooking oil, ferry fees, tools, and truckloads of firewood that our budget or womanpower could not possibly allow. We reluctantly signed up for welfare. As frustrated as we were to be reduced to be sucking at the big mother's tits, we were also grateful for our monthly cheques. One added advantage to receiving them was that, sometimes, we had a bit of money left over from one month to the next. We deposited whatever little money we had in surplus in a shared savings account. Over the years, we had womanaged to accumulate $4,020.19. This stash was to be used at a vague, perennially retreating future date for a trip somewhere yet undetermined on our blue planet. Or maybe even the moon or Mars. We were careful to keep our savings below $5,000. If the amount was more than that, welfare would start giving us smaller cheques, defeating our purpose in trying to save up.

Julie also had her own little stash. Some distant relative had left her an inheritance several years before, prior to our meeting. I didn't know the exact amount of Julie's little fortune, but somehow, I had estimated (from clues gleaned over the years) that it would have added up to somewhere between $12,000 and $15,000. I'm not sure how she had womanaged to hide her loot from welfare except that her brother was somehow involved in the con-spiracy. In fact, this money was the only issue we ever disagreed on. We did not fight often but on the rare occasions that we did flare up, usually when we were having our periods, it was always about this loot. I had lots of great ideas about how to spend Julie's unearned money. I felt that we should invest it into our little homestead to make it more comfortable, maybe even to have solar panels installed. I tried not to be greedy, but I could also see us spending Julie's money to buy a luxury form of transportation, like a scooter or a sailboat, not that either of us knew how to sail. We could have learned.

We could also, for example, have taken a sabbatical from our little homestead and roamed the planet much as Julie had done in her exciting past. But Julie kept firm. Her untouched capital, cunningly hidden from welfare, accumulated interest in a term-deposit at the Bank of Montréal, drop by drop.

CHAPTER 2

Julie disappeared on the night of June second. I received the red Buddha on June fifth. Did she actually go to Japan and send me the package as soon as she arrived? I had no other clues whatsoever as to what Julie might have been up to. From what I could see, she had only taken her passport, a few clothes, and a backpack. I sunk into an intense grieving phase. Tears would stream from my eyes at the slightest reminder of her. Her favourite work-gloves, our videos, and especially our animals. I still did not have any idea of what to do next. I had not realized how much Julie's and my free time had been spent with our lovemaking. There was suddenly too much time and not enough activities to fill it with. I roamed around the house. I dragged myself to the seashore, looking for answers from the glistening pebbles letting themselves be licked by the soft edge of tides.

For lack of anything else to do, I thought of making the long journey to the second-nearest town and going to our bank. I figured that the amount of money that would be in our joint account might provide me with an indication as to whether Julie was planning on returning home anytime soon. If the amount was intact, I figured I would see her soon. On the other hand, if she took only a portion of her half or our money, she would be gone on a short holiday of sorts. Without me. Of course, she could simply use her own account only. There was no way I could find out anything about that. All I was certain of is that, if she was going to be really gone—that is gone indefinitely—she would have taken her entire half from our shared account, in addition to the contents of her own. This was perfectly in line with her personal interpretation of fairness.

I didn't go to the bank. I wanted to be home at all times in case Julie came back. Another reason I made up for myself was the huge expense of going to town. Also, it could have been that I could not bear to go off-island alone. The real reason, and I see it now, is that I was afraid to face the possibility of finding out for sure that Julie was not coming back. Ever. I stayed put. I continued performing the most basic chores, vaguely looking for clues as to Julie's disappearance. Without our lovemaking, I realized I had too much time on my hands. I could have gone next door to the Naiad commune. I didn't. I was too proud. I did not want the Girlz to see me in my desolate state. Julie could even have moved in with them and I wouldn't have known. The way I was feeling, and knowing Julie, anything was possible.

There was a chameleon side to Julie. It wasn't so much the cold-blooded part but more of the colour-changing aspect. During the almost seven years we had spent together, I witnessed her losing or gaining up to five kilos, hacking at her clothes, cutting, sewing, even embroidering them, until she would change her whole wardrobe into a completely unique, different style. She would let her hair grow, then cut it short in a totally unusual new way. She could even alter the tone of her voice and change her vocabulary from cultured to vulgar, to artsy, add an accent or two, and all this just for the sake of what she called "starting anew." Her talents at metamorphosis amazed me. I was getting a completely new girlfriend from time to time. I thought that re-inventing her personae was the way she had found of bringing a bit of excitement into our monogamous life.

For lack of anything else to do, I continued to wait. For what, I was unsure. I immersed myself in waiting. Two weeks went by, then almost three. On June twenty-fourth, the Québécois *Fête Nationale*, I woke up knowing, somehow, that the time had come for me to get proactive. I had to get off the island or I would go crazy. For some reason, on a whim or by intuition, or maybe because of it being a Québécois holiday, I decided that day that I would have to go to Montréal for a while. Who knows? Maybe I would even find Julie there. At best, I could lick my wounds in the company of a few friends I hoped to still be able to track down.

The first step was for me to contact welfare. I had to let them know that the cheque I was going to receive from them in a few days would be my last one, at least for a while. I had briefly considered making a trip back East, then back home to the West Coast in the same month. That way I would not have missed a single cheque. But something told me that, once I was off the Island, I would not have any desire to return for a long while. So the next day, on Monday, I walked to the post office and phoned welfare. I told them I would be leaving soon. The reason I gave them was that I was moving to the city, to Montréal, in the hopes of finding remunerated work. The person at the end of the line was courteous and wished me good luck. I walked home in a daze. I had, with a single phone call, changed the course of my destiny.

On Tuesday, the day before everybody's welfare cheques would arrive on the Island and be distributed in our mailboxes, I was shaking in my boots. The next day would give me one more clue as to whether Julie intended to come home or not. Maybe Julie was going to show up as if by magic, much as the first scapes of garlic in our garden. If Julie did come home to collect our cheque, I would cancel my plans to leave. We would need to talk, for sure, but at least she might be willing to do so. We would have a chance to work things out, whatever they were. Or maybe, if all Julie wanted was a change, we could go to Montréal together. Maybe.

On the Wednesday afternoon, welfare day, there were two envelopes in Julie's and my mailbox. The first, a thin one, contained a cheque for July. The amount was made out to my name only and for a bit more than half of what Julie and I used to receive as a couple. The second envelope, much thicker, contained another cheque also made out to my name, for about half the amount as the first, and a form in quadruple copies printed on thin pages of colourful carbon paper. There was also an empty stamped envelope, pre-addressed to the welfare office. The first page of the form was white, the others pink, yellow, and green respectively. A blue post-it-note on the top of the form informed me in hasty writing that the second cheque was intended to help me cover my costs of moving to Montréal. The person who wrote the note also wished me good luck in my new adventure.

Most of the form was already filled out by hand with the writing on the last green copy, somewhat blurred but decipherable. It seemed that all I had to do was sign on the solid line at the bottom of the top page, date it, put the form in the envelope, seal it, and send it off. An easy enough procedure, much easier than it had been for Julie and I to apply for assistance years previously. I didn't even take the trouble to read through the form to make sure it had been filled out correctly. I had all the reasons in the world to believe there would have been no mistakes. Welfare had all my personal information. They knew the exact amount of money Julie and I had in our bank account—well, at least the one we shared. Somehow, they even knew we were vegetarians. They also knew, of course, that Julie and I lived "maritally, in common-law" or however they put it. In simple words, welfare knew we were lovers. Since they had knowledge of the most private details of our life, I wondered if maybe they could also enlighten me as to Julie's recent whereabouts.

There was nothing in the mailbox for Julie. She must have contacted welfare for them to cancel her portion of our cheque. I had no idea what she might have told them. I also couldn't figure out how she could possibly have called them without my knowledge. We had been inseparable. It would have been impossible for Julie to sneak away to the fire hall or the post office to make a phone call while we were together. Unless she somehow womanaged to write and then send a letter or maybe a voicemail while I was asleep. I imagined a half-naked Julie sneaking out into the night, taking advantage of my post-coital snores to cover the creaking of our front door. The reality would have been either that scene or the more plausible explanation of Julie having advised welfare after she had already left. She'd now had a good three weeks to do so.

I thought of calling our worker and asking her if she could give me any clues as to what Julie had told them. Then I thought the better of it. It was very unlikely, even though she knew we were lovers, that our worker would have given me any information about my girlfriend. I felt enraged that some bureaucrat two ferries and a bus ride away possibly knew more about Julie's intentions than I did. Unfortunately, my rage did not change anything in my situation. The garlic scapes would have to emerge without Julie; the world would move on as best it could, unperturbed by my distress.

✳   ✳   ✳

The next day, Thursday, I walked, hitchhiked, ferried, hitchhiked, and ferried some more, then bussed all the way to the first town, where the welfare office was. I skipped the line-up, went right up to reception, and slapped three pages of my filled-out and signed form onto the desk. I had kept one copy for myself at home, the pink one, for no other reason than an odd sentimentality.

I also slapped down the stamped, unsealed envelope on the chipped counter on its own. I had not filled in a return address on the envelope so that the office could reuse it and save themselves the cost of a stamp. The receptionist gave me a slightly puzzled stare, as if she were wondering if she should call security on account of my strange behaviour. She didn't, though. I was able to leave on my own accord unescorted.

Next stop was the bank. I bussed to the second town. There was no lineup inside the huge marble-lined hall. My teeth were rattling, not so much from the over-zealous, unnecessary air-conditioning but more from pure terror. The moment of truth had come. It would womanifest itself in the form of numbers. Instead of going to the counter, I trudged over to the cash machine near the entrance. On the way, I almost peed my pants.

It turned out that Julie took almost half the money from our joint account. There was exactly $2,020.19 left. Most of the blood drained from my brain. With my teeth still rattling, I somehow womanaged to limp over to the closest teller's counter. I inserted my ATM card in her machine. I entered the wrong PIN number. After my third unsuccessful try, the teller asked for my birth date, my address, and a sample of my signature. By some miracle, I was able to remember most of my address except for the postal code. However, my shaky lopsided signature did not, even from the most lenient perspective, seem to match the sample on her screen. I even got my own birth date wrong. I gave Julie's instead. The teller looked benevolent. She could obviously sense my distress. She gently offered for me to sit down in the lobby, help myself to a paper cupful of cold water, and wait for someone else to help me.

Eventually, after an agonizing, embarrassing, cold-sweated hour of psychological and emotional self-inflicted torture at the bank, I somehow ended up out in the street with a huge wad of twenty-dollar bills neatly filed in the zippered inside pocket of my backpack. I had emptied our bank account and closed it forever. Julie, I had been informed, had already taken her own name off our joint account. The situation was more serious than I had anticipated.

Still, the sun was shining. It was a beautiful day. In my stupor, I attributed evil intentions to the weather and thought that the sun was thumbing its nose at me. There was little else for me to do than to go home, pack my bags, and leave my goddess-forsaken island.

On the following day, Friday morning, I woke up with an annoying headache, the kind one gets from dehydration. Or withdrawal. I remembered I hadn't made myself coffee since Julie left. It had been our special, weekly little ritual. Even though I could probably make a better brew than Julie ever could, there was no way I could get myself to make only one miserable cup.

I scooped myself a glass of water from the bucket on the kitchen counter, then glanced around the inside of our little cabin. The logs piling up to make the walls were sweating with a stale fever. Like a dying woman who sees her entire life in an instant (I had no idea yet how appropriate this was to my case), I remembered all the cabin-feverish times I had felt like setting a match to the entire place. We had embroidered ourselves into an idyllic little cocoon with a sly tranquility. The fabric of our nest was ripped throughout. We had agreed to ignore the frayed edges of our existence. We had been determined to see ourselves as ecstatically happy. Thanks to Julie's recent disappearance, my chance had come to pierce through the lie, as alluring and as irresistible as it had seemed to me for so long.

Still in my birthday suit, unwashed, I promptly started to put our things away in the same boxes that they had come in seven years previously. My initial enthusiasm soon worked itself into a frenzy feeding on a rage that I didn't know I possessed. I attacked our most intimate objects first. I had to be strong and resist at all costs sinking into the slimy pond of nostalgia. I was doing moderately well until my hands brushed against the little pile of love-notes we had accumulated throughout our seven years spent in beatitude. A thickened, viscous sadness, heavy with discouragement, poured over me. I piled our writings into one of the rare paper bags that had miraculously escaped our assiduous recycling. It was only the same conscience of an organic recyclist that prevented me from flinging the whole bag into the cold ashes of the woodstove and setting fire to them despite the intense afternoon heat. Instead, I abandoned the bag in a corner with the intention of deciding its fate later.

Suddenly, just like in a movie, a thunderstorm as violent as it was unexpected broke out over our house and garden. I saw there some kind of rapport with the emotions raging through me. Blindly obeying a scenario I thought was inscribed through each of the drops of rain pelting from the dark sky, I crumpled tragically into a heap, onto our fake polar-bear rug made from the wool and not the skin of lambs. I slid an avid hand in-between my thighs.

In Julie's flagrant absence, I took my revenge of her. I stole my own pleasure to the rhythm of the rain thumping down on our tin roof and single-paned skylight. My tactic failed. Despite my thunderous climax and my vegetarianism, I was ready for the kill.

I rolled off the rug. I dragged myself out to the garden on all fours, bare-assed. There I heinously tugged at the huge buttercup colony that had invaded the spaces in our asparagus beds, impervious to the rain falling on my back in big, fat frigid drops. The weeds hung on in their typical, utterly undesirable way. I could obviously not, with my bare hands and nails, dig out the recalcitrant roots of the hard-headed flowers. The persistence of buttercups is a well-known fact to whomever has had them in their garden. I was perfectly aware of this fact. It's just that I had thought my rage was so immense that it would overcome even the hardiest of weeds. Not so. Seething with frustration, I crawled back to our shack, still four-legged, an animal unchained by fury, hair plastered to a face contorted with bitterness, indifferent to the sticky mud I was trailing behind me, to continue, with grinding teeth, my destructive undertaking inside.

I was still enraged. I grabbed anything that dared fall under my muddy hands. I threw whatever it was into the closest box, haphazardly. Some of the most fragile objects shattered. I pushed the broken pieces into a corner of the box and continued filling it. Some things I smashed on purpose. This activity oddly ended up calming me. I continued packing with some softer, quieter things. All our food reserves except for a handful of lentils ended up on our compost pile. I filled two big burlap bags with work-clothes, with the intention of leaving them to the Naiad Girlz. The bag of letters was still hovering in the corner like a hunted animal. I tied the whole thing with an old scarf and flung it in the closest box.

I went back outside. The rain had stopped. The smell of green filled my nostrils with all its freshness. Slowly this time, I toured the garden. The season had been late, and the roses had just started to bud. An army of busy little black ants were scuttling over the sweet round buds of the peonies mere days before the flowers would burst open. The lilies showed their promise in clusters at the top of whorls of pointed leaves like spokes of green sun-rays. The peas, past the obligatory initiation bites from the weevils, were deploying their new, perfectly oval leaves. Their delicate tendrils, cajoled with a patience verging on mania, had finally wrapped themselves on the fishnet, like baby opossums to their mother's bellies. The garlic fronds cleaved for the eager scapes, ready to push up into their characteristic curl.

I had taken up the habit of talking to plants, birds, earthworms, and even the slugs before killing them. Now everything was eerily silent except for the trill of a robin. As if all beings were waiting for me to speak.

Every goodbye is a little death. It takes a chunk out of you.

A piece of your heart, a gash out of your liver. If you're lucky, it only takes the little toe of your non-dominant foot. Either way, you can never get any of it back.

I tried to console myself with the thought that the Naiad Girlz would easily profit from the fruits of our labours. I felt bad about all the dry food I had thrown into the compost bin. Absentmindedly, I started to snap off the beginnings of the garlic scapes, even though I had to almost break the fronds apart to get at them. I pulled a few blades of couch-grass erratically, as if it would have made a difference. Then came the animals' turn. They all got an extra serving of food. I turned my back while I could hear them eating with their habitual gusto. Usually I would derive a vicarious pleasure from seeing them so eager to devour their ration. This time I couldn't let myself partake in their innocent enthusiasm. It would have been like stealing, somehow. I also didn't want them to see me cry.

Back in the cabin, I filled the same backpack I had arrived with all those years ago, with the same clothes except for the latest acquisition from the local free store that made up my "party" or "town" wardrobe. It was a rayon dress, one that Calypso from the Naiads had called a "banquet dress." Colourful, with ruffled sleeves, the wide waist was ruched to accommodate a little banquet-belly, if the need ever arose. I laid the dress carefully on Julie's favourite chair, ready to wear the next day. I put the handful of lentils I had saved from the compost into a glass jar that I filled with water to soak overnight. The legumes would sprout nicely over the next few days and provide basic nourishment. My day done, without even taking a bite for dinner, I slid into our bed for the last time. I spent a sleepless night, flooding my pillow with bitter tears.

The next morning, the last Saturday of June, the designated day of my departure, I got up with the first light of dawn, around four thirty, eyes puffy and limbs heavy from turning over and over all night long. I dragged an ice-cold cloth across my face, then over my whole bruised body. Julie's touch was missing from my strokes like a rotten tooth. I looked over at her chair where I had lain the banquet dress the day before. It looked too bright in the dim morning light, too provincial. It would not do for the journey into the civilized world. I grabbed the dress, stuffed it into one of the burlap bags sitting in the middle of the room, and looked for the least shabby work-clothes I could find. I extricated a pair of black Capri pants and a long, crumpled black and white t-shirt. The pants' zipper was broken, but it also had a drawstring. It was made of some unknown material. The added advantage was that the pants didn't crumple. They would travel well. The t-shirt was long enough to hide the pants' defect, if I didn't tuck it in. I shook the pants to refresh them. I didn't bother looking for underwear. Julie and I hardly ever wore them, even for going to town. We certainly never wore or even owned a single bra between the two of us. I put on my gum-boots and stepped outside.

The rooster must have heard me. He started crowing even before I got within his sight. The chickens were probably oblivious to the fact that this was the last time I was going to feed them. I scattered them their feed, augmented with seaweed, a special treat. Their egg-yolks would turn that beautiful shade of rich bright orange. The seaweed would be my parting gift to the chickens and also to the Girlz, who would be sure to appreciate the special eggs.

As for Ralph the Pig, contrary to his habit, he was trotting very slowly towards me. I saw in his demeanour that somehow, with his animal's intuition, he knew. My eyes started to smart. My throat tightened. I walked up to him and fell to my knees. My good pants were getting smeared with mud. I hardly noticed and didn't care. I wrapped my arms around Ralph's thick neck and rubbed his snout with the tip of my nose. That's when I noticed my own nostrils were almost as sticky as his. He was staring at me placidly with his tiny soft eyes. I thought I saw a glimmer of profound sadness there. I scratched him behind the ears, then along his spine. His hairs were so hard and sharp I could have cleaned under my crusted-up nails with them. I continued to rub in the direction of the hairs. I was blurting out all sorts of stupid things about my leaving. I told him I would be back soon. I reassured him that the vegetarians would take good care of him and that the carnivores would not eat him. I even confided in him that I would have loved to take him with me, even though this would not be possible. I assumed he did not believe me anyway. I finally fell silent.

We looked into each other's eyes for a good minute or two; I'm not sure how long. I got up with difficulty and turned my back to him. I walked away and did not turn around. I was trying to convince myself that I would be coming back soon—maybe even accompanied by a repentant Julie. Deep down in my heart, I knew this was a lie. I wiped my knees as best as I could, then dragged my soiled hands as well as my dripping nose across the soft fresh fronds of salmonberry, which would soon open to look like maple leaves.

I went back into our cabin for the last time. My stomach was too tight to accept even the most frugal of breakfasts. Anyway, there was no food left anywhere except for the lentils that had been soaking overnight. They were still at the promising phase. I rinsed them and let them drain while I was giving a last check to make sure I did not leave any food around, not even the odd crumb for the mice and other undesirables. Satisfied, I took the jar of lentils from the sink, then slid them upside-down in an exterior mesh-pocket of my backpack. The other side of the pack would hold a water-flask. It was an odd accessory, the horror of vegetarians, cut out of suede, lined with plastic, and shaped like the stomach of a goat. It had been a gift from an old hippie friend of mine. I had not used it for years, maybe a decade or more. The thing only held a vague sentimental value for me. Julie hated it as much out of jealousy as for the fact that it irritated her vegetarian sensibilities. Miraculously, the insides of my offensive container didn't smell bad. I rinsed it at the water-pump and filled it with fresh water.

I called Sam the Cat to show him the large pile of food I had left for him until the Girlz would take over his care. No answer. Ever since Julie left, Sam had made himself scarce, volunteering to show up at most once a day to feed. I knew he was wild enough to be able to take care of himself quite well. He was the best mouser. I did not worry that he would go hungry. Still, I missed his regal, condescending presence. I could only hope that he was okay and that he would eventually show up for his breakfast, according to his peculiar cat-logic, only once I was gone. It was almost like he knew I was going to disappear for real, just like Julie had done. He might have been too offended by our double abandonment to suffer the humiliation of being left behind.

I fished out an old receipt from our paper-recycling bag. A lone lime-green pencil was hovering on the counter. It had escaped my packing. I used it to write a hasty note to the Girlz. My piece of paper was small. I had to write in minuscule characters. Luckily, the pencil was well-sharpened, but still, my note would be hard to read. I could only hope that the Girlz would understand that I had decided to leave and had no idea when I would be back. I did not disclose my destination. The garden would be there for them to harvest, with the hopes that they would also adopt the animals. Ralph was a friend, I thought it wise to remind them. He had been saved from slaughter and would offer kind companionship. I did not mention Julie on the note. Maybe the Girlz knew she had gone, maybe they did not. If they didn't know, they would surely find out whenever they decided to drop in on our homestead. I concluded my note with the promise—a lie, really—that I would contact them as soon as I was settled. I folded the thin piece of paper and put it in my pants' pocket. I heaved my pack onto my back, stepped out onto our threshold, and closed the door to our cabin. We had no key. I made my way along the path towards the Girlz' mailbox next door, leaving an erratic trail of water-droplets from my jar of lentils.

The Girlz' mailbox would be full of welfare cheques. They would probably not have made their monthly trip to town yet, as per their habit. They liked to go on Monday when the ferry-traffic would be less busy. I unfolded my little note and slid it in between a crack in their mailbox with the hope that my bright-green-coloured writing would attract attention. Turning my back to the letter box, I walked the two-kilometre trek to the paved road, where I would display a hopeful hitchhiking thumb.

As I was walking, I sent my usual prayer to be picked up by a gentle, non-smoking soul. I added that this person would not know me. This was to avoid too many embarrassing questions. My prayers were doubly granted. An octogenarian, non-smoking lady that I barely knew picked me up a mere ten minutes after I had put my thumb out. She did not ask me any questions. The added bonus was that she was going to the airport herself. Her great-grandson was coming to spend the summer with her. She was very excited. It had been four years since she had seen him. The whole trip to the airport was spent with my driver excitedly boasting about all the wonderful attributes of her youngest descendant. The chatter was a welcome distraction from my immense grief.

★　★　★

29

Since I had not made any reservations for my flight, I didn't know what to expect at the airport. It turned out that I got lucky. There was one seat left in the small airplane that would take me to Vancouver that same day. It was due to leave in half an hour. The attendant seemed a bit surprised at first to see me take out a pile of twenty-dollar bills to pay for my fare. Then, after a short moment of hesitation, she painted on her polite face, one that she may have been keeping in reserve for the feeble-minded. She accepted my money with a wavy smile. I didn't care. I was just happy to be leaving.

The first wing—some would say leg—of the journey was truly magical. The air was clean, with just a few clouds puffing here and there. I even caught sight of my island for a few short minutes before it disappeared from view. Genus Island was only one of dozens in the northern Salish Sea. We flew over many of them, more than I knew the names of. I could see the beautiful dark spires of evergreens, ink blue, almost-black lakes, sandy and rocky beaches, and the tops of a few houses, all woven through by fingers of scintillating ocean dotted with the odd ferry or sailboat. Then the scenery was replaced too soon by the sharp claws of khaki-coloured polluted water. We were preparing for our descent into Vancouver.

I got lucky again at the Vancouver airport. A Montréal-bound passenger had cancelled at the last minute, and I got their seat. It was a good booking, with only one forty-minute layover in Toronto. The attendant at this counter did not flinch when she saw me extricate my large wad of banknotes. She watched patiently as I counted out my pile in front of her. She had to re-count it before she was satisfied. However, I was not so lucky with security. They took exception to my all-purpose penknife. It was a good one, with everything I could possibly need, such as miniature sharp scissors, a toothpick, a nail-file, and three sizes of screwdriver heads in Philips, square, and flat. And, of course, the perfect three-inch blade, sharp enough, with a bit of exaggeration, to slice through a sheet of paper if said paper might have been dropped on it. After making me fill out an elaborate form in quadruplicate, the security guard confiscated my precious penknife. She ripped the third, pastel-green page off the form and pushed it into my hands. With a fake smile, she mumbled something that might have been meant to reassure me that I could retrieve my security hazard at the Montréal airport.

Incredulous, I cried out, "In Montréal? Do you mean I will actually get my knife back in Montréal??"

She only hissed, in English, already looking at the next victim behind me, "Yes, just go to the airport customer service. It should be there. But hang on to your receipt. It's your only proof. Next!"

At least she did not seem to mind about my jar of lentils. This was, after all, before the fall of the towers in New York. As I was running towards my departure bay with my backpack bobbing, my arm twisted behind me to prevent my jar of lentils from falling out, I could hear my name being last-called for my flight. I tried to run faster but could not. Still, I made it. Just. The other passengers had already boarded. I was whisked away, panting, to join them. I stepped into the passenger cabin, sheepishly smiling at all the passengers who looked up, curious who this dishevelled person was who had caused all the commotion and delay in departure.

I had been assigned a window seat. I slunk into it and obediently folded myself in half to push my backpack under the seat in front of me. As I emerged, I locked eyes with a little girl who was staring at me from in-between the seats in front of my nose. That's when I noticed how grumpy a mood I was in. My compassion had completely left me. To rectify the situation, I sat back as far as I could on my narrow seat and closed my eyes, trying to send benevolent energies all around, even through the stewardess's annoying safety performance. I sang John Lennon's "Imagine" in my head to cover her voice. A baby in the seat in front of me, presumably the quiet child's younger sibling, started wailing. My inner song failed to muffle the cries. The girl was still staring at me, even through the times we had to wear our seatbelts. Then she would twist her body and continue her silent *manège*.

I was starting to feel uncomfortable to be the object of such quiet, focussed attention. I tried to smile at the child. Whatever expression she saw must have been frightening, by the way she retracted like a startled turtle. I felt bad. I fumbled in my bag and took out three coloured pencils from my precious special artist's selection: Fire-engine Red, Lemon Yellow, and Periwinkle Blue. Maybe the little girl would know about the magic of primary colours, how one can create entire rainbows by layering or mixing them. If she didn't know, maybe we could discover their power together. I carefully ripped out a few pages from my journal and slipped them, along with the pencils, in between the seats towards the child. She seemed hesitant. A woman's harsh face appeared over the seats. She grabbed my meagre offerings with one hand with barely a hiss of thanks and handed them to the child herself. End of art lesson. The woman's face sank and disappeared from view.

The animosity remained. A palpably hostile, perhaps protective energy permeated the entire three-seat row ahead of me. However, as if she had needed this protective shield, the little girl seemed content with her drawing. Every now and then, she would show me what she had done, through the gap in between the seats. Flowers, a house, a child amongst some puffy trees. She did not mingle her colours. The bark of the trees was yellow, and the cloud of leaves blue, and the little girl in the picture all red. The house was drawn as an outline with all three colours. The last picture she showed me was also drawn using all three pencils. It had a blue person of indeterminate gender with a shag of yellow, unkempt hair and a fire-red wavy mouth as seen through a hole, or a slit. Oh yes, the gap between the seats. The person on the picture was obviously me. Not very flattering but honest.

In my head, I added up the drawings she had shown me so far. If I had calculated right, she must have used up both sides of all the paper I had given her. I was just wondering if I should sacrifice another few pages when the woman made the child give back my three pencils, as if she had been reading my mind. I must say I was happy about this as I had been wondering how I would fare without them.

When the airline attendants crowded the aisle with their food cart, there was nothing for me. I was a last-minute replacement passenger. There had been no time to accommodate me with a vegetarian meal. I had not eaten for more than twenty-four hours. My stomach suddenly reminded me how ravenously hungry it was. My lentils were not quite ready. I had to content myself with stale pretzels and even staler unsalted peanuts that the attendant dug out from the recesses of his cart. After I finished munching on them, I gathered myself into a grumpy bubble.

The woman in front of me did not accept food from the cart either. She had brought sandwiches, vegetable chips, veggie sticks with hummus, and fresh cherries. I saw their entire lunch menu because of the little girl, who did not fail to show me her prizes through the gap between the seats, item by delicious item. It all looked so good and healthy. It smelled heavenly. I bet it was all organic. Even the chips must have been from the health-food store. They were green, orange, and red, speckled with fragrant herbs. The smell of my fellow traveller's lunch activated my salivary glands to the point of searing pain. The woman forbade the child to share any of it with me, of course.

The worst of it was the realization that Julie would have found a way to make the situation fun. She was very creative that way. She would probably have figured out how to engage both the adult and the child in some interesting interaction from the beginning of the flight, and later score a healthy sandwich out of them. My longing for Julie sank all the way from my heart into my belly. I slunk even deeper into grumpiness. Pretending to sleep, I tried to ignore both my hungers. I could feel the little girl's gaze on my slumped form. I did my best to ignore her too. When the baby started crying again, I stuffed my ears with toilet paper I had snatched. The makeshift earplugs did not do their job well. I could still hear the wails. They lasted through most of the entire rest of the long flight.

In Toronto, I lined up with trepidation with the two hundred or so other passengers for the flight to our city of choice. Just a few more hours and I would be back in my home town. The woman and her two children from the previous flight were also on the same plane. They had scored a front-row seat, right behind business class. Again, I was in the row behind them. The little girl resumed her staring at me from in between their seats. The baby was quiet. My stomach was rumbling from hunger. I fed it some tomato juice, no ice, when the attendants came over with their cart. I immediately felt nauseous.

We finally arrived at the PET airport. I left the little trio still fumbling with their stuff in the seats in front of me and followed a short line of important-looking business-class passengers through a maze of corridors, escalators, and rolling carpets. I was travelling light. I did not have to wait for the checked-luggage carousel. I was looking for customer service. At the first counter, they sent me up and down stairs to Lost and Found, where they directed me through a complicated set of further twists and turns. I arrived, more from instinct than anything else, at a soiled counter at the end of a sombre, wide corridor.

After extricating the copy of the pastel green receipt I had been given in Vancouver, I handed it over, jubilant, to the attendant sitting on a high stool. They appeared to be some sort of a pale version of a homunculus from a science-fiction movie. Maybe they only understood another language than our two official ones, as they gazed at my paper upside down for too long.

Finally, they turned it right side up. And then the staring started. This was a different stare than that of the little girl on the airplane. Whereas hers seemed motivated by an innocent childlike curiosity and wonder, the look of this being in front of me was a stubbornly neutral version, as if they wouldn't accept any suggestions from the brain. I tried to expose my predicament in three and a half languages, one of them being the use of universal, frantic hand motions. My gestural description of the knife was starting to take on an increasingly threatening appearance.

The attendant was mushing my paper with hammered thumbs, as if they wanted to make the writing disappear. Panicked, I insisted too loudly in French, English, and a mix of Latin tongues to talk to someone else, a superior, maybe. They seemed to perk up as if moved by a hidden spring. They jumped off their perch, the sudden action overthrowing the stool. Without taking the time to pick up this piece of furniture, they twirled on their left heel with a surprising, almost alarming dexterity and disappeared through the door at the back of the small cubicle. They were gone for several bewildering minutes. I could hear some muffled sounds from what sounded like a whole tribe of small beings, but I could not make out a single word.

My attendant finally re-appeared, alone. They had disposed of my form. Instead, they slapped a new, virgin but crumpled set of thin, paper sheets on the soiled counter. After fumbling through some drawer concealed from my sight, they produced a pen, which they slapped, triumphant, on the top of the form, hard enough to make a mark through all the copies. Then they picked up the stool, moved it away from me, and perched on it, staring at me from the far end of the cubicle with a rapacious look.

I obediently put myself to the task of filling out the elaborate form on the spot. Luckily, I had all the required documentation either on my person or etched in my memory: my flight numbers, passport, BC Health Care, SIN number, age, and gender identity. And of course, the brand-name and close enough dimensions of my knife. I even remembered my library card number, although it seemed to be the only information not required on the form. I only hesitated in front of the "permanent address" box. After careful, silent deliberation, I thought it best to give the house number of my friend Charlotte's. I didn't know yet for sure if she had space for me in her apartment, but she was the only friend from Montréal that I had kept in touch with on a regular basis by letters over the years. Finally, exhausted but

34

content, I pushed my duly filled-out form towards the attendant. The pen fell to the floor on their side. The attendant jumped from their perch, grabbed first the pen and then my form in their claws. They spoke. Or rather, some strangled, jumbled sound came out of this being, not from the mouth, but from somewhere else, as from a bad ventriloquist's puppet.

"Trrrrotto"

Pardon excuse me?" I blurted out.

A greasy, crooked index finger was pointing at my flight numbers on the form.

"TRRRROTTO," they repeated.

Oh. I got it. They were saying, "Trop tôt." Too early. My knife obviously had not made it yet from the plane to this strange, remote office. Of course. I rolled my eyes at my own idiocy. I cranked out a half-apologetic smile. My attendant started to look endearing to me, like an ugly newborn of some mutant species. I could kiss them. Instead, I asked humbly if they were going to send me my weapon at the address I had just filled out on the form. After an imperceptible nod, they returned my half-smile without the apology. They disappeared again through the door at the back of the room where the mumblings from the small beings resumed for a few minutes. Then they came back with a hurried sort of look and nimbly climbed on the stool, gathering their body in a way strangely reminiscent of a giant sleeping bat, except that they were right side up and not the other way around. They seemed to have gone to sleep immediately. I concluded that our interaction had come as far as it would go. There was nothing left for me but to initiate a parting ritual.

"Au revoir, mon ami!" I said, smiling in a friendly sort of way. They obviously could not see my smile, but I knew it must have been audible.

The creature twisted their face up towards me, opened a top eye, and grinned, revealing a perfect row of gleaming white teeth with maybe a few extra added in. They assured me with a melodious voice in plain English, no discernible accent, and told me—even though it was obvious to both of us that they were lying—that I would be contacted within the week. Then they pulled their neck in, reaffirming that we were done. I had no other recourse but to leave. I repressed a strong urge to ask if I could adopt them.

CHAPTER 3

The airport had been renovated since the last time I had been there. I felt thoroughly lost. I had to activate my emergency rat-like directional ability. Only then did the visuals come back to me like a maze seen from above. I remembered each corner, each advertisement in sequence, backwards. Trotting along the interminable corridors, I fled past the Lost and Found counter, down and up stairs, all the way to Arrivals. Once there, as I was looking for the *sortie*, the exit, I picked up some food smells. I followed my nose to a short row of restaurants. The darkest of them beckoned me. I went all the way into the deepest recesses of the shabby place. Since the establishment turned out to be a bar, I ordered a draft beer. "Anything, surprise me." A bock.

The huge retro-style Coca Cola clock on the wall informed me, if it was correct, that we were locally close enough to four o'clock. My body was still on West Coast time, which would have been one p.m. for me. Too early to drink. Too late to stop. Apart from me, there was only one other patron in the bar. Slumped across the aisle a mere two booths away, facing me without looking my way, she was fixated on her coffee-cup, gripping it with both hands as if she were trying to prevent it from flying away. She seemed completely oblivious to anything or anyone else besides her cup. There was the most intriguing creature I had seen for a long time. Being close enough to observe the tiniest details about her person, I gazed on.

She had the kind of face that would not age, as if she had been frozen at about Shirley Temple's era, retaining her childlike innocence through the deepest of old ages without any surgery or miracle creams. She also reminded me of Lillian Gish, my favourite actress from ancient silent movies. Her face, which could be called old-fashioned since it reminded me of long-gone eras, attracted and repulsed me at the same time like a fascination with a fresh wound. In contrast, her eclectic clothes, her well-worn Docs, the metal jewellery she wore scattered over her eyebrows, ears, and septum, multicoloured ribbons flying even as she was immobile, all were screaming: contemporary urban artsy bohemian, maybe guerrilla, maybe Goth with a sprinkling of fairy dust. Plus, a personal, category-defying touch. My spontaneously activated gaydar remained stubbornly non-committal as to any alleged gender preference on her part.

A single chain wound around her endearingly delicate, swanlike neck. From said chain, the thickness of which contrasted with the slenderness of the wearer's traits, hung a miniature metal skull. I recognized it right away, even from where I was sitting. The skull was almost exactly like mine. The tiny stones that made up the eyes on her skull were red (Ruby or garnet or glass?), whereas mine were amethyst. Even though hers was immobile at the time of sighting, I knew it to have a moveable jaw. This girl's pendant seemed a bit more articulated than mine. It was gaping open almost to dislocation. In my jet-lagged, fuzzy mind, I thought it was smiling at me with a macabre maliciousness.

I had gotten my own tiny metal skull at a flea-market in the suburbs of Santa Fé in the early nineties. It was a vaguely bohemian time, mostly in between eras. It was also an era when a lot of the Boomers, such as my mother, for lack of anything else available to extend the peace and free-love movement, would have gone punk and underground. Except that my mother died in 1990. In a way, I had acquired the little skull in memory of her. I was all of eighteen at the time. I had to grow up fast. I had not seen anyone other than me wear such a skull until that morning at the airport.

The girl still seemed oblivious to the *émoi* she had provoked in me. She kept staring ahead of her, clutching her cup, intermittently bringing it to her pretty wavy lips and slurping in an almost audible way. Usually, I hate slurping, but on her it felt endearing. Horrified, I noticed I was falling in lust with her. Against my better judgement, I was already planning an approach. I was just lucid enough to remind myself to retain a certain nonchalance-tinted chastity to honour the memory of the ambiguous nature of my visit in the area.

To give myself courage, I downed the rest of my beer. This was a mistake, which I regretted instantly. The beer started churning in my stomach, sending sour bubbles into my jet-lagged brain, making it impossible to score an infidelity, albeit one in my hopes and dreams. It would be better to slink out of the bar before she noticed me.

I discreetly patted my backpack to remind myself of the limits of my monetary funds. I had no idea yet when or where I would find a job to justify my existence. I looked around. There was no waiter or barman anywhere in sight. For a moment, I deliberated if I should jump on the opportunity and leave without paying. My meagre *pécule* would only fatten the bulging pockets of some horrible bourgeois capitalist pig anyway. On the other hand, shrouding my visit with bad karma right off the start might not have been the best idea.

Just in case, I sent a generic wave of goodwill throughout the place, being careful to wrap the girl with the skull in an extra dose of anonymous love. Then I slapped a big blue five dollar bill and two loonies on the badly graffiti-scratched table and got up without looking back to see whether the girl had noticed me. In this case, it would be better to slink off unnoticed since I had nothing of interest to offer the intriguing person. My attempts at invisibility failed miserably. My vision, blurred by jet-lag, must have mistook the big faded rose on the carpet for a real one. I tripped, trying to avoid crushing the obviously already-flattened flower. Two chairs turned over. The barman came rushing in, reeking of smoke. I felt more than saw the girl's body shaken by a small tremor. Blushing, I squeezed out a crooked smile all around, pointed to my money on the table, and stumbled out of the bar.

*   *   *

I called Charlotte from the first phone I saw. She did not pick up. Her answering machine kicked in instantly, so I figured she must be on the phone. I didn't bother listening to the message. I promptly hung up. Generally speaking, my friend was an amiable and gregarious person. She was also, as I remembered her, usually up-to-date with any gossip that would circulate across the country and beyond, within our intricate web of friends and lovers going back more than a decade. She used to know, even before they realized it themselves, the electricity mounting between any two, three, even four persons that would lead them to infidelity, teeth-gnashing passion, and breathtaking swoons. She knew about break-ups and comings and goings in and out of sexual and gender-preference closets long before the people concerned knew it themselves. She might know what happened to Julie. Especially if Julie was indeed in Montréal.

Charlotte attracted bohemians, eccentrics, and marginals. I had no idea how I would fit into any of these categories. I probably didn't belong anywhere. Actually, I have never understood why Charlotte kept me in her colourful *répertoire* of interesting friends. I am as ordinary as they come. Nothing interesting ever happens to me. Nobody would be inspired to write poetry or to jump out of a window because of me.

This is true, and I have proof. I once had an acquaintance, a female artist, who had invited me to participate in a performance she was working on. Her idea was to paint portraits of her friends and acquaintances dressed in prototype characters according to the way she saw them. There would be a Pierrot, a Van Gogh, and a tiger, among many others. Then once all the portraits were finished—about a dozen or so, maybe more, according to her time and inspiration—she would have a show. On the day of the *vernissage,* all the people who'd had had their portraits done would circulate among the guests, dressed in costume, just as they appeared on the portraits but live.

It was a great idea. For me, the artist had chosen a ballerina costume. She was going to make me wear a pink tutu, my face painted white like a sort of female Pierrot. I remember being very flattered to be chosen. I liked my character. As a child, I had always dreamt of becoming a ballerina. I liked the added Pierrot theme as well. It contained a certain androgyny, a certain mystique. I was delighted. Until the artist told me one day, about a month into her project, what had made her choose the ballerina character for me. It was her banality. I still see her face in front of me, as she spit that word into my face, "BANAL. She is *banal.*"

The artist never did my portrait. The show never took off the ground. I doubt the cancellation had anything to do with me, but I was secretly happy I was off the hook. Up till that time, I used to consider myself a calm, reasonably jovial and reliable person. It had never occurred to me that I could be seen as banal. That artists' impression of me grew insipidly into my entire being all the way into my bone-marrow. It took me years of counter-affirmations to break the curse of the word she had used to describe my person. Actually, I have never been able to entirely shake that dreadful appellation from my consciousness. It would rear its ugly head whenever I would feel uncertain or weak. Like on that day I arrived in Montréal after seven years' absence.

That day at the airport, my resolve to give Charlotte another call evaporated in a deluge of self-doubt. I felt uncertain if Charlotte would even offer me shelter. I started questioning my friendships and relationships all the way back to my childhood. I mistrusted even the very attraction that had brought Julie and me together in the first place. Judging from her stories, she had had some pretty wild relationships with lots of other girls and women. They all sounded much more interesting than me. Had she kept me as a lover all those years only like some sort of "control" subject, like they have in scientific experiments? The normal subject, the one that all the interesting hybrids and mutants get compared to?

I loved listening to Julie's stories. She would choose the most unusual times to tell them, such as when we were cleaning the outhouses or right in the middle of brushing her teeth with the black foam of roasted *aubergines* spilling out of the corner of her mouth. The companion activities to her tales would lengthen them, easily stretching them for hours or even spanning out over weeks. Over time I was able to weave the stories together until I got the sense of personally knowing all the picturesque characters and situate them in time and space. I knew that I would not measure up to the excitement factor. I would not appear in any of Julie's tales even if we split up. In that case, I bet she might describe in detail to her new lover our living conditions on Genus Island, the Naiads, the nomads, but nothing personal about me.

Julie was not a traveller. True, she had been in some pretty exotic-sounding places. But even according to herself, she did not travel in a mainstream sort of way. She claimed that she simply plucked herself off the map. Then she would reappear somewhere else like an alien flying squirrel that had just landed on earth. It was, as a matter of fact, just after one of her unexpected appearances that I met her for the first time.

✶　✶　✶

I could say that the occasion of my very first meeting with Julie had a fictional aspect to it. This is just a polite way to say that I felt our getting together had been based on a lie, pure and simple. Julie never agreed with me on my theory. I think her take on the matter was this: If I went along with her story at the time, it was, in effect, absolutely true. Kind of like truth residing in the eyes of the beholder, like beauty.

We were in 1994. I was all of twenty-two years young. At the time, I was living with a man—an older man I had been silly enough to marry. We had been hitched for almost two years. A psychologist might have said I got together with him mostly to fill the void left by an absent father. I also mistakenly thought I was heterosexual. I was not, nor ever had been, bi. It was just that the idea I could be a lesbian had never occurred to me. My mother, in her light-headed hippie sort of way, had been into men. I had no reason to think I might be different than her.

My sex life with my husband turned out to be like a desert, without even the odd Joshua tree. He was not very macho and didn't seem to care that we could go on for months without intimacy. In fact, I think he preferred it that way. We had mostly married for companionship, because it seemed a fun thing to do at the time. His social life was what mattered most to him, and he never missed the occasion of calling a party. Sometimes I think the main reason I got attracted to my husband was because of his friends, who were, of course, all very interesting. You could say that my attraction to people who have interesting friends was a pattern of mine. My friendship with Charlotte would be another example of this habit.

So, I was at this party at Charlotte's, in Montréal where I was born, raised, and still lived at the time. There were a lot of people at this party. The music was enchanting, Latino-urban and World, a bit hip-hop-ish with a splash of Motown, my favourite mix. My husband, George, according to his habit, was deeply engrossed in conversation with a pretty woman. I assumed they were talking about political New Age Enviro-urban-pagan-guerrilla philosophy. I knew that whatever words they were uttering were just a cover for flirting with each other. I was not jealous. I knew he wasn't macho enough to get into any serious relationship that might have threatened our arrangement. And if he had, I would still be curiously neutral. I was young. George might have been a mere *hâvre de paix*, a safe harbour after my turbulent life of debauchery following my mother's death. But that is another story.

Charlotte's place was packed. Several people had pushed most of the furniture aside, rolled up the carpet, and started dancing. I looked for a free space where I could unite my body with the joyful mob, hopefully far from the enthusiastic arm-swingers and foot-stompers. It was not easy to find a free space, but I eventually thought I had seen one. First, I traced myself an imaginary itinerary all the way to the desired spot. My choreography included (but was not limited to) ducking, with perfect timing, under arms swinging to the music, then twisting my body around a group of enthusiastic people before finally landing on my chosen spot near the middle of the room. I had just completed my planning and was on the verge of letting myself fall into the pack when two small *mamitas* who seemed to have been beamed from some extraterrestrial pueblo landed exactly in my chosen space.

I decided to squeeze in anyways. I figured that if they had somehow womanaged to jam the two of them in the area I had intended for one person, namely me, there should be enough space for the three of us. I grabbed all my courage with both hands and plunged into the *cohue*, eyes closed, nostrils palpitating, spurring myself on with some sort of psychic sense, directing my movements with sound and heat reverberations like a bat. When I opened my eyes, I was sharing a circle of dusty light with the *mamitas* in the middle of the dance floor. The music had changed to New Age. Everything, from the particles of dust in the blue cone of light we three were in, to the ethereal sounds, to the fact that the other dancers had mysteriously given us a lot of space, all contributed to an other-worldly aura. I started wondering if the diminutive *mamitas* might have been descendants from the Lemurians or whichever extraterrestrials might have helped build the temples at Machu Pichu.

An irresistible urge to make contact with them kicked me in my solar plexus. Seemingly nobody else had yet formally welcomed them to our blue planet. Someone had to let them know we meant no harm, and it had to be me. I knew from watching enough science fiction movies that extraterrestrials often have ways of instantly mastering local languages. Taking clues from their physical appearance, I decided to try my rudiments of Spanish on them.

"*Holà!*"

"*Holà!!*" answered the taller one of the two.

She didn't seem surprised at my seeming familiarity with her tongue. I decided to push further into conversation. Spanish was not the easiest language for me. Having grown up in Rosemont, I was more familiar with Italian. Still, I found myself extricating from my brain the twenty-three or so words I knew in Spanish, trying to come up with short sentences that would show off the maximum number of them.

"*¿ De donde vienes?*"

My question seemed to confuse her for an instant. I assumed she might have been deliberating between telling me her real origins somewhere in a distant galaxy or fake it and produce the name of an earthly Latin country. She smiled, shrugged her square shoulders, and waved her hands in a vague sort of way. To help her along in her subterfuge, I offered her an *échappatoire*: "*¿ Vienes de Sud America?*"

She hesitated some more, then still smiling, said, "*Si,*" firmly but politely, indicating that our conversation was done.

She actually turned her back to me and resumed dancing with her shorter partner with a slightly too frantic enthusiasm. Just in time. The shorter partner—who was pretty much the exact same height as me—had started to throw more and more bad-energy darts at me. A few more minutes and one would have hit me in the eye. I left the two women to work out their interaction, whatever it was, and made my way towards the back porch. It was summer, and there was a *super-écoeurant* joint going around. All of us out there turned instantaneously into lifelong friends.

Unbeknownst to me, the fate of five people—the two *mamitas*, a stranger, my husband George, and me—was being decided right there on the dance floor while I was unconsciously smoking away on the porch. As it turned out, the two *mamitas* had broken into a jealous fight. Maybe I had triggered it, but I wouldn't flatter myself. All that I found out later, according to the shortest one at least, was that the taller one had dashed out to the kitchen and daringly kissed the first man who got in her way. However, the man-kisser's version of the story was a little different. It went like this:

"We are soulmates. We just found each other, as simple as that. We have some pretty heavy karma to work out. So, this is the way it's going to be now."

Nonplussed, the shorter *mamita*, who must have followed my movements, eventually appeared by my side on the porch. She was quite alone. Her power might have been so great as to send everybody scurrying into the house to give us some space. This would have been her version. Or maybe they just left because all the joints had been smoked. At any rate, in my stoned stupor, I fell clumsily into her open arms. I stayed there for seven years.

Now here comes the lying part. Neither of the two women were originally from South America, or even Mexico. They were actually from Montréal, just like me.

The shorter woman—the one I ended up with and who had rebaptized herself Julie—was originally called Shoshanna. The other one was called Pearl. Over time, I was to find out that they both came from Anglophone Jewish third-generation Canadian middle-class families, steadily climbing towards nouveau-richism. After they met in an Israeli Kibbutz at the tender age of sixteen, they'd become inseparable.

They'd quickly adopted a nomadic lifestyle, moving haphazardly as their whims suggested, following whatever alluring opportunity presented itself. To earn their living, they made themselves useful wherever they happened to be. Sometimes they paid their own fares on the mode of transportation itself, such as by working on luxurious yachts bound for evocatively named places: Ischia, Bora-Bora, or Arros Island in the Amirantes.

During the relatively slow periods, they assembled trinkets and jewellery with objects they found in ditches, on beaches, even in garbage heaps. They claimed to have processed more volumes of these findings than the total mass of anything else they owned. Seashells of all shapes and colours, broken wind-up clocks and watches, toys, bottle caps, buttons … anything was good for them. Except plastic. Pearl and Shoshanna did not use plastic in any form, including common household objects that had the offensive material in them, such as napkins, paper-towels, and disposable handkerchiefs.

In really slow times, when they had exhausted all opportunities, they "harvested" their food off grocery shelves whenever they got really hungry. This was, of course, as a very last resource, and they usually only targeted large, big-corporation-owned stores. Pearl and Shoshanna were not greedy. Once they had no more than a single snack's worth in each of their pockets, they would sneak away and hitchhike out of that situation as fast as they could.

The women slept wherever and whenever they put down their weary heads. This could be under the stars or sitting at a table in a library or sprawled out in the four-post, canopied bed of a millionaire's castle. Sometimes they came upon a curious soul, living in solitude in some mansion, who would shelter them in exchange for their jovial company. The rich but bored host would perk up and listen with rapture to the travellers' exotic stories. The more they kept their audience of one captivated, the longer the women got to bask in the lap of luxury.

Other times, when all the stories were sufficiently told, the women might further their relationship with their host by romping in their bed, showing him or her new tricks and a good time. The host's gender did not matter, as Pearl swung both ways. Shoshanna was a bit more conservatively gay. Caught in a bisexual setting, she preferred to watch or would mostly abandon ship once the humping got going. Anyway, the willing participants barely noticed that they were left to their own resources. They would usually bring their session to its satisfactory, albeit predictable, conclusion without any problem.

At the time of the party when I met the *mamitas*, they were passing through Canada after having raked through South America. To be more precise, they had been deported back to their home country for illegally selling their wares in a Bolivian village market. Shoshanna had even done some jail time for their petty crime. She was just lucky she got almost decent treatment by her jailors, and then been let go after being made to promise not to *reincidencia*. Shoshanna suspected that her parents helped her get out of trouble by paying a large ransom to the Bolivian *policia,* but they never mentioned this fact to her, nor did her parents ever ask for repayment, if they did in fact disburse any amount for her.

Undaunted by the turn of events, the two women took advantage of their deportation by visiting their families. They renewed their passports, recharged their batteries, had a few affairs each, and started looking for ways to earn a wad of quick cash so they could resume their wanderings. They thought Japan might be a good next destination. But Dame Fate decided otherwise. Pearl got herself spontaneously hitched up on the spot at Charlotte's party. This was supposedly not like any of her occasional flings, like she had treated herself to many of in the past. This was, she claimed, "it." He was an older man from New York who had been expecting her after he had been told by a clairvoyant that he would meet his soul mate at a Montréal party. He had even made the three-hour trip that weekend to meet his fate. The new pair, convinced they were siblings who had met a tragic fate and been cruelly separated in a former life, flew off together in a whirlwind romance. They spontaneously decided to have a go at carving themselves a whole new life together and set their karma right. There was talk of marriage. Maybe they could even breed.

With Pearl suddenly gone, Shoshanna instantly realized she was ready for a change in partner herself. All those years spent in constant intimacy, along with the fact that she had felt abandoned by Pearl when she had to do time in that dreary Bolivian jail, had taken its toll on their relationship. Without losing a beat, Shoshanna immediately jumped on the opportunity for freedom of choice. She renamed herself Julie to commemorate the occasion and hitched up with me. Just like that. All in one night. That, I would find out, was the kind of woman she was.

I was easy prey. My relationship with George was on the rocks. I didn't even realize, until I felt Julie's pheromones envelop me, that I was ready for something other than the too-short, sparse, emotionally barren arrangement my husband and I had been living during our two years together. Besides, George had confided in me, as a sort of warning before we got married, that he thought himself incapable of sustaining long-term relationships. Our marriage would have been, according to him, a sort of experiment. Not very flattering for me. At least he was gentlemanly enough to give me the opportunity to be the one to leave.

As we had been preparing for an inevitable break-up, George and I had kept our bank accounts separate while we had been together. We split the food and utility bills exactly in half, despite the fact that he earned three times what I could ever come up with. To even out the inequality, he paid the rent in full. He also occasionally took me out to dinner and a movie. Sometimes he even bought me a new outfit for these occasions. I figured it was because he liked being seen in the company of pretty women. I have never seen myself as pretty by any means. I guess I simply had the freshness of youth on my side. That way I could get away with not wearing makeup. George had tried once, and only once, to get me to paint my face. I flew into a rage. He never brought up the subject again. I eventually compromised with occasionally drawing a line of Kohl at the base of my lashes. Everybody has to draw the line somewhere. That is where I drew mine as far as makeup was concerned.

Once George got over the jolt to his ego caused by my leaving him, he ended up thanking me for having had the courage, he said, to leave a dying relationship. I didn't feel particularly brave or courageous. I was just ready. Two years of virtual celibacy had primed me for falling into Julie's welcoming arms. I was not disappointed.

* * *

The fourth thing Julie and I did after we got together was to pack and high-tail it out of the city. The first one had been, of course, to start exploring our bodies to their full, mesmerizing potential. Pearl and Shoshanna—now Julie—had found a caretaking situation: a quaint little pad in the Plateau. With Pearl gone to New York with her twin soul-brother, Julie and I had the place to ourselves. We used it well. Julie and I drew the curtains shut, locked the door, and cocooned ourselves for over two weeks, ordering out whenever we were hungry for food. I only tore myself away from our embrace just long enough to phone my workplace. I told them I quit. That was the second thing I did. It was only a low-paying job as a messenger for an investment company anyway.

Julie and I only emerged from the apartment when we ran out of my meagre funds, our eyes puffy and our pores saturated with the pervading scents of sex. Then we did the third thing. We got dressed as nicely as we each could and applied for welfare. Since I was penalized for quitting my job, Julie was the only one who got a small cheque from them.

The apartment-caretaking situation was coming to a close. Julie and I started to pack our meagre belongings, the ones we had brought to the apartment. I phoned George to ask him if I could leave the bulk of my stuff with him. He obliged. I had always lived frugally. There was not that much anyway, just some clothes, books, and CDs. The sound system, the furniture, and the kitchen stuff were his anyway. He was even gentlemanly enough to eventually finalize our divorce and pay the lawyer's fees. According to the lawyer, it was the most amicable divorce he had ever seen. I told George he could pass on the fancy clothes he had bought me. I would have no use for them in my new life. All this took a whirlwind of a few days.

Julie admitted she did own some odd pieces of furniture and some sentimental *tchotchkes*. They were stored indefinitely at her parents' place. She just left them there. Pearl showed up some day with her beau, and they moved her own stuff out. In order to avoid any weirdness, Pearl and Julie had arranged for them to come at a time when Julie and I would be out. Thus, the move-outs went smoothly, with no awkwardness or flying fur. Everybody's eyes stayed intact.

A mere three weeks after we met, Julie and I were all packed, including her smattering of lesbian videos. We flexed our thumbs and hit the road. The idea was that we would head west, hitchhiking, and keep moving until we found a place that would have us. After a few unsuccessful tries in Creston and Kaslo, we got to the end of the line: the remote, fabulous island of Genus, hovering in the middle of the Salish Sea. This was a lucky find, as the next stop would have been Hawaii or even Japan, neither of which I would have been ready for, not even with resourceful, exciting Julie as companion.

The dwelling we found on Genus was a small octagonal log-house made from driftwood and crowned by a Buckminster Fuller-inspired geodesic dome built with Plexiglas triangles badly framed together with slats of wood and lots of putty. It had been assembled by some hippie squatters who had raised a family there and moved on. The land belonged, coincidentally, to a Montréal-based businesswoman who was quite aware of having had some unpaying tenants but who didn't seem to mind, as long as the integrity of the land was not significantly altered. The previous tenants handed us a tattered letter, a contract of some sort, which specified, mostly, that no trees were to be cut without her permission.

An added bonus to living on the property would have been the lovely presence of the neighbours. Julie and I were delighted to find out that there was a women's commune next door. They showed us the ropes and gave us the businesswoman's home address for us to contact her. But most interesting of all was the next-door women's Sappho-Tantric energy that caught our attention. It was immediately evident, as soon as we directed our palpitating nostrils in their direction. We were very excited at the prospect at getting to know them and them us. We were all fresh blood for each other.

Julie contacted the Montréal businesswoman by letter. Her name was I. Côté, and she lived in Westmount. Julie insisted on getting a new contract written up with more details. She said it was for our protection, so that we would not get evicted without reason or warning. I didn't know about such things and was proud of my girlfriend, knowing that she would have done the right thing, and properly. I. Côté seemed delighted with Julie's seriousness, and after she gave us her enthusiastic written permission to stay on her land, we properly settled in.

Then Julie wrote a letter to her parents to ask them to send an assortment of her belongings. Apparently, they said they didn't mind sending the stuff, and even paying for shipping. But still, the tone of their letter showed some reluctance on their part. Julie knew her parents had enough money for them not to mind paying for the move. She figured their hesitation had to do with them seeing her leave again, so soon after she had just come back to Montréal. Knowing them, she said, they had probably been hoping to keep her belongings as a sort of bribe to get her to keep coming back. With her things moved to the West Coast, Julie would not be settling back in Montréal anytime soon. The shipment never arrived.

Julie also suspected her parents had not given up on her popping out some grandchildren one day. This was despite the fact that her parents were perfectly aware of her being gay. Julie did have an older brother, but he was gay too. In that way, both siblings had been a disappointment to their parents. The parents had tried to be proud of their offspring, boasting about all their accomplishments to whomever would listen. Still, it must have been difficult for them to find something to be proud of, when all their friends had wads of baby pictures to show off.

Eventually, I had come to realize I was a sort of new toy for Julie. A rebounding ball to distract her from her sudden separation from Pearl. I offered her my Sapphic virginity with no expectations of a lasting relationship. I took the risk of throwing my heart into the package in exchange for being initiated to the delights of oxytocin-fuelled bliss. It came as a gigantic surprise that she kept me as her lover for seven years, long after she had seemingly gotten over her break-up with Pearl.

*　*　*

I only realized all those years later, standing in that Montréal airport, that Julie had surreptitiously but steadfastly cut me off not only from my past but from any possible new friendships. As it turned out, we had never fully made the best of the presence of the women in the commune next door. Instead of enjoying them to their full luscious potential, Julie and I had ended up, in the space of our years together, in quasi-total isolation from the world.

For a while, I had thought this isolation to be a desirable thing. I assumed it would have helped us to grow into independent, responsible adults. Our constant proximity to each other, and only to each other, could have helped me with a fear of intimacy I didn't even know I had but which Julie insisted we were all afflicted with. I was ignoring the fact that human beings are basically social. In retrospect, I think I was a fool for letting myself be cut off from the possibility of being close friends with the gaggle of amazing, interesting, smart women from the commune next door.

Left to my own devices at the airport, I had no other choice but to take full responsibility for not having gone over to the Naiads more often when I had the chance. I suspect that, if I would have gone over for some visits, Julie would have broken up with me earlier. Either I was exclusively her friend, lover, companion, confidante, partner, and basically everything, or not. Those were the unspoken rules. I chose Julie. I chose lots of sex.

At the beginning stages of our relationship, Julie amused us with taking on different personalities at the whims of her fertile imagination. There was the leftist news reporter, the pill-popping bored housewife, the jaded millionaire yacht-man, the hobo, and even animals, such as the aging circus lion and the rebellious teenage dog. She created the illusion that I was living with a succession of fascinating, exotic characters. Of course, as I interacted with the different personalities, I felt different too.

Still, over the years, even the novelty of Julie constantly coming up with different characters had become routine. Julie had eventually locked herself into a sort of taciturn sex-maniac robot *personnage*. The only good thing about this character was that sex was surprisingly satisfying. Some new element, maybe the fear of intimacy Julie seemed to take for granted, had installed itself in my personality. I found the new lack of the human element agonizingly exciting. Sinking deeper and deeper into the role of a crazed sex maniac, I found a strange kind of balance.

I should have seen the signs. Just like the *avènement* of the reversal of the Earth's magnetic poles, or the promise of the new Avatar, a radical change was preparing itself. The change may have experienced some delays due to technical difficulties, but it was inevitable. I must have been deaf and blind to the clues that something was preparing itself. Over the years, the clues had nevertheless been multiplying at the same rate as the kangaroo mice under our conjugal bed, with the exception that kangaroo mice were said to be endangered. This appellation might have referred to populations of said mice anywhere other than under our bed, as it was certainly not the case in our experience of them. Anyway, suffice to say that I cannot pretend that, on some level, I was unaware that something had been stewing. All I can claim in my defense is that I had no idea what might have been the nature of the coming change. Most of all I did not guess—could possibly not guess—that I would not be invited to its unveiling.

And there I was in Montréal, not knowing really why or what I was looking for, or even if Julie would still want me, if I miraculously found her.

CHAPTER 4

I did not know yet if Charlotte would have me in her apartment. I could at least trust her to stay put in one place. Ever since I've known her, she has always lived at the same address. She survived many attacks to her chosen abode, such as the invasion of a swarm of giant cockroaches. Apparently, a friend had inadvertently introduced the first specimen from an extended stay in Chiapas. The insect was a superb example of its species, measuring an impressive seven centimeters long. As the story goes, it disappeared promptly in a very large crack in Charlotte's kitchen wall. I am not an expert on insects, but I can only presume that said cockroach must have been a female, and pregnant to boot. Or parthenogenetic. Or maybe there had been two cockroaches, one of each gender. What did I know about how cockroaches did these things? At any rate, two weeks later, not only Charlotte's apartment but also the neighbouring houses were infested by close replicas of the giant exotic pest.

The cockroach incident was just one of a series, much like the Seven Plagues of Egypt, that could have chased Charlotte from her apartment. For example, there had also been the gentrification-fuelled rental hikes in the neighbourhood and the pitiful state of the noisy plumbing in her own unrenovated place, plus the improperly installed electric wires sagging alarmingly towards the kitchen sink and all the other funky solutions illegally set up by a succession of previous tenants. But Charlotte held fast and strong. She even womanaged to save from slaughter a solitary Silver Maple that chose to grow in the minuscule yard in front of her building. The tree was leaning precariously towards the sidewalk and had been deemed "dangerous" by the city. Charlotte put a convincing petition together, pointing out the importance of preserving green urban spaces. She won. The city did not even prune the leaning tree. As if to prove Charlotte right, the maple never dropped a single branch on any passersby. Charlotte was a very powerful, determined, and smart woman. I tried to call her again from the airport.

She was still not answering her phone. This time, though, I listened to the whole message on her machine.

"Hello, *bonjour*! *Vous avez rejoint,* you have reached Charlotte's place. We are not available at the moment, *s'il-vous-plaît, laissez nous un message.* Message, please."

The message was normal enough, especially for Charlotte, but the voice was not hers. At first, I had thought it had been one of those computer-generated messages where one can choose the gender, even the accent of the voice for security purposes. But the tone of the message was too personal-sounding, too intimate to have been that of a machine. For one thing, the speaker's gender was not quite clear. The pitch of the voice was too high for a male, too low for a female. It was both sweet and assertive. It also had an odd mixture of accents I couldn't quite place. And why did the person leaving the message not identify themselves? I declined the offer to leave my own reply and hung up, puzzled.

Who was Charlotte living with? My friend was a very independent woman. She would never share her apartment with anyone long enough to have them put a message on her answering machine. Unless she was head over heels in love. I was disappointed. The idea of having to put up with another person in Charlotte's life disturbed me. I could only hope, albeit with mixed feelings, that this mysterious person would actually be sharing Charlotte's bed. That way, I could still have the only other place available in the minuscule apartment: the space under the kitchen table.

Sometimes, when the other half of Charlotte's bed had happened to be unoccupied, she had gotten lonely enough to invite me to a sleepover. When I say "sleep," I mean that she would sleep, and me not. Long before I even realized my own sexual preference, I already had a mean crush on her. Being invited to share Charlotte's bed was a great honour for me, even though ours was an entirely platonic affair. On her part, anyway. There I was, not knowing yet that I was a lesbian, and her, who knew (adamantly) that she was not. So, I spent my share of nights in Charlotte's bed, tossing and turning, not knowing what to do with my controversial torment, a wanting that I thought to be impossible to act upon for lack of equipment. I would lie awake for hours on end, listening to the soft whisperings of her breath verging on snoring, while I was slowly being eaten alive by my own all-consuming, burning desire.

Trying to reassure myself in those unconscious days, I had told myself that, at least this way, Charlotte would never have me overstay my welcome. If I had stayed too long, I would have fizzled into a smouldering pile of red-hot coals fuelled by my useless, excessive want. One morning, she would have woken up to a small pile of gently smoking ashes.

This time, assuming I could crash on the kitchen floor, I could only hope that my friend would not be as noisy as she had been with Fernando. As happy as I was for her—had to be, given my spiritual affiliation—I didn't rejoice at the prospect of being reminded how much fun I could have had with her in bed. She was, I was sure, what in popular French they call *un vrai pétard*. Roughly, one could translate it as a "firecracker." Add to that colourful gases, sparkles, and a series of explosions...

✳ ✳ ✳

If I had put more thought into planning my arrival in Montréal instead of packing up and leaving Genus Island on a whim, I would have chosen a better day to arrive. We were in the middle of the Canada Day weekend. There was a subdued sort of frenzy all around me at the airport, with red and white maple-leaved flags dotting the metallic landscape. I could not help but wonder if there had been some blue *Fleur-de-lis* hung all around the week before for the *Fête Nationale*. I did not get an answer. Besides, there were more pressing things to attend to, such as bracing myself against what I thought would be sweltering ambient heat outside the terminal. Also, the precarious condition of my stomach was vacillating between hunger and nausea. I took a deep breath, the last relatively fresh one for a while.

I walked through the two sets of electronic doors, still holding my last breath. Stepping outside, I exhaled. I was expecting, with my next breath in, the hair in my nostrils to sizzle as if they had been anointed with an acid-saturated Q-Tip. This did not happen. The temperature that day would have been almost tolerable. Well, for a local that is. For me, it was still too hot and heavy, with a dusty humidity I had grown unaccustomed to. A misty stench of diesel, the international scent of travel, immediately stuck to me like a giant octopus.

Most of the passengers around me were piling into air-conditioned taxis, unaware that I was snubbing them. Even if I had felt I could afford a taxi, I thought I would still use public transit as it was more ecological. Then I saw the woman from the plane with her two kids in tow. The girl was gripping her mother's skirt with both her little hands, and the baby was wailing. They must have stopped for a snack or bathroom break as well. The woman seemed to be painstakingly making her way towards the *Aérobus*. I almost waived my principles. I wanted to give her some money for a taxi just to make her life easier for a change. But I wasn't so sure, given my own meagre financial situation. Instead of spending the money, I sent love all around, even to the people who had chosen the easier but more polluting way to get to their destination. Who was I to judge?

One single *Aérobus* was stopped at its station. For some reason, the bus reminded me of a female housefly in heat. We, the passengers, would be the eggs she was waiting for to fill her belly. Funny sort of metaphor, but anyone who has taken a Montréal bus midday in summer would know what I mean. The bus also seemed very, very far away. I would have to walk on hot, steamy pavement with no hope of any shade. I was afraid that, egg-like as I was, thanks to my own metaphor, I would get hard-boiled in no time. I let the woman and her children walk ahead of me. I followed them at a turtle's pace, huffing and puffing with my suddenly heavy pack on my back, fixating on the bus the whole time, my only hope being finding the air cooler inside.

What a disappointment. The driver had turned the ignition of the bus off. This included air-conditioning. The door was open. I had a choice between outside pollution or inside staleness. The heat was not optional. The woman and her two children chose to wait outside for a while before they went in. They eventually settled themselves at the front of the bus. I decided to follow them in. I didn't notice if the woman had paid. For my part, I thought I would not and went to hide all the way at the back of the bus. Hopefully the driver would not come and bother me there. I couldn't figure out anyway if I was supposed to have a ticket or to pay cash. As I slid past the little girl, she looked at me with those serious eyes of hers. I felt guilty. Sweat started pouring down from my forehead. Some of it got into my eyes. It smarted.

My chosen seat was so hot that I took a towel from my backpack to sit on. The driver came back into the bus. I could smell smoke on him even from where I was. He jumped up on his seat and opened a book. He didn't seem inconvenienced by the sweltering heat at all. I thought of getting out. Anything would be cooler than what I was going through. But if I went out, I would have to come back in and face the driver. He would be sure to demand payment. I resigned myself to my fate. I let myself sink into a hot sweaty doze.

By the time I came to, the air-conditioning was working full tilt. The air had gotten considerably cooler, almost too cold. We were rolling at full speed on a new highway. The bus was now quite full, and I found myself sharing the wide seat that ran across the back of the bus with a young man in dreads, a mom nursing her baby, a couple necking, and right beside me, a large person with a very strong body odour. If I moved from my seat to avoid the affront to my nostrils, I would have to stand. I took the towel from under me and discreetly wrapped it around my throat and lower face, pretending to be wiping the sweat off but really covering my mouth and nose. I turned my face to the window.

Intermittently, from in between trees, factories, and overpasses, the tall buildings rose from downtown like so many fingers. The only building I recognized was Place Ville-Marie. It had been erected before I was born, but I remembered my mother once having explained to me that it had been shaped in the form of a cross in an attempt to revive a Catholic faith that was crumbling with the advent of feminism and the accompanying birth-control pill, and also with the general cultural awakening called "*la Révolution Tranquille.*" There had been a widespread dissatisfaction and malaise with religion in general, and the clergy in particular. La Place Ville-Marie wasn't just a building; it was a monument. One charged with meaning.

I had also gotten to know the interior of the building quite intimately in my own lifetime when I worked as a messenger. Not only had I ridden the Place Ville-Marie elevators frequently, I also knew about the intricate subterranean corridors that networked, like a giant spider-web, below all of downtown. Some of the passages had been shown to me, cigarette in hand, by the seasoned older messengers. Some other secret channels I think I discovered myself. I was very proud of my underground knowledge, and it helped me many times in making my deliveries at record-breaking speed.

One enchanting day, the scene in the Place Ville-Marie lobby had turned into a vision. I forget what day of the week it was or even the season, although I suspect it must have been spring. That day, at the end of my shift as I got out of the elevator on the ground floor, I stopped in my tracks. While I had been making my last delivery on one of the higher floors, the whole downstairs had been flooded with a flock of young, colourful women. Their voices, more of a cackle, a trill, or a warble than actual words in any human language, echoed throughout the cage formed by the granite floor, the tall glass windows, and the metallic ceiling.

To me, the women and girls all looked like some strange yet-to-be-named species of exotic birds. I stood there, jaw gaping like that of a freshly-hatched ugly gosling waiting to be fed, eyes popping out of their sockets. Instead of receiving pieces of worm in my throat, it was only my eyes that were being filled with the fluttering, intoxicating vision. I remained standing near my elevator, mesmerized, until the very last two women-birds had flown through the revolving doors in a quiver of flying hair and feathers, leaving me nothing but an echo, not even a single fleck of down. That very night, as soon as I got home, I drew a huge picture of them, from memory, using all my coloured pencils. Some of the women ended up looking completely like birds, their original long human legs—made longer by high heels—transformed under my hands into far-reaching, heron-like stilts extending all the way to their personal zenith. Some girls and women had retained their human breasts, their adornments clearly visible through a sheer top, while their lips had turned into beaks. One sported a crest like those California quails have on their heads. There was not a single humble sparrow in the lot.

I was very satisfied with my drawing. I submitted it as well as another one of my favourites to an art show at Concordia University where I was attending evening art classes. The second picture had been a full-frontal, very realistic coloured-pencil drawing of my own vulva. That one I had done as a manifesto to commemorate the first time I had the courage to look at my own genitalia in a hand-held mirror. I had been surprised to find that my lips reminded me of a rooster's comb. My discovery had impressed me so much that I had to draw a picture the next day, from memory. Those were very experimental times for artists, an era when "anything went." And go my pictures did. They actually got taken, who knows by whom, why, or where?

I was left with no other choice but to interpret the stealing of both of my art pieces as compliments. The girl who exhibited her used menstrual pad was not subject to the same treatment as I had been. Maybe it was simply because the pad and the bloody slime on it lacked archival quality. I have no idea what the person or persons who took my drawings might have done with my creations. For a long time, I shuddered at the thought of my images, especially that of my vulva, having ended up in the wrong hands. Like some pervert's, or worse, in the claws of a woman who wished me ill. For a while, all sorts of kinky, gross images had invaded my paranoid mind. Eventually, the only way I had found to exorcise my own evil thoughts had been to do a ritual to release said drawings. It took the burning of a whole lot of sage, incense, and even some old photographs of myself to finally make peace with the feeling of having been violated.

As seen through the grimy windows of the bus I was in, on my way downtown on Canada Day, the cross on Mont-Royal was still perched at its usual spot. I wondered if all its electric bulbs were in place and working. My friend Rémi had told me that the bulbs were, in certain circles, considered collector's items. For one, they were difficult to steal, and two, they lasted a long, long time. I didn't hang out with Rémi long enough to find out if he eventually managed to get one (or some) for himself, or how long the bulbs actually lasted before they ran out of whatever gas they were burning. I was quite certain that his brother Patrick at least would have figured out how to nab a few for himself. He would have used them to light his grow-op, for sure. I made a mental note to try and find Rémi, not so much because of the lights but just out of curiosity. I hadn't seen him for close to ten years.

We were nearing downtown. My own impatience was growing at an alarming rate. I decided to get off at the first stop, whatever it might be, and walk. I was getting more and more panicked with every smooth turn of the bus's wheels, as if anticipating disaster. Despite the frigid air-conditioning, sweat reappeared on my brow. Frantic, I slung my backpack on my shoulder and got up in the moving bus, determined to get to the front and eject myself at the first opportunity. I didn't see the bag spilling softly into the aisle. I tripped. I caught myself from catapulting just in time. I swore. Then I realized the bag belonged to the girl with the skull I had seen at the bar at the airport. Too late to swallow my offensive words. I bent down to gently push the bag out of the way. She did the same, simultaneously. My own bag slipped from my shoulder. It fell on the girl's head. Confused, by now red as a cooked lobster, I fell to my knees with a plethora of excuses spilling, foam-like, from my mouth. The girl's face was an uncomfortable-few centimetres from my own. She was wearing a neutral expression. I would have preferred her to be mad or something, anything. Her delicate lips drew me in like a sweet apple on the verge of falling to its inexorable destiny if not picked, smashing and being burrowed into by worms all the way into its core. Only a kiss would save the forbidden fruit from doom.

Attention à la tentation!! Beware of the temptation!! I did not kiss her. Instead, I blurted out some more stupid excuses that were not even funny.

"*Tellement désolée. Je ne suis qu'une maladroite, une tête de linotte, une nouille...*"

My breath still reeked so much of alcohol that I could smell it. The girl stared at me for too long. Then she bent back up with a graceful shrug of her frail, vine-like shoulders, curiously glabrous despite the coldness of the ambient air. Her face lit up with the most magnificent, most superlatively angelic of brightnesses. She blossomed out into a beautiful smile, like a kalei-doscope. For an instant, I forgot that I was trying to get off the bus. Later, as I was recalling the endearing scene, I realized with a touch of guilt that Julie had been nowhere to be found in my consciousness at the time.

By the time I finally found myself outside in front of the *Hôtel Reine Elizabeth*, the ambient air seemed even sultrier than it had been in Dorval. How easily I had gotten unused to the Montréal summer heat. A small group of female workers, who seemed to have escaped from their office a few minutes before rush hour, were speed-walking, chatting like seagulls, towards the closest Métro station. Unlike their counterparts of many years before, their colours were subdued, almost drab. I caught a whiff of their new scent as my hair lifted slightly with the whoosh of their passing. They left me feeling dizzy. One of them had dropped something, a hair clip maybe, with a single small white feather on it. I didn't pick it up.

I made my way to Sainte-Catherine Street, heading east until the next message would arrive from my inner urban-survival guide. I felt frumpy. My black Capri pants were still smeared with caked-up mud from Ralph's pen. To this, some indescribable moisture had been added, probably from the floor of the bus. My striped t-shirt that I thought so chic on Genus Island stuck to my heat- and hunger-swollen abdomen like I have seen in sad pictures of refugee children. Gertrude Stein once wrote that, in the city, people have to get themselves ready before they go out, whereas in the country, they simply went out, end of story. I had gotten out of the habit of going out in the big city. Especially since Julie and I would wander around at home in our birthday suits.

I would have to get new clothes. And wash my hair with shampoo. How unappealing. On Genus, we used seaweed. I would have to get a job, the sooner the better, and go shopping. Better still, I would have to borrow clothes first since I had not budgeted for such luxuries as new clothes and toiletries. All I had brought in my backpack in lieu of grooming tools was a toothbrush and a single stick of Kohl for emergencies.

A cajoling smell of fresh croissants filled my nostrils. It was coming from somewhere down under, where it was dark and cool. I followed the aroma into the entrails of the city, all the way to a tiny, brand-new shining kiosk. It looked like a chain of some sort. My political beliefs usually forbade me from supporting such establishments. Too late. My stomach, blindly obeying the commands given out by my reptilian brain, triggered by the smell, had turned me into Pavlov's bitch. My stomach didn't care about ethics. It demanded to be fed. I gave in.

The service was efficient. I was soon grasping a sort of greasy little pillow in my paw. I made my way back out into the street. The consuming of the croissant, to be an authentic urban experience, had to be done in a bustling crowd. I took a huge bite—half the croissant. It was disappointing. Even the cajoling, buttery smell of my pillow had evaporated. It was as if the alluring aroma had been originally piped into the kiosk from a gas-tankful of emissions manufactured in a smell-factory in Lachine. I needed something else. Like coffee. There was this cute little place under *La Place Bonaventure* that used to make a decent Cappuccino. I wondered if it was still there.

The belly of the *Place* had been transformed into a European-style train station. My café was nowhere to be seen. Reluctantly, I stood in a long line at a *cafétéria* that was selling an astounding variety of healthy-looking food. Very healthy and scrumptious looking but prohibitively expensive. Fortunately, I could hear the characteristic hiss of a huge espresso machine. I contented myself with a double espresso. It was what I imagined a perfect Italian coffee should taste like. Not that I've ever been to Italy, but I have read many travel books, just in case I might have enough money to go one day. My coffee was appropriately strong and piping hot. All sorts of exciting ideas rushed immediately into my brain and left just as quickly. I got frantic. The only way I found to prevent my head from spinning itself off my neck was to start walking again. This time, I was walking faster. Really, I was just moving at the same pace as everybody else.

The big clock I remembered from my messenger days was still in the same place. It was also still giving the wrong time. Despite my jet-lag, I knew it was locally somewhere in the mid-afternoon, and not ten past nine as the clock insisted on displaying. I got lost temporarily in thinking about time—the futility, the illusion. To defy time, and waste it, or better yet, kill some of it. I decided to get lost in the labyrinth of the underground.

All the false riches, the costume jewellery, the piles of handbags, the racks of shoes of assorted shapes, colours and sizes, the mountains of colourful paper and plastic, the profusion of things only people who have everything would need, all that simultaneously fascinated and repulsed me. I imagined a scene, maybe not as far into the future as one might think, where our human race would have consumed ourselves into extinction. Then a UFO full of alien archeologists would come to study our planet, now empty of human Earth-beings. How thrilled they would be to make their way amidst the armies of cockroaches, the extended families of rats, the flocks of cooing pigeons, the murders of crows, and the march of mutant reptiles! The aliens would don our ridiculous frocks and laugh at each other. They would attempt, probably without success, to figure out some possible uses of our multiple gadgets. Hilarious theories would be speculated about what such strange objects, such as souvenir key chains or rhinestone-studded shoehorns, might have been used for. The aliens would have a grand time at our expense.

For a moment, I was almost ready, if it had been possible, to trade in Julie's and my entire collection of lesbian *vidéos* just to see their faces. Or better still, to watch the films themselves together with the extraterrestrials on our archaic, scratched TV with the purple circle on the top right corner. I started to wonder, if not popcorn, what appropriate munchies our visitors would have come up with for the occasion.

The thought of the *vidéos* unfortunately brought me back to thinking about Julie. They were hers, really, and not ours. Who knows if she would have wanted the aliens to watch them? She was very particular about who she accepted as audience to her treasures. Better to say goodbye to my imaginary friends and focus on my present mission in Montréal. My first stop, my spring-board, would be Charlotte's apartment. Maybe by the time I got there, she would be home. I resurfaced to street level and returned to Ste-Catherine Street. There were so many tourist shops on this stretch of road that, disgusted, I turned left as soon as I could and zigzagged my way up towards Sherbrooke.

The big, round apartment building was still perched on top of the hill. That is where Rémi and I had lived for a short while ten years or so before. He was going through a deep depression at the time as I simultaneously got into a manic phase in a futile attempt at filling the void created by his apathy. Among several other activities, I was attending art school at Concordia, plus working as a messenger and as a live model in my attempts at supporting the three of us: Rémi, our crazy cat Minuit, and me. I was also working on my first novel. I have to give credit to Rémi for giving me all the space I needed to focus. As soon as I sat at my desk facing south, he would leave me alone to chase the elusive whims of my creativity. There were no tall buildings yet to block the view from our eighth-floor apartment. I could, if I wanted, transport myself over the city and fly all the way to Mont Saint-Hilaire, which I could see from our window. And fly I did, whenever I could. Sometimes Rémi would slip a steaming cup of coffee by my left hand. No thanks, no acknowledgements were expected, ever. I had no idea at the time how privileged I had been to be living with such a supportive partner, despite his depression. By the way, I have never finished my novel.

That day, looking up at the "*Colisée*" building, almost expecting to see Rémi waving at me from the eighth-floor window, I wondered again what he might be up to. I had to track him down. Soon.

Further on, I walked through the student ghetto. I must have lived on each and every one of those streets after my mother died. I called them my crazy years. I was all of eighteen springs when I lost my mother. I had to grow up overnight. I chose to do this by piling up all the experiences, hippie drugs, lovers, and even orgies that I could, just to forget who I was and where I came from. And forget I did. That time is a big blur. I only remember a face or two here, a faded flower there, a particularly spiritual hallucination, maybe.

I did recognize the window at street level on Milton Street. My friends Kent and Robert had once shared that basement flat, eleven years previously. It had been their first urban dwelling as they had both grown up in the west-end suburbs. The apartment was also where Kent discovered that he was gay. The two young men had thrown a party and a lot of their friends had stayed over through the sleepless night, including me. Eventually, at dawn, most people settled down on whatever surface they could find, be it an old chair, the floor, or on top of someone else. Robert and Kent ended up sharing a bed. Side by side.

Days later, I heard two versions of the same story. Kent related to me that he had been horrified at waking up with a massive erection. He said it was not one of those "routine" morning occurrences. He had taken one look at an endearingly beautiful, sleeping Robert, and there it was, the turgid, peremptory proof of his own sexual attraction towards his friend, pointing its eager head. Kent tried to gently kiss Robert. Robert woke up. Robert jumped and almost hit his amorous friend. He apologized, but it was too late. Kent's feelings got hurt. Badly.

Robert's story also includes the aborted kiss but his focuses mainly on his own embarrassment at being caught as a homophobe and having seemed to find his friend's advance repulsive. But, he assured me, he was not gay himself. It made no difference to me either way.

Kent eventually shacked up with a bisexual man. Kevin. I lived with them for a couple of months in another apartment on Saint Urbain that they called the Egg House. It is in this love-nest that Kent finalized his gayness status. I had the dubious honour of having been the last woman he tried to have sex with. Since I had had sex with bisexual Kevin, Kent figured it was only fair I would sleep with him too. However, Kent and I failed to get excited about each other. We agreed that we were each in his or her way, very sexy persons. For other people. Thus, Kent came to the conclusion that he was exclusively gay. I did not know yet I was a lesbian. I just thought I was better off to have Kent as a good friend. I had to wait a few more years, including doing time being married to a man, before I faced the lovely truth of my own prefer-ence. Who knows? If Julie hadn't saved me from heterosexual dissatisfaction, I might still be looking for my soulmate in the wrong clan, like a dowser searching for water in the desert.

My walk was taking on a decidedly nostalgic aura. I felt like I was the main character in a movie, revisiting the streets I had roamed in my younger days. The streets were still the same but different in some indescribable way. For one thing, the trees were taller and lusher than I remembered, and there seemed to be more of them. Wild vines were growing everywhere, covering balconies and entire building walls. Even though we were still close to downtown, the whole area was eerily quiet, dark, and green. In the humid heat, the odours of a rain forest were so intense that we could have been in the tropics.

I finally emerged from the jungle at the complicated maze of streets, overpasses, and lights of the Park Avenue and Pine intersection. I felt confused, having re-emerged without warning into a wildly urban panorama. To settle my nerves and orient myself, I started looking for a tunnel a block or so away that I remembered as having been near Duluth. It used to traverse Park Avenue underground. It also used to reek of piss. I hated to have to use it, but at the time, it had been the easiest way to cross to the other side of the busy avenue. I would run for my dear life through the dark and dank passage, hoping I would not come face to face with a pissing maniac.

That day of my return to Montréal, I realized I was, in a bizarre way, almost looking forward to seeing the tunnel. This may sound gross, but I was even anticipating with faint trepidation my nostrils being stung with the acrid smell of human male animal scents. This weird anticipation was not so much because I was looking for a perverse thrill. It was mostly because the tunnel and its accompanying odours, as offensive as they were, would at least have been something familiar. Also, and mainly—and I don't quite know why—the tunnel, complete with its urinal smells, would be certain to remind me of Julie in a full-frontal kind of way. Maybe it had something to do with her obsession with learning to piss standing. She would position herself, legs akimbo, opening her labia, defiantly watching the golden stream spurt out without messing her thighs with a single drop. Seeing her like that never failed to get me wonderfully excited.

★　★　★

I thought Julie and I understood each other. It wasn't a given at first, but at least we were determined to make our love work, whatever it took. I remember a scene at the very beginning stages of our relationship. We happened to be in the bathtub with no water. I forget how we got there and why we chose that particular receptacle for our libations. I don't think we had been wanting to take a bath even. Maybe we wanted to feel contained in some way, like in a womb. At any rate, Julie was busy caressing my clit, expertly, thanks to her vast Sapphic experience. I remember gently nibbling at her left ear, according to what I thought would be an act that might have been complementary to hers. I was just a few seconds away from my point of no return. It was taking all my willpower to remember not to bite Julie's ear off, when she said out of the blue:

"Is that my laundry spinning around in the dryer?"

This was happening during our very first two weeks of being together at the apartment Pearl had conveniently vacated to hang out with her new beau. I didn't fully realize yet that Julie was very particular about her own clothes. I thought I was doing her a favour by throwing her same-colour garments into the washing process along with mine. I didn't crane my neck to listen for the sound of laundry turning. I already knew that, yes, I was doing laundry. OUR laundry. I was mad. How dare she interrupt our lovemaking to ask such a stupid question?

After all the sex—some bad, some almost good—that I'd had with men during my brief but busy hetero phase, I had learned one essential fact: never, EVER interrupt one's crescendo to orgasm. It is difficult enough for women and men to try and coordinate their timing with each other, given the sad fact that the average male climaxes within two to five minutes of entry and the average woman, twenty. Minimum. Add to that hours, months sometimes, of courting and foreplay, romance, caresses, flowers, and bonbons.

In my humble opinion, the odds of physical gratification in heterosexual lovemaking are generally in men's favour. I guess women compensate with our ability for multiple orgasms. Still, one often needs a dedicated partner. I can hear the protests of millions of fiercely heterosexual women who stand by their men. Oh well.

I have wasted a lot of useless time recreating, in my imagination, a fictional movie scene that looks like this: One woman and one man are frantically ripping their clothes off. They face each other. Their feverish eyes are locked. The man pushes the woman to a wall, preferably made of old brick. His gesture is not violent. Just determined. A shade this side of rough. The man is wearing a leather jacket. His face shows a day's old beard. The woman is wearing a tight skirt, short, easy to pull up. Miraculously, she's either not wearing underwear or the taking off of it is not a problem. She is not having her period. We are to assume they go at it. Hungrily, with much huffing and puffing and moaning. So far, this scene might be familiar to the audience. It has been played over and over in countless movies with only a few slight variations.

But then something different happens in my movie: The man, satisfied, pulls his jeans back up. The woman, furious, scratches his face, bites his ear off, or yanks a tuft of hair off his head. Why? Because she is frustrated. And there he is already looking for a cigarette while she needs more loving. Lots more. If I ever get to make a film, this is how I would end the scene. With the woman slapping his face. I would add to that the soundtrack of mechanical applause, as after a mediocre guitar solo in a room with bad lighting.

That's why I love women. We understand each other. We would never leave the other person hanging. We finish the job of love, and we love doing it. That is why I was so mad at Julie that day in the bathtub episode. She should have known better. Fortunately, she figured out what was going down and never left me on the brink ever again. She picked up our lovemaking from where we had left off and took me to Nirvana no problem. She didn't even answer the phone a few minutes later, even though she was expecting one from a prospective employer. The call could have been for a job Julie wouldn't have wanted anyway. The company could have ended up moving to Toronto a few months later, being mostly made up of Anglophones. They could have their job, and Julie and I could continue with our loving.

The rain brought me back to the present moment. There were still seven long blocks to walk from where I was to Charlotte's apartment, and then that downpour. Hard. The cool, heavy drops were washing the sweat off my face. I could taste salt. My t-shirt started to stick to my feverish body. It felt good. Then I remembered I wasn't wearing a bra. This was no Genus island. As cute as my erect nipples may have been in a country-like setting, I had to hide them or run the risk of being followed by some maniac. Not that there were many around, but there was lots of car traffic on Park Avenue. Someone might stop and offer me a "ride." It was better not to take any chances. Julie would not have had the same problem. She would have her own breasts bound tightly or hidden behind a loose shirt. No one, not even the Naiads, had seen them in their full splendour for many years. No one, except for me. I knew how absolutely exquisite they were. Too bad she did not share my opinion. She would hardly even have looked at them in the mirror, if we had had one.

I was leaving the green stretch of Park Avenue and getting close to Mont-Royal with its lineup of *restos* and shops. I fumbled in my bag and took out a sarong, which I reluctantly wrapped around my wet shoulders. I hated the idea of having to be modest, but the alternative would have been worse.

The telephone booths kitty-corner beckoned me to try calling Charlotte again. A human voice that was still not my friend's answered in English. I recognized the voice as belonging to the same person as on the answering machine. They didn't seem surprised to hear from me, a stranger. The voice was unusually friendly. There was no time to try and determine if this person was intimate with Charlotte or not. Either way, I immediately felt at ease.

"Charlotte did come back, but she is lying down already. She was tired," they said.

"*Euh* … can I spend the night … at your place?" I was reluctant to ask for shelter from this stranger, but I had no choice.

To my immense relief, they replied, "Friends of Charlotte's are my friends too. Of course, you can stay. As long as you want. *Mi casa es tu casa.*" It was as if my staying was a given, the most natural thing to do.

I still couldn't quite place the accent. It definitely had a twinge of Parisian French. Not as a mother tongue but as from someone who has spent some time there. I imagined us in a *ménage-à-trois*, not necessarily in a sexual way. We would attend a selection of *vernissages*, *flânant* casually, leaving floating tassels from our silk scarves behind us as so many slippery fingers. We would utter very *à-propos* comments about the exposed *oeuvres d'Art*. There would be sightings of us in the trendiest of cafés, sipping the latest concoctions. We would get invited to the coolest of parties, walking the fine line between politically correct and provocative. At first, I would mostly listen. Then I could sweep up the latest jargon nonchalantly spilled on the shiny floors like so many scintillating sequins to be used appropriately later, showing off my new coolness and cultural erudition. We would eat little—in public, at least. We would peck at our food sublimely like exotic birds. In our intimacy, we would *empiffre* (stuff) ourselves like pashas, our fingers dripping with unctuous day-old marinade.

Maybe Charlotte finally got lucky in love. If indeed she was enthralled. The person on the phone sounded fun, educated, and easy-going. A relationship with them would be a change from the succession of talented but lost souls Charlotte had been supporting over the years. In this way, I felt lucky I had never shared her bed. If I had, I would soon have been let loose on the

Sargasso Sea or somewhere, ending up on that weird island of plastic garbage floating, drifting aimlessly on the wide-open waters of our planet. Discarded.

Speaking of being let loose, I thought of Julie. Again. Insecurity came to get me under my wet sarong and tightened its grip on my solar plexus. What if she simply got tired of me? I had no idea if I was going through some kind of a test of our love. Was I set up to prove my adoration by having to go clear across the continent, do some intensive searching—including soul-searching—and finally get her back? Of course, she could have gone anywhere on the planet. Maybe she even went on an odyssey to find the legendary Island of Floating Plastic Garbage. She could easily have left on a quest like that. But by some strange telepathic phenomenon, a skill that we had developed over the years, I was almost certain she was here somewhere in Montréal. That almost-certainty in itself may have been, I innocently thought, a sign that I was supposed to find her. And then, supposing I did find her, what would happen? Maybe Julie wouldn't know the answer either. The decision of the next step would have to be made on the spot like a hummingbird choosing the perfect flower.

If reincarnation exists, and if we have a choice, I think I'd like to try and come back as an orchid. I would be beautiful. Unquestionably desirable. I would shamelessly exhibit my availability when I would be ready. All that I would have to do is wait to be served by a succession of pollinating insects. No questions asked, no mind-games, no soul-searching. Easy.

In the meantime, I had reached Bernard Street. I turned right towards Esplanade. Adrenalin was coursing through my veins like a speedboat on choppy waters. Soon I would be basking in the enchanting aura of one of the sexiest women I knew. After Julie of course. My own sexual experience with women was limited to my life with her. I was not an expert by any means. Still, one never knows. With my fresh Sapphic experience under my belt, Charlotte might be willing to give me another chance.

The adrenalin sank right down in between my legs. I frowned. I scolded my useless desire. I told my down-theres they would get us all into trouble. My little pearl had better behave or we would both end up lost somewhere in the Land of Unused Talents and Opportunities, like pens out of ink, like lone socks whose twins mysteriously and irritatingly got lost in the wash. If I was going to stay sane, living at luscious, delicious Charlotte's, we had better keep cool and level-headed. Breathe deep and slow. Release any hopes of hanky-panky, buttress all our cells against pheromone-fuelled bright eyes and bushy tiger-tails peeking out from under innocuous-looking frumpy housecoats.

The date of the building in front of me was etched in stone: "1911." If nothing had changed much since my last visit, I guessed that the plumbing and electricity would still be dating back to that era as well. Fortunately, the outside stairway had been renovated, and I climbed the steep rungs with relative ease. I was still fit, thanks to my recent country-living. My heart was beating wildly with trepidation and badly contained exhilaration at soon being at my long-time friend's door. Just one more floor and I could marvel at her beautiful presence. I paused on the first landing and caught my breath before I opened the door in front of me and clambered up the next set of stairs to the landing on the second floor, near her personal door.

I was so excited that I almost knocked at the wrong address. Some sort of instinct, some vague memory of what the neighbour was like in the older days stopped my knuckles from rapping at the door on the right. The visuals poured in. I remembered this neighbour who lived across the landing. She once greeted me with an extremely sharp-looking knife, mouth twisted in a snarl, eyes aflame, ready to strike. I had no idea why she had even opened the door for me if she was that suspicious of visitors. Maybe she had been anticipating someone other than me, her ex perhaps, the father of her only girl-child.

I knocked at the correct door. After a short pause, followed by long fumblings with the loose lock that still hadn't been fixed, the door opened wide. A superb, tall woman was standing in front of me. It wasn't Charlotte.

My mouth gaped open. As soon as I noticed this, I shut my trap but too tightly. An inhuman sound meant as a greeting croaked out of a tiny passage through my compressed throat. The face of the woman in front of me showed an expression that didn't match the benevolence of the previous voice on the phone. Who could blame her? She had no way to guess at the inner beauty, loveliness, and discretion of this greasy-haired, wet, live imposition on her conjugal beatitude. Because beatitude it had to be. Charlotte would not allow anyone to put a message on her answering machine who was anything less than sublime—in her own eyes at least.

The person who was not Charlotte did not invite me in. I almost had to push past her to slide my body into the minuscule anteroom. Somehow, despite the awkwardness of the scene, I found a smile floating around. I caught

70

it and pasted it on my face. She replied in kind. Or maybe I had imagined it all, wishing. I stepped back slightly and tilted my head up to get a better look at the tall person's face. She had an almost transcendental beauty with a hint of severity due to the pronounced, aquiline nose. The lips were slim but not thin, firm and well-traced, a perfect match to the gently arched eyebrows that had been drawn on dexterously after a rigorous removal of superfluous hair.

The person returned my scrutiny of her face with a slow, restrained sweep over my whole body with her immense, almost bulging blue eyes adorned with sets of long, real lashes. She did this coldly at first, then gradually her expression took on a slightly more benevolent air. The whole face, large and angular, transformed to reveal a grace verging on nobility, with a matching hint of ill-concealed disdain.

And what a voice! Now that I could see the face that went with the message on the phone, I understood the harmony that existed between the two elements. With its slow, unctuous and deep tone, and the *je-ne-sais-quoi* of a foreign accent, the result was perfection personified. Intrigued at where the sound was coming from, I couldn't help but look at the throat. A distinct Adam's apple still lurked there as a relic from a distant past, as if this person had truly forgotten to swallow the coveted fruit from the original Garden of Eden. Charlotte had finally found her perfect match. I had no idea what stage of transition this person in front of me was at, but wherever they were, it seemed to me that Charlotte and them must be enjoying the best of many exciting, promising transient worlds.

I must have gotten myself lost at sea on my sailboat of fantasies. Now the person was staring at me with head slightly tilted, a single eyebrow raised. An answer to some question I didn't catch was definitely expected from me.

"Oh, excuse me," I blurted out in English with remnants of my Québécois accent. "I did not hear you."

"I said," they said with a hint of a sigh of exasperation, "my name is Josie. That's all."

Fortunately for me, the enormous blue eyes were now glimmering mischievously. I must have been looking quite pitiful.

"Uhm ... hello. So sorry to show up like this, unexpected. My name is Claire. I am indeed enchanted to meet you. Also, I am completely exhausted. Would it bother you very much if I took a nap?"

"But of course, sweetie. I can make you a little nest under the kitchen table. You will be comfy there until Charlotte wakes up."

All this was said in a benevolent tone. I didn't like the allusion to my size or maybe even my inferior status with being called "sweetie," the reference to a "little nest," and the use of the word "comfy." Three expressions that were offensive to me all at once. While Josie was busy with assembling my bed, I thought of replying to their comments with something witty to offset what I judged to be condescending remarks. My brain only offered the buzzing residual sounds of an airplane. I had exhausted all the caffeine I had ingested at the train-station downtown. There was nothing else for me to do but drag my wet carcass into the kitchen and hide under the table like a generically guilty dog that never knows what it did wrong. My clothes, drenched by the rain and slimy with sweat, clung to my body like a shroud. Without even peeling them off, I collapsed on the makeshift bed—indeed, it was small, perfectly adapted to my size, I had to admit—and sank into a feverish slumber.

CHAPTER 5

The sun had just set by the time I woke up. The air all around me seemed as muggy as when I had arrived. The back door was wide open, letting in the remains of spicy bouquets of mixed ethnic foods: curries, tortillas, *pommodori* sauce, and lots of roasted garlic. I realized I was hungry. I got up and bumped my head. Oh yes, I was under Charlotte's kitchen table. Once again. She had welcomed Josie into her boudoir, sparing me the agonizing delight of sharing her bed. I half-clambered out of my lair, grabbed the edge of the table, and looked over the top to see if Charlotte's clock was still at the same place it has always been. Indeed it was, nestled within a small jungle of Ficus vines, and spider and "Wandering Jew" plants. The clock-face indicated that it was nine thirty. If it was accurate, I had slept a mere half an hour. The apartment was quieter than a mouse. My hostesses had either sequestered themselves in the bedroom at the front or they had gone out.

Also on the table, beside a bowl containing a few seemingly inedible, bruised cherries surrounded by a busy swarm of fruit-flies, a note and a single key had been left behind, presumably for me. I hoisted myself up to standing and opened the folded note. This is what it said, in large, noble, carefully formed letters that matched what I had observed so far from Josie's personality:

Welcome, sweet friend! We have gone out for dinner so that you
can nap in peace. Here is your key. Please remember to leave
the downstairs door open, if you go out. Otherwise it would

lock itself, and there is no key for that door. Charlotte says hi.
Au Revoir!

Charlotte was apparently basking in the cozy stages of newly discovered domesticity. She didn't even take the time to write the note herself. I took a few moments to deal with my creeping jealousy. Credit was due, it is true, to this marvellous creature who had captured my long-time friend's heart. Josie obviously had many advantages over me. Her blue-hued variation of Audrey Hepburnesque eyes, her sultry, deep voice, her all-around exoticness made me look like a domestic rabbit in comparison. I might have been agile, but I was nevertheless a mere rodent.

True to my self-appellation, I noticed my hunger. Again. My lentils did not take the trip well. They had turned into a slimy mess. Since there didn't seem to be a compost bin anywhere, my sprouts went into the garbage to keep company with a pile of equally disgusting moldy waste. I grasped the old fridge door-handle with both hands and yanked. Ferociously but with a certain special twist to the right. The handle had either gotten worse since last time or I had lost my touch. It only opened after my fourth try. Inside, the same foods that Charlotte used to eat or shelter hovered on the grimy shelves: plain full-fat yoghurt, lots of fresh exotic fruit like star fruit, mangoes, and guava, a few chunks of badly wrapped expensive cheese that was drying up at the corners, and the obligatory few wilting carrots, broccoli, and celery. A lone giant of an eggplant bearing a fist-sized, caved-in brown spot was staring at me from its nipple-end.

I have always had the impression that Charlotte bought vegetables only as a sort of duty, and that she kept them as mascots to ward off disease by their mere presence. In the summer, she would go all the way to Jean-Talon Market to buy a selection of local, more or less fresh produce, cheap because it would already be slightly past its prime. Then she would lovingly harbour the rescued vegetables in her fridge, replacing them only once they were rendered unrecognizable. In the winter, she would still buy vegetables but closer to home: potatoes and carrots mainly. They would inevitably suffer the same unfortunate fate as the summer ones.

It seemed like Josie had easily adopted Charlotte's culinary habits. Except for beer. The three bottles and three cans on the shelf were all imported from Belgium instead of my friend's usual local, proletarian brands. This indicated a social climb from working-class to foreign, educated class. Not a surprising change given Josie's aura, but I was nevertheless disappointed. I held myself back from revenge and did not empty the guilty alcohol into the sink or even my throat. I grabbed a slice of under-ripe mango, chipped off a random piece of dry-cornered cheese, and closed the fridge quick, before I changed my mind about the beer.

I shuffled towards the bathroom down the hall, leaving a trail of still-damp clothes on the floor as if I were going to meet a lover. The bathroom was, alas, empty of lovers. I remembered from years ago that the shower acted a bit funny. I was in no mood to find out if it still did. Instead of experiment-ing with it, I sponge-bathed with a grimy hand-cloth, except for my privates, which I wiped with my fingers, for hygiene. Then, avoiding using any of the towels hanging on the rusty hooks, I made my way back to the kitchen, picking up my clothes as I went. I grabbed the first country-garb I could find in my backpack, put them on without looking, and went out onto the back porch to hang my dirty and still-wet clothes on the line, hoping the next rain would rinse them. Then I grabbed a pocketful of change out of my bag, took the key from the table, and went out into the night.

The ambient air had finally cooled down into a comfortable, balmy tem-perature. I was happy to see that the neighbourhood health-food store was not only still open but thriving. Only the name had been changed. It still smelled the same. I got myself a lentil-sprout salad in memory of my own defunct meal and sat down at the only available small table. A youngish, pretty woman and a man about the same age as her were sitting at a table near me. I could see, smell, and hear them whether I wanted to or not. It was obvious that they were very interested in each other by the way she let him reach for her hands, but also that they were in the beginning stages of court-ing as indicated by his shyness and gentleness as he gingerly touched only the tips of her long fingers.

"I have not had a lover for a very long time," she said, staring dispassion-ately into his eyes, which were riveted on hers. "Several years, in fact. I don't know how long, exactly. I tried to forget. I did not have many relationships anyway, but they have all been disastrous. I just gave up dating altogether. I gave up trying. In fact, I think my body must have shut down. I haven't had periods for quite a while..."

The young man kept looking into her eyes, silent as she talked. He didn't reply when she was finished. Their silence stretched out for a long time. Actually, it lasted for the entire time it took me to slowly enjoy my copious-sized lentil salad. But somehow, there was no awkwardness between the couple. From what I could witness, he just kept staring at her, and she, in turn, would alternate between shyly lowering her gaze and then giving him an odd, softly neutral glance. I figured they might try their luck with each other soon, maybe even that night. Maybe she was truly going to get lucky this time. He seemed like a kind, good match for her. I left them wrapped in their private cocoon. All three of us would be at peace with the world.

Once out on the street, I turned towards the Orthodox Church, otherwise known to the non-orthodox as the "Penis and the Tit." The set was indeed still there. The dome—the "tit"—had gotten a makeover. Its original copper showed beautifully through, even in the dim early evening light. The steeple might have been harder to climb as it had not yet gotten the same beauty lift. Its own cap—shall I say glans—appeared firm and proud in the soft, dull hues of pale green leaves that had been caught by dryness before they'd had a chance to turn yellow. Then as I was still admiring the subtle hues of the church, and as if by some divine intervention, the bulging cumulus clouds in the sky slowly parted, showing the suggestive structures in their full dramatic glory against a background of the most beautiful shades of dark Cerulean blue. If I had been religious, I would have seen it all as some sort of redemptive sign of God's influence on us mere mortals. As it was, I was simply nailed to the pavement in awe at being witness to an amazing and absolutely free light show.

Inspired, I decided to visit a certain shrine of sorts that I knew. It was a watering hole, really, Montréal's first official women's bar, which had opened in the seventies. Julie had taken me there two weeks after we met, just before we set out on our adventure out west. I remember how awed I was, even more than I had just been at the sight of the Penis and the Tit. The first thing I had noticed seven years previously, as I had set foot in the lesbian bar, had been the confidence all the women seemed to have. They all showed to me an air that I could only qualify then as one of propriety, of belonging. An air of being home. I could not share this feeling at the time, being myself on the way out of town with my new-found lover. But on that Canada weekend's

Saturday, upon my return to the city after a long absence, I desperately needed to find a place I could belong.

The lesbian bar was no longer there. In its place, a straight establishment was proudly displaying its clusters of happy hetero-beautiful people. My heart sank into my heels. There was no time to waste standing there, wondering why so many women's bars across the country seem to be so short-lived. I decided to take my ruminations on the road and walk all the way to the Gay Village. Maybe there would be a welcoming bar for me there.

By the time I had gotten to the village, it was properly dark. Instead of the Canadian flags I had seen at the airport and the few that had been brazenly fixed to a smattering of select balconies, here it was rainbow flags that flapped proudly at every excuse they could find. All the bars' terraces were jam-packed with happy, boisterous, and very cute patrons. Unfortunately for me, as alluring as they would be for each other, they were all men. One of them reminded me of Julie. How could that be? I was completely puzzled. I walked on, shaking my head.

Out on the street, finally, a butchy-looking woman was clambering towards me, her shoulders held scrunched high. She looked as if she were cold, both in temperature and attitude. I surmounted my fear and asked her in French, as innocent-looking as I could, if there was a women's bar nearby. She sighed loudly enough to slice a wedge into the hot pavement. Staring out into a space beyond me, she gestured vaguely, flashing a dangerously sharp-studded, ringed hand over her shoulder towards the direction I was already going. End of conversation. She pushed past me and was gone in a flash. Maybe she took me for a straight tourist looking for a thrill. I walked on. Whatever confidence I might have had now lay shattered at my feet.

After two long blocks, I was almost ready to give up when I finally saw a bar that seemed a touch more feminine-looking than the others. I hesitantly crossed the threshold. Inside the dim, cavernous atmosphere, a few groups of young women were huddled in small clusters. Their number altogether would have totalled a mere dozen or so. Otherwise the room was loosely packed with men of all shapes and sizes, and a sprinkling of people of undisclosed gender. I focussed on the women. They all seemed happy, their prattle and chuckles rising above the din of the techno music. The dance floor was empty. Too bad. I had been hoping to hide the fact that I was alone by mingling with a sweaty, boisterous dancing crowd. As it was, I stuck out like a dandelion in fruit in the middle of a well-tended lawn. I might as well leave.

Then I saw her. She was quietly sitting at the chrome counter at the far end of the room. Alone. The woman was not Julie. She was the girl I had seen that morning at the seedy bar at the airport, then later in the bus. Suddenly everybody else in the room turned out of focus except for her. I walked closer. She was sipping some sort of an opaque bright-pink beverage of the same disquieting colour as children's Milk of Magnesia. From my vantage point, I could see she was still wearing her skull that was just like mine. Except this time, it was attached to her ear. Somehow this detail informed me that she would be out of my league. My intuition meekly, barely audibly, suggested I had better leave. In response, my heart instantly switched into fight or flight mode. She probably hadn't seen me yet. It was not too late to run out of there. Then, surprizing even myself, I rebelled. Caressing my own miniature skull for courage, I threw all caution to the wind and decided to jump in.

Both seats on each side of the girl were empty. I chose the one on her left and sat down as gently as my lingering jet-lag permitted. I murmured something in her exquisite ear below the din of the strident music. I forget what I said, but whatever it was, she turned her elfish face towards me with a blank look. I had no idea if she had simply not recognized me from our collision in the *Aérobus* or whether she did remember and declined to engage. Hoping for the first and least-depressing alternative, I leaned towards her, took the chain on my neck in my clumsy hand, and shook the miniature skull on it towards the girl in the hopes of getting a smile of recognition and approval.

My ploy was met with mitigated results. She finally smiled at me quizzically. I was still not sure if she remembered me. Maybe it was better she didn't, as all she would have known about me would have been my clumsiness and maybe my bad breath. I wished I had a mint in my pocket. She deigned to offer me about ten minutes of her attention. I was not about to divulge the real reason for my impromptu visit to Montréal, so I encouraged her to talk about herself with a few non-compromising questions.

Her name was *"Bourgeon."* Literally translated, the name would be "Bud" in English. Unfortunately, the sound of her name in English loses all its original charm in the translation. You lose the puckering of the lips in the *"ou"* sound, the guttural *"r,"* the juicy, rolling *"g,"* and the sensually nasal *"on."* And mostly, you lose that feeling of the first shoots bursting at the seams in spring, evoking freshness, an eagerness to swell with the callow promise of youth. All these attributes seemed to define so well the young woman I was getting to know as Bourgeon.

The short story Bourgeon told me was in some ways similar to mine, except for the Julie part. She was born and raised in Québec. As a young adult, she decided to seek refuge in British Columbia to get away from the long seven months of Québécois winters. However, despite all the local rain, she found herself thirsty. She tried big city living in Vancouver, she picked fruit in the interior for a few seasons, she traversed an island-living phase. Wherever she had sought refuge in the beautiful province, she found only alienation. The Lotus Land left her wanting. Bourgeon missed her own culture. After six lonely years on the "wet coast," she gave up and decided to come back to Montréal.

I told Bourgeon that I was also from Montréal and had lived on a remote island for seven years, and that I had come back to my home town for an extended visit. Maybe I was going to stay for good, like her. I did not mention Julie. To fill the gap left by Julie's absence, I lied. I droned on and on about all the imaginary friends and family I had in Montréal that were allegedly so happy to see me. The look on Bourgeon's pretty face informed me that I had gone too far. She had obviously lost interest at least two sentences previously. My voice trailed off. I shut my trap.

After a few minutes of awkward silence, I tried to engage her to talk some more about herself. She just quietly sat on her stool, answering my opening lines only with shrugs of her tanned shoulders, absent-mindedly drawing pink bubbly squiggles on the shiny counter with the miniature shovel-end of her straw. The silence separating us grew into a fuzzy opaque mess. I offered her another drink. She said, "No," softly, turning her delicate face away, sweeping the air with the back of her right hand across her chest towards me as if shooing me away like a fly. Her gesture flashed a set of impeccably mani-cured, long pink and white nails, a surprising feature on this Punk-Goth-elflike creature. I couldn't help but surreptitiously crane my neck to look down to her other hand, her left, the fingers of which were carelessly wrapped around her glass. The nails on this hand were also very clean but short. I deduced from my discovery that Bourgeon was either a right-handed guitar-ist or a left-handed lesbian. Or a left-handed lesbian using her long nails on her right hand to hold down her guitar strings, hoping the nails—and the neck of her guitar—would stand up to the treatment. Or a right-handed, very careful lesbian. But then I would have no logical explanation for the short nails on the left hand other than an artistic temperament that might be attempting to defy common sense.

I did not ask Bourgeon which one of the above variations of people she might have belonged to. Instead, I reluctantly bade her goodbye. Slipping away alone into the opposite end of the bar, I folded myself as small as I could into the creases on the walls.

✶ ✶ ✶

Three beers later, still half-hidden in my lone corner of the bar, I dared look up towards the counter where I had last sat beside Bourgeon. To my immense relief, she was gone. The bar had started to fill up, and the music was a little more danceable. A few people were already squirming on the dance floor. I joined their happy cluster. It took me a while to get somewhat comfortable amongst this group of strangers. I closed my eyes. Ignoring everything else except the entrancing music, I tried out a few fancy steps that I had been practicing on Genus over the past few winters. Before long, I was happy and confident enough to lift my eyelids and glance around me at the other dancers. Then I saw trouble coming.

A medium-tall and extra-wide diesel dyke had sprung up from the table where she had been sprawled out with a small group of friends. She was making her way towards the dance floor with an exaggerated deliberation. No mistake. She was coming for me. As she was advancing, she ran a hand, roughened no doubt from generations of proletarian drudgery, through her thick, black, pomaded hair. She found my eyes and threw me a look saturated with suggestive meaning.

By this time, there was only one couple left between me and the amorous woman. She was still confidently priming me for her advance. Rounding her wide shoulders slightly forward, she simultaneously pulled in her stomach. This double gesture exposed, oh so briefly, a flash of a silver buckle with a western theme on a belt that was encircling her generous girth. She yanked at her black jeans and stuffed her impeccably-ironed, crispy white shirt inside them, maybe with the hope of extending the flashing of her fancy belt-buckle.

Too late. The unwieldy, flopping belly had already spilled back down into its most comfortable position.

I don't think I really had an aversion to this person. My policy towards all beings is that we all have a right to be here on Earth at this time. We all have a right to be whomever we want to be, which is nobody's business. It's just that I also reserve the right to be with whomever I want to be with. I happen to prefer feminine women. One could say that Julie, with her flannel checkered shirts and boy's manners, might have been an exception to this preference. Maybe. But that would be discrediting her natural appearance. I'm talking here about her beautiful body. Naked. In her Eve's costume, over and over, I found my Julie shining with all the exquisite glory of feminine beauty. Too bad she did not share my admiration and that she was constantly wishing she had been endowed with fewer curves.

The amorous woman was by then standing right in front of me. She didn't even pretend to be dancing. She was openly staring at me, her head slightly cocked, sizing me down from her seven inches or so of vertical advantage. Like a spider, she had already swiftly wrapped me in the web of her phero-mone-laced scent. And like a drugged victim, I felt myself falter and relax. I shook free of her spell a mere few seconds before it would have been too late. I stopped in my tracks. As much as I had just begun to have fun dancing, I wasn't prepared to face an awkward scene with this person. I turned my back to her, grabbed my sarong, and ran out into the balmy night.

The holiday weekend was galloping into its boisterous, wild peak. Everywhere, from all the bars spilling out into the busy streets, happy, increasingly drunk people meandered together in friendly or romantic pairs and clusters. I felt like a loser. I tried to avoid the busier, bright avenues and took my loneliness to the darker side-streets. Walking slowly, I was not quite ready to return to Charlotte's and Josie's love-nest. I zigzagged, I shuffled, I sniffled. Tears were running down my cheeks. I didn't bother to wipe them off. I licked my upper lip. The salty, bitter taste gave me a peculiar comfort. On and on I wandered until I ended up in front of Charlotte's. I still wasn't ready to face whatever would have greeted me, or not, but I had run out of places to go.

Much too sober despite my three beers, I climbed the dark and steep set of stairs ahead of me. I was happy the lovers had remembered not to pull the downstairs door locked. Inside, I didn't bother to turn on the light for fear of being found, bad breath and all. The door to the bedroom was closed. Complete silence. No snoring, no tossing in the bed emanated from the lovers' nest. I started wondering if they were even there. I wasn't going to open their door and find out. Instead, I groped my way along the buckled and polished floor of the corridor all the way to my cot under the kitchen table. I fumbled in my bag, in the dim orange light beaming in from a telephone pole in the alleyway. The pole was the one that doubled as a support for Charlotte's clothesline. There were the same two sets of bed sheets and the assortment of women's panties hanging from the line as before, plus my own clothes.

I made a mental note to myself to hand-wash my garb as soon as possible the next morning. I extricated a pair of 100 percent silk pyjamas that I usually reserved for extra-special occasions and changed into them. Then I got out a home-made sleeping bag of sorts, the kind you are supposed to use in youth hostels and cheap hotels to protect yourself from bedbugs. I tucked this makeshift bag made from 80 percent cotton and 20 percent unknown fibres under my armpit and dragged my skinny mattress of sorts out to the balcony. I lay down and immediately sank into a dreamless slumber.

✯ ✯ ✯

A fresh, damp breeze carried on a very pretty pinkish-orange light woke me up at dawn. I was in no mood to admire the beauty of a pollution-enhanced sunrise. Still half-asleep, I dragged my meagre bed back to the kitchen and resumed my sleep. A brutal mechanical sound woke me up a few hours later. I rose to check the time and bumped my head. Cursing, I peered out from under the table and checked Charlotte's clock. Seven thirty. On a Sunday morning, during Canada Day weekend. Must be some emergency, I thought. By then, I was fuming and fully awake.

I tossed my anger aside to feel the full excitement of being in Charlotte's apartment in vibrant, exciting Montréal. I was even looking forward to getting to know Josie. I hoisted myself up to Charlotte's favourite chair. On the table in front of me, a sesame-seed-sprinkled bagel was spilling out from a small bag. It was still warm. There was also a note, written in Charlotte's lively, childish scrawl:

My Beautifullest, Dearest of Claires!

Welcome!!

So sorry we are not here for your awakening, my gentle Sleeping Beauty. Josie and I have decided to go up North for a few days to escape the heat. We considered—briefly— inviting you as well but we don't think we would have been very fun to be with. We are still—giggle—on a honeymoon of sorts...

Help yourself to anything in the fridge. See you Monday evening maybe?

Yours Always, Allways

Your Charlotte

Oh yes. "Your Charlotte." Right. The two were joined by their navels, stars in their own private movie. I would be an extra—an out-of-focus faceless body in the background. Who was this Josie anyway? What stage of transition were they at, and most importantly, how did this person manage to steal my friend's heart? All these questions irritated me. My only consolation was that at least my friend was happy. For the time being. I had seen her before in this state I guessed her to be in. The effect could last from a few minutes to two months. She would fly high until the oxytocin of new sex ran out. Then she would look the other way towards the next lover from her perennially replenished list. How did she do it? There always seemed to be a lineup snaking up to her door.

I tried to guess how long Josie would last. I couldn't come up with a figure. As far as I knew, Charlotte has never been with a trans person before. I felt sorry for myself. I started chewing on the sesame bagel. With the bagel hanging from my teeth as if I were a dog, I got up and carefully grabbed the fridge handle. Unlike a dog, I opened the door right with the perfect grip of fingers and twist of the wrist on the first try. Already I was getting the hang of being in Charlotte's apartment. Behind the six imported beers and the lone rotting eggplant lay an old tub of cream-cheese spread. The cheese inside was covered with a miniature garden of green fuzz. I put the tub back where I found it and finished my first bagel. Then I ate a second one to make up for the fact that there was nothing to put on it. There was only one other bagel left in the bag, a poppy-seed one. It wasn't my favourite, but I ate it too. Not only was I hungry that morning but I wanted to fill another, insidious craving that was acting like a vacuum-cleaner in my throat.

Charlotte on a honeymoon. The words kept dancing in my brain until they made me jealous. I chased them away, trying to replace them with wimpy alternatives from my yogic vocabulary. Once I realized the futility of that exercise, I decided to spring into action. I could do something exciting. The big city has so much to offer. I could go see a movie. Too early. For lack of anything else to do, I decided to have a shower.

I peeled my 100 percent silk pyjamas off and let them softly fall to the floor. I went to Charlotte's bathroom, stepped into her claw-footed bathtub—there was no shower curtain—and turned on both taps full. The perforated head at the end of the rubber hose lurched and covered me and the floor with cold water. Cursing, I lowered the pressure on both taps. Oh yes, I remembered now. There still didn't seem to be a place to hang the shower-head, so I held it with one hand as I adjusted both taps in turn with my free hand. It took me a long time to get the temperature just right, and when I finally did, the steamy chlorine smell almost toppled me over.

I had either forgotten how many chemicals the city puts into its water or they had augmented the dose, maybe as a tribute to Canada Day weekend. Either way I tried to neutralize the chlorine smell with the power of my mind. I let the water flow over my love-thirsty body like the first spring rain cascading over the swelling sprouts of a field of asparagus spurred by the selfishness of vigorous growth. I was surprised to see how refreshing the water became. Maybe the city had also put something invigorating in their water on top of everything else. I peed in the tub. My pee turned a sickly pale green. They must have put blue colouring in the water as well, like they do in swimming pools. That probably meant that my insides would turn blue also.

I had forgotten to bring my towel to the bathroom. After I gingerly dried myself with the least-grimy towel hanging from one of the rusty hooks, I proceeded back to the kitchen. I sat, naked and half-dry, on Charlotte's chair. There was no newspaper on the table. This surprised me, since Charlotte was a big fan of reading the Sunday edition of the *New York Times*. She even attempted sometimes to do their crossword puzzle. Charlotte and I disagreed on her habit of buying the *New York Times*. Not only was it, according to me, full of bad or else trivial news but it also used up too many trees. I forget the figures, but I used to know them back when I was trying to convince Charlotte to save our forests and get her news from the radio or from the neighbours. I told her that, if the world was going to come to an end, we would know soon enough. But my environmental efforts had been in vain until seemingly recently. Unless she had taken the paper with her.

I was, however, unusually irritated by the lack of a newspaper that Sunday. In a perverse kind of way, I had been looking forward to catching up on what was going on in the allegedly civilized world. Disgusted, I crumpled the empty paper bag the bagels had been in. A cockroach scuttled away. I hate Sundays in the city. There's a sickly-sweet inertia that descends from the sky, a massive cloud of boredom that suffocates me from my solar plexus up to my eyeballs.

Coco Chanel, I read or heard somewhere, hated Sundays too. She dealt with her dislike of them by ignoring the idleness imposed on just about everyone on the Day of the Lord. "Idleness is the root of all evil," says the proverb. The Church seemingly made an exception for one day of the week. They did that, I guess, so that people would go to church. My mother once told me about a story she had heard in religion class when she was a little girl in the fifties. According to the story, a farmer went out in his fields on a Sunday. It was wheat-harvesting time and huge dark-blue and purple clouds were looming in the sky. It definitely looked like a big storm was imminent. Rain on the ripe wheat would be disastrous. The farmer could lose his entire crop to mold. So, the farmer, instead of going to Mass, went out in his fields to harvest the ripe wheat threatened by rain on that particular Sunday. He got struck by lightning. End of story. My mother and her classmates were left to draw their own conclusions.

Coco for her part seemed to ignore all warnings of a religious nature. She worked diligently on Sundays, just as she did on any other day of the week. She even worked on the day she died. It happened to be a Sunday.

Julie and I rarely observed any mainstream holidays. We ignored birthdays, our own or anyone else's. We had no anniversaries to speak of. The only calendar days we were aware of, really, on a regular basis, had been cheque days. Our welfare cheques always arrived, rain or shine, on the last Wednesday of each month. We would go to town on the next day, first to the bank and then to do some absolutely essential shopping. We would never miss a visit to the chocolate shop. Julie and I loved to celebrate Life. We made up our own holidays. We celebrated whatever we fancied, be it the changing of the moon, the roll-over of the seasons, or just because.

Thinking of Julie gave me an idea as to how I could spend my free time until the lovebirds came back. I was going to clean up my past and start afresh. I was going to do this by fasting. My fast was going to be a complete experience, like a total deprivation of the senses. I would do nothing for the rest of the weekend. I might clean the kitchen but not necessarily so. In any case, no food would pass my lips. I would drink only water, the strict minimum required to survive the heat. I would stay naked to complete the clean effect. I would not read, or at least try not to, so as not to fill my mind with someone else's thoughts. I would observe the wanderings of my own mind and let go of the polluting distraction of thoughts. By the time Charlotte and Josie came back at the end of their honeymoon, I would be clean as a whistle inside and out, thanks to my austerity.

I found the largest empty glass jug, cleaned it, and filled it with city water. I put it uncovered on the table, hoping that the chlorine would evaporate. I got my sweaty clothes off the clothesline, my silk pyjamas off the floor, and rinsed them all in the kitchen sink, wrung them out, shook the crinkles out, and slipped out naked onto the balcony to hang them back on the line next to the bed sheets and panties. There seemed to be nobody around in the alley nor on the other balconies. It was early. People must have been either in Church or still in bed.

The rest of my Sunday and the following Monday went by uneventfully. I slept a lot. I slept in my own space under the table, even though I could have luxuriated in Charlotte's bed. This was in keeping with my voluntary asceticism. When awake, I wandered around the apartment just to shuffle my toxins out of the recesses where they might have been hiding. I drank water, lots of water. I went to the toilet. I slept some more. It's amazing how much time there suddenly is if one has nothing to do. I got bored. So bored in fact that I even spent some time looking for something to read. Having found nothing that sparked my interest, I tried to sit and watch my own thoughts. I fell asleep.

* * *

Tuesday morning, finally, I woke up early as according to my nature. The first thing I did was to take all the clothes and sheets off the line. They were quite stiff but bone-dry. I folded them and put the lovers' stuff in their room. Charlotte and Josie had not come back from their honeymoon. Looking for clues, I re-read Charlotte's note. That's when I noticed the ambiguity of the ending:

... "See you Monday evening maybe?"

When I had first read the note, I had thought the "maybe" was referring to me, that "maybe" it was I who was going to be away when the lovers returned. Instead, they had reserved the ambiguity for themselves. They had given themselves an open ending, an opportunity to come back whenever they wished. How unfair.

However, the advantage of having the apartment all to myself, albeit for an indeterminate period of time, would be that I did not have to look or even pretend that I was looking for alternate shelter right away. I could concentrate on my plan of action of womanifesting money. This, of course, would mean finding a job, but even before that I would need to apply for welfare to hold me over until the perfect job would show its opportune self. For all this, I would need some decent clothes. My own would look too shabby. A visit to Charlotte's closet was in order.

From behind the damask curtain in the hall closet, a cacophony of colours and new smells greeted me. Apparently, Charlotte's style had changed, presumably to match Josie's. On the left, a slew of slightly smaller garments hung from wooden hangers; on the right side were longer ones. All were feminine, of course, and somehow exaggeratedly so. All would have been too big for my petite frame. I concentrated my search to the left, which I guessed to be Charlotte's side. In the past, I knew my friend and I to be of similar proportions, with the exception that Charlotte had a good six inches of height over me. On a computer-generated image of our bodies side by side, I would have been her, 75 percent. Her pants were too big for me, but shirts and dresses were passable as long as I folded the sleeves up.

I pulled out one of the least garish dresses. It was a purple Indian rayon number gathered at the waist. I tried it on. The waist fit me perfectly, though it was positioned a bit too low for me. The loose top puffed out. I didn't bother checking myself in the mirror. Feeling like a mushroom was enough warning. Next, I pulled out a pink rhinestone-studded pair of jeans and held them against my midriff. Same thing. The waist would fit but the legs would be too long. Just for good measure, I tried on a bouncy, flowered, cotton-spandex fitted shirt. Again, the waist was too low but the shoulders and hips were good. Charlotte must have lost a good twelve pounds at least. She must have been really in love this time. And she must have expected to stay in love, since she seemed to have gotten rid of all her previous urban-gypsy clothes.

After having scanned the entire half of the overstuffed wardrobe, my choice fell on an eighties-style, royal-blue, short-sleeved cotton dress with fake-gold buttons down the back and two deep and wide pockets at the hips. I was sold on the pockets. Since I don't carry a purse, I would need them. The dress's cut was of the type known as "princess," with a high waist. I tried it on in front of the hall mirror. Other than making me look vaguely like a transvestite, the dress fit me well enough.

I filled the pockets with my dog-eared notebook, plus the luxury of two five-dollar bills and two pencils: one 4H to accommodate my tiny writing and for detailed sketching, and a 4B with a flat and wide nib for soft shading and making curls and waves. I would not bring my colouring pencils. This had to be a serious sort of outing. I could tell.

I looked at myself again in the mirror. The reflection was that of a young-ish and small clump of a person, probably a woman or at least trying to appear as one but with unkempt hair. All the chlorine and who knows what in the water had not neutralized the grease in my thin, dusty yellow hair. In this light, the sun-licked colour I was usually so proud of looked greyish. I stepped back away from the mirror, afraid to find more flaws. Too late. My peripheral vision had already offered me the pitiful sight of sagging, defeated shoulders, a chin tilted to the left, a few insidious lines unflatteringly scattered around my eyes and mouth, and puffy eyelids. Plus, even if I could not see them, I remembered that my legs would be quite hairy.

Something had to be done if I was going to show myself to the scrutiny of the world and especially to welfare. I marched to the bathroom. Scraping a wet comb across my unruly mop, I made a parting line from the left side to counteract the tilt of my chin with more hair on the right side of my head. Then I drew a thin line of Kohl on the interior of the bottom edge of my eyelids to make my eyes look bigger, more eager, and to hopefully distract from my greasy hair. The grey-green hue of my eyes would be put to an advantage. I grabbed the dull razor on the edge of the shelf and unceremoniously shaved my legs, dry.

It was not easy to submit myself to the dictates of feminine beauty, lies propagated by excessively rich multinational companies using women's insecurity to augment their own already-stuffed coffers. But *"à la guerre comme à la guerre."* I guess one can translate that as "when times get tough, the tough get going." If I was destined to become an urban guerrilla, I might as well don my war-paint. I would claim back some of the money that belonged to me and that had been stolen from me and my gentle kind by greedy capitalists. I did not add "pigs" to the word capitalists. I had a great fondness for pigs, starting with Ralph. They were intelligent and fun animals. I tried to remember my hoofed friend, his smell, the feel of his ears, his smile. My mind drew a blank. Panicked, I tried to conjure up an image of my dear Julie. She appeared, but her contours were blurry.

I took a last look at the mirror. This time what I saw was a bit more ego-satisfying. In the cracked, hazy bathroom mirror, a tanned young woman, determined, sparkling with a touch of healthy wildness was looking back at me. I threw myself a confident kiss, skipped to the kitchen, fumbled through my bag, and took out an old vial of Neroli. I dabbed some of it behind my ears and ran my scented fingers through my hair to complete the effect. With an added trickle of small change in my dress pockets and the key to my new, albeit surely temporary home, I was ready to confront the world.

By then, it must have been about ten a.m. The promise of a sweltering day hung over the street as soon as I emerged from the coolness of Charlotte's staircase. The sun's rays, augmented undoubtedly by pollution, mercilessly pummeled the top of my head. But there was something else in the air that morning, something far more agreeable than the initial brutal onslaught on my senses. Indeed, a subtle aroma of something flowery, exotic, and sweetly edible insinuated itself into my nostrils. It wasn't my own Neroli I was detecting, although this new smell seemed to complement my own scent in a gentle sort of way. I looked around. The only possible sources of agreeable smells around me would have been the silver maple in front of the apartment and maybe a neighbour's minuscule garden of leafy, over-nitrogenised tomato plants reaching desperately for the filtered sky. There was nothing remotely edible around at that time; nothing exotic, and certainly no fragrant flowers were present on the scene.

I concluded that some exciting woman must have passed by recently. Some woman whose smell seemed to match mine to perfection. I looked up and down the street. There was no one else but me as far as I could see.

We were well past rush hour. Maybe the alluring woman had been late for work, and in her haste, she forgot to take her smell with her. There it was, the scent, lagging behind, comfortably hovering over the sidewalk at a short-person's nose-level (such as mine) for anyone five-feet-not-much to smile at with delight, nostrils quivering. For a while, I followed the scent down the street. It seemed to be going in the same direction as I was headed, which was on the way to the place where I had known the welfare office to have been.

Eventually I felt self-assured enough to abandon the delicately scented but too-hot sidewalk trail to bravely tackle the cooler, darker back alleys. I perambulated under the bed sheets clacking from the clotheslines in tune with the foraging steps of errant dogs and cats seeking the same shade as I was. I didn't encounter any human maniacs nor rabid dogs. Only one single fat rat crossed my path. No one was following me except maybe the new scents of fresh garbage and excrement. I didn't find Julie either. This surprised me. I had been so sure to find her there, competing with the animals for a heel of bread or cold pizza remains. To cope with my disappointment, I had to remind myself I was not in a movie.

CHAPTER 6

I arrived at the welfare office without any remarkable incident. Or rather, I arrived where the offices had been many years previously. The decrepit, seemingly abandoned building in front of me was overgrown with lichen and vines. A faded notice on the old front door barely hung on, pinned as it was behind a camouflage of the graceful branches of a negundo maple. I had to push the boughs aside to read the text. I could decipher with difficulty an address not far away, which must have been the new location of the offices. After memorizing the number, I made my way more by instinct than anything else towards what turned out to be a menacing bunker out of a World War II novel.

The newly familiar sweet scent from earlier that morning seemed to float around the building like a swarm of worker bees trying to get home to their hive. Or maybe it was simply the feverish result of an over-fertile imagination fuelled by futile hope. I had to circumnavigate the monstrous building a couple of times before I found the tiny door. It was too stiff for me to open it any wider than a slit. Exhibiting a miracle of flexibility, I made myself as flat as possible and slipped in like a single piece of mail. Given my body's bloated condition caused by the sweltering, humid heat, I felt more of a padded envelope.

The building's interior held as little promise as the exterior had. Only a static, putridly lukewarm, vaguely buzzing atmosphere badly disguised as air-conditioning hinted at a certain human presence. At the end of a long corridor, plastered with tiny black and white matte tiles that might have been left over from a public toilet project from the nineteen fifties, loomed the hesitant beacon of a reception booth. The promise I had been waiting for. I made my way towards the pale light, my heart swollen with hope. The corridor opened into a vast waiting room painted in a greasy hepatic green.

An overly made-up large woman spread herself complacently at a counter behind a scratched, grimy plastic window. She was on the phone. Without covering the receiver, she barked at me with a familiar Rosemont accent to sit down and wait my turn. I was exhausted from the intense heat I had grown unused to on my idyllic West Coast Island, as well as leftover jet-lag and my recent fast. Still, I demurred from depositing my carcass on any of the numerous seats covered with questionable plastic that were circling all around me like emaciated hyenas poised in mid-air, ready for the kill. A quick glance around informed me that the five other clients, slumped here and there on the plastic hyenas, were each clutching in their own paws a crumpled slip of damp paper with a number on it.

One of these people, a person of indeterminate age and a gender I was unable to categorize, revealed a semblance of willingness to communicate. The being leaned awkwardly towards me with what could have been a smile, half-exposing a single grey tooth. A cavernous hand slowly floated up in a wary gesture that might have been interpreted as friendly. One single, arthritis-deformed finger indicated the reception booth. Dangerously tottering between compassion for this human being and a certain reticence to return to the reception desk, I carefully turned around and gingerly made my way back over the black and white tiles as if on a badly tensed tightrope over the tumultuous waters of the Saint-Lawrence River.

The receptionist had been waiting for me. With an impatient gesture, without either of us uttering a squeak or a squawk, she pointed towards a little distributor at the end of the counter with its mocking paper-tongue spilling out. I couldn't figure out how I had missed this object as it was bright red and rather rude-looking. Sheepish, as if I had been caught shoplifting, I extricated my own damp ticket. All this of course without my receptionist taking a break from her telephone conversation nor lifting her garishly painted eyelids even once from her popular tabloid.

Let us note again that this entire scene occurred without a single peep from me. My muteness was probably to my advantage. Thus, I didn't run the risk of submitting myself to the thick sigh and the rolling eyes of my adversary.

Her reaction would have been uttered in international body language in response to my over-literary French (having read too much and spoken too little) tinged with a recent British-Columbian accent that had wickedly glued itself to my tongue after seven years of forced Anglicism. My receptionist was surprisingly not chewing any gum. This detail was blatantly missing from the integrity of her character. It got me wondering if there might have been a regulation that forbade civil employees from chewing gum during working hours. If this had been the case, it would have been a great loss. A little bit of rumination might relax said workers a bit and consequently render them more productive.

My turn came sooner than I had expected. I heard my number being called by a mechanical voice over the crackling stereo speakers before anyone else's in the room. No one looked up to complain. I started wondering if the other beings, the starving hyenas and their charge of tired riders, were alive. Maybe I had stumbled into a mausoleum of beings who had died while waiting for their feed. Even the person with the crooked finger seemed to have been transformed into a bag of grey cement. They were all eerily immobile, frozen in time while still clutching their numbers. I whipped my ribcage to attention for fear of being turned into an inanimate object like them. The air I disturbed made no one budge by even a hair.

My jubilation at having been called so early was short-lived. I would have to present myself in front of the receptionist again. This time, I would have to blurt out the reason for my disturbing her chatting and reading. I recruited all my strength of character to amass any crumbs of compassion and courage hidden in the darkest recesses of my being. I proceeded with explaining my situation as briefly as I could to this glorious manifestation of the goodness and generosity of the Goddess.

"*Ahem ... euh ... je suis ici pour—*"

Without letting me finish my already shortened utterance, decorated with my famous double accent, she took my moist ticket and—oh surprise—still without giving me as much as a glance, handed me another one of a different colour. It had a letter on it this time. The receptionist had managed to execute this movement by multiple-tasking, adding it to the reading of her tabloid, her personal conversation on the telephone, and an almost imperceptible sideways nodding towards a sombre corridor with her generous crown of platinum blonde hair. Her up-do seemed to have been immortalized in

93

an eternal instant at the epicentre of some private tornado. I noticed the curved incline at the uppermost tip of the stiff hairdo. How brilliant. Since her hands were busy, she could use the tip of hair as an extra finger of sorts to indicate directions.

I steered myself in the direction indicated by the stiff wisp of hair. Being so relieved to be free of the emotional grip of the receptionist, I had forgotten to ask her the meaning of the letter "J" on my slip of paper. The letter, it is true, could have constituted a clue as to the person I was supposed to see. But maybe not. Precariously armed with the piece of paper clamped tightly within my fingers, I advanced into the sweltering corridor, searching for the famous letter "J," or failing that, for someone, anyone, disposed to see me. I slid past a series of closed doors completely bare of letters. Instead, they proudly bore enormous bronze numbers that seemed to have been picked at random like in the lottery.

The long corridor led me to the top of six steps descending into a large room. From my vantage point, I could see that the front of the room was divided into four grey three-foot-high partitions covered with a material that made me itchy just looking at it. Past the four partitions, a flurry of mostly female typists were softly clicking on their keyboards. Their finger-nails painted in an astounding range of sanguine tints moved in a subdued frenzy akin to a school of guppies in an aquarium at feeding time. The air was permeated with a slimy, nauseating thickness infiltrated with irritating musac tones stuttered out through speakers saturated with static.

Inside each partition at the front of the room sat a civil servant, each affirming the same infinitely bored expression. Two of the employees each had a trembling, fumbling client sitting in front of them. From the two remaining, one had a paper bag with the rim carelessly turned down, revealing the neck of an open brown bottle. I chose the other person. Crumpling my piece of paper with the letter "J" in my hand, just in case I would be reprimanded for not going to the right civil servant, I made my way towards my chosen person. He was an older gentleman, bulging with the roundness of a paunchy middle and an advanced stage of baldness on his head. I could detect, even from several metres away, his breath tinged with stale tobacco. I asked him with my pronounced accents, the only ones I had at my disposal, if he was free. *Libre*, in French.

"Libre??" said he with the dreamy gaze of an armchair philosopher. Then he continued in English. "If I were free, my lady, I wouldn't be here."

Okay. A true patriarch. And sarcastic to boot. I slumped myself as comfortably as I could on the chair, which was upholstered with the same itchy material as the partitions were covered with. My posture was borrowed from one that I had developed a long time before, in my adolescent days. It was designed for letting the sermons slide like water over a duck's back as they spilled from the mouths of assorted men who made it their duty to replace my absent father. For good measure, I added a psychological brace, ready to deflect the obligatory discourse on manners and morality.

My civil servant started to play with his government-issued pen. I flattened, as best as I could, my damp and crumpled piece of paper with the letter "J," and handed it to him just to see his reaction. He took it mechanically and threw it towards his waste-paper basket without a glance. While he was momentarily struggling with the slip having stuck to his fingers, I explained to him with grammatically impeccable French, but with the famous revealing accents, that I had just arrived in Montréal, that I was a very assiduous worker, and that I only needed a little bit of money to tide me over until I found work, which was going to be very soon.

The slip with the letter "J" finally landed on the floor, joining crumbs of an unknown nature. My worker suggested, still in his English bewildered by a pronounced Québécois accent, that maybe I should take my time to find the perfect job instead of throwing myself into any boring occupation. My prospective employer would not want to have an employee as smart as me. I flattered myself briefly to be considered smart. My civil servant added that I would probably be "fighting for my rights" of some sorts. I would be trying to improve my working conditions as well as those of my colleagues. Or fuelled by boredom, I would put subversive ideas such as ecological or pseudo-feminist ones into my co-worker's heads, thus seeding discontent in the whole place.

I was flummoxed. Fortunately, my spiritual reflex kicked in. I suddenly saw my person as he really was, an Infinite Being of Light, a superb manifestation of the Goddess' infinite wisdom. A flow of positive energy showered on me. While I was at it, might as well wrap the whole place with it, the typists, the clients, the plastic hyenas and their immobile riders, even the receptionist with the tornado hair. A hippie song from Genus Island started playing in my head:

"We are one..."

"Would you accept my application as an employee in this very office?" I asked my worker, music still humming in my mind's ears.

"Sweetie, you don't want to work here," whispered a woman's marvelous contralto voice behind and over my left shoulder.

The hippie music in my head stopped. Forgetting how I abhor being called "sweetie," I slowly lifted my gaze, tinted it with a coquettish curiosity toward the languorous voice that already sounded like a soft melody to my suddenly virgin ears. When after a moment that seemed interminable, our gazes met, I had to congratulate myself. I really believed I had conjured up the apparition of this angelic being thanks to my recent incantations.

She was petite, and not short like me. Whereas I usually wore my stunted stature like an embarrassment, she wore hers with grace and dignity, like a crown. Hazel eyes sparkling with flecks of gold dominated her delicate face. My gaze slid towards her mouth, which revealed itself exquisite in its tininess, floating in soft curves over a playful chin. If she was wearing makeup, it didn't show. To crown it off, an unctuous mass of curls of a warm golden brown matched her laughing eyes. If she was dying her hair, it didn't show either. Curls drive me absolutely crazy. Julie had them too. Except that she hated them and chopped them off with rage.

I dug deep into my rapidly dwindling energy reserves to face the imminent situation. Soliciting my superwoman strength, the only one remaining, I somehow womanaged to repress a crazy, spontaneous desire to lunge toward her and kiss her, with no fear of consequence. I could have invited her to dance to the sound of the musac punctuated with the soft clicking of the nails of the guppy-typists. Alas, I did not do any such things. I contented myself instead with biting my lower lip. This contributed to a muteness that was inappropriate for the occasion but habitual in my case in such situations.

I tried to produce a smile, despite the fact that I had forgotten to relax my grip on my lip with my upper row of teeth. I did notice, however—Oh horror!—that my eyes were left riveted on her cleavage, albeit legitimately displayed directly in the very epicentre of my visual field, leaving me to guess at an astonishingly generous bosom on such a delicate-looking frame.

Confused, I reluctantly levitated my gaze, blushing and dripping with sweat the whole time, towards her eyes, which were waiting for mine with a gently mocking patience.

She slightly turned her exquisite head towards her ungrateful colleague to utter a few words to him in a jargon incomprehensible to me. This is when I finally noticed that I was still biting my lower lip. I instantly released my grip with an audible exhale, leaving my lower jaw slightly gaping in awe. The lovely apparition sauntered away after having thrown me an effervescent swig of her sparkling gaze. The mass of bubbles gathered immediately into an electric mist that sank through my optic nerves, made its way downwards through my oesophagus, then—crossing my stomach—travelled past seven or eight meters of intestines, and after traversing them, went to wedge itself in the very heart of the warm shaggy animal coiled up between my thighs.

My nostrils were still quivering from her sweet female scent, cleverly accented with vanilla mixed with coconut and the famous *je-ne-sais-quoi*, evoking simultaneously home baking, tropical beach, and mystery, and—oh delectable surprise—I recognized it as being the same fragrance I had detected on the street near Charlotte's apartment that very same morning. I applied myself, however (with much difficulty), to filling out the interminable application form that had been placed before me. I surprised myself with my own sagacity when I noticed that I had had the presence of mind not to answer an enthusiastic "YES!" in the "sex" box.

CHAPTER 7

My civil servant entered my vital statistics on his computer. He warned me with a stern tone of voice to make sure I was going to be home on the Thursday of the following week. All day. A worker would come for a home visit—read: inspection—and if all was well, I would be granted my first cheque. But that is only, he reminded me, if I was accepted in the first place. He seemed to believe me, from my filled-out form, that I only had the few dollars of cash I had declared to my name. I had no bank account, having closed the one Julie and I had out west. He must have already discovered this from a few simple clicks on his keyboard. I wondered if the worker coming to visit me at Charlotte's would test the mattress to see if I had stashed huge wads of bills there.

We were partway through Tuesday. Somehow, I had to make it through to the Thursday of the following week. Ten days in all. It wasn't going to be easy. No beers, no outings. Despite my worker's suggestion, I could not really be looking for a job during my waiting period. I did not own any decent job-searching clothes. In a way, I was happy that I did not have to submit to an interview with the lovely apparition of a few minutes before. It would have been an impossible feat to be begging for money and keeping my dignity at the same time.

The interview with my male civil servant was concluded. I extended a cordial right hand towards him, surprising myself with my own friendliness. A little taken aback, he nevertheless responded with an equal civility. His own hand felt limp and moist, much like the ticket with the letter "J" that was already decomposing on the floor beneath our feet. Our eyes did not meet. In certain cultural circles, this fact could indicate that we would never be compatible in bed. In other cultures, this omission would be interpreted as neither of us having honest intentions towards each other. I scurried out of the partition as fast as I could.

The lovely scented woman was nowhere to be seen. Sighing, I slunk back through the long corridor past the waiting room, still occupied by the same patrons frozen in time distractedly overseen by the lady with the tornado hair. I pushed my body through the stiff front door into the street with the image of the lovely woman still in my mind's eye, her scent caught in my nose-hairs. My heart was wildly beating. I knew it would be better for me to forget her. If she really did live somewhere near Charlotte's, as her scent-trail would indicate, we might be fated to meet again. My original liking of her person could easily turn into a full-blown obsession.

I was and still am not certain at all that each of us is mistress of her own destiny. On that day in Montréal, I thought myself ready to face any possibility with equanimity. I thought I could accept whatever, whomever, came my way … be it Julie or the beautiful civil servant or maybe even Bourgeon. But just one at a time please.

That day was beautiful, the sky blue like it could only be in my absolutely favourite city in the whole world. Not that I've seen them all. Far from it. Anyway, the thirty or so cities that I did get a chance to visit in my lifetime were all my favourites in one way or another. Just like my small bouquet of girlfriends, those that I had foolishly wasted my time on in my lost hetero phase by trying to be just friends. If only I had known. Each of those girl-friends, as platonic as our relationship might have been, were my number one of the moment. Until they were not, of course. Same for any man I've ever had actually.

Julie never understood this principle of my serial *numéro unes*. We wasted a lot of time and saliva in our efforts to reconcile our differences of opinion on this crucial matter. As far as Julie was concerned, each person gets one, and only one, number one per lifetime, or maybe even in eternity. I think that by affirming this over and over, she wanted me to admit that she was my one and only, ever. And that she reserved the right to have, in the past or in the future—I was never clear on this—someone other than me as her own number one.

The realization of our inequality in the desirability order could have been enough for me to have let go of Julie from the start. But something, call it shame or some perverted guilt, had kept me paralyzed in the relationship. As an orphan hooked on longing forever for the absentee parent, I had kept coming back to Julie for more, for something that wasn't there. And the crooked wheel of my dependence kept turning, askew. Over time, I glossed over it with a patina of denial. Despite all odds, I had to admit that I was still hooked on Julie. Until further notice, she would have to stay as my *numéro une*.

I brought myself to the present moment. It was a beautiful day. I was free. I could do whatever I wanted. Whatever didn't cost money, or hardly any at least. Just at that moment, two little girls skipped by, laughing. The taller of the two had her arm tenderly wrapped around the other's shoulders. Overhead, a woman from the baby-boomer generation was leaning out of her second-floor window. She was watering, from up above, her lone giant sunflower growing at sidewalk level from a tiny square of cracked earth surrounded by a plastic fence. The plant had grown so tall that it almost reached her window. Across the street, an orange dog was sniffing around with a lovely, wide-brimmed-hatted, ageless, genderless person at the other end of its leash, singing a falsetto, solo version of the flower duet by Délibes. I could find in response to these charming vignettes of everyday life only one response: "And so what!?"

I wandered aimlessly through streets, avenues, and alleyways for over an hour. Eventually, I found myself on Ste-Catherine Street, squeezed in the middle of a crowd. It took me a few minutes to realize that I was actually caught in a long lineup for ice cream. The sun above was hot. People were willing to brave the mid-day heat for a temporary treat. I decided to dig into the deep pockets of my borrowed dress and treat myself too. It would have to be cherry, in Julie's honour. By bringing Julie into the scene, I was hoping to redeem myself for not having thought of her for the last hour or so. My reprieve was short-lived. The guilt I had almost chased away came back with a vengeance, wearing another face. I was about to fall prey to an evil multi-national chain and harm the physical temple of my soul with unhealthy chemicals. I halted my brain's message with an irritated frown. Enough was enough. I was determined to enjoy this cherry ice-cream against all odds.

Eventually, I walked away with a cherry-chocolate-chip, double-scoop extravaganza bursting triumphantly out of a hand-made sugar-cone. The price had gouged a significant dent in my savings. I was determined not to let my sacrifice to the altar of money get in the way of my pleasure. Eyes shut, I slowly dragged my hot tongue across the unctuous white matter, polka-dotted with wine-red fruit and dark flecks of bitter-sweet chocolate. Just as I was getting close to forming a soft, curly peak of cream at the tip of my cone, someone hit me. Not hard but enough to startle my eyes open. The person, just a few centimeters from my nose, seemed totally oblivious to the fact that they had run into me. Eyes half-shut, this being reminded me of flotsam or jetsam—I never could tell one from the other—already reeling away, carried by the twirling waves of the surrounding crowd. Androgynous, exotic, the stranger stood out despite their short stature without seeming to especially want to. Following a discreet few feet behind my spaced-out alien, another person emerged from the human ocean. This second person did not hit me. She was alert. She seemed to be holding a connection somehow to the first person with an invisible thread of a kind that only psychic persons familiar with auras can see. Also, this person was blue. Blue of hair, extra-terrestrial bluish-white of face, royal blue sunglasses. Blue throughout. She smiled at me. I dropped my cone.

The wonder and curiosity about the two enigmatic persons took prece-dence over any potential irritation at having lost my cone. Not eating the forbidden fruit was probably better for my health anyway. Maybe, instead, I could follow the intriguing pair for a while. But then I realized this wouldn't be such a good idea. Somehow, I felt that my time hadn't come to meet them, and most importantly, that I would see them both again. The meeting would happen on its own, in its own predestined time. I wouldn't have to do any-thing. I knew this infallibly. My telepathic message had come through clearly, through some osmosis caused by the proximity of the strange creatures. Our fates were linked. There was nothing for me to do. There was no escape. Destiny would just have to figure out a way to bring us together again. And destiny would do that. I kicked the remains of my fallen, already melted cone into the gutter. Immediately, it got run over by a taxi.

*　*　*

My ice-cream was lying in a mess in the gutter, dirty and squashed. As much as I didn't want to admit it, and once the enchantment of the two intriguing creatures had faded, I felt angry. I stuffed my sticky hands into the deep pockets of Charlotte's dress in a futile gesture of desperation. Luckily, my two pencils were still there, as well as Charlotte's keys and my notebook. And a few useless coins, of course. Probably not enough to get me another cone. Then a mischievous smile split my face in half. In the fumbling through my pockets, my fingers had found my BC welfare cheques. I had completely forgotten about them. They must have fallen out of my notebook.

Just like in a fairy-tale movie, a Bank of Montréal building conveniently appeared across the street. I crossed the *Catherine*, slipping in between the cars like an eel migrating through the Mediterranean Sea. Two giant, stern-looking matrons had been positioned at the entrance of the forbidding temple to the God of Money. A pair of massive, sword-like arms almost met in the centre, blocking my way. Then they seemed to soften somehow. Maybe I was too insignificant to pose an actual threat to the institution they were defending with such devotion and loyalty. They allowed a temporary passage to cleave between their metallic-looking arms. Despite all the vast openness of space they had given me, I felt compelled to further reduce my Goddess-granted, already undersized form to slip by the formidable figures they presented.

Inside, it was so cool that I started to shiver. I seemed to be the only aspirant in the large hall. From behind their bullet-proof windows, nearly a dozen bank clerks were sizing me up, each already swollen with the confidence of an easy victory over me. According to a popular French song, I took the prettiest one without actually choosing her. And probably the least friendly one. I could have changed my mind halfway through. Amidst the clerks, there was also a fatherly one who might have been somewhat more helpful. And then there was that clean-cut young man, looking almost kindly. But fuelled maybe by my experience with the civil servant in the welfare office, and remembering my beautifully-scented apparition in the same office, I remained faithful to my initial choice of pretty girl. It turned out to be a near-fatal mistake.

An uncertain smile had settled on my slightly trembling lips. I slid my left hand with the cheques into the frigid stainless-steel bowl, quickly, as I didn't trust the guillotine-like bullet-proof screen to spare my fingers. The cheques, sticky with dried-up ice-cream, came back to my side. Taking my right hand, I peeled off the cheques and gingerly inserted them again under the guillotine. The clerk watched my manoeuvres with a neutral expression on her pretty painted face. She whisked the cheques away. Too fast, as if she had wanted to catch up on the time we had wasted with my clumsy fumblings. The look on her face changed as soon as she unfolded the two sticky pieces of paper. My cheques came back. The clerk looked triumphant.

"*Hello bonjour!* So, what is it you wanted to do with those cheques?" she said in French.

"But ... to cash them, please," said I, also in French but with my disastrous accents. The rest of the conversation continued with her disdainfully speaking a perfect, accentless English and me insisting on continuing in French.

"Do you have an account with us?" she said.

"*Euh* ... yes. Well ... I did in BC, until very recently—"

"I mean here, at this branch. In Montréal."

"Well, no ... not exactly. But I can open an account here, can't I? Surely, I can. I have been banking with the Bank of Montréal in BC for over seven years, and before that I did have an account right here in Montréal—"

"You need a local address. Current. And local ID. Do you have that? Do you have a bill, like one from a telephone company or electricity? Library card? Credit Card?"

Just a few more minutes and she would have crushed me into a miserable little heap of ashes. It seemed the whole bank had gone quiet, anticipating the moment where I would flip out and they could push the security button. The expression on my pretty clerk's face had softened into one of sweet innocence. Her giant, heavily mascaraed-eyes bulged out with feigned concern.

I was not quite ready to give up. I whispered, so as not to usurp the sanctity of the venue, "Okay. I get it. Let me at least try my ATM card? It might still be good," I said, meekly. I was bluffing. I had no such card in my possession.

"Your card. It's been issued in *British* Columbia?" She said this with an emphasis on the "British." She wasn't going to bother looking at the fictional card unless she was sure it would be worth the effort.

"Well yes ... but it's from a Bank of Montréal—"

"Then no."

There was a long silence. Then with the wide-eyed look of a pure and innocent mule deer, she said, "Sorry."

Our interaction was over. I took my cheques and inserted them as best I could into my notebook and turned my back to the clerk. The rapid click of her fingers over her keyboard, like applause after an ace performance, accentuated her triumph over me.

The two matrons were waiting for me at the door. I offered no threat. They uncrossed their arms by a mere few inches to allow me to shuffle past under their scrutiny. Their knowing looks from almost a foot overhead burned through my skull.

Once I had safely catapulted myself into the street, I landed on a park bench at *le Carré Philips*. It was obvious that I would need a local address. Maybe Charlotte could write a recommendation letter of sorts for me. If she ever came back that is. Then there was the visit from welfare the following week. Maybe it would offer me the legality I needed to exist.

I looked at my hands. They were tanned, almost to the point of being leathery, criss-crossed with slightly bulging rivulets of greenish veins. I had short fingers, small without being stubby, and my nails were well-trimmed but still perennially stained with the remains of rich garden soil. Real worker's hands. Proletarian, even pioneer hands. I was proud of them. They had served me well. And now these same hands laid idle, their potential, their talents unrecognized. My hands were made to work. I had kept them supple and soft, mostly uncalloused. This was so they could shamelessly transmit the pleasure of caressing a loved one's smooth skin. Frustrated, I took out my 4B pencil, the soft one, and started to write.

I wrote about Love, about the pleasures of touch and feel. I wrote about some delicious moments that I'd already had and also those replete with promise or at least hope. I wrote about the wonder of bringing new skin to light, all the immensely infinite ways two people can navigate uncharted private territories, smoothly sailing through caves, caverns, folds, crevices, vast plains, and forests, all the way into the other's soul. And most of all, I wrote about longing, un-belonging, and the desperate ache, the futility of want.

Three pages had to be covered before I could feel better. I finally closed my notebook and slid it along with my pencil into the pocket of Charlotte's dress. I did not look for my cheques at that time. If I had, I would probably have discovered they were missing. They might have fallen out at the bank or anywhere along the route back to Charlotte's. Incidentally, I never found them. All around me in the *Carré,* people were milling about in an eerie silence. It was as if some giant hand had turned the dimmer up to a painful brightness and pushed the mute button.

☆ ☆ ☆

The memory of my lost ice-cream cone, the beginning of pleasure I had experienced then lost, the very frustration of it all was still clinging obstinately to my tongue with its milky oversweet residue. I decided to offer myself the luxury of some fries to appease my hunger. They had to be piping hot, thickly flopping with grease in the body and crisp at the tips. Golden. Fortunately, the handful of change that was still weighing down the bottom of my pocket would suffice to get me at least a small *casseau.* I walked to a certain stand I remembered from seven years previously, on Rue Saint-Laurent. It was still there. An assortment of characters vaguely reminiscent of the ones I had seen in the lobby of the welfare office earlier, but maybe a touch more colourful and slightly more animated, dotted the greasy proletarian setting. The fries absolutely met my expectations and cancelled the sickly-sweet aftertaste in my mouth with the first salty bite.

A retro-style *cinéma* was calling me from across the street. I walked into the steaming hot lobby to investigate. The film offered that afternoon was *Barbarella.* It was going to be dubbed in French. *Barbarella* in its original English version had been one of the vidéos in Julie's collection of pirated films. The film's status as a good example of feminine power was a bit controversial in our opinion. Even though Jane Fonda had proven that she eventually became a staunch feminist in real life, it was debatable that she had sufficiently come into her militancy at the time that the film had been made by her then director-husband Roger Vadim.

Besides, I have never been a great fan of Jane Fonda. From that era, I was more sensitive to the feminine charms of Vadim's first wife, Brigitte Bardot. She was not a Québécoise, but at least she spoke a very sexy French. BB didn't need to be a feminist. Her undeniable power lay in her savage beauty and unapologetic sex-appeal. She perfected the French pout with those delicious pink lips of hers. I also secretly harboured a crush on two Italian actresses from the fifties and sixties, Gina Lollobrigida and Sophia Loren. Anything, anyone, but the products of colonial English-American culture. To me, those were all cold. Frigid, even. So, Barbarella blew the pleasure machine in her movie. To me, she was still passionless. Like a Barbie doll.

The choice was obvious. I abstained from wasting my money on the movie. Still munching on my fries as I pondered on what I remembered from my Film and Feminism Studies 101 from CEGEP, I turned my back to the *cinéma* and pushed further east all the way towards Park Lafontaine. It would be the perfect venue to observe the contemporary, live movie of everyday action. Then I remembered that, unless things had drastically changed, I might be subjected to harassment in that particular park due to the fact that I was alone, shaved, and wearing a thick smear of Kohl on my eyelids. As far as I could remember, Park Lafontaine was a notorious pick-up site. If one did not have a baby carriage to push or someone to hold hands with, one was fair game regardless of gender. I turned left up the street towards Sherbrooke and points north.

Rue du Prince Arthur had changed. I still felt the urge to write, mainly so I could take a rest from walking and not be disturbed rather than from a real desire to put words to paper. It seemed bizarre to me that one would have to look busy in order to deter most forms of male harassment. I thought maybe the dress I was wearing might help in being left alone. Most of the times I had been grabbed, followed, or whistled at had been, curiously, times that I had felt frumpy. It was as if men were intimidated by clean-cut women. Well, in my experience anyway. Julie, on the other hand, had a set of totally different stories. She claimed to have never, ever been prey to *des maniaques*, whatever she wore in public. She said that she didn't care about her clothes anyway. I knew this was not completely true, because she was very aware of her appearance. She just didn't dress for men. She dressed or undressed exclusively for women. In fact, I had discovered that, on our island at least, she preferred to walk around naked. Still she liked it very much when I would get all dolled up. Julie again. I sighed.

The laid-back café I had remembered on Prince Arthur was nowhere to be seen. Some fancy-looking establishments had taken the place of the once-bohemian street. In other words, gentrification had put an end to cultural diversity. All around me, I saw nothing but rich-looking, generic people all wearing the same self-assured, entitled air. They were the new owners of the *Quartier Latin,* boisterously enjoying their privilege. I tried to be compassionate towards them. The only person that would benefit from my intentions would be me. I couldn't do it. My resentment gnawed at my own heart.

Strictly speaking, and based on my physical appearance, I could easily have been confused with one of the educated elite. A lot of people think I am Danish, and therefore European. Except for my hair, I don't even have a Nordic sort of colouring. Maybe the confusion arises from my compact, naturally muscular body-type. I have always enjoyed, without looking for it, an excellent physical fitness. This natural attribute seemed to have been bestowed on me by a simple twist of fate, or DNA, a luck of the draw. I have never needed (nor been attracted to) extreme, strenuous sports like running, going to the gym, or engaging in any other form of aerobic activity. My particular body type meant that I wouldn't have to join the army of Speedo-clad, clenched-jawed, obstinate fitness-aware body-builders crunching their faces as they pushed themselves towards a further and further unattainable goal.

Julie was gifted with more of a full, curvaceous sort of body, the type most popular in the era of Classic Greece. Like I said, a real Goddess. She was also naturally inclined to sleeping long nights and basking leisurely in luxurious afternoon naps. Yes, generally speaking, Julie was a mellow sort of person. Her own disposition, of course, caused her a lot of grief. She fought it like a lioness in a cage. She didn't like running or working out any more than I did, but she was perennially searching for opportunities to be active so that she would develop more muscles. At our homestead, she was usually the one to tackle the tougher jobs while I did the delicate, detailed work.

Thinking of Julie made me feel hot. I craved the coolness of water. There used to be a swimming pool nearby, but I would need a bathing suit, which of course, I did not have on my person nor in my dress pockets nor even back at Charlotte's. The idea of squishing my body into a synthetic casing repulsed me. I would also have to submit my sun-licked West-Coast-fresh skin to the assault of extra-nasty chlorine. Quite a drastic change from basking in the slimy embrace of a swaying forest of seaweed at high tide, warmed up by the afternoon sun.

On the plus side, I might meet an interesting, seasoned woman. After frolicking blissfully in the chlorine-laden foam, we could go out for fries and an orange soda. Or maybe I would meet a younger person with whom, after watching her do at least twenty laps back and forth like the Energizer bunny,

I could share an organic carrot-alfalfa smoothie while staring in wonderment at her pallid complexion, achieved with the use of the most potent sunscreen. But the promising encounters would have to wait. I did not have a bathing suit nor could I justify splurging to get one until I got my first cheque, wherever it might come from. I did the next best thing. I walked to the fountain at the Carré Saint-Louis.

All the benches were occupied. I slumped onto a handkerchief-sized area of short, hard, plastic-feeling grass. Finally, I could let my inspiration loose on paper. A flow of words spilled out without me having to do anything other than take the dictation. Twice in a day. A bonus.

My dear darling Julie,

But where the hell are you? Here I am turning my life upside down for you. You, you, and only you. Tell me you don't love me anymore, and I will know where I stand. Your silence is driving me crazy. I promise you, if you show yourself, to exhibit my full unabashed appreciation. If you perchance want to give us another gift of your involvement and for us to move back in together, wherever that may be, I promise to do more dishes. Don't you miss my tofu Stroganoff?

I know I didn't tell you enough how beautiful you are. Please forgive me for having spent too much emphasis on your majestic aquiline nose instead of sliding down its perilous flanks to emerge onto the sinuous curves of your lips, always wanting for a softening balm, or lack thereof, a soft kiss. I could easily let myself sink into the bottomless abyss of your deep, somewhat slanted eyes, only to get lost in the corridors of your entrails at the risk of exiting through the wrong orifice.

Oh, holy maybe-ex, give me a chance to teat softly and respectfully at the inexhaustible source of your creamy bosom, your turmeric-scented orbs, with the hopes that my enthusiasm might be contagious and that you may also fully profit from our shared experience. Let me descend past your sweet belly to breathe in the musky scent of your short curls!

I beseech you, folded over my crackling knees: Let out a howl, a shriek, a squeal, a whisper, or a cry, say, "Yes!" with your raspy voice that sends shivers up and down my spine. Leave me a note written with your abundantly dextrous short digits. Send me a whiff of your deliberately fermented crevices. Don't let me languish, my love, hanging as I am to a coagulated chain of spittle twisted around a heart that has become marble-cold by pure want of your impact!

You can find me at Charlotte's, that is as long as I can support their super-sweet bliss. Otherwise, you can reach me through the telepathic post-office. You know the address.

Yours until eternity,

Your adoring Claire

All I needed was an address to send my letter to. And a shore to throw my bottle of hope from, into an ocean fuelled by humanity's folly. Very poetic but impractical. There were no notice boards nearby, but convinced I would soon find one, I slipped my note into my left pocket, the heart side. Everywhere in the park around me, happy pairs or clusters of people, mostly young and seemingly in love with each other and with life, were tenderly taunting, fondling, and grooming each other. Mortified, I got up, dusted off Charlotte's dress, and walked back to the "Main" without saying goodbye.

As soon as I turned the corner, my nostrils were assaulted by a rank, vaguely smoky odour. It had been a while since I had smelled it. Memories of my childhood flooded in. Simultaneously, the disgusting vision of animal body parts, stuffed intestines, even an entire head, eyes blind, filled my vision. There they were, the remnants of past lives, at once victim and defiant, hanging in the shop-window from giant metal hooks like so many white and red banners to the glory of carnivoracity. I passed a predictable judgement over this blatant aggression towards my vegetarian sensibilities. I sent my friend Ralph the Pig back in Genus a prayer of sorts. Then the time came for the next stage, the forgiveness, and the acceptance of my own genetic heritage. My own flesh, my DNA, would have been assembled thanks to the carnivorous habits of my ancestors. Plus, I had to admit that I actually used to like eating such things. Embarrassing fact but true.

Somewhere, somehow, somebody has declared that people taste like pork. How did this person find this out? Did they have a chunk of themselves or of somebody else? There was also a popular saying going around that one "is what one eats." That would mean that vegetarians would taste like vegetables, nuts, and fruit. Add to that milk, butter, cream, and eggs, for the lacto-ovos. But then someone would have to have a bite of a vegetarian, since by definition a vegetarian could not have a bite of themselves.

My mother, after my birth, ate the placenta her body had produced. This, I guess, is the closest I got to hearing a true-life account of someone actually having eaten human flesh. Eating placenta also happens to be the only way to eat meat without harming any living being. My mother said it tasted wild, like game. Julie and I, with our diet composed of a lot of seaweed, might have tasted like the ocean...

The smell of women's genitalia has often been compared to that of fish. I would make a distinction here and affirm that we smell more like the ocean. There is, in my humble, unique experience at least, absolutely no resemblance in what I remember of the smell of Julie's treasures to a stack of limp dead fish lying on a bed of ice. I loved to bury my nose in Julie's *touffe*, especially after she emerged from a dip in the vast salty water. The pleasure was incomparable. The letter in my pocket weighed as heavy as was my heart.

The raw scent of fresh kill eventually gave way to that of cheeses sweating through diverse stages of fermentation, of over-ripe fruits and vegetables rendered limp by the afternoon heat, and unidentified garbage. Eventually all other odours were overpowered by seductive scents emanating from a bakery. I crossed the street to get myself a fresh bun. It cost seventy-nine cents. I assumed that the raise in price had resulted from a rent hike. It could not have been corresponding to a raise in the employees' salaries. They were just as grumpy as I remembered them seven years before. I was too embarrassed to leave the store without buying anything, so I chose the smallest bun, one that cost sixty-nine cents. It turned out to be oversweet and laced with too much anise. I hate anise, except traces of it in a blend of Chinese five-spice. Julie hated anise too. I slipped the uneaten bread remains in my right-hand pocket to be disposed of in the nearest garbage can.

The tombstone place was still at the same location on the street, as were the famous public baths. I walked up the worn, ancient stone steps and grabbed the handle of the massive front door of the *Bains* Schubert. The door opened easily but with a dignified screech straight out of a Halloween cartoon. A violent smell of chlorine immediately filled my throat with its sharp grasp, stinking of contagious sterility. I marched up the interior steps anyway, trying to ignore the assault to my senses. A desk of sorts had been placed along the wall as an afterthought. Its placement didn't appear to fulfill its purpose, which might have been that of welcoming prospective swimmers. A rachitic-looking stoic young man who had been planted behind the desk didn't seem to have caught the friendly "hello" I had carelessly thrown into the stinky draft. I could have taken pity on him. I was unable to do so. The only attitude I could drag out of my repertoire would have been one, dusty from lack of use, that I reserved for lost causes.

After a short silent prayer to Saint Jude—patron saint of lost causes—I cleared my throat. Too loudly. The young man jumped. He gave me the haggard but innocent look of a lost angel. I asked him for a schedule. This simple, direct request seemed to throw him into a fit of panicked incredulity. It was almost as if he couldn't understand how my scattered brain was not permanently engraved with this information that was obviously essential to the very survival of our species. He let out a sigh that lifted his heavy, greasy bangs. He fumbled lazily through a small pile of assorted pamphlets, slimy and worn from the fingers of several generations of attendants just like him.

He finally extricated the most soiled piece of paper of all. It was the schedule that I was asking for. He handed it to me with calculated revulsion as if he regretted having found it. By pushing the evidence towards me with one sharp, long, cigarette-stained index fingernail, he would presumably save himself from the possible contamination of my ignorance. I accepted the piece of paper with, I hoped, an attitude equal in revulsion to that shown to me by this Infinite Being of Light.

My efforts at mimicking were lost on him. He had already hidden his face behind some magazine, the cover of which had been torn off. The stained, complicated schedule was printed in tiny characters almost impossible to read. I could decipher, however, that there were no longer any women-only sessions at this pool. I sighed with disappointment. The images of me miraculously delivered from my aversion to chlorine and splashing gleefully around with other members of the feminine persuasion within an erotic sub-context all vanished into vapour.

A greedy hand that appeared in my peripheral vision made me jump. It belonged to the receptionist, obviously wanting to recuperate his precious schedule, as soiled as it was. I tried, but in vain, to memorize its contents. I knew I only had a few seconds at my disposition before he would tear it from me with a sense of propriety that his kind had possibly earned since prehistoric times. All I womanaged to achieve was to make a mental note of the present day and time to make sure I was not going to return on the same shift. That way, maybe on my next visit, I could come face-to-face with a more agreeable receptionist.

Just as I was about to exit the building, something made me stop in my tracks. It was a large notice board. There was a slight possibility that Julie, if she was indeed in Montréal as I was hoping she would be, would pass by this same notice board. Julie loved swimming. She would frolic in all waters, freezing, crystal-clear, or slimy-murky, salty or sweet, in all seasons. There's even a picture somewhere of her swimming unprotected in a pond with a nuclear heavy-water plant in the background. When it came to swimming, Julie was brave and unabashed. Julie was not allergic to chlorine.

This notice board seemed the best place for me to pin my message onto. There was the added advantage of it being inside, therefore protected from rain and sleet. Also, some of our friends and acquaintances might see that there was a message for Julie and let her know. That's if she was in Montréal. At any rate, I knew I had to act quickly. Julie had this annoying habit of changing her friends' circle as easily as peeling off a sweat-saturated t-shirt. It turned out I was right about Julie having cut herself off from any contact with our friends. It's just that I didn't—couldn't possibly—know the reason why ... yet.

The receptionist, still perched like a rare bird at the top of the stairs, seemed deeply absorbed in his magazine. I knew his attitude to be a cover-up. He would be watching me like a hawk. He would not miss any of my gestures. This feat of clairvoyance, I knew, would be achieved by a certain vacuousness, a kind of deficit in the gaze. In yoga, a more compassionate variety of the same look may be called a "soft gaze." Try as I might, I have never been able to perfect either variety of look. When I looked at someone, whether I knew them or not, I could not help but do so with a particular intensity in my stare. For a while, I was proud of my power. I actually worked hard at developing it to its maximum potential. Until some well-meaning friends trying to feel comfortable in my presence confessed that they could actually feel the piercing of my gaze right through them, even if they had their back turned to me. They asked me to stop doing whatever it was that I was doing.

I realized to my horror that I could no longer look at someone normally, try as I might, without compromising the personality that I had worked so hard on developing over the years. The best I could do was to lower my gaze whenever I felt the urge to stare at someone I found especially alluring, be it on a bus or at a party. I would have to work on my charm, surreptitiously wrapping the person in my scent and energy-field instead.

But for the most part, I obviously hadn't needed to work on my powers of seduction for the last seven years, comfortably nestled as I had been in a steady, committed relationship. Julie's and my mutual attraction had been a given fact. Or so I thought. With her gone, the time had come to dust off and develop any talents at seduction I might still have had left. Maybe. I hated not knowing where I stood.

In the meantime, until I found Julie—if I ever did—I could get in touch with my friend Rémi. I could take lessons from him. Rémi was one step ahead of me with his gazing talents. Even though he could do the soft yogic kind of look, he could also stare one down into a willing heap of submission. He could tickle you just by looking at you. Actually, Rémi could give you a full-on orgasm without any physical contact. That is, if you let him. He could send a flow of energy funnelled into one single sharp ray from his steel-blue eyes and sweep you off your feet. All you had to do was ask. Unlike myself, Rémi did not use his gifts on anyone unless they wanted him to. Rémi was discreet. He was also psychic and very, very sensitive. Too much so. He could have benefitted from using his own powers on himself to ward off evil. This never happened. Somehow, he seemed to be unable to stare his own demons away. Rémi was bipolar. I had to track him down to see if he was okay. Unfortunately, his last name was Lauzon, a very common one in Québec. Finding him would be a bit of a challenge, a bit too much to take on since I was already preoccupied with the Julie affair.

And yet I knew in the deepest of depths of my innate knowledge that not only were his and my fates linked somehow but that the same fate would bring him to me one day. Soon.

Dear Rémi. The last time I had seen him was in the depths of the cold winter of 1990 at the reception desk of the Sir Albert Memorial mental institution. I had led him there myself at his own request. We had been living together for a mere few months when he got overwhelmed by a deep depression. He quit his job, he quit school, he quit everything. I was in the middle of art school, working two part-time low-paying jobs. My mother had just died, leaving me, an innocent eighteen-year old, to fend for myself.

I was not equipped to take care of Rémi, support both of us, plus our crazy cat Minuit. We moved out of the tower we had been living in, and into a cold and dark basement apartment. Our meagre student loans were long spent. Surviving on just a few dollars a day for food—thirty-two dollars a week, to be exact—we were managing on plain yoghurt and potatoes, me walking to work and school to save on bus fare. Rémi just stayed home, his body glued to our bed by a heavy weight he just couldn't lift.

One day, after I almost fainted in the *Banque de Montréal* lineup, I gave up. I decided to leave the relationship. There was no one else to look after Rémi, so that's when he asked me to bring him to the mental hospital. I had run out of anything else I could have done. On a sad January day, we braved the snow banks and made the pilgrimage up to the mountain where the Institute stood. Leaving him there was one of the most difficult things I have done in my life, and the one I am most ashamed of. The image of him hovering, so tiny, so resigned, at the front desk of Sir Albert Memorial was etched by my guilt forever into my heart.

Shocked, riddled with an overpowering sense of grief and remorse that I had no idea what to do with, I had callously resolved never to see him again. While I assumed that he was still interned, I moved out of the tiny apartment we had been sharing with our cat. It took me a single day to move. I hardly took anything but a canvas bag full of my school-books and art supplies and one backpack crammed with my favourite clothes. I took the cat. Whatever else was left in the apartment was of no interest to me. I was in shock. We didn't have many friends, but still, I hid as best as I could from the few areas we used to frequent so that Rémi could not find me when they let him out, if they ever did. I checked into a rooming house in Saint-Henri.

Eventually Kevin and Kent, my two gay friends, despite my efforts at being invisible, somehow heard about my sad story. They took me in immediately, almost for free, at their place. They called it Egg House. It was a party house. And party I did with every kind of drug, a plethora of sexual partners—mostly men as I didn't yet know how to do women and neither did they know how to do me—and lots of whipped cream. It was only once I had become a crazed maniac with huge dark bags under my perennially-red eyes that I got scooped up by a man old enough to be my father. That was George. We got married five days after we met. We were so sure. He's the guy I divorced two years later to be with Julie. I was so sure about her too.

Ten years later, back in Montréal, I was finally ready to see Rémi. I was still feeling guilty about having abandoned him but strong enough to ask him humbly for his forgiveness. That is if he was alive.

I went back up the stairs and asked the baths' receptionist for a phone book. To my surprise, he swiftly produced one without any problem. It was in pristine condition. I flipped through the pages nervously. There was no *Rémi Lauzon,* but no less than eight listings for *R. Lauzon* in the directory. I could have asked the receptionist for a pen and paper but thought the better of it, not wanting to push my luck. When I gave the book back to the receptionist, he seemed triumphant at seeing my disappointment. Disgusted, I made my way back down to the notice board. If Rémi was alive, I would have to conjure him up by telepathy. Same as Julie, really, except for the hopeful letter I had in my hand.

CHAPTER 8

First things first. Before I was going to activate my telepathic call to Rémi, I would need to know if I was free. Not that I wanted to be his girlfriend again, but maybe he could be the friend I badly needed. Julie had always disliked any mention of my infamous "lost hetero phase." She had wanted us to start afresh and forget everything and everyone prior to our relationship. Of course, this rule, like that of the number ones, was somewhat askew. It applied mostly to my past, not hers. I didn't care about the inequalities. I took them as a sign of her interest in me.

The board seemed at first glance sadly underused. We were, after all, at the rise of cell-phone popularity. Julie and I severely lagged behind in that department. It seemed that we were not alone. Apart from a half-dozen or so faded new-age health-related business-cards, there were five fresh-looking personal messages carelessly pinned on the board. All of them seemed to have been scrawled hastily, with an urgency similar to mine. I tried to extract the only available thumbtack from the cork panel. The tack was jammed. After some concerted effort on my part, it finally fell out into my hand with a nasty squeak. Crooked. While I was struggling to make the best use of the only implement I had without actually breaking its point off, my attention was distracted by the contents of a message just a few inches from my face.

"Hé Bougresse ! Ça roule ? Tu es ma Karma. Une lampée sam ? Tsé où...

La Nouvelle Toune"

This language would be untranslatable into English, as I barely understood it myself. All I could figure out was that the cryptic message might have been an invitation to have a drink in a place familiar to both sender and receiver. The note also featured a colourful cartoon-drawing of a sort of extraterrestrial creature with antennae and fluorescent green bug-eyes. Another scrawled piece of paper also had a sort of animal drawn on it, maybe a frog. It read:

> "*Vue la Toune hière. Elle te tende la brasse, mais pas autre chose. Oublie pas que moé je suise dans tes pensées. Meilleure chance quande tue serasse prête.*
>
> *Signée: Ta Prêtresse d'Amoure*"

In order to make any sense of this one, I had to come to the conclusion that the author must have feminized the message. All the words in it, even the verbs, had feminine endings. There seemed to be a reference to something about a doubly unrequited love, maybe, where A might have liked B, and C would prefer A.

The names signed on all five personal messages appeared to be female. I might have come upon a secret communication board of a wildcat urban-guerilla network. My imagination took off on a ferociously wayward tangent. As I was struggling on tiptoe, crooked thumbtack and my letter still in my clutches, trying to decipher the highest-pinned note, I felt a presence behind me.

I pivoted on my left big toe, finding myself face-to-face with empty space. Below this space, Bourgeon was quietly waiting to be noticed. I lost my balance. The only option that my brain laced with adrenaline had offered me was to let myself fall into the arms she had extended towards me, amused perhaps, but probably mostly by a simple reflex. The tack fell somewhere to the floor. It luckily missed both of us.

I tried to squeeze out a smile despite the fact that she was close enough to probably not have seen it. I took advantage of our fortuitous intimacy to look deeply into her eyes, trying to establish if she had any interest in me at all. There was no indication either way. She gently steadied me on my feet. She took a step back and smiled a smile I guessed to be much more pretty and serene than mine would have been a few awkward instants before. Then she threw a proprietary glance towards the notice board as if she had been expecting a special message. Apparently not finding it, she slid towards the undressing rooms, completely ignoring my presence. I promised myself on the spot to get a bathing suit and have it with me at all times, ready for any eventuality.

It could have been obvious to anyone watching the scene that Bourgeon didn't have the least interest in me that day. She was visibly looking for much bigger fish than the small fry that I was. And what was I doing lusting after her anyway? I already had my own mermaid. Maybe. I was angry at myself for having succumbed to codependency with Julie enough to feel paralyzed. I let her have a grip on me despite the fact that I didn't even know if we were still together or not.

Fuelled by rage, I bent down, found the lone crooked thumbtack, and applied myself to pinning my letter to Julie on the board. For good measure, I zapped the message with a sort of ambivalent voodoo spell. On the one hand, I wanted Julie to find the note and to contact me, but on the other, I did not ... and only wanted to appease my conscience that I had done all I could possibly do to find her.

★ ★ ★

Back out in the street, the heat hit me in the face like an insult. I looked for an opportunity to be angry at someone, something, anything. There was nothing around me but everyday life, running its ordinary course. If only I had been a cow, a bird, or a leaf, I wouldn't have to care about anything. And since I was doomed to be human, why couldn't I be with someone? It didn't have to be with Julie. Anyone would have done, maybe even the receptionist I had just left. He must have some redeeming features. We could have found something exciting to do, or failing that, we would have done nothing, but together. Two idle people are not doing nothing. They are doing something by the mere fact of being together.

I slumped onto the nearest bench. I could watch my thoughts and let them scatter away until I found inner peace. Almost immediately, a cottony cloud wrapped me in an insulated cocoon of muffled silence. Nothing could touch me. Then a crunch jolted me. It was the sound of the remains of the anise-laced bun. Disgusted, I took the bag out of my pocket and took the squished bun out, putting it on the ground for any bird that might have wanted a snack. A flock of pigeons immediately came out of nowhere. Ignoring them, I sank back into oblivion.

A well-placed kick on my shin, done on purpose or not, woke me up from my meditation. I had no idea how long I had been lost to the street-life around me. Apparently, it had not been long enough. My temporary sense of peace flew away like a murder of cawing crows. My jaw tensed, ready to bite whomever had brutally or carelessly interrupted my peace. I tried three complete breaths to ease and bless whomever had kicked me and to welcome the interruption for what it really was, being a sublime manifestation of fate operating in a world absolutely perfect in its magnificence. Who was I trying to fool?

The stranger had left a smear of grey mud on my leg. I didn't want to wipe it off with my hands, so I used the other foot to try and rub it clean. It didn't work. I yawned, trying to look nonchalant to whomever might be watching, stretched my limbs in an exaggerated way, and got up. Around me, people were perambulating with full grocery bags in hand, looking happy or at least busy. Nobody paid me any attention. I realized I was hungry enough to eat the crumbs from my discarded anise bun. As I grabbed at my bag, my face split into a smile. There was a twenty-dollar bill and some change in it. Some generous person must have thought I was begging. I gazed up at the sky as if the money had fallen from there. All around me, people were still bustling around. Now I could be one of them. I would belong to the shopping community.

There were lots of bargains to be had in the surrounding shops. Pretty soon, I was walking around with several plastic bags full of goodies: smoked tofu, half-price but still two full days before its expiration date, a day-old whole-wheat baguette, a small wheel of Brie with just a little brown around its perimeter, an impressive assortment of almost fresh fruits and vegetables, and for dessert, an Easter egg stuffed with hazelnut crème. I had done well. That night I would have a feast, the first one in weeks. I walked on Saint-Laurent towards Charlotte's with new confidence.

Something odd happened near the Saint-Joseph intersection. It started with the bizarre feeling that Julie was somewhere nearby. I could almost smell her but not quite. I was so sure she was around, close, that I started wondering if it might have been her who left me the money in my bag. Ears pricked, eyes sharpened, nostrils quivering like a deerhound, I looked around. There was no one who could even remotely fit her description.

And then suddenly there she was, like a mirage floating over the hot pavement in the humid afternoon. Julie the magnificent, slippery like an eel, was crossing the street a mere half-block before me. She must have been coming from the park. Maybe she even saw me approaching. The apparition was so unexpected, so incredible, that I squinted, I blinked, half-wanting for it to go away so that I could get back to reality. To no avail.

There she was: Julie with the Greek fisherman's cap on her head that she wore almost all the time on our island, even if it was the only thing she wore. Since she now had to wear something on the rest of her body too, given that we were in an urban setting, Julie was concealing her glorious torso with her favourite flannel shirt, the one that she had cut the sleeves off of with a hunting knife. It was one of the shirts she would wear on our town days, like a sort of vest. Her beautiful hairy thighs were encased in a soft pair of khaki shorts. The shorts looked new but all the rest was painfully familiar. My heart felt like it was going to jump out of my chest.

Despite the heat, despite my tiredness, I started running. My plastic bags twirled around and stuck to my sweaty, freshly-shaved limbs. It was as if I were in one of those nightmares when one is supposed to run or fly, but can't. I was swimming through molasses. I yelled her name at the top of my lungs:

"JULIE!!"

She did not turn around. Somehow, with all my efforts, I had managed to get close enough to recognize the tear on the edge of her shirt, on the left shoulder. The rip came from the time Julie's shirt got caught by a branch as she was chasing a mule deer that was trying to get our half-wild apples. Julie was a worse seamstress even than me. Still she had insisted on repairing the damage to her shirt herself in a sort of ritual. The tear to the flesh on her shoulder, however, had taken a long time to heal. Julie did not want to go to the clinic to get stitches. She claimed that hers was a superficial wound. We covered it with poultices of plantain first to get the pus out, then myrrh and golden seal as antiseptics, followed by a cannabis poultice to lessen the scar. The cannabis didn't quite work. She was left with a four-inch scar. Julie wore it like a trophy. It changed colours with the seasons. Purple in winter, pink in the spring, and shiny gold like buttercups in the summer, matching her tan.

This time I did not see the famous scar. I was close enough, maybe a dozen feet away or so, but a little bit of sleeve left over on her shirt was hiding the scar from my view. Still I was sure this person was Julie.

She was not turning around. I stopped flat. Maybe this person was not Julie after all. The shirt and hat were undeniably hers but the body wearing them was, in a subtle way, different from that of my lost girlfriend. One could have said that this person filled Julie's clothes in a more compact way. The walk was different too. I couldn't help getting the sense that the gait had a more masculine feel to it. Even the smell that had enveloped me in its enchanting trail was different from Julie's scent. It vaguely reminded me of after-shave. The eel-like being that I thought I knew had mutated into another animal, I didn't know what, just that it was somehow more angular.

Julie's butchiness had always been obvious to me, despite that fact that she moved with a lightness of step, a carelessness that seemed to contrast with her great physical strength. Instead of just walking, she would float. She would slide and glide; she would skim and slither like an eel. I have never seen an eel swim, but that is how I imagined it to be. It was this combination of power and lightness that also made her a great dancer. I loved how she could twirl me around with the greatest of ease. In contrast, the being a few feet ahead of me would certainly have crushed my toes if we had been silly enough to be dancing together. Determined to solve the puzzle, I called again, loud, but not using Julie's name this time.

"Hello! Excuse me? *Allô!?*"

Maybe this person wearing Julie's clothes might lead me to her. I knew that my girlfriend would not have let any stranger wear her favourite shirt and beloved hat so easily. She would have wanted to get acquainted first. Well. Intimately, actually. Maybe even sexually. Julie never let me wear her clothes. I felt betrayed. My resolve to catch up grew with each torturous step that I took. The person in front of me accelerated into a wider stride.

"*Hé! Vous là-bas! Attendez-moi!! Wait!* Please!!*" I screamed, frantic, until my throat ached.

All that yelling would have made anyone else turn around. Passersby had started to look towards me, concerned. Except for this one person who kept walking, faster. The distance between us grew exponentially. My legs, encumbered by my plastic bags, were slowing me down.

Then one of my bags burst. I watched, bewildered and helpless, as an almost-still-good melon slipped out, rolled off into the street, and got smashed by a passing car. The Brie, melted by the heat, was sprawling on the sidewalk at my feet in an irretrievable smear. The smoked tofu had tumbled out of sight. And worst of it all, the distance between Julie—or whomever it was—had increased to such a point that I couldn't catch up if I tried. I had to admit defeat. Letting myself slide down the brick wall beside the window of an orthopedic equipment store, I landed cross-legged on the hot sidewalk, threw my head back, my hands upturned in a gesture of surrender. I sat, defeated, for several panicked breaths, my throat on fire.

That's when I got a message. It could have been a telepathic dispatch from Julie, or it could have come from outer space or from my own intuition. I had no idea. All I know is that the voice said, loud and crispy clear, "It's not time yet."

Not time for what? For me to find out about Julie? Not time for us to split up? Or for us to get back together again? I was angry and confused. Angry to be confused. And most of all, I felt immensely helpless. And alone. The imperious energy of the message I had just received, the square aura of the person who might have been impersonating Julie, even the feeling of Julie's own presence via her favourite clothes … all this had vanished as quickly as it had appeared. It all left me questioning my own sanity. My limbs felt heavy. I couldn't find the strength to get up. I don't know how long I spent slumped on the sidewalk, eyes shut. A loonie pressed into my upturned palm shook me up. I looked up only to see the donor gone. Two donations in one day. Maybe I had found my calling as a beggar. Embarrassed, I picked myself up and started walking.

Going across the street where Julie or her *sosie*, her double, might have come from, I slumped myself on a park bench to try and figure things out for myself. I didn't resolve anything. Instead I got lost in memory.

✮   ✮   ✮

It was one of those crazy exhilarating April days that make you peel your shirt off in one swoop, drowning your cells with *Prana*. You bathe in your own sap, intoxicated by the scent of the swollen fresh-blown buds all around. Birds you haven't heard all winter long would call each other at the top of their little lungs over your head.

Julie and I were at home on Genus. It was maybe our second year together or our third. All I remember is that my woman was resplendent beyond compare. Actually, we both were. We donned our gum boots, flannel shirts, and work gloves and decided to attack the huge mound of slash abandoned the previous fall when we had cleared a space to enlarge our garden.

We felt strong enough to move a whole mountain. And that's exactly what we did. First, we built a fire. Starting with some kindling, we then piled on it some of our precious dry firewood. Soon we had a nice hot fire going. Then we added branches and roots from the slash, still saturated with winter dampness. They took a while to dry on the pyre, and when they finally did, they would smoulder in red-hot smokeless coals. It was a slow steady burn that would take two full days. At night, the fire looked like the crimson, molten lava from the mouth of an active volcano.

On the second day, barely an hour into our strenuous work, our bodies had already started shimmering with sweat. We took all our clothes off except the boots. That's when it started raining in huge fat droplets, one of those heavy April showers that are said to bring the May flowers. Surprised, we stopped for a nanosecond. Then exploding in peals of delighted laughter, we resumed our work with twice the determination. The liquid energy pouring from the sky was inundating our heads, pelting over our shoulders, drawing greasy black rivulets of water-logged loam around the curves of our arms. The exponentially growing heat of our bodies sublimated the freezing rain into an almost imperceptible film of vapour surrounding us.

We kept on shaking, pulling, tugging, lifting, and piling the dirt-laden roots. With hair plastered on our foreheads and around our cheeks, cosmically joined through our solar plexuses with each other and with all that was around us, we breathed in the cool wet air. We exhaled soft heat in unison with resonating cries of *"Hahn!!"* Delighted to be alive, made stronger by our togetherness, we were utterly powerful. Invincible.

Our momentum crescendoed into superwoman strength. We threw increasingly huge branches, entire small trees even, into the smouldering cauldron we had created. By this time, it was mid-afternoon. The rain that had subsided for an hour or so started pelting down again. Delivering a contented exhalation, we joined our wet hands as we contemplated the birthing of our fertile promised land. The dark soil, rising from its own ashes, soft and inviting, ideal for harbouring fat red worms, would soon lie ready to receive our seeds, lovingly saved from the previous year.

Instead of running into the house to get our precious reserves and start planting right away, we looked at each other. Then in a common accord, laughing with delight, we slid our boots off and let ourselves fall onto the cool, dark, damp soil at the edge of the fire.

We rolled around, smearing our faces, limbs, and loins, carefully at first, then with increasing boldness until we were completely covered from crown to foot-soles with sticky black loam. Fuelled by our accomplishment, inspired by all the bursting growth around us, we made love with an urgency, a frenzy like we had never known before and probably never would know again. Yes, right there in the black mud, we had found Nirvana.

Somehow even the Naiads next door found out about our tryst. Maybe they heard our whoops and yelps and checked to see if we were okay. I don't remember seeing them. All we knew is that the incident of the two diminutive women who could move mountains became carved like a legend into our collective herstories. It might become an inspiration for generations of young women yet to come. Unwittingly, Julie and I had become beacons of light in the turbulent seas of Sapphic love.

But for me—and I have kept this secret up to this non-time called the present, due to some residual modesty—this incident threw a new light on Julie's and my relationship. It made me realize the enormous power of the mind. Or in this case, of two wills joined into one. And in love to boot.

You see, on that memorable mountain-moving day—and maybe on other occasions too, but definitely in this one—I have felt superbly, completely, profoundly ... penetrated. I even got an electric shock, like lightning. It climbed all the way up my body, past my crown chakra, past our galaxy, into the vast infiniteness of the universe.

And this was simply with her energy. No hands, no tongue, not even a big toe. I know this. We were completely covered in mud. There was absolutely no way either of us would let the other dare enter her sacred sanctum with digits in any state other than pristine cleanliness.

I still haven't the faintest clue how Julie was able to execute such an exploit. Or more precisely, how I let her do this to me. I have no illusions whatsoever about my state of mind at the time, nor even now. I was and am still entirely conscious of the anatomical, biological, geometrical even, impossibility of such an occurrence. I am fully aware that other women have been imprisoned, burned at the stake, or tied into straightjackets and left to scream in a lone corner of a mental asylum for affirmations far more anodyne than mine. Still, I persist absolutely and unequivocally in my declaration.

As a yoga practitioner for several years, even before I met Julie, I was familiar with all sorts of prowess that the mind, despite being harboured in a mortal body, was known to come up with. Stories abound of spiritual masters from the Yucatan to the peaks of the Himalayas who can levitate, be in two or more places at once, or whatever else they can do. Some even choose the time of their own death.

It shouldn't have surprised me in the least that my girlfriend could penetrate me with the sheer force of some bizarre electromagnetic energy. We were psychic. And hot. Maybe I had received the gift of a Kundalini rise. From the way I heard and read it described, my experience might have matched that. It's just that I have always thought that a person would have to devote themselves body and soul to their spiritual practice for years, for lifetimes even, to be able to eventually execute themselves with such dexterity as Julie had. There she was, wriggling about like the Tantric priestess that she had suddenly become, as if she had been practicing all her life in an ashram lost on some remote mountainside. I have no idea if she even knew how amazing she had been, how astounding a performance she was exhibiting on me with her electrifyingly penetrating talents.

Apart from odd remnants of modesty, there was one other reason why I have not told my experience to anyone, especially to Julie, even once the aftershocks had finished going through our bodies. It had to do with one of Julie's pet phobias. In fact, she abhorred anything that even remotely made allusion to any object, gesture, or action at all that might have been construed as copying what heteros take for granted. Penetration deeper than the length of a middle finger would unequivocally have to be avoided at all costs.

Our home-woven toy-basket only contained one lone object that could have passed as a dildo. There she was, sleeping peacefully, gathering lint under our bed amidst well-used oils, creams, and feathers. She was carved out of blue calcite in the shape of a beautiful life-like dolphin. She had been a going-away gift to us from Charlotte. The palm-sized carving might not even have been designed to serve as a dildo in the first place anyway. Given its hardness, it probably had been intended to be a massage wand. We exclusively used it as such, and due to its vaguely phallic shape, only very occasionally.

So, I never talked to Julie about my having felt penetrated by her. Who knows? She might have accused me of trying to fantasize about scenes from my hetero phase. Disgusted, she might have left our relationship then and there, prematurely.

Julie's obsession with us only using our own resources included, but only perfunctorily—and it turns out for a limited time—the act of tribadism. Before I met her, I used to have fantasies of two women joining their vulvas together, matching their clitorises. It seemed a most exciting thing to do, one that was specific to Sapphic love. Obviously tribadism was the first thing I wanted to try with Julie. She protested, saying we would look too much like two heteros. It took me years to convince her of the contrary. I reminded her that no one would be watching. I told her we could be hands free, leaving our pearls to commune like the true sisters they were. Finally, she relented. Since I had the more flexible hips of us two, given my years of yoga practice, I exceptionally got to be on top.

The idea was for her to eventually get so much pleasure out of the act that she would forget that our position would look like that of a heterosexual couple, in the unlikely event that someone, anyone, would have been watching. After much squirming, trying different angles, sideways and up and down, we finally seemed to have gotten the hang of it. Eventually I would hear Julie moan and groan, matching my pelvic thrusts with her own. I got aroused like I never had before. It was during this phase that I let myself ejaculate for the first time. I executed myself with glee, over and over and over again. I was hooked.

It was unclear to me if Julie and I had ever achieved genuine simultaneous orgasms with our tribadism, but I assumed we must have been at least pretty close. Julie seemed to derive as much pleasure out of the act as I did. She never was as demonstrative as me at the best of times, but I had learned to look and listen for signs of pleasure on her. A particular pitch in her groans, a sigh deeper than the others, a puff followed by her gently pushing me aside, any or all of these clues would inform me that she had come to her own. It appeared that I was getting a grasp of the art of tribadism. I had lured Julie over. She offered every undeniable indication that she was genuinely enjoying our new activity as much as I did. Or at least that's what I thought for years.

Actually, Julie had faked orgasm every time we engaged in tribadism. I only found out by accident one day as we were having one of our rare fights. We didn't usually fight. Instead, we discussed things in a New-Agey, passive-aggressive way. But that day—and I forget what stupid argument we were having—Julie threw a slew of spiteful words at me. Maybe she was trying to show how gullible I was, how easy to fool, how malleable to the point of being spineless, and mostly, how irritating these characteristic traits of mine might have been to her. She also accused me of all kinds of other offenses. One of these extra faults of mine was that of having tainted our pristine relationship with some of my bad heterosexual habits. I asked for an example so that I could do better next time.

I shouldn't have asked. What I found out is that I had apparently missed her clit by a good inch and a half every time. She had let me execute myself for months, years even, and she didn't let me know I was embarrassingly off. She also added that since we were doing a het kind of thing anyway, she figured she might as well do what hetero women do and fake orgasm to get the other person off their body.

"But then why did you keep letting me climb on top and do this thing on you?" I whined.

"Because you seemed to have so much fun. I didn't want to ruin your pleasure."

"But aren't we in this together?"

"My point exactly."

How disrespectful of me to have carried on, fuelled by my own rush to orgasm. How disrespectful of her to have deceived me. And mostly, how utterly, gut-wrenchingly, paralyzingly humiliating.

To this day, I am convinced that, if we had just had better communication, we could have eventually womanaged to coincide our tiny but delightful pleasure-points. I love a challenge. And so did Julie. So why did she give up trying? Maybe we were getting too much into technique, another one of Julie's peeves. But we could have had fun trying. We both loved to experiment. Why not with tribadism, the practice of which gave lesbians one of our names?

As long as I can remember, I have always owned my own penetration fetish. I am talking here about the one where I get to enter another being. Even throughout my het phase, I used to have this urge to enter my male partner, somewhere, almost anywhere. Ears, nose, mouth of course, and especially the small flat part between testicles and anus, where a vagina would be on a woman. Unfortunately for me, when it came to my relationship with my girlfriend, I was at a loss. In my fantasies, I would imagine my clit swelling enough that I would be able to feel, with my own sexual organ, her soft interior all the way to the little slit of a smile on her cervix. An obvious case of penis envy? Not so simple. I had never felt any desire for the secondary characteristics of penis-carrying persons. Extra facial- or chest-hair, a deep voice? Oh horror! Bulky, muscle-bound body? No thanks. Give me softness, gentleness, thin corpus-callosumed, two-hemisphered joyful chaos, nurturing tendencies, yes. Oxytocin. Check.

I don't remember ever wanting to be other than whatever I was assigned with at birth. Maybe a bit more hair on my head would have been welcome, but that's where the puck stops. It's just that, when it comes to sex, I cannot resist the invitation of sliding in-between another person's inviting thighs. This desire has little to do with any given being's anatomical configuration. It is simply a natural response to the call of the wild, the call to the source of life itself. I know exactly what I am talking about. I used to have one of those sources myself. I remember her thirst.

As for the logistics of penetration, I would have been content with a sort of sensitive probe. A dildo would not do the trick, as it fails to transmit sensation to the penetrator. *"A penis!"* some might say. I would patiently like to repeat what I've said. I would not have wanted to walk around with such things attached to my body. Always lolling around between my thighs, plus a pair of balls flopping in a hairy sack. And then poking its head out embarrassingly at the slightest hint of arousal. No thank you. I might have fondled some while I had the opportunity, if that was all that was available, but I wouldn't want to be burdened by such apparatus myself. Unless maybe we all got to carry the same equipment on our bodies for the sake of fairness. And then we could all give birth too, to satisfy the needs of those who are so inclined. We could all be hermaphroditic. Or maybe we could all wear something removable. Some insects, I forget which, have that. They have found the perfect solution to my altruistic idea with their detachable sperm-sacks.

Except that I am not an insect. It would be fun if we, as a species, would evolve in that direction. We might as well grow wings too. Just for extra fun.

In a perfect world, we might have one sex with a multitude of variations. Or as many sexes as there are individuals. Our exchanges might purely and simply be of love without the use of any apparatus. No one would be left out for not having the right thing. I think that Rémi had the right idea with his talents of making me come with a simple directed gaze. And even Julie, with her hands-off talents described above. Except, in Julie's case, her allergy to anything that she saw as het. *But maybe, if I ever find her for real, we could try again,* I thought.

Meanwhile, I had a whole new science-fiction novel in my head. All I would have had to do is sit down and take dictation from my imagination. Then I would have gotten published. My book would have been made into a great movie. It might have been a bit like a remake of *Barbarella* but less polarized. I would have become famous, maybe even win a Nobel Prize for my altruistic contribution to humanity. I would have created a craze, a fad. No, more than just a fad. A revolution. An evolution. A revevolution. Claire's Theory of the New Love-Being. I would have inspired a lasting free-loving new humanity like the hippies had tried to do but failed.

Everyone would make love with pure energy. No one would be left out. I would have gotten laid. Often. Whenever I wanted, in fact. And well ... I would have been immortal on account of my book. But there was one small problem: I was too lazy, or scared, or both. I didn't bother to take the dictation from my own mind.

All I did that day, instead of surrendering to the compulsion of the Idea and furiously starting to write, was regret not having seen the movie *Barbarella* earlier that day when I had the opportunity and taken notes. And then there was all that almost-fresh food I had lost too. What a bad day. Getting up, I dusted my ideas off and started walking towards my temporary home.

✯   ✯   ✯

Once I arrived at Charlotte's apartment, still shaking from my weird aborted encounter, I pulled out the first can of beer from the fridge, ignoring my proletarian sensibilities. Cracking it open, I pasted on a nonchalant face. The look was useless for lack of witnesses. I dusted off the ancient radio on top of the fridge and turned it on. A western song lamented in a minor, nasal twang. I usually love most kinds of music. This one was just not fitting my mood. I turned to another station. Then another. All that I found was talking and more talking. Some heavy metal. None of these matched my peculiar frame of mind. I was still too confused about the scene on the street to allow the radio to offer me an answer to my riddle, or at least a distraction.

I checked the radio's CD compartment. It opened slowly, as if reluctantly. A disk lay inside. The label, instead of a name, only had two hearts drawn on it. I closed the little door and pushed the "play" button. Cesaria Evora's distinctively rich voice filled the kitchen. I remembered that Charlotte only ever had two CDs to her name. Cesaria Evora was one. I rummaged on top of the fridge until I found the second one. Carly Simon. Some things never change. I guess stocking up on contemporary music did not figure in my friend's priorities. True, we were similar in this situation. I hadn't exactly kept up to date either on my lost island. I promised myself that, if I was going to be in Montréal for a while, I would catch up with popular women's music and share my discoveries with my friend. I might even buy her a new CD player. My heart swelled with good intentions towards her and Josie.

I was not in the financial position of being able to put my altruistic idea into action immediately, so I decided to make myself dinner. It was a bit early, but I was hungry. That's when I remembered the groceries I had carefully bought earlier. One bag had burst. Then there was the other one with the veggies now sprawled out on Charlotte's table. But what happened to the day-old bread and the Easter egg filled with hazelnut crème, the *crème de la crème*? And the giant biodynamic peach with just a single bruise? *Where are they?* I went to the antechamber, found nothing, opened the door, and looked on the landing. Nothing. The only answer to my riddle must have been that I left my bag with some of the best goodies either at the orthopedic-equipment place or at the park. How *tête de linotte* of me! The sight of would-be Julie had shattered my nerves so much that I completely forgot about checking to see if I had picked up all my groceries. What a waste.

There was no way I was going back to wherever it would have had to be. Some weird memories were bound to assail me. Instead I hoped someone else would have picked up my treasures, someone who needed them even more than I did. The money I had bought them with had been generously given to me. *Easy come easy go.* I might as well do a clean-up through Charlotte's

131

victuaillles instead. I rummaged through my friend's cupboards, ignoring the scuttle of cockroaches. An old half-empty box of curry spices hovered at the back of the top shelf as if ashamed to be discovered. I opened the fridge door and shovelled a pile of soft vegetable mascots into a big pot along with the spices. As far as I knew, the city did not have a compost program. The produce that was obviously rotten beyond recognition I threw in the garbage. Then I added my own veggies I had amassed that day, poured some oil (probably rancid) into my cooking pot, and topped the unsavoury-looking pile with city water and set it on the gas stove.

The food cooked for a long time, but my concoction was surprisingly good once it was ready. I ate heartily to the sounds of Carly Simon. I dragged my full belly to the front balcony with a second beer in my paw. The evening's light-show of a sunset was just starting. I admired it, lulled by the greasy odour of decomposing garbage on the street below me. The sanitary engineers hadn't come yet. The bursting black plastic bags stacked up in unkempt rows along the sidewalk reminded me of baby elephants waiting to be picked up from the nursery. Their diapers must have been full, judging from the warm stench.

Once darkness had settled and the garbage-collectors had done their disappearing act, I wandered down to the street. For a while, I zigzagged alone like a drunk while everybody around me seemed to have someone else or a joyful group to be with. I cursed Julie for leaving me dangling, and myself for playing the game. Disgusted, I returned to Charlotte's. I stumbled up the stairs, fumbled with the lock, and finally let myself fall into her favourite chair. I tried to meditate. My efforts to empty my mind were in vain. I wished the garbage collectors would return and take my dark clouds with them as just some more forgotten trash. I wished I were a baby elephant welcomed back into my herd.

✶　✶　✶

Eventually I fell asleep in Charlotte's chair. A particularly noisy gang of presumably very drunk people woke me from my dreamless slumber. I wiped the saliva from my cheek and rolled my stiff body down the long corridor all the way to the front bedroom. Carefully, so as not to disturb the coverlet, I lay on the bed, deathly inert. Their bed. It was impossible to resume sleep. I grabbed the first book that my groping hands could find. It was *The Satanic Verses* by Salman Rushdie. It turned out to be so hard to read that I fell asleep almost instantly.

My week had started off being quite eventful with my encounter with the lovely woman at the welfare office, seeing Bourgeon again, and the strange apparition of Julie's double. The rest of the week, plus the following weekend, proved to be quite boring in comparison. Nothing to declare, no major incidents. I locked myself in the apartment. I even checked that I had indeed bolted both the downstairs and the upstairs locks. Time passed through my comatose awareness like an out-of-focus slow pan of a cloudy sky. I alternated reading my densely provocative book with bouts of dreamless slumber. To appease my sporadic hunger, I chewed passionlessly on some old and hard bagels saved from the cockroaches, alternating with leftover cold curry. I didn't even bother heating up what felt more and more like a bitter witch's brew.

I attacked the remaining of the lover's small stash of imported beers. One per day, four in all. I left the empties on the kitchen table without even rinsing them like I was supposed to. Unconsciously, I had created three cockroach and wasp traps, but not fruit-fly traps, as the mouths of the bottles were too wide. There they were, the little flies, scattering in irritating swarms as soon as I passed them by. I started avoiding the kitchen as much as I could. I avoided the bathroom too, except for the obvious visits. I did not wash myself nor brush my teeth. Nobody except for me was around to be offended by my stink. I owned my own.

One day, I forget the date, I woke up early to a soft, almost imperceptible rustle that came from the top landing. I got up, but by the time I opened the door, an urchin was already one flight of stairs down and disappeared in a flash. An English-language local daily paper was lying at my feet. From that day on, a new paper would show up every day. Maybe it was a promotion of some sort. Or maybe it was a sign that Charlotte was coming back any day. It was possible that she had cancelled her subscription while she was away and then had recently renewed it, anticipating her return. They must have even given the kid a key to open the door on the first landing.

Not knowing what was happening, I got into the habit of neatly stacking all of the papers one by one in the entrance hall without reading them. Eventually, when the piles would get high enough to topple over, I would tie the papers together with whatever lengths of string or knitting wool I could find and put them out at the curb come recycling day.

By the time I was ready to face the world again, a week had passed. I knew this because of the date on that day's newspaper: Tuesday, July 10, 2001. Still no sign of Charlotte and Josie. The "maybe" at the conclusion of their note had started getting bigger. Especially the question mark. That little squiggle gave them a lot of leeway. Really, except for the newspaper delivery, the date of their return was open all the way to infinity. That was fine with me. It gave me more time to get my act together.

I skipped over the titles screaming at me from the front page of the latest newspaper. I wasn't going to waste my time reading the articles that every-body else would be talking about that day. The section that held my interest was the classified ads. I extricated them and set them aside. After allowing an invigorating assault of chlorine and other lethal chemicals to drip down over my body, shampooed, shaven, and teeth brushed, I dried and talcum-powdered myself, then applied a fresh line of Kohl to my eyelids.

From Charlotte's side of the overstuffed closet, I chose a flowered skirt. It had two giant pockets. I dribbled a few scant handfuls of change into each, then added a five-dollar bill and a pink magic marker. A white blouse, also with pockets, would complete the travesty. I love white shirts, although I rarely feel like I belong in one. There is something very classy and pro-fessional about them. They proclaim that the person wearing them means business. A good choice for someone looking for a job. The shirt's pockets over the chest were an added bonus. Thanks to them, I would not have to wear a bra. What a relief. Let's not push conformity to city dress codes to uncomfortable extremes. On my feet, I had no choice but to wear my old sandals. At least I would be comfortable. I slid the apartment key into the skirt pocket, and with the classified ads under my armpit, I closed the door and ventured out into the street. Unbeknownst to me, the black ink of the newspaper immediately started to stain the white cotton of Charlotte's shirt.

The corner café had changed owners, but it was still a café, much like it had been several years previously. I picked up a copy of a French local paper from one of the empty tables just to be fair to both languages and asked for a double espresso. It was a luxury but worth the expense, since I was sure to be getting a job soon. I sat down inside at one of the small round tables. As much as I tried avoiding reading the news in any language, this time I couldn't escape the front-page titles demanding my attention. I knew I would feel vaguely guilty if I didn't at least pretend to care. It was almost as if, by not being aware of the news, living in oblivion, I would be letting the rest of the world down while society would be rushing to its own collapse. Here was my second chance to get updated and become responsible. The news articles were talking about municipal elections. I didn't know any of the participants, having been gone too long. *May the best party win,* I thought. There was not much else I could do.

CHAPTER 9

Once the ordeal done, of trying in vain to acquire a sense of belonging from reading the front-page article of the French newspaper, I set to attacking the *Annonces Classées* with my pink magic marker. There was not much that I was even remotely interested in, let alone qualified for. My marker lay unused. I pulled out the English classified ads that I had, until that time, forgotten under my armpit. Luckily for me, they offered a few options. Three, in fact. One was as a server at a well-established Hungarian café downtown. The other was as a clerk at a tourist shop, and the third for a cleaner in a new metaphysical bookstore. I marked all three postings in pink and put my marker away in my shirt pocket.

Another classified ad attracted my attention. It was not a job advertisement but rather an event announcement. Apparently, the local branch of a provincial scatology club was to hold their AGM on the following Thursday. *Thursday ... Thursday...* That day seemed familiar to me, but perhaps because of my recent week lost in limbo, I couldn't remember why that date would be so special. I took out my marker and circled this fourth ad in pink. Then I carefully tore out all four ads as best as I could with the help of a butterknife. After folding them, I slid them in the pocket of my skirt. The marker went in my shirt pocket. The point was down, a habit I'd learned as a messenger. That way the ink flows to the point, ready for the next use. Unfortunately, I had forgotten to put the cap on. I didn't notice my mistake until several hours later. The bright pink ink immediately started spreading into a small circle like a low-placed nipple.

It was barely eight-thirty in the morning. I decided to start applying to the place closest to me. It was the Hungarian café. Since I knew it to be a lunch and dinner establishment, I had lots of time to get there. I could easily walk and have time to spare.

The morning rush-hour traffic on Avenue du Parc hit me in the face. Combined with the surge of caffeine in my veins, the two irritating elements merged into an effect I had forgotten. The feeling came back with a vengeance. I used to call it my early-morning-urban-phenomenon. It consisted of an extreme oversensitivity to bright lights doubled with a sort of sharp metallic pinching in my sinuses all the way into my brain. Then there was the enervating tinnitus, featuring some vague mechanical sound. My nostrils would be crammed with some leftover scents of after-shave mixed with the equivalent female current scent-fad—coconut that day—all stewing in a vat of pollution. And most urgently, to top it all off, the alarming feeling that I would have to perform a superhuman task of looking and acting normal within the next hour or so. Obviously not being up to the task myself, I should somehow morph into somebody totally else before it was too late.

I would much have preferred to catch the scented trail of my beautiful social worker. Now that would have motivated me to surpass any expectations that may have been bestowed upon me. I would show my good intentions by finding a job on the spot. But then I would cut my chances of seeing said worker on a regular basis. In any case, there was no such scented trail like hers that day on Park Avenue. Instead of feeling inspired into action, I was paralyzed by tension.

I returned to Esplanade Street. It was a bit of a detour, but my sanity demanded it. I walked until Marie-Anne, crossed the park and the busy avenue, and ended up face-to-face with the angel statue. The monument was curiously devoid of graffiti that morning. I followed the dirt trail across the foot of the mountain towards the McGill's student ghetto. The itinerary was familiar to me from when I used to live in the area so many years before. Nothing much in the scenery had changed since then.

The Parc-Pine intersection, however, was much different. All the bicycle lanes plus the lights scattered in unexpected places were very confusing. I almost turned around with the intention of climbing some of the mountain and walking on the traffic-free wide path until I reached the top of Peel Street. That way I would descend directly into downtown, avoiding this intricate intersection before me. But then I remembered how often I had been accosted on that same traffic-free path by some weird maniac or another, supposedly suffering from a chronic lack of loving. No thank you. I suffer too, but I'm not going to soothe my desire with the likes of you.

The light in front of me showed red, but one-third of the way through the intersection, another one was green. Then the one after that was turning yellow. The path frequented by maniacs was starting to have some appeal. It might be easier to deflect a weirdo than avoid being hit by a moving vehicle. I just stood there, pondering. I felt the presence of someone near me. Without looking around, I assumed it wasn't a maniac as they usually come out of the woods. I figured this someone near me would know how to navigate the intricacies of this intersection. All I had to do was follow them to get safely across.

As if the person near me had read my thoughts, a reassuring hand landed on my shoulder. It was a very light touch, like a butterfly's. Still, I jumped. He excused himself. The voice was familiar. I looked around. The shortish man's delicate face was hidden under the pointed shadow of a bicycle helmet, his eyes difficult to see behind a pair of goggles. He had dismounted his bicycle to cross the complicated street. My new guardian angel laughed. Leaning his mount on his hip, he gracefully removed his helmet and goggles and shook his generous mane free. That's when I recognized him.

I was face-to-face with my friend Kent. For a few delicious minutes, we stared at each other's faces shamelessly. We were amazed at the coincidence of our encounter. We hadn't seen each other since we lived together, along with a slew of transient, horny cronies at Egg House, shortly after he had come out of the closet. The Kent that was before me had changed enormously. Yes, I did recognize him, but mostly because of his voice and manner. He had always had the pale colouring of the British. This time, he was even paler. He had also lost a lot of weight. I didn't think this would have been possible. I remembered him as having the body-type of a person who could wear an undershirt, a shirt, a sweater, a vest, a suit and a jacket piled on at the same time and still appear svelte. That is if he had been willing to wear a suit.

Kent, as I had known him in our bohemian-anarchist, urban-pagan-intelligentsia days, would have categorically refused to be seen in such a bourgeois symbol as a suit and tie. At the time, he only owned a single suit that his father had given him out of his own vestimentary vocabulary. Kent was supposed to wear it at funerals to show respect for the ancestors. But on that Tuesday morning, I understood why I had not recognized my old friend at first: He was actually wearing a normal suit and tie. And it was not old-fashioned or even retro. The suit that Kent wore seemed to be of the latest cut. It fit him well. I assumed the outfit had become his daily garb and that he was on his way to work, not to a funeral. I bemoaned the fact that he had presumably given up our anarchist lifestyle. As much as I tried avoiding pinning any judgement on my friend, I couldn't help thinking that he had sold himself out to the establishment.

It was only once I caught the glimmer in his eyes that I could fully recognize the true essence of my long-lost friend. I instantly felt at ease. He told me that he worked in a market-research company downtown. Actually, he was a bit late and didn't have much time to talk. He swiftly extricated a business card out of a side-pocket of his jacket along with an expensive-looking pen. On the back of the card, he wrote his home phone number and handed it to me. I had to promise to contact him soon. We pecked each other on one cheek, then on the other. Kent flew away as quietly as he had appeared. I was so much in shock that I forgot to follow him across the intersection. Instead, a slew of images flooded into my brain. Especially the orgies at Egg House.

I have never enjoyed orgies to their fullest potential. My dislike of them is, I know, contrary to some popular myths. These myths might be, in my humble opinion, possibly broadcasted by people who have never participated in a single session of group sex. I can appreciate the merits, as imagined by an innocent orgy-virgin, of finding oneself in the presence of assorted intertwined body parts, some identifiable and some not, all twirling and squirming. Sweaty. And anonymous. But what can I say? That kind of thing, despite all my attempts at fitting in, never did work for me.

Invariably—and I must add that I am only talking from a personal experience limited to about a dozen occurrences—a certain hierarchy of desirability seems to arrange itself in the pile. At least in the orgies I have been in. Maybe there exists somewhere a calibration of orgies. If that's the case, I have only had the doubtful honour of having participated in the mediocre ones. In my loser orgies, the fascinating chaos would invariably concentrate into a certain focus, a sort of energy funnel. A focus that would squeeze me, smeared with everyone else's sweat, out into the cold.

Like a flock of seagulls moved by a mysterious, instinctual force, they would go, all flying up with perfect synchronicity, abandoning on the moist, firm sand only traces of their feet, scattered piles of excrements, and the odd lost feather. And leaving behind the lone bird-version of me.

One human variation of this flocking phenomenon could take shape in the tacit complicity of respecting the sacred bubble created by a single couple. They would have found each other at last. They would suddenly have become the apex of their personal funnel of energy. Everyone else may as well content themselves with licking their behinds. Another example of directed focus would be that of a young woman or two or three, often the youngest and most beautiful in the pile. The chosen would get everyone else's undivided attention, the occasion soliciting all participants' cooperation in collectively bringing her or them to orgasm, faked or genuine.

In my worst-case scenario, once the funnel phenomenon is engaged, I would find myself left face-to-face with an undesirable, a reject like me. Recognizing a kindred spirit, he (or sometimes she) would then proceed to pursue me like a maniac. Relentlessly.

I remember one of these maniacs. I even found out his name, a rare occurrence in such events: Albert. As soon as he introduced himself, Albert proceeded to actually admit to being mentally ill. He never let me out of his sight, literally drooling onto the carpet like a dog while I was trying to extricate myself from the sundry mass of bodies that I had let myself be entangled on the periphery of, as a sort of accidental accessory. The horny satyr pursued me all the way into the sanctuary of my room, which was perched in a tower two flights of stairs up. This was happening in a castle of sorts, where I had been staying in passing. I also happened to be going through my heterosexual phase. With a vengeance. I was trying to prove to everyone, including myself, that I was normal. I would engage in free love, peace and all, like everyone else around me. In my enthusiasm for proving myself to be someone I was not, I rebuked only a very few men. Albert was one of my rare rebuttals. Nonplussed, he offered to share his medications with me. I declined. He pointed out that he could easily beat me into submission. Albeit shaking inside with fear, I refused him. However, I could not get rid of him completely.

For lack of defenestrating him, I let him talk. Which he did. All night long. He finally fell asleep after an interminable, weird lecture of sorts gleaned from a mixture of Marxism and futurist, apocalyptic science-fiction. He continued to drool on my shoulder, which had temporarily turned maternal for his benefit. I did not dare move for fear of waking him and his aggression entwined with a diarrhea of confusion. It was only many long hours later—by lunch time the next day, to be exact—that my host, the castle owner, found us in my lair. I looked at him accusingly. He apologized for having invited this mad satyr to his party as he untangled the crooked claws of my sleepless night's companion from my dishevelled hair. Then my host invited us both to join the rest of the guests at a gargantuan table set with a lunch worthy of a fairy tale.

My one-night's companion, displaying a Quasimodo-like appearance, performed at the table like a true gentleman for all to see. Albert offered his gratitude for my good behaviour during a night that had been difficult for him. Congratulations flew my way about how I had humoured this sick man all night long. Nobody seemed to be aware of or willing to believe that his behaviour towards me had been grossly inappropriate. My host, my one and only true witness, left them with their error. Apparently, the satyr was a prominent psychiatrist and university professor.

Another cyclist jarred me out of my *rêverie*. He had just missed hitting me and mumbled something in English about spaced-out cadets. I didn't know him. I had never met him. Probably not even in an orgy. I followed him safely across the chaotic tangle of the intersection.

✯ ✯ ✯

Trying to get away from my bad memories of Albert, I found myself almost running. It was only once I was safely ensconced in the shady shelter of the student ghetto that I slowed down. Every street corner, every block, offered its own set of memories. Again. I let the familiar movies pass in front of my eyes until I found myself almost downtown, in front of a three-story restored heritage building that caught my attention. I pulled out the business card Kent had given me. This address before me was indeed the same as on the card. How intuitive of me! Since I was in front of Kent's office, I might as well go in and see if he wanted to do coffee that very same day.

The three wide stone steps led to a massive carved-oak door. It evidently had been recently lacquered, as indicated by a faint scent of turpentine. It also looked very heavy, making me feel small and weak. I used all my strength to squeeze the latch and pull. The door opened easily, without a hint of a squeak. Actually, it flew open in response to my excessive efforts. After I recovered from tottering back and almost falling, I propelled myself forward into a cool and dark lobby, rolled past a sober arrangement of expensive-looking leather furniture, and almost toppled over a vase full of exotic flowers. At the far end of the vast room, a tiny wisp of a woman was perched above a huge reception desk. She seemed to be waiting for me to regain my composure.

The receptionist was sexy without looking slutty. She did not chew gum, nor was she manicuring her nails, nor reading a magazine. Something in her demeanour made her look busy without her doing anything at all. Her delicate face lit up in a carefully rehearsed solicitous smile with traces of a respectful reserve before I could even emit a squeak. She apparently had been anticipating my arrival for days, weeks, maybe all her short life so far.

Immediately, I felt messed-up and dirty. All the shampooing, all the care I had put into making myself presentable, had evaporated. What remained was the true peasant that I was underneath, complete with pig-dung still clinging to the soles of my hippie sandals. I thought of Ralph, of how I was being a traitor to him in some way. The tension I felt in that moment rapidly grew to unbearable heights. I tried to erase the image of my pig-friend. The only escape I could find was another memory from a remote past.

It was during my time as a messenger for a broker company. One of the other messengers, a strapping young buck, had warned me that there was a particularly seductive receptionist at so and so's company on one of the higher floors of Place Ville-Marie. He wanted me to pay attention next time I would have to do a delivery at the office in question. Then I was supposed to report back to him with my opinion of her. I figured that he had a crush on her—not an infrequent occurrence in our line of work—and that he might have wanted to know if I thought he had a chance of a date with her.

The next time an errand to this particular office came up, I accepted it, even though it meant I would have to skip my coffee-break. The receptionist was cute indeed, almost as much as the one in front of me that morning at Kent's office. But the girl of several years ago was definitely sluttier. She would cross and uncross her legs several times during my short pick-up and delivery. Her little *manège* was performed with such dexterity that I was treated, with an astounding precision in timing, to a single flash of her crotch. She was not wearing any panties. And then, the soft clearing of the throat that made me look at her face and notice her beaming smile, acknowledging the effect she would have had on her solitary audience.

My reaction may or may not have satisfied her. I still don't know. All I remember is my confusion. True, I was very thankful for having been witness to such a delectable spectacle of her nether parts. Even though I thought myself heterosexual at the time, I could, even then, appreciate a good show. It's just that I didn't get it. Was there supposed to be a follow up? Was she signaling that she wanted to go for coffee? Or maybe something a little more potent? Was I expected to jump on her on the spot, and if so, what about someone—anyone else—showing up, which was inevitably bound to happen? Did she do this to all or only to a select, judiciously chosen few? Would she content herself with, instead of immediate contact, simply the knowledge that she might invade my feverish sleepless nights with her irresistible presence, sticky as I was bound to be with my desire?

The new receptionist at Kent's office was staring at me. She would already have noticed the grey half-moons of sweat smeared with newspaper-ink oozing out from under my armpits. Then there would be the extra pink nipple from my magic marker in my pocket as well. I was yet oblivious to said superfluous nipple, but it must have been present by then and still growing. For her part, the extra colouring on my shirt would have been impossible to miss.

I felt as if all the moisture from my body was exiting through my face, hands, and armpits, leaving me with an annoying dryness in the nostrils, a sort of spontaneous mutation of my urban anxiety phenomenon. I could only hope that my receptionist was not particularly eager to look for any effects she might have had on me. Instead, she might be polite or kind enough to pretend not to have noticed my discomfiture. I asked her as nonchalantly as my situation allowed if I could see Mr. Kent Farrell.

She didn't reply directly. She invited me to sit instead. Meanwhile, I was not offered any coffee. A counter, nipple-level for me, waist-high for the average North-American male, exhibited a giant samovar exuding whiffs of delicious coffee ready for immediate consumption. But apparently not for me. For one thing, there was my vertical disadvantage, making the pouring of the delicious fuel an awkward maneuver. Also, something about the set-up screamed that this taller person would obviously have to be more important than me. True, I could simply have jacked myself up on tiptoe and tried to pour myself, without spilling a drop, some of the precious liquid in one of the many travel-mugs stamped with the company logo. I did not dare. The receptionist might give me one of those disapproving glances I knew her to be perfectly capable of. A certain fragile complicity had installed itself between us. It was a sort of underlying tacit understanding of the lowness of my position on the corporate hierarchy that she herself was a member of. In other words, I knew my place.

In another life, on another planet perhaps, she would have been a Holder of the Order of the Garter, and me, a lowly lackey. Or maybe the court buffoon. She started clicking on her keyboard. I tried to reply in kind by exhibiting an appropriate countenance. There were no magazines, not even a pamphlet anywhere in sight. Maybe I was the only one ever left like this to wait. Everyone other than me would be ushered in immediately to see whomever it was they had come for. I did not have an appointment. The receptionist had not asked me if I had one. My case must have been highly unusual. Instead of looking busy with a magazine, I got lost in a movie in my head, of my past life at Egg House.

I was just at the part when Kent and I had tried for the very last time to have sex together when my friend appeared in the lobby. In the flesh. His face bore a preoccupied expression that he tried to hide behind a film of polite professionalism. I have never seen that look on him. We had always been like open books with each other. He was my soulmate. He didn't used to think he had to fake anything with me. Like on the memorable day we tried to have sex.

Now I had two images chasing each other in front of me: one of this Kent disguised as some sort of a professional poodle, and the other one of him younger but especially naked, rigid not only with that particular segment of his anatomy but also throughout his whole body. I could still feel his chest, his buttocks, and his muscled arms like a smooth stainless-steel sculpture coated with a thin film of the softest silk, his buttercup-blond pubic hairs sprouting out from below his firm belly like a cloud of vapour. Both images, the one from the past and this one before me were undeniably similar because of one huge embarrassment factor.

The main difference, really, between the two scenes would have been that in the older one we had both been naked and in this present one we happened to be wearing clothes. Oh, and a little detail—well, not so little in fact, anatomically speaking, but a detail anyway, if only in significance. The Kent standing before me was utterly devoid of an erection. His pants, snug enough to kill any sperm manufactured in his testicles, fit him very well. They would also not allow any room for an erection, should one happen. Or in the case of one occurring, and given the size of my friend's endowment—if memory serves me right—he would be extremely uncomfortable. And embarrassingly exposed.

It was not my habit to lower my eyes towards good peoples' crotches, especially men's, even if they were harmlessly gay. I don't know what came over me. It could have been the impeccable cut of my friend's pants. Or maybe it was the simple fact that his crotch was the closest thing to my vision from my sitting vantage point. I decided for the last alternative. No one could read my thoughts, so there was no one to prove whether I was lying or not.

I felt just as exposed as if I had been naked myself. More naked, even. In this lobby, Kent and I both knew that we had long lost our opportunity to hide behind the inquisitiveness of our fresh, virginal beauties *vis-à-vis* each other. Our carnal knowledge weighted us down like meat on a hook for all who cared to look and see the shame. Even though we did not (could not) carry our experiment to its completion in the past, we had tried. Hard. It had been a fiasco, true. We had used up our once-in-a lifetime opportunity of climbing the Tree of Knowledge and of coming out radiant and victorious. Instead of consuming the luscious Fruit of Good or Evil, we simply threw ourselves out of the Paradise of Innocence. Forever.

No wonder we couldn't do it. On his part, he was flamingly gay. And me, a lesbian without knowing it—the worst kind. How did I delude myself into thinking I could get away with murdering our innocence? All I knew at the time was that I had my soulmate in front of me, the man of my fairy-tale dreams. We were best friends and also the worst possible sexual partners. Fortunately, our friendship was strong enough to withstand such an affront to our respective dignities.

I couldn't help but wonder if Kent was having the same movie as I had unfurling in front of his eyes. According to his new persona, he exhibited no clues whatsoever as to the content of his thoughts. He affably invited me to go out for coffee in about an hour's time. He suggested a Hungarian café nearby. As it happened, it was the same café where I had planned on applying for a job that morning. I accepted Kent's invitation, wondering if I should apply before or after my rendezvous with my friend.

I arrived at the Hungarian bistro a good hour earlier than what was suggested in the newspaper ad. The place was closed. A handwritten note scotch-taped on the inside of the glass door suggested to "NAK HARRD." The phonetic spelling threw me off. I would have to act as a sort of interpreter between the boss and the clientele. Then there would be the corresponding expectations from said clientele.

Giving the patrons good, cheerful, and efficient service would be no problem. I could easily fake an extroverted personality for a few hours. What might have been a bit more challenging would have been playing the part of the Hungarian-girl cliché. Pretty, cute even, a little flirty, bouncy, street-smart without being rude, at once vivacious and quiet, and above all, showing a generous cleavage. And preferably blonde. Not my mousy variation of non-descript lightness of hue but golden like the full wheat kernels on the *Puszta* at harvest-time. This would be the classic stereotype of the east European female played up by the sisters Gàbor in the fifties, and adopted even by dissident Hungarians themselves. Despite the fact that we were a good two generations later, I sensed that the expectations remained, especially within the old refugee community. These patrons, self-rescued from the 1956 Uprising, would want to see a waitress that reminded them of their first love.

Inevitably, despite the impeccable service I would give the clientele, I would prove to be a disappointment, cultural stereotype-wise. Never mind the looks. Besides I was only one quarter Hungarian. Past the usual requests for beer or the location of a toilet, I have yet to master the language. The other employment possibilities in that day's paper were starting to look much more promising.

Despite my hesitation, and since I was on site, I knocked obediently on the thick glass door. *Harrd.* Hard enough that I got scared I might crack it. A shuffle could be heard coming from inside, but I saw no one. I waited, imagining what my potential new boss would look like. I decided he would resemble the blurry black and white photo of my paternal grandfather. I have never met this grandfather. His photo, kept with an exaggerated care by my mother, was one of the few items that comprised the totality of my tangible inheritance. Other than the blurry photo and a few others, there was a hand-embroidered pillowcase and a ring. The ring was mostly of sentimental value.

It had a big fuchsia-red stone, probably glass, and was mounted on a thin 14-karat-gold band. On the inside, one could barely decipher, other than the carats, the brand: "Lido." As for my inheritance of non-commercial value whatsoever, I had been left with an iron-clad health, blondish hair, copper-tanning skin, and a mistrust of all capitalist bourgeois pigs. And the story of the ring, which was more of a legend.

The memory of the ring brought me brutally back to reality. The husky Hungarian man filling my whole field of vision did vaguely look like the blurry photo of my paternal grandfather. Except that this one was in full focus with all the tiny details on his face of pimples and stubble. He must have been looming in front of me for most of the time I had spent musing about my tangible inheritance, as he was showing the last stages of annoyance just before an outburst of anger.

Seeing he had finally caught my full attention, he promptly recovered and invited me, with a theatrical sigh, to enter his bistro. I assumed, due to his demeanour, that he must be the big boss. I climbed onto the nearest stool, facing the high chrome counter. The man compressed himself behind the same counter and unnecessarily wiped it. He leaned his hairy muscular forearms on the immaculate, cool surface. His naturally jovial face, already sprouting a five-o-clock shadow, was so close to mine that I could have counted the hairs in his nostrils had I been inclined to do so. I could smell his pipe-tobacco breath that he had tried to mask, unsuccessfully, with cheap minty chewing-gum. This vaguely offensive combination of scents, as well as a physical proximity typical of Europeans' interaction, felt a bit like a *déjà-vu*. For the run-of-the mill Canadian, such intimate *exiguïté* could easily have been interpreted as aggressive. In my case, I found that it put me surprisingly at ease. Maybe my nostrils had also picked up on some of his male pheromones. I have heard that they often have a calming effect on females. This would be, unfortunately, in complete disregard for said female's sexual preference. Oh well. There's no harm in feeling relaxed.

As if conforming to a tacit rule that one should always have something in one's hand in an establishment such as his, boss or not, my interlocutor straightened up and started to polish a wine glass. The glass was, of course, already crystal-bright, but his conviction seemed so genuine that it gave the scene all the credibility that it might have needed. He offered me a coffee. I accepted. He spun on his heels with an astonishing agility, shaking the remains of a once generous mane of hair that he had proudly retained on the bottom part of his skull well into his middle-age. In record time, I had a perfect, frothy double espresso in front of me.

The man was watching my reaction to the beverage, surreptitiously tilting his head, squinting a little. I had graduated, without saying or doing anything, from the role of potential server to that of patron of the establishment. Somewhere, somehow, we had both realized I would never have passed the test of becoming a waitress. I was fully conscious of the fact that the vast majority, if not all, of Hungarian restaurateurs throughout our planet are convinced that they make the best coffee in the world. After all, they have learned from the pros, namely from their neighbours and sometimes cousins, the Turks and then the Italians. I decided a bit perversely to make him languish. I accepted the froth-rimmed beverage with a detachment worthy of a well-seasoned countess. This would bring his gesture down to what it really was: a banal event, really, being offered a cup of coffee. It was too late for him to counter my nonchalance with a weaker beverage.

I had won. It was unclear to both of us what I had won exactly, but enough that I did. I could then afford to offer him some simple words of thanks with a smile as innocent as that of any uncultured ignoramus. Just to dig my victory in, I slapped, like an insult, a softly worn five-dollar bill on the counter and told him he could keep the change. Then signifying that our interaction was finished, I took out the pink marker from my pocket. At this point, I was still totally unaware of its having been without a lid since morning and that it had been bleeding onto my shirt for the best part of two hours. The boss didn't say anything. He simply swept my five-dollar bill away, then scattered some change on the counter without seemingly having kept any tip for himself. Having thus somewhat recovered some of his dignity, he painted a smirk across his face.

Still ignoring him, I snitched a pencil that had been hovering on the counter and started doodling on a napkin in black and pink. I could feel the weight of his disapproving gaze on me. I didn't care. I didn't owe him anything, nor did I need to make a good impression on him. What a relief. Unfortunately, it meant that I would have to rely on the controlling generosity of welfare to survive, and this, for an indeterminate length of time. Or try my luck at the other jobs, of course.

Yes, I know. I know. I was so fortunate to have that option of the generous monthly cheques to fall back upon. I owed it all to the taxpayers. Thanks to them, I could eat three meals a day. And mostly, thanks to them, I could maybe meet the delicious auburn-haired creature with the enchanting scent. The thought of possibly seeing her again almost cancelled the shame and humiliation that I was feeling at the prospect of being labelled a parasite by certain righteous citizens. The bistro's boss turned away, disgusted, as if he had been reading my mind.

With the help of the double dose of caffeine, I was confident in the fact that the universe would take care of me much as it was already looking after the Biblical lilies of the field. I continued doodling in the deserted café. The boss had disappeared into the back to deal with business more important than me. Once he was gone, I got lost in the review of my genealogical background.

I was only partially left with remnants of a Hungarian heritage. And also, French, Basque, and Mauritian, 25 percent of each, statistically, at least, give and take a few percentages to account for whomever came before my grandparents. One might think I would have had dark curly hair, given my part-African background. I wish. Alas, things turned out otherwise, and I was left with a more northern look. To my great disappointment, I was gifted with that perennially dishevelled headful of mousy-pale, lanky hair that seemed not to be able to make up its mind what colour it wanted to be. However, I used to be very proud of the fact that I would tan rather easily. Give me just a few hours of sun and my skin would turn into a copper-*café-au-lait* hue that I was very proud of. My mother often said I got it from my father.

I was born in Montréal, in working-class Rosemont. I saw the light of day in the kitchen, to be exact, on the second floor of a duplex on 25th Avenue. My mother, in having a home-birth, might have been way ahead of her time. Or maybe she was backwards, doing it like her own long line of women had done for centuries. At any rate, she did not give birth to me in a hospital. Maybe she didn't really plan it that way. If she had deliberately chosen to have a home birth, there might have been a midwife on site and possibly a brow-wiping husband who would have taken classes with her in Lamaze-style breathing. There might have been a photographer. No flash, just ambient light. And lots of clean towels.

Instead, in the real and raw reality, I was coming so fast that my mother barely had time to alert Mrs. Babikova, our landlady who lived downstairs.

All that my mother said she could find to do was check if our back door was unlocked, then bang on our kitchen floor with the tip of a broom-handle. The broom-messaging did not figure in the two women's shared vocabulary. Mrs. Babikova, a Russian immigrant herself who had undoubtedly had her share of hardship, understood right away that she'd better go up and see what was going on. She took the needle out of the pillowcase that she was embroidering. Then she climbed up to the second floor, her ancient knees creaking in protest, still gripping her handiwork in her weathered, crooked fingers as if she had forgotten it there. Somehow, she knew to use the back door. By the time she made it into our kitchen, my mother was already pushing me out to my brand-new destiny.

The Russian landlady arrived just in time to slide her half-embroidered pillowcase under my mother's damp bottom, providing me with an improvised litter. Later, the pillow-case, once carefully washed and the embroidery dutifully finished by the Russian lady, became my first gift from her. Because she had been presiding over my birth, Mrs. Babikova appointed herself as my godmother. Over the years, she added half a dozen other objects to the gift of the pillowcase. The presents were mostly of a religious nature. There were statuettes of the Virgin, pictures of Jesus and the Saints embroidered in petit point, and even a keychain-reproduction of an icon of St. Clare. As she had given me the keychain on my first communion, Mrs. Babikova had proudly told me, with her son translating, the story of my patron saint's name. St. Clare had been a thirteenth-century nun who had shunned her luxurious upbringing and a promising marriage to a wealthy man in order to follow Saint Francis of Assisi and found the order of Poor Ladies, later to be known as the "Poor Clares." I had been aptly named, it seemed.

All the gifts' purposes were to punctuate assorted stages of my initiation into the world from a religious point of view. That is how I got baptized into the Russian Orthodox religion, which was my landlady's church. My mother did not seem to mind the fact that our landlady took over my spiritual upbringing with her toothless insistence. She herself adhered to the path of least resistance. It was just easier that way. Besides what would my mother have claimed to know about the afterlife? It was better to let me be baptized. Just in case.

There were no Orthodox schools nearby, and the closest corresponding church was a forty-five-minute bus ride away. I got sent to the nearest learning establishment instead. It happened to be a Catholic school. I was to be indoctrinated in that religion instead of that of my landlady. Nobody seemed to mind what religion I was being raised in, as long as I did not turn out to be a heathen. I never learned Russian. I grew up in a triangle of females where we all communicated with a sign language of sorts, punctuated, as the need arose, by some choice onomatopoeias gleaned from our surrounding cultures.

My biological father was absent from my birth. In fact, he had disappeared forever a mere few months after my conception. I never knew him. My mother did not speak about him much, except for a few details, mostly of a genealogical nature. She thought it was better I knew about such things in case I might want to have children of my own one day. The rest of the details from her stories could eventually be fashioned into a cautionary tale. Over the eighteen years I spent with my mother, I was able, eventually, one clue at a time, to weave the following tapestry of my lineage:

My genitor was born in 1926, on Île Maurice. His father was Hungarian, white, issued from an ancient line of aristocratic families that had made their home in Transylvania in the seventeenth century. My paternal grandmother was Mauritian of Creole origins. My own mother made sure I knew that theirs was a story of true love, and that, despite the differences in their economic and racial backgrounds, it could rival in romanticism and chivalry with any fictional love and adventure novel ever written.

My grandfather Béla had been born by no fault nor merit of his own to an aristocratic family in one of the most continental areas of Europe. Much as other families of their class, they were educated, land-rich but financially austere. The upkeep of the land demanded a lot of work. This was done mostly by some local peasants in exchange for food and shelter but little protection against the ruffians still marauding the area in those days. My great-grandfather Jànos also put himself to the task of helping to care for the estate, joining the peasants in key planting and harvesting times, in felling and splitting trees for firewood, and in attending any difficult births occurring with the livestock. It was assumed that his one and only son Béla would inherit the land and keep up the maintenance of the estate.

But things turned out otherwise. To the great chagrin of his parents, Béla, my grandfather, seemed to have been gifted with a spirit for adventure. Instead of showing any interest in managing the ancestral lands, he rebelled and got himself employed on a merchant marine vessel at the strapping age of sixteen. It is during one of his trips that he met my grandmother Rosalie in Port-Louis.

According to the story, and to their fate, they fell into a legendary and genuine love. Since an interracial marriage would be less frowned upon in Mauritius than in backward continental Europe, the young lovers initially kept their union a secret from the Hungarian contingent. My grandfather Béla abandoned his passion for seafaring adventures so that he could spend all his time with his beloved Rosalie. The lovers eventually settled on Agaléga Island. The story does not divulge my grandmother's age at the time she got married. There is, as far as I know, no marriage certificate in existence anywhere. I have not a single picture of her. I can only imagine my grandmother Rosalie as being not only beautiful but also very gentle.

Béla had to resign himself to renouncing his noble status, thus avoiding the shame of being disowned by his own parents. He was not afraid of hard work. From his father, he had learned a deep respect for the land. Béla bought a few acres from his seafaring savings and set up a coconut plantation. He was a fair landowner, much like his father had been. Eventually he would send letters to his parents, telling them about his new wife and their adventures on the farm. They never answered.

Despite the great love between Béla and Rosalie, they only had one single child that made it past infancy. It was their last born, my biological father. They called him Csoda, the word for "miracle" in Hungarian. Béla tried one last time to get his parents interested in his own life. He sent them a letter extolling Csoda's robust health and how he was such a beautiful and alert child. A real miracle. The letter came back unopened. After much research, my grandfather Béla found out that his father had, by that time, died, and that his mother was interned in a mental institution for dementia.

Baudelaire said it so well: *"Homme Libre, toujours tu chériras la mer"* (Free man, you will always cherish the sea). Indeed, it happened that Csoda (pronounced "Tchoda", as in the word: "Tchèque"), much like his father at the same age, got the restless bug. Csoda had always been a dreamy and romantic child. Now he had become a superb young lad. Fuelled by his hybrid vigour, Csoda got himself a job as a deck-hand on one of the pleasure yachts that came to visit Agaléga Island. He sailed off never to return home.

It was undoubtedly due to his acute sense of observation and a talent for mimicry, augmented with his obscenely good looks, that Csoda must have learned the art of gallantry and seduction. Triggered by his new affluent environment, some aspects of his genetic memory must also have emerged, providing him with a taste for luxury and refinement. And a liking for beautiful women of all ages. Using his charms, Csoda eventually climbed to the position of being more of a guest than a worker. He would sail the open seas in the company of his generous hosts and hostesses, knowing when to show his wit and vigour and knowing especially when to slip away from the wrath of a jealous husband and move on.

The exotic nature of my paternal genealogy makes my mother's ancestry look quite simple in comparison. It might be, however, just as romantic. My mother was born in 1952 from the union of a French mother and a Spanish father. Both of her parents were of Basque origins, issued from middle-class families who had emigrated legally to Québec after the Guernica massacre in the hopes of forgetting the horror and starting themselves a new life. My maternal grandparents, according to family lore, had met at the Jean-Talon market. More precisely, they allegedly collided in front of a tumbling tower of tomatoes as ripe and ready for consumption as they were themselves. They became so convinced that they had been brought together by destiny that they got married almost on the spot.

The tomato-growing season was still in full force when my grandparents vowed fidelity to each other for perpetuity in front of God and Man. Their respective families sealed their union by providing the young couple with their own time-honoured, jealously guarded *Piperade* recipes. The recipes turned out to be identical right down to the amount of thyme needed. This was seen as a good omen.

My maternal grandparents' marriage had been a happy one. According to a tradition that seems to run in my families from both sides, they only had one child, namely my mother. She was their pride and joy. She was gentle and kind. She was obedient and helpful with household chores. She mastered the art of twirling the perfect *Piperade*. She went to mass most Sundays. My grandparents hoped she would eventually become their *bâton de vieillesse* when the time would come. All was going well. Well until August 1969 that is.

At the tender age of barely seventeen, my mother defied her parents' careful and patient indoctrination. On a whim, she hitchhiked down to Woodstock with a cluster of friends. When she came back to Montréal, she had changed. Metamorphosing her catholic exaltation into a hippie flower-child-make-love-and-peace-not-war belief system, she had, almost overnight, lost all patience, obedience, and tolerance towards her parents' generation. She scornfully started calling them bourgeois capitalists. It was only the scanty residuals of her innate kindness that prevented her from calling them pigs as well. It was an awful time for my maternal grandparents, one that my mother eventually regretted. Too late.

From Woodstock on, my mother would wander around perennially stoned, real flowers scattered in her disheveled hair, a beatific smile floating on her lips. She would crash in a random succession of hippie pads, communes, and hovels, wherever the whims of the moment took her. Sometimes she slept on the street.

Meanwhile, my father, Csoda the miracle boy, had just landed in Montréal. My mother was all of nineteen years old by that time. More or less innocent, despite or maybe because of her nomadic lifestyle, pretty without a trace of a doubt, my mother was also more-or-less still a virgin. And very naïve. These last two attributes might have been surprising to Csoda, given the hippie-inspired promiscuity that was prevalent in America at the time and the fact that my mother was a flower-child. But my mother's naiveté was in effect not so surprising, given her Catholic education. According to her own confession to me, she was more of a spaced-out waif than a slut. I imagine that her careless nonchalance, her child-like sensuality that I myself had witnessed in her, must have given her an irresistible sweetness like the first strawberry of the season. But somehow untouchable. And easily bruised.

My parents met in Le Carré Philips in the merry spring of 1971. My father-to-be was watching the antics of a newly met friend of his, a street performer, when my mother caught his attention. According to her own story, she had been dreamily playing with her flower-decorated clouds of wavy hair as if nothing else mattered. He slid over and touched the tips of her fingers. My soon-to-be genitor lit stars in her eyes with stories of his voyages through exotic destinations bearing evocative names. He seduced her easily with his tanned, vigorous good looks, his shock of impossibly golden hair, and his refined charm. All his courting was excessive anyway. My mother had already fallen in love at his first touch.

Csoda took my mother to his busker friend's pad in Mile End, where they disappeared in a room for two weeks, emerging only to eat and take lengthy lavender-scented milk baths. Csoda busily put himself to the task of initiating my mother into the secrets of Tantra. It was not to be the Tibetan kind of Tantra where you mostly meditate and observe celibacy. No, the Tantra that Csoda and my mother practiced was the one more popular in western culture, where the couple get to explore the human manifestation of the path of Divine Cosmic Love. Together in *Maïthuna*.

However, in the fever of spiritual rapture, Csoda the golden miracle forgot he was supposed to control his emissions. Instead of letting his sexual energy rise past his third eye out the crown chakra and into the universe, he released his life-giving seed via the usual way of mortals. Oops. He made this *faux pas* only once, but it was enough. The stage was set to attract a little soul that might have been floating in the nether land waiting for the right opportunity to take human form. My parents' cells immediately united. The egg in my mother's fallopian tubes cheerfully must have started to roll at the first spasms of their orgasm. At this point of the story, my mother thought it wise to share that said orgasm had been simultaneous, as if such detail would have made a difference in the magic of the moment of conception. My conception.

My biological father was forty-five years old at the time. Had he bothered to wait and see what happened to his carelessly released seed, the story might have been completely different. Instead, he simply disappeared one day as quickly as he had appeared, leaving no other traces of his passage than his DNA contribution to the few weeks-old embryo that I was in my mother's belly. The story does not divulge if he even knew that my mother had gotten pregnant on the first dime. She never attempted to find him, nor did she try to track down any of his family members. She figured that, judging from Csoda's stories, his family might be too difficult to find anyway. It is, according to the story she gave me, thanks to her calming pregnancy hormones that my mother was simply content with us living the miracle of being two persons in the same body for a while.

Once my mother fully accepted the reality that my father would never return, she burned everything that could even remotely remind her of him. She only kept, without really knowing why, the one faded and blurry black and white photo of my grandfather Béla. There he was, young, good-looking, his square jaw accentuating his serious expression. Bedecked in what must have been his Sunday best, mustachioed and solitary, he seemed to be floating awkwardly in front of an in-focus coconut grove as if the coconuts were more worthy of a picture than he was. On the back of the photo somebody had scrawled a name and date: Port-Louis, 1925. The photo must have been taken on or near the time of his marriage to my grandmother Rosalie. For some unfortunate reason, however, she does not appear on the photo.

My mother died in 1990, at all of thirty-eight years of youth. The official diagnostic was heart failure. I would say, rather, that she died of a broken heart. I did not put a lot of effort into finding any of my living relatives just so that I could tell them the tragic news. If I didn't know them while my mother was alive, they would be of no use to me when she was gone. A few of her old hippie friends and I were the only ones who attended her funeral. I was eighteen years old.

I found myself alone, lost in our tiny apartment on 25th Avenue Rosemont, the one where I was born. I gave away, sold, or threw away just about everything. Only a few photos escaped my cleansing, namely that of my paternal grandfather with the coconuts and a few other pictures, a simple handful, of my mother and I, and a few of Mrs. Babikova and us. I also kept the embroidered pillowcase that had been my birth litter, and the Lido ring with the fuchsia stone.

When the apartment lease was up, I moved out with Rémi for a few months. Then, after I guiltily accompanied him to the loony bin, I moved to Saint-Urbain Street with my very gay and very eccentric friends at Egg House. That is where, wanting perhaps to pay tribute to my mother's old bohemian lifestyle, I lived my life of debauchery for two years with my friends of small virtue. I thought I was going to recreate a similar lifestyle to the one my mother had enjoyed, but with more potent drugs and less flowers in our hair. And more sex. Lots more. Except that it all happened with scrupulously diligent condom-use. I had no desire to get pregnant like my mother did. Or sick. The new threat of AIDS was looming over our promiscuous heads...

CHAPTER 10

A light hand on my shoulder made me start. It seemed that the café had officially opened, and Kent was standing right beside me. There were no other patrons but us two. I had, while lost in my thoughts, covered my napkin with an elaborate drawing of a superb bionic woman. She was wearing garb similar to that of Jane Fonda in *Barbarella* but her face had, thanks to my talents as a caricaturist, an uncanny resemblance to my welfare worker. Kent showed no interest in my sketch. He asked for an espresso and suggested we move to a table. I folded my decorated napkin and slid it into my skirt pocket.

Kent didn't even wait for us to be sitting before he started to give me updates about our Egg-House friends' whereabouts. Almost everyone had found their place in middle management. This news seemed quite predictable to me. What could I say? For all the bohemian lifestyle they had tried to lead, they had all come from comfortable families.

Chassez le naturel…

The coffee arrived. Sipping from his tiny cup, Kent went into further details. It turned out that one of the women from our promiscuous tribe had married a man three times her age, then divorced him once she found out he was not as rich as he had led her to believe. She was an editor at a small publishing house. Another, Rose, who had been a self-proclaimed nymphomaniac and who became a sort of madame in her own free house of ill-repute, was gone. I remembered being at her red-velvet decorated apartment. We enjoyed a mutual respect, as unlike most everyone else, we both came from working-class backgrounds with the only exception being that Rose came from Boston, and I was a local.

We liked to brag about our sexual prowess. I remember one day, on a dare, I somehow womanaged to actually have intercourse with two sailors at the same time. Don't ask me how this acrobatic feat happened, just trust me that it really did. Maybe the double penetration was simply these two men's specialties and they did it to whichever woman was willing in each port they had lined up for themselves. I do remember that Rose was very upset. One of the sailors was supposed to be her boyfriend. Or rather, she was supposed to be his exclusive *pied-à-terre* in Montréal. I might have won the bet with Rose due to the successful double penetration, but I lost her friendship forever. I was banned from her house of ill-repute and never saw her again.

Kent informed me that Rose had died of breast cancer. Amongst the dead, he also added our friend Kevin. Kevin had been found dead recently in the alleyway behind an underground gay bar in Fiji. Apparently, he had been done in by a blow to the head with something hard, maybe a baseball bat. The murder suspect was a pretty young man, a local, probably a jealous lover. He disappeared that night, never to be found. The local police didn't bother to go looking for him. They had no interest whatsoever in homosexual cock-fights.

When I think of the circumstances of Kevin's death, it should not come as a surprise. He had always been confrontational, always looking for exotic thrills. It has been said that people often die as they have lived. Actually, one could say that the one astonishing thing about his death would have been the fact that he had managed to live as long as he did, given his taste for risk.

I had certainly not been the first person to have suffered from betrayal on his part. As long as I had known him, he had always relied on his boyish charm, his acerbic sense of humour, and his androgynous beauty to get himself out of the most awkward situations. Kevin could have shown more discernment in his choice of acolytes. He could have let himself be pursued by love-sick calves like Kent and I had been. Instead, Kevin loved to play with fire. His life would have been much less exciting with the likes of us barn animals. But at least he would still be alive!

At this point of the story, Kent and I took a silent pause to shed a few nostalgic tears. The Hungarian boss broke the awkward hiatus by offering my friend a second steaming cup of espresso. It looked even more potent than mine had been. Kent took it absent-mindedly, as a given. As for me,

I declined the boss's offer of a refill, leaning closer to my friend and wrapping us in an intimate aura. I asked him in a whisper about his present life. He told me softly what I already knew, that he was working for some pro-capitalist entrepreneurs.

"But one has to make a living, does not one?"

He added that he also engaged in what he called "creative pursuits." Namely, he would visit a certain corner of Mont-Royal on weekend nights. That is where he would choose the object of his trysts anonymously. There were, he said, quite a generous variety of stereotypical types exhibiting their wares, from the preppy collegiate to the bears, passing through the girl-boys and even a python trainer, sometimes.

I knew of this corner of the mountain. As Kent was droning on about the wonders of this special place, I got lost in my memories of a hetero friend of mine, Mike, who had taken me there one enchanted summer night. Mike loved the unexpected, the bizarre, the stuff that makes for good stories. His taste for the extraordinary seemed to attract the most incongruous of situations. Like that day when he happened to take me to the cemetery in broad daylight on an ordinary day and someone, obviously not an employee, was digging up a grave. They looked more like a transvestite than any legal grave-digger, muttering, enraged, and furiously shoveling away. We never found out what that story was about. I made a mental note to look up my friend Mike. Charlotte would know where he was. Charlotte knew everybody worth knowing.

Shaking myself back into the café, I took a good look at Kent. Given his lifestyle, I would grant him a dozen years of life maximum. But it was not for me to grant. Destiny would take care of that. Part of me was jealous of his careless abandon, of his passionate recklessness against all odds. I confessed that I was envious of him. Bashful, he changed the subject of our conversation.

"By the way," he said in English, "if you are looking for work, I could help you find what you want. You choose your own hours. You can even work from home, sometimes. The salary is quite generous—for what you would be doing." He added the last bit in a tone of voice he might have wanted to be less condescending than it sounded.

"Oh yeah!? You have a job for me!? What are you suggesting?" My ears perked up. My eyes lit up like a squirrel's clutching a nut. I swept away, with an assured but invisible gesture, my aversion to working in an office, and oh horror, for a bunch of horrible capitalist bourgeois to boot. Maybe I could stand being a traitor to my own principles if the pay was right...

"It's easy. All you have to do is scan some newspapers. Canadian ones, from all across the country. Not the big ones, they print too many syndicated columns. The ones from the small towns. You cut and paste the articles that seem interesting into a file. Then you group your articles according to subject. Finances, management, culture, health, and so on. Then at the end of the month, a team of analysts, including yours truly, studies what you came up with and do a report. It's a study of popular trends if you will."

He repeated, still trying not to appear condescending:

"The salary is really not bad for what you would have to do. So, what do you say? Are you in?"

"Reading newspapers? M-me?

"You still haven't gotten over your allergy to the news, have you? Don't worry. You wouldn't have to actually *read* the articles. Nobody does that. You *scan* them. Then you categorize according to subject. Like I said, easy. Our team takes care of the rest."

"Okay... I guess it's a job like any other. You are very nice to offer it to me. Why don't I go back to your office and make an appointment for an interview or something?"

"You have just passed the interview. You can start today if you want."

"Oh! Wow!! You're right. It's much easier than I thought."

Voilà. In about an hour or two, I had gone from being a potential server to a countess (briefly) to a welfare recipient to an official newspaper-clipper. Why not? I could earn my living in the midst of people I would have called crooks just yesterday. I reassured myself with the thought that, if I didn't take the job, someone else would. There is no such thing as a clueless job, just clueless people.

I would infiltrate the system. I would rub shoulders with the executives, private secretaries, CEOs, and administrative assistants. I would eat expensive hors d'oeuvres and get sweetly drunk on the best booze at office parties and all-expense-paid conferences. I would work hard until I got promoted for being Best Employee of the Year. I would climb the corporate ladder one rung at a time. I would earn everyone's trust. I would be given the responsibilities I deserved.

Then, one glorious day, I would crack the code. I would take off with the loot, the tax evasions, the *pot-au-vins*, the goods stolen from the proletariat, the unjustly awarded promotions, the rip-offs, and the taken-for-granted benefits. I would distribute it all where it rightly belongs, with the people. But not before I would plant a juicy kiss on the bewildered lips of our pretty receptionist, or better, on the firm mouth of my boss, who, of course, would be a lesbian... I could even run away with my boss (ex-boss, really) as we would be equal at last. And then, once the money was properly distributed among those that truly deserve it, my ex-boss and I would homestead on a remote island far from the rat-race...

"Let's go?"

Reality helping, I looked down on my body to check the clothes I was wearing. I still did not see the pink blob under my breast. I ran my fingers through my lifeless hair, freshly washed with Josie's or Charlotte's shampoo. Kent was watching my manoeuvres with a glint of irony in his blue-grey eyes. If he saw the stain, he did not mention it.

"There's no need to primp yourself up. The boss is a lesbian. Well, let's just say that she is but doesn't admit it. Yet. Just a word of warning: Don't let on that you know! At this point, she's still hanging on to her men like they were life-saving buoys. Seems to me she should have figured it out by now. She's one smart cookie..."

"Oh..."

"And by the way, she's also very, very private. She kind of hides out in her office. She only sees her clients mostly, and a few of us analysts like me. Chances are that you might not see her for months. Or ever."

I was too preoccupied with my delight at the prospect of having guessed that I would have a lesbian boss to realize how unrealistic I was being with my fantasies. All I was thinking of were the many advantages of having a superior who would be on my side. Then I let myself wonder if the rest of my fantasy would come true as well. Could I really crack the company's code? And more importantly, would my boss and I really end up on a remote island?

Still dreaming, I inserted my sketch-covered napkin in one of my skirt pockets. Kent and I rose up from our chairs in unison as the real soulmates we had never ceased to be. My friend's face lit up with that smile of his I knew and loved so, kind and with a trace of mischievousness. We had finally broken the ice that had grown between us. Exploding into peals of laughter, happy to have found each other after all those years, we interlaced our arms. With a last wave to the bewildered-looking Hungarian bistro-owner, we took our leave.

When we got to the lobby of the office, we passed in front of the pretty receptionist. I couldn't help but smile at her with complicity, even going as far as feeling a daring sense of propriety towards her, since now she would also be *my* receptionist. Kent ushered me into a largish room. The heritage character of the building had been preserved, and the high ceiling of the room rose above our heads, reminding me how small I was. In the centre of the room, a huge, heavy, long, and dark table, the kind you see people dining at in historical movies, loomed like an ancient alligator in a swamp. The top of the table was littered with several cups of cold-looking coffee and last-bites from expensive-looking pastries.

Around the table, six employees comfortably ensconced in their ergonomic chairs were boisterously bantering. Nobody, except for one person, seemed to bother to work. I wondered if the cohesiveness that seemed to tie them together as a group had been the result of the fact that they had all tried each other out in the biblical sense. An office that sleeps together stays together? I hoped not. As soon as they noticed Kent and me, one by giggling one, they stifled their laughter into badly repressed chuckles. I could only hope they would accept me as one of theirs without me having to be intimate with either of them. But for now, I had other things to worry about than sex. Each employee was sitting in front of a computer screen. I hadn't used one of them since high school. I imagined we would be cutting real paper newspapers with real glue and scissors like we had on Genus Island. Silly me.

While I was contemplating the scene before me, a complicit silence had descended on the small group. I could tell I would have to work hard at being well received, especially by the butchy-looking woman sitting at the head of the table. From her sober demeanour, I assumed she must have been the supervisor. She had been the one that hadn't been participating in the little party. Unlike her co-workers, she was wearing a permanent-looking frown on her square forehead.

Behind her stern look, I sensed a kindred soul. As if to make things easier for me, her short hair was, oh miracle, very much like mine in its natural un-shampooed state. I smiled. She smiled back, still a bit reserved but staring at me with a benevolent curiosity.

I had recognized the tribadist's twinkle in the corner of her eyes. I couldn't help but wonder if she had tried to seduce the big boss, the one reputedly still hiding in the closet. I could only hope this supervisor would not try her luck with me. My heart was already occupied. By whom I was unsure, but it had to be. If my heart was no longer filled by Julie, then it could have been open to the welfare worker. There might have been Bourgeon also, but I had a sneaky suspicion that I had better abandon all hope of getting anything serious going on with her. She was too elusive. Plus, she didn't seem to have shown any interest in me.

The person who was probably to be my supervisor pushed a steaming cup of coffee my way. I declined as graciously as I could, having already imbibed three shots that day. I got offered a cup of herbal tea instead by someone else. I accepted, especially since I was informed that it was organic and fairly traded. Another one of the employees who introduced herself as Natalie explained to me the simple but potentially fascinating procedure of newspaper-reading and clipping. All that I was supposed to do was avoid the syndicated columns, whether they were national or international. The local, quainter articles were what our analysts were looking for. "That's where the real trends are," I was assured.

She explained all this to me, her fingers clicking away the whole time with astonishing rapidity.

"Ahem... It's just that I'm not the best with computers... on my island..." I said, sheepishly, m voice trailing off.

She shot me an incredulous look. The supervisor took over. "It's okay, Nathalie. I got it," she said, smiling at me.

She was very patient. The work was not that complicated. She opened a site, stopping after each step to make sure I understood. I was to begin with small local papers. They were dailies and weeklies from British Columbia. By an uncanny coincidence, the first one I picked up came from the town closest to Genus Island. It was as if home had been beckoning me all the way from this Montréal office. It was only by sheer willpower that I did not let the tears escape from the flooded rims of my eyelids. The article featured on the front page of my newspaper was talking about a case of welfare fraud. A single mother of three, instead of looking for paid employment while her children were at school, had been caught using her so-called free time to play Bingo in a church basement. I did not know the woman in question. The name of the church was, however, familiar to me. It was in the lower-income area of town. I couldn't help but wonder who had turned the mother in and why.

I was just going to ask where such an article might have been categorized when, at that very moment, another employee poked a smiling head through the door. Svelte and clean-cut, he wore a naturally reserved and distinguished air. His elegant appearance belied his short stature and made him seem a good twenty centimetres taller. He seemed totally oblivious to the fact that he bore a compulsively intriguing face, one that only androgynous persons can carry off gracefully. His beauty, far from being conventional, must have come from the kindness and intelligence that animated his face. He was vaguely familiar, but I couldn't quite place him. He also seemed to recognize me, but just like me, he seemed clueless as to where we might have known each other from.

Kent was still in the room. I could feel his energy behind me. He must have stayed on as a sort of guardian angel, making sure that my new co-workers would treat me kindly. His hands, which he had placed on my shoulders in a protective kind of way, had grown heavy. It was as if they had contracted like the dense mass of a black hole. One degree more and I would be absorbed in the vortex. I interpreted the sensation as a sign that my friend was immensely attracted to this other unusual-looking but beautiful person. I also concluded from the way my friend's hands were weighing on my shoulder that his attentions were not reciprocated. My cup of tea started shaking in my hand.

The androgynous apparition whispered something in the supervisor's ears and vanished. To my great relief, Kent released his burden on my shoulder. It was about time. One more fraction of a second of pressure and I would have had to peel his fingers off my frame. And this despite the awkwardness such action, as necessary as it would have been, would have caused to both of us. I turned around, trying to offer him a smile that I hoped would express all my sympathy towards him.

"That was Adam," whispered Kent, letting out a dejected sigh. "He is an accountant and *homme de confiance* of the big boss. He is very discreet. As for the big boss herself, I will introduce you. Later."

Adam's name did not give me any further clues as to where I might have seen him. I had to let go of trying to figure it out. Oh! But wait a minute! Wasn't he the careless person who bumped into me previously, causing me to lose my ice-cream on Sainte-Catherine Street? And most importantly, was this the simple reason for my feeling that our fates were linked? Or was there more? Only time would tell. Meanwhile, I thanked Kent with all the sympathy I could put into my tone of voice. Then I cautiously rested my hot cup on the table and sat at the edge of the one unoccupied ergonomic chair. I immediately put myself to the task without a peep.

The other workers followed my example under the approving look of the serious person. This is when she introduced herself. Her name was Helga. Indeed, she was our supervisor. She told me where the toilets were and to address her with any other questions I might have at any time. She smiled and bade me welcome. After that, the room sank into an artificial silence. It was possible that I was being classified as a party-pooper, an over-zealous ass-licker by the suspicious little crowd. I didn't care. This was my first day. I had to show at least a semblance of good will towards my tribadist supervisor. In a few days, I would prove to my co-workers that I could be as much fun as they were, given the right opportunity. I would find the perfect balance of diligence and joviality and be worthy of my generous pay.

All I could have hoped for was that I would not have to pass an intimacy initiation into the group. I supposed I could hide behind an obvious gender-preference. But then I would be expected to be flirting with the supervisor. Unfortunately, even apart from the fact that I considered myself taken by at least two other love interests, she was not my type. Too masculine without being butch enough, she did not turn my crank in the least. I felt uncomfortable. I started squirming on my chair. Helga, who had been visibly observing me, offered me a cushion. I accepted it, despite the fact that I didn't really need it. It might have seemed hostile on my part, after I refused her offer of a coffee, to have declined her advances twice in the same day. I retracted my neck into my shoulders and worked like that for three full hours. Eventually the others more or less ignored me and relaxed a bit. Someone put the radio on to help dissipate the slight tension my arrival had brought in.

It was only by the time I arrived back at Charlotte's place with very sore shoulders that I noticed the pink and grey stains on the white shirt. No one had said anything about them all day. It was understandable that Kent would not have had any interest in my bosom but what about the supervisor? And if she had said something, what would I have done? If I had run to the toilets, rubbed at them frantically, then returned to my place with a wet white shirt,

I would simply have been adorned with another pink circle, that of my own erect nipple, instead of the stain from the marker.

It was better to ride on the illusion that nobody had noticed said stain. Disgusted, I threw the guilty pink marker in the trash along with the ads for jobs. I only kept the notice for the scatological meeting and my cartoon of the bionic woman. Then I tried to wash the shirt. The newspaper ink eventually disappeared at the armpits, but a faint trace of pink remained on the pocket.

The next day went by without any unpleasant incidents at the office. I had instinctively found my balance of work and play. I noticed that, as long as we talked about the articles we were reading, we could be as loud as we wanted. Sometimes I even allowed myself to read the odd comic strip, and this under the indulgent eye of my supervisor. I was in. Or so I thought.

✭   ✭   ✭

Thursday morning, I was trying to sleep in. It was to be a day off. I had been up until the soft light of dawn with an interesting book I had found on Charlotte's bookshelf. My short slumber was rudely interrupted by a peremptory door-bell ring. I barely suppressed a juicy succession of all the swear words I knew and threw on my bare shoulders the first thing that fell into my hands. It happened to be Josie's huge silk kimono, embroidered on the back with the obligatory dragon. In a flurry, I wrapped myself with it as best as I could.

Only a single arm had truly found a sleeve. The other was embedded who knows where. The whole *accoutrement* was only held in place by a precarious miracle. I ejected myself thus rigged out onto the balcony to see who this person was with the audacity to visit me at such an early time. It was 8:37 a.m. I saw the top of a head covered with auburn hair. I had never seen her from this angle yet, but I recognized her immediately thanks to her scent, which activated my salivary glands, transforming me on the spot into Pavlov's bitch. There was not even time for me to clean the crust from my sleepy eyes.

I raucously tried to clear my throat in a way that was intended to be discreet but ended up excessively loud. The head winced. A beautiful face turned up in the direction of the strange noise. Her soft golden-brown gaze landed on my balcony, light as a sparrow. I exhibited the best smile available to me that morning, which was not saying much. I invited her to come up. Since I already had found a job, there was no longer a need to impress her with my zealousness at landing myself another one. I was thus free to focus on at least trying to seduce her with my charm and maybe even a certain erudition. My kimono would be an asset in this scenario. I was counting on it to give me at once a serious and sexy look. The kind that only needed a pair of black horn-rimmed glasses. No such prop was available to me on that morning. I would concentrate on the kimono, my one and only trump card.

There still remained the inconvenient situation of the recalcitrant sleeve. In my haste, the second arm still hadn't found its proper place. I had to act promptly. As I was rushing towards the door, I frenetically fumbled through the mass of disobedient silk hovering over my otherwise naked body. Once I arrived at my destination, I stopped in front of the locked door. I quickly fluffed my hair. In that gesture, I was relieved to realize that both of my hands had emerged, as if by miracle out of the eel-like slippery garment covering my cool shoulders.

Alas my triumph was short lived. I still had no idea where my second hand had come out of, but it certainly was not from the right place. Without even needing to take the trouble to visually check my attire, I had recognized the unmistakeable freshness of the morning breeze on my gluteus maximus. Still standing in front of the closed door, feeling the patient but slightly intrigued presence of my visitor on the other side, I cried out, in French and English and much too loudly, still struggling with my kimono:

"J'arrive! I'm Coming!"

Despite my heroic attempts, my compromised dexterity offered me only one of two choices: Either I had both my hands free but my ass bare or I covered my behind and had a single hand at my disposal. I opted for the second alternative. It was with my only available hand that I finally turned the door-handle, and in French, with a gallant bow, invited my beautiful visitor to enter all the way into the kitchen, where I pulled up Charlotte's favourite chair and offered my guest a coffee while tossing a bowl of fruit on the table in front of her. I regretted this last gesture, as soon as I noticed the small herd of cockroaches that I had disturbed. The poor dears driven wild with panic scattered in all directions.

My visitor's delicate face showed no surprise nor disgust to the point that I could be hopeful she hadn't seen the insects. I lit the stove under the kettle half-full of yesterday's water. Grasping as precariously as at a straw, in the hope of still holding my visitor's interest, I slunk into the closest chair as best as I could, facing her, in a move that I would have liked to appear languorous but that ended up feeling like something else completely, I didn't know what but certainly something disadvantageous for me. I sprang up, pretending to get the hot water. The kimono slipped somewhat. A quick glance revealed the welcome presence of a seam, then of a sort of silken tunnel.

"Ah! The sleeve!" I said with private jubilation. My triumph was to be brief. In order to insert my second arm in the new sleeve, I had let go of my grip on the slippery kimono. The whole garment spilled onto the kitchen floor in a soft, silent cascade. I found myself, in a manner alarming by its prematurity, in all my inopportune splendour. Egg-naked.

Nonplussed, serenely ignoring my extreme malaise, my interlocutor chose this instant to calmly lay down her visiting-card on the table. There she was, smiling in the most natural way, as if she were used to women routinely letting their garments fall to the floor in her presence. She offered me another *rendez-vous*. I must add here that all our conversation was done in French. My worker was tactfully respecting my right to speak Molière's tongue, even though I spoke with an irritating, slightly anglicized accent. At any rate, she said, still in French and still smiling, that it seemed to her I wasn't ready to have a visit at that particular moment. Excruciatingly conscious at this point of my very naked state, all I could find to do was duck under the table. This was done in the hopes of both retrieving my garment and hiding for a while.

I repressed, by some primal instinct, my initial reply to her, which would have been that on the contrary I was indeed ready for her. Very ready. And desperately willing. Instead of my impulsive reaction, I gave her another, more sedate version of the truth, which was that I had actually found myself a job and that I would not be needing welfare's assistance. All this was still uttered from my refuge under the table.

My task of trying to put the kimono on properly kept me so busy that I forgot to take advantage of my position to steal an inquisitive look at the gap between my worker's knees. Meanwhile, I was obviously losing the battle with the kimono. It was time to admit final defeat and emerge. I hit my head hard as I tried to get up too soon. Rubbing my crown chakra, I slid out from under the table and clambered onto a chair, clutching my kimono to my breast. My beautiful welfare worker was examining with interest the two bits of paper I had left on the table, namely the ad for the Scatological Society meeting that very night and my caricature of the bionic woman that looked like her. I still have no idea if she recognized herself in the flattering drawing. She simply smiled wider than before.

Then she picked up, with hands so delicate as to melt the most hardened heart, her folder decorated with an array of colourful flowers. The same folder in anyone else's possession would have been embarrassingly tacky. But in her hands, it was perfectly at home. She sauntered out of the kitchen, leaving only her scent to continue lighting up the place with its tenacious softness.

"But I still need a place to stay!" I said (in French, and I translate), frantic at the thought that I might be losing her forever.

"(Translated) Finding housing is not really in my department, nor in my job description, but I will see what I can do." She stopped to slide this sentence in like a secret, turning her face slightly around towards me.

That's when I noticed how close I had been following her. Her lips were at such an immediate proximity that we were only separated by a kiss. I must have fainted or something at this moment, because by the time I came to and opened my eyes, she had already passed the threshold of the door. She was offering me an almost hardened, professional sort of look. Then she turned her back and flew down the two sets of stairs.

I clutched at the slippery garment that I still had not quite womanaged to wear properly and waved her retreating back a sad goodbye. I softly closed the door. The kimono fell off my shoulders as I slumped my sad body onto the entrance-hall floor, feeling like a Kabuki *heroïne* whose lover had just left her never to return. In the following scene, I would have to save face by performing Seppuku, the ritual where I would be piercing through my guts with the ceremonial sword. No such dramatic event occurred. With the true banality of my pathetic situation, I picked myself up. The kimono stayed on the floor. Rubbing my head the whole time, I made a futile attempt to slide a healing balm on my bruises. One bruise was to my head and the other one, more serious, was to my ego.

I went back to the kitchen. The business-card that my visitor had left informed me that her name was Sonia. What a perfect name for her. There was no *nom de famille*. I made a small pile with the card on the top of all the pieces of paper on the table, namely the scatological meeting, the bionic woman, Charlotte's notes, and some grocery receipts. Then I buried everything under Charlotte's ancient phone. The table became my clean slate. I was ready for a fresh start. A cockroach scurried away into a crack in the wall. The hot water in the kettle had almost boiled itself dry. Just noticing there was no tea to be found anywhere in the kitchen, I turned the stove off, barely dodging the remains of the hot steam.

My plans of having a day off were ruined. What would I do? The only option that remained was to go to work. It seemed like an arduous, almost impossible task. My heart and limbs felt heavy. The only advantage I found to my slow movements was to catch a whiff of her scent every time I displaced some of the air in the kitchen. I started moving with bigger, faster gestures to enhance the experience. Her scent soon wore off but this did not put a damper on my enthusiasm as far as she was concerned. I had it bad.

I went back to Charlotte's room, lay on her bed, and closed my eyes. Almost immediately, a scene played itself out in front of my eyes like a movie.

Urban environment, obligatory malfunctioning neon sign blinking bright pink from the street below and lighting up a dilapidated room in a slow strobe-light effect. At each flash of light, the intermittent shape of two women emerge, prancing about on the unmade bed. I am obviously one of the shapes, and I am in great shape! The other person is a sort of three-way hybrid of Julie, Charlotte, and of course, the superb Sonia. There we are, gambolling about like there is no tomorrow, rising, spiralling collectively into crescendos of pleasure. At the peak of our collective climax—because of course it is simultaneous, it being in a fantasy—I hear a sort of wail, an inhuman scream from another life, the one that is called "real." The sound jolts me out of my movie. A strident alarm slices the atmosphere in the room from directly under Charlotte's window. I recognize it now. It is the siren from an ambulance, so close I feel I should move over somehow. The ambulance has arrived extraordinarily precisely at the robust and delicate instant of the apotheosis of my orgasm in its purest state.

Opportune in a certain way because the clamour of the siren could have masked, and thus given us the space, to accentuate our virtual cries of victory. Not to mention my own real wails. I even forgot to pray as I would usually have done for the unfortunate neighbour whom the ambulance had come to get. There I was, still quaking from my own climax, jubilating inside from the serendipity of such a coincidental occurrence of siren and orgasm at the same time. Deep spasms of laughter rose from my guts in fat jolts like a torrent at the first thaw of spring. Inspired, hypnotized, and saturated with a fresh tide of oxytocin, I tried to put my experience to paper. It must have taken me a good hour to get it right to my satisfaction.

Refreshed, thankful that my new job would permit such luxury as to be able to give in to spontaneous creativity, I was finally ready to take the urban bull by the horns. I walked to work. The effects of my oxytocin lasted pretty much for the rest of the day. They certainly lasted long enough for me to completely forget about the scatology meeting that was to take place that very night. It will forever remain on my bucket list.

✸   ✸   ✸

At work, an article relating to statistics on couples' infidelities especially attracted my attention. I read it all attentively, even though we were not supposed to, feeling vaguely wicked for wasting my remunerated time. And mostly wicked for hoping for the possibility of cheating on Julie.

And then the shroud of oxytocin that was still enveloping me took over. I smiled. It was obvious to me that Sonia and I had known each other since time immemorial. Maybe we were even soulmates separated by fate, destined to meet again and again. That's just the way it was and had nothing to do with my past life with anyone else.

In the meantime, there was the business at hand. It was obvious I had to settle the Julie affair once and for all. The best strategy—the only one remaining, really—would be to call Julie's parents on my coffee break. As soon as I started dialling the Goldbergs' number, my fingers knew automatically where to go. Memory is a strangely selective thing.

The telephone, strident at my end but no doubt discreet at the Goldbergs', rang for a long time. I could imagine Julie's mother reading an unknown number on the display, wondering if she should pick up. Maybe I should have called her up from Charlotte's. Then Mrs. Goldberg would have recognized the number and picked up in a flash. Julie and I had insisted that Mrs. Goldberg and our friend meet. The two women had hit it off like a house on fire. Charlotte, with her charm and distracted joviality, almost lofty, matched Julie's mother's sophistication to perfection. The two women, past the first introductions, immediately started talking about choice things, as in trendy and expensive. They spontaneously offered to the unsuspecting onlooker, and despite their age difference, the image of two long-time friends. They even had the same laugh. I have to say that my friend's demeanour surprised me. She had never shown that aspect of her personality to me, that sophisticated ease of the well-to-do. With me, Charlotte had always played, instead, her proletarian, urbano-gypsy, politico feminist cards.

After too many rings, probably just before the answering machine should have kicked in, Mrs. Goldberg (Sandy) picked up the phone. She didn't seem surprised in the least to hear my voice. She had already heard from Charlotte that I was in town. That meant, I was sure, that she already knew about Josie and their honeymoon. I felt irritated that my girlfriend's mother knew at least as much and maybe more than I did about my friend. Charlotte was *my* friend after all. What business did she have blabbing about her own personal life to a woman twice her age? However, if I could just overcome my anger, I would still have a slim opportunity to save face. Maybe I could get some information out of Sandy about her daughter. There was only one way to get Sandy to divulge her secrets. I had to meet her in person.

Instead of hanging up, I let our conversation meander through boring details about the weather and about how long I was planning to stay or if I had come home for good. I told her I was calling from work, so she should have let me keep our conversation brief. She didn't seem to care though. It was as if I should have been well-placed enough in my employ to allow myself as much time on the phone as I wanted. As our conversation droned on, I started to realize that Sandy seemed perfectly aware that Julie and I were no longer living together. It was also very clear that she would not debase herself to talk to me about her own daughter, let alone ask me any questions about her. Not on the phone anyway. I was, consequently, left in the dark for the time being. Maybe Sandy had no clue either where her own daughter was.

Neither of us knew at this point how much information the other one had. All I knew was that, if Sandy didn't have enough information, I would be invited for dinner so that she could *tirer les vers du nez* from me. I won the prize. I got my invitation to a delicious and healthy supper that was undoubtedly going to be cooked according to ancient family recipes that had been adapted to current trends. The dinner would, of course, have been prepared by the perfect cook, a rare pearl, efficient and suitably humble who didn't yet know her true worth, poor thing.

The price I would have to pay for this rare privilege would be to divulge all pertinent information that I had about Julie. I had to play my cards right.

Instead of letting on right away that, in fact, I had no clue as to where Julie was, I would have to pretend at some knowledge and let Sandy languish. The dinner would become a sort of perverse and merciless duel with each of us trying to get as much information as possible from the other without leaking out any significant news ourselves.

Obviously, I had no experience at all in this kind of exercise. A direct approach, a raw honesty tinted with a certain innocence, maybe even naiveté mixed with guilelessness would be my best bet. That is how, on Friday after work, without even going home to Charlotte's for a shower, I took the Métro and the bus all the way to Côte-Saint-Luc. I walked, following a trail well-etched in my memory, the long blocks that led me to the Goldbergs' house.

Except for a few changes in landscaping, the front exterior of the house seemed essentially the same. I tried, mechanically but unsuccessfully I'm sure, to tame my rebellious locks before raising my index finger towards the doorbell. A dark circle of sweat revealed itself in my armpits.

It was in this compromising pose, my finger pointing in mid-air, that Sandy caught me. She must have been watching me from behind the sheer curtains, anticipating the exact minute of my arrival. The door was only opened a crack, and she was already explaining to me that she had deactivated the doorbell because she was waiting for a new chime, perfect in its imperative charm and suave discretion that was supposed to arrive all the way from Sri Lanka.

All this was said before she even uttered any words of welcome. And then, as if she had just noticed my presence, she managed to hug me in a narrow embrace in a way that made me feel like an errant dog, endearing only because of its pathetic situation. Then grabbing me by my index finger that I had embarrassingly forgotten in mid-air, she swiftly pulled me through her front door before any contamination that might have followed me from the outside world had a chance to get in.

The temperature and humidity of the interior were, as usual, perfect. The two damp circles in my armpits dried in record time. Contrary to the exterior of the house, I barely recognized the vast lobby where I was standing. I must admit that my hostess' talents at interior decorating were impressive. From the little bit of reading that I have gleaned from second-hand architecture magazines, I recognized the live application of Feng Shui principles. I let out an appreciative whistle. Meanwhile my hostess' gaze was burning into me all the way to my bone-marrow. My hair felt messy and dirty, even more than it usually did downtown. My skimpy little summer dress, which I had bought recently at *le Château* on sale, did not do its job of making me feel pretty.

I tried to slip my brand-new shoes off discreetly. They hung on for dear life. I had to bend down and struggle with the things. Finally, I succeeded in yanking them off, revealing a reddened pair of damp feet covered with talcum powder that had turned into a white slimy mess. I tried to create a diversion from the prints I was leaving on the cool dark tile floor by fiddling with the oversized sequinned handbag I had borrowed from Josie's side of the closet. Maybe Sandy would approve of my talents at accessorizing. One look at her badly disguised smirk of disapproval informed me that I had made the wrong choice. I felt like an outdated object that one stores in the garage only because not even the garbage collectors would take it away. Something so disgusting that she would not want to take it to the landfill in the family SUV herself, because it would mess up the upholstery.

I lavished my sincere compliments on her decorating talents. She accepted them gracefully as a given. Father appeared at the top of the impressive white and probably Carrara-marble winding staircase. He cut a meek figure, perfectly suited to his wife's ebullient personality and his own profession. He was a gynecologist. Seeming at ease with his role of genitor as well as unconditional moral support, he would also be an inexhaustible source of funds for his family. I also knew him to be a good host, discreet and affable. However, a certain weakness, a new paleness in his complexion, made me immediately worry about his health. There was no time to enquire about his well-being. The conversation, skillfully orchestrated by his wife, was meandering away from him.

Due to my rapidly sinking blood-sugar level, I was starting to feel faint. Sandy must have noticed, because she abruptly stopped talking and ushered us into the living-room. There, comfortably sunk into an overstuffed chair, I was given the opportunity to exhibit my dietetic discipline. A colourful array of delicious *hors-d'oeuvres* was already on display on the glass coffee-table. Somehow, I knew that I had to be careful. The appealing morsels were actually baits set out to test me. I sensed that I was expected to nibble at them in a nonchalant way, using a polite restraint but carefully letting out the occasional breath of praise. Additionally, I was to lavish compliments not only on the cook but mostly on Sandy herself for having chosen the menu with such discernment.

I tried my best to follow the unspoken rules. I reined in my proletarian instincts with both hands. Wishing I were a horse with its nose buried deep in its feeding-bag, I somehow succeeded, instead, in refraining from shovelling as much of my food as I could fit into my mouth and from slipping the rest into Josie's sequinned handbag. Too bad. The morsels deserved more than to be merely admired. They would have fared better had they been devoured, all holds barred, with much lip-smacking and finger-licking.

The torture finally took on a welcome hiatus as we were invited into the dining-room. The table was set for five. That meant, hopefully, that brother Allan might show up. And who would be the mysterious fifth person? Julie herself? My heart started beating so hard that I was wondering if Sandy and Julie's dad could hear its hysterical drumming.

We did not wait for the two mystery guests. The food was already on the table as we seated ourselves at our assigned places. Finally, we could dig in. But we had to do this very carefully and only with the tip or our forks, using the same hypocritical reserve as before. Actually, the eating was to be done with more of a gentle scraping of the food on the plate before making tiny bits disappear, as if forgotten, in between barely opened lips. Meanwhile, we always had to be ready to pretend there was no food in our mouth at any given time. This way we could immediately respond to any question with no visible morsels being churned around in our respective mouths.

I was so busy being careful that, honestly, I cannot recall any of the food that was served. All I can say is that I could trust it was all prepared then displayed with infinite care and that it would have been perfectly balanced in colour, shape, texture, and nutrients. I do remember that our conversation was thankfully interesting. Sandy and I shared a passion for the arts, literature, and cinéma. And yoga. Although I was at a bit of a disadvantage, having lived the past seven years captive on a remote island, I luckily remembered some of my art history and literature classes from CEGEP. Also, my recent perusing of the arts and life sections of my newspapers came in handy at this point. And of course, there was my ongoing yoga practice. True, I had not stood on my head for a few weeks, but I knew I could get back to it whenever I wanted.

Once I got the hang of playing with my food more than eating it, seeing it as a particularly aromatic form of malleable art, I was almost enjoying myself. Except that the most challenging period of our encounter was yet to happen.

So far, neither of us had mentioned the subject dearest to our heart. We had to wait before we could start the duel. Wait for what, I was unsure.

I knew from our recent telephone conversation that Sandy was seemingly aware of Julie's and my separation. How could she have known already? Charlotte must have figured it out and spilled the beans. A pang of jealousy, guilt, and remorse ripped at my guts. Just in case I had forgotten, a quick glance at the pictures on the wall confirmed the sad fact about Julie and me. In effect, amongst a good few dozen or so of family pictures that had been watching over us, I was featured in only one. It was the one that had been taken by Calypso from the Naiad commune, from when we had just arrived on the island. There we were, smiling ear to ear in the rain with the tumultuous ocean as our backdrop. I always hated that picture. My scanty wet locks pasted onto my face, I looked terrible. Julie, on the other hand, was resplendent as always. My left ear started to ring. I noticed Sandy had been watching my reaction to the pictures. There used to be more with me in them. In some, I had almost looked good.

Something in Sandy's demeanour slipped into my awareness that Julie was not going to show up that night. In fact, I sensed she had not yet contacted her parents at all. Doubt crept in, a foreboding that Julie might not have been in town at all. Yes, there had been the incident where I thought I did see Julie on Saint Laurent Street that other day. But then I had come to the final conclusion that it had not been her at all. And now a certain sadness in her dad's eyes, an extra dose of arrogance on the part of the mother, both of these facts accentuated my doubts about being able to get any new information about our beloved Julie. I felt dizzy.

Since I now had nothing to lose, and suspecting that Sandy was as much in the dark as I was, I decided to pile on an extra ladleful of pistachio ice-cream. The half of my first portion, delivered by Sandy herself into my toy tea-set sized bowl, had melted while I had been trying to be polite. Now I could finally make myself a tower of dessert and devour the unctuous delight with all the gluttony it deserved. Which I did, insolently, noisily, and with much flourish as some of the surplus dripped green onto the ironed, white-linen tablecloth. Sandy pretended not to notice. She completely ignored me and asked her husband about his day. This was the first time she had addressed him throughout the whole evening. Looking a bit surprised at her attentions, he played her game in good faith with a touch of compassionate resignation.

Just as I was reaching for a third dollop of ice-cream, Sandy announced we were to retire back to the living room and look at some family albums. The family-album viewing was a ritual usually reserved for a new prospective addition to the family. I remembered Julie and me looking at the same pictures seven years before, just as we were getting ready to leave for the West. It had been both our hello and goodbye dinner with the Goldbergs. I was made painfully aware at the time of the parents' sadness at handing me their beautiful and talented daughter on a silver platter, so to speak.

And then, as I was sitting in the same overstuffed chair as before, with Sandy and Julie's dad wistfully poring over the old photographs, I found myself thinking and talking about Julie in the past tense. I had no news at all. Neither, it seemed, had her parents. I am sure that, by this time, they also realized I had nothing recent to report about their daughter either. There had been no need for a duel between Sandy and me. At some point, each of us must simply have admitted our private defeat. It was as if Julie were dead. Maybe she was. Allan, her brother, would be my only chance of possibly finding out anything about her. I remember Julie saying they had been close. I had to contact him without their mother finding out.

As if he had heard my thoughts, Allan appeared at this very moment. He was accompanied by a very cute Latin-looking buff companion. Neither young man apologized for being late for Shabbat, and neither parent reprimanded them. At most, Allan absent-mindedly mumbled something about having already eaten. The two men seemed to have landed from another world. They probably did. A fresh, raw sexual energy surrounded them with an insolent complicity. Allan was not one of my intimate friends and relations. His sexual preference made absolutely no difference to me. I smiled at him, showing my blanket approval of his person. He beamed back. I suspected Sandy would not have been happy when she'd found out her one and only son was gay. Now with both of her children being homosexuals, her chances of one day becoming a grandmother would have been seriously compromised.

The obvious facts that Sandy was not very maternal, plus that her children had been raised by nannies so she didn't know how to hold a baby let alone wipe up its secretions or put up with its cries, or that her house was not child-proofed, made no difference at all. The most important fact here was that this branch of the Goldberg family was at a dead-end. And that, in her world, would be a disgrace.

Emboldened with what I considered to be an unexpected victory over my well-bred adversary, my mission accomplished as far as it would go, I was only waiting for the best moment to leave the crime scene. But first I had to corner Allan somewhere private and fix a meeting with him to talk about his sister. Not easy with Sandy watching everything and everyone like a hungry hawk. To top it all off, Luis, the boyfriend, a *véritable fauve en rut*, seemed to detect without even consciously knowing it himself the familiarity that had spontaneously settled between Allan and me. He could have started licking his paws like a wounded animal, or worse, sharpening his claws, and he would have fit right into the surreal scene we were all privy to.

The complicity between Allan and me was not strong enough to counteract the tension that was rapidly rising in the room. There was nothing else left for me than to take my leave as soon as any remnants of politeness would permit. I got up. Sandy half-heartedly went through the usual protests, insisting that I stay longer. Then, as if resigned to circumstances beyond her control, she suddenly got up also and started ushering me towards the door. I thanked her for the meal. She droned on about me not being a stranger and to come back for more. I lacked the language to return her niceties. All I could come up with was a pitiful little smile.

And that's when it happened, in a completely unexpected way. Just as I was about to open the door, my fingers already wrapped around the cold steel handle, something made me turn around. I slowly raised my gaze towards this proud woman who was a good eighteen centimeters taller than me. Once I got to her face, I froze. My fingers let go of the door handle. My gaze lost itself in the periwinkle-blue, infinite ponds of her eyes. They were the windows to the soul of a broken, dethroned woman. In that moment, I only saw a mother who had just realized that all she had worked for her entire life was crumbling into a pitiful, useless heap.

A shiver at once icy and scalding raised the hair on the back of my neck. My eyes, just like hers, filled with hot tears. Maybe I had lost my girlfriend, but this woman in front of me, this mother, finally stripped bare of any pretense, had been deprived of the fruit itself of her womb, her one and only daughter. And of any hope of ever knowing the joys of hearing the crystalline laughter of her little descendants. Silently and of a common accord, we hugged in an almost tender embrace. Two women united at our navels by our grief.

CHAPTER 11

It was only once I was in the company of an army of strangers in the *Métro* that I realized I could have put more of an effort into fixing a meeting with Allan. I remembered where he worked seven years before. Maybe he was still employed at the same place. I made a mental note to myself to try and track him down.

On my way back to Charlotte's apartment, I decided to get off at the Saint-Laurent *Métro* and walk up the hill. Of all the ways of getting up to Mile End from downtown, this was one of my very favourites, especially in the early evening. It's the time of day when, reaching the top of the hill, the Montréal sky appears suddenly in an explosion of that indescribable blue that everybody should see at least once in their lifetime. And there it was, the sky doing its awesome display, and me. Nobody else with whom to share the wonder of it all. I didn't know if I should smile or feel sorry for myself.

When I got to the Bains Schubert, I thought of checking the message board just in case. My letter had disappeared. My heart skipped a beat. Maybe Julie took it! But then again, maybe somebody else did, like the receptionist. Maybe the messages on the board each had an expiry date known only to the cleaner. Or maybe a stranger had taken an interest in my note. I tried to remember if I had written anything incriminating in my message. Just as I was racking my brain, I felt a quiet presence behind me. Julie! My mouth gaped open, ready to yell out her name. I turned around, beaming. It was Bourgeon.

In shock, I had nothing to say. My brain had to change tracks. Quick. I knew instinctively that, if I wanted to keep Bourgeon in my life, this was the last chance that fate would give me. I had no idea what I was supposed to do or say, just that it had to be done fast. But then again, my same instinct also told me that she and I would never be quite compatible, ever. Still, a perverse curiosity took over. I needed to find out more details about her. Maybe we could at least be friends. Breathe. Be in the moment. Feel the LOVE.

This time, it was obvious that Bourgeon had recognized me right away. I had no time to ponder if her recognizing me was a good thing or not.

"Do you want a beer?" I heard myself asking. It was the first thing that crossed my mind.

"No thanks. But maybe we could share a plate of fries? I have been working all day and I'm hungry. There's a new *pataterie* that opened a few blocks down the street, and I am curious about it. I could use the company..." she added casually.

I hesitated. Not because I didn't want to spend time with Bourgeon. The reason for my needing to ponder her offer was another, embarrassing fact. I hate sharing food with anyone, let alone a relative stranger. My distaste for sharing food has nothing to do with the person I am with. It comes up with anyone. It had even come up time and again with Julie, and this despite a profusion of accusations I would be showered with about being selfish. Ah Julie. I didn't even know if I missed her at that moment. Were we still together? Would the fact of having a beer while watching a fascinating young woman eat her *frites* be considered playing with fire? Would being in the presence of a cute, presumably single pixie as she consumes some greasy food be considered an infidelity?

I could have applied the "what would you do if the roles were reversed" rule. In that scenario, yes, I had to admit, I would have been jealous. The thought of Julie sharing a plate of steaming fries with Bourgeon—or any other cute woman—grabbed me right in the guts. But maybe in that scenario I would mostly be jealous because Julie, had she been in my place, would have been able to share a plate of *frites* with Bourgeon. No problem. Aha. I had just resolved my own dilemma. Since I was not going to share a plate, the "what if" rule was not applicable. Easy. I decided to accept the opportunity that fate had just thrown my way. I said yes to the *pataterie*. The rest of the world would just have to adjust.

All the while, Bourgeon had been patiently watching me, smiling, the question still sparkling in her eyes. I jumped, hoping that I had not been talking out loud to myself. I closed my mouth. I tried to smile.

She spoke. *"On y va?"*

Music to my ears.

So, we went. We walked almost in complete silence. With someone else, this quietness might have been awkward. With Bourgeon, it was natural in a simple and gentle kind of way. Besides, we were almost strangers to each other. But somehow, I knew that any disclosures about who we were, where we came from, would only have made sense as answers to the most profound of big questions. Instead of revealing our geographical places of origin or our ways of making a living, the dialogue would have had to be about the universe, and time, and eternity. That's the kind of person Bourgeon was. I could tell. I suspected her to be an old soul. Somehow, I felt I was not up to par with her. I could only hope she would not discover this unfortunate lack of the required coolness factor on my part, at least for a while. I was ready to do anything just to have her at least like me. Maybe I could even do something I have never done before. Maybe I could share a plate of food with her. If Julie saw me, she would be proud. Well, except that she would surely be jealous too. Suddenly, I felt voracious.

The little resto offered three pages of food options, most of them poutines. There were some with peppers, hot or sweet, some others with chicken, with beef, with mushrooms, and one "all dressed, like a pizza." There was apparently something for everyone. I tried to choose a dish that I thought Bourgeon would be least likely to want. That way I would not be expected to share. She looked like she would probably be vegetarian, but I couldn't push my perverse plan so far as to order meat. Grossing her out was not necessary. Besides I was mostly vegetarian too. It would have to be the poutine with the sweet, half-cooked peppers and chewy eggplant on top.

There were too many peppers in my order. The skin of the eggplant was like leather. I had to ask for extra sauce and extra cheese to make it all remotely edible. However, I had made the right choice from the point of view of undesirability. Bourgeon did not covet my disgusting pile. She had chosen what I had secretly set my heart on, the tamari-marinated tofu burger with green salad and yam fries. It turned out I had ordered the repulsive vegetables for nothing. They would not have been what turned her off. The cheese would have. She was vegan.

The restrained dinner at the Goldbergs' had left me wanting. I was determined to get the most out of my poutine. I tried to lick the sauce and cheese off my vegetables with a certain vicariousness towards my *convive*. As if my bites and licks would merge with the lustful morsels that were making the trip from her own plate to her cute little mouth and would arrive as kisses from me to her. This was a dangerous game. To change my mood, I ordered a locally-crafted beer. She asked for an orange soda. Once again, she had chosen better than me. It turned out that my beer was too bitter. Actually, it was undrinkably vile. Bourgeon laughed at the face I made. She offered to share her soda. To my delight, I was able to indulge in this intimate moment with her. I was hoping it was a good omen.

Halfway through our meal, and for reasons known only to herself, Bourgeon started talking about her life. I felt honoured that she chose to share more than her soda with me. Maybe she was starting to feel comfortable in my presence. I was all ears. It turned out that she had had an unusual childhood and adolescence. I would have expected nothing less than that from her. This is her story, paraphrased, and with my translation from Québécois:

"I was raised by more than a dozen mothers in a Sapphic commune near Sutton in the Eastern Townships. The commune had no name. There were just a bunch of women in it. I was the only child. No man was ever welcome on this 'Women's Land.' None, ever. Only one woman, the *coureuse*—loosely translated as the "runner"—was allowed any contact with the man's world. She was the eldest and trusted by all the other women not to bring any male '*contaminationne*' into the community. Yes, the women in this commune had even invented their own language. They feminized all the nouns. "*Jardin*" became '*jardine*,' '*frigo*,' '*frigo-e*,' '*savon*,' '*savonne*.' Some feminine words that were considered too 'male-sounding' had been enhanced, such as was the case of '*contaminationne*.' The women even changed the masculine nouns that happened to end in a feminine-sounding 'e.' They kind of 'enhanced' them. So, '*arbre*' became '*arbresse*' and '*livre*' became '*livresse*.' The women had, of course, especially re-claimed their body parts. So, there was '*Poile*,' '*brasse*,' and inevitably, '*vagine*.'"

At this point, I remembered the feminized messages on the board at les Bains Schubert. I wondered … but Bourgeon seemed to be on a roll, so I did not interrupt her.

"I never knew my father, if father there even was. The story of my very conception as it was told me was bizarre. You see, I was told that I was born almost ten months after my mother joined the commune. If my mother knew that she was pregnant at the time she joined the commune, she certainly didn't let on. All that anyone knew is that my mother—Louise—always maintained that she'd never had any sexual contact with any men from the moment she arrived at the commune. The 'no hetero sex' rule was very strictly supervised anyway. It would have been pretty much impossible for my mom to have had sex with a man after she moved in...

"Then a week or so shy of ten months later, I appeared on the scene. I was born on the commune with a dozen midwives attending. They called me 'Mésange' (tit-bird in English, but also a play on words implying some sort of a non-angel, a misunderstood one or something). Anyway, I was treated like a miracle-baby, kind of like a baby Jesus, but a girl. Actually, the women came to the conclusion, obvious to them but bizarre to me now, that my mother must have gotten pregnant by parthenogenesis. I don't know if you have ever heard of this phenomenon. Anyway, there is only one gender. Reproduction happens with the spontaneous division of the creature's own unfertilized eggs. As far as I know, you can only see this phenomenon in some reptiles and plants like dandelions. Not people. It's never been recorded in humans. But as the women in the commune said, 'Why not!? Who knows?' Anyway, according to this theory, I would be a clone of my own mother..."

Bourgeon's voice trailed off at this point of her story. She gave me a crooked smile, almost apologetic. I didn't know what to say. I usually liked to consider myself a pretty open-minded kind of person. Even to the point that I often said that I believed everything. It was just that, as I was listening to Bourgeon's story, my eyes must have been like giant saucers. I thought of Julie and me, about our fantasies about making a parthenogenetic birth happen, of the Naiads' attempts at the same thing and how they would have embraced Bourgeon and her story with a flourish. I wanted to share all this with Bourgeon just to make her feel better. Difficult without mentioning Julie. I kept quiet. An awkward pause wrapped us in cotton batting for a while.

Then almost reluctantly, she started fumbling in her pockets. She extricated a worn cotton wallet decorated with one of those Egyptian, or Tibetan—I'm not sure which—all-seeing eyes. Just like mine, of course. I automatically reached for the little metal skull with the articulated jaw dangling from my neck. Yes, it was still there. I looked for hers and didn't find it. Anyway, she pulled out a scratched and worn plastic sleeve from her wallet. Inside was a piece of dog-eared cardboard, barely larger than her minuscule palm. It was a photo that might have originally been in colour but that had faded into an almost monochrome blue. A young, attractive woman was leaning, smiling, onto a flower-decorated surface, maybe a hippie-style van. A crown of leaves, laurel maybe, sat on her long braided hair. She was wearing a checkered shirt and holding a hammer in her left hand. Her right arm was flexed, showing off an impressive bicep. She reminded me of a hippie version of the "We can do it" propaganda image from WWII so dear to feminists.

But the most remarkable thing about the woman on the photo was that, except for the haircut and missing all the piercings, she looked exactly like the Bourgeon I had in front of me. Despite the small size of the face on the picture, the resemblance between the two young women was unmistakeable. It felt like we were in some bizarre time-warp.

"She's my mother…" whispered Bourgeon unnecessarily.

She did not wait for any comment I might have wanted to make. I would probably not have been the first one to express their bewilderment, and she might have heard it once too often. Bourgeon slowly put the photo away and continued her story.

"…I was homeschooled by all my mothers in the commune. They felt more like fairy godmothers, actually. Whenever I asked any of them where people came from, they always told me the same story about parthenogenesis. Well, all the women except for my biological mother. Whenever I asked her about my origins, she got quiet and kind of weird, and she told me to ask the other women. So that's just the way it was.

"There were lots of books around in the commune. Some were about biology. There were, of course, some with mentions of parthenogenesis. But funny enough, there was no mention of the phenomenon occurring in humans in any of the books.

"Some of the pages relating to human biology had been ripped out. I didn't—couldn't—know what the ripped-out pages had contained. All I know is that there were only pictures of female anatomy in any of the books. Not a single penis or anything remotely male in sight anywhere. As a result of the missing pages, I was led to believe all through my childhood that only certain animals had two genders in their midst. Some birds, insects, and some reptiles, but not all. And never humans. All humans were female. Only some animals had males in their midst. Or said another way, all males are animals..."

She looked at me with a quizzical smile. Then she went on. "But once I got to be a teenager, the story of my conception got to be way too bizarre for me. Somehow from my mother's silence, from the mischievous glint in the eyes of the other women as they were keeping me hostage with their lies, I suspected something was wrong. Besides, if parthenogenesis exists in feminine land, why was I the only child in the commune? My question went unanswered. I was told to wait ... that the miracle would happen again in its own good time.

"One day, I must have been thirteen or so—a bit late, I know—I stopped waiting. I had passed the threshold of some sort of self-initiation. Kind of like when a child decides the Tooth Fairy does not exist. I got wanderlust. But the women would not let me go.

"Then around the time I turned fourteen, one sad day, my mother died. I think it was cancer. I'm not sure. She'd been sick for a while but didn't want to see a doctor, not even a female one. With my mother gone, I saw no reason to stay in the commune. The whole fairy godmother thing had gone out the window with the other fairies from my childhood. Besides, the commune was falling apart and some of the women had left already.

"I was still a teenager. I packed some stuff—not much—and just left one night. It was an easy escape. I think the women had seen it coming and had loosened their surveillance on me. I wish they had prepared me for life in the big world, but they didn't. Anyway, somehow I ended up in Montréal. It didn't take me too long to figure out that human animals are classified into two distinct genders, just like insects and birds. I was in shock. I got scared. I hid in dark alleys at night, in libraries during the day. I even briefly considered going back to the commune. Then I got over it. That's when I changed my name to Bourgeon. I learned how to live on the street, shoplifting or dumpster-diving for food. I didn't go to shelters or soup kitchens, because I was still a minor and didn't want to be caught. But a welfare worker found me anyway. They placed me with a *famille d'acceuil*. They were nice and everything, but I felt awkward and alien. I got treated by some very nice counselors for insomnia and anxiety. That was a good thing. Most of them, except for the weird ones, were very nice to me. Then I ran away. I still couldn't sleep, so I worked under the table at night-jobs. Mostly restaurant work. I got bored. I got myself some spray-paint and started tagging old buildings. Eventually, I got known in the graffiti underworld. I got 'discovered.' Businesses started paying me to do murals on their walls. The work was less exciting, but at least I was able to get myself a studio to live in and pay my bills. One day, I got myself a *cinécaméra* and taught myself to make films. Kind of like documentaries...

"Funny how one of my favourite subjects ended up being on parthenogenesis. Especially Komodo lizards. I'm actually working on a documentary about them."

"Komodo lizards! YES! YES! I'm fascinated by them too!" I wanted to clamour. I stayed quiet.

Bourgeon had the stage. I have no idea why she chose this particular moment to share this next fact, nor did I want to figure it out: "And I have no sexual desire at all. I am not a lesbian or het or even bi. I've always been like that. The therapists that they made me see for a while ... they all said it was a phase. They said that, once I got over the trauma of having been raised in an 'unusual' atmosphere, I would get my healthy appetite back. But I've never had an appetite for intimacy. Not with anyone. I feel happy as I am. Asexual. If I'm anything, that's what I am. That's what 'normal' is for me, if there is such a thing."

Looking at Bourgeon, smiling in that quizzical way of hers, her asexuality was completely believable. I had to admit that despite my *incontournable* attraction to her, she seemed more like a fairy, a pixie, than a potential sexual partner for me or anyone. That fact actually made her even more attractive to my eyes. I was completely fascinated. And in a funny kind of way, relieved of my compulsion of trying to seduce her. I glanced at her hands. She still wore her nails short on her left hand and longer on her right. This would identify her, as per my theory, as a right-handed guitarist, since we had just ruled out the option of being a left-handed lesbian. I repressed the urge to verify my hunch by asking her if she played the guitar. The question would have been out of place. Plus, she might have said no, in which case I would have been very, very confused. Her little metal skull appeared from around her wrist. Seeing it there gave me some comfort.

The *resto* was closing. Bourgeon and I got up and walked out through the door. I felt that we still had so much to say to each other. We had, I felt, so much in common. Both of us had been raised by single moms, our fathers non-existent. We were both orphans. I had seen her wearing her little skull pendant just like mine. We even had the same kind of wallets. And then there were the Komodo lizards. Could we become like them and synchronize our fertile periods in an opposite kind of way, and would she then batter me, and me her, at the appropriate times and release little clones of ourselves?

But our interaction was over. Much to my chagrin, we said goodbye without a kiss or even a handshake or a hug, and turned in our different directions to each be swallowed by the balmy night. I thought the only reason Bourgeon told me her story was because she figured I would never see her again. Fortunately or unfortunately, I am still not quite sure which, I was wrong in my assumption.

★   ★   ★

In my abundant spare time, with no friends or interests other than part-time employment, I had read all of Charlotte's books. Well, the ones I considered even remotely readable, at least. I would usually try to give each author a chance, given that they had taken the trouble, unlike myself, to write something, anything, and to have it published. But I must admit that I did take exception to long complicated novels. And Harlequin romances. Het or lesbian. Too much gasping.

It was time for a visit to the library. I walked the two long blocks to our local Mile End branch. It being a Saturday, the place was packed with a young boisterous crowd. Gone were the days of studious, respectful quiet. A young woman was reading a story to a group of about twenty children sitting distractedly on the bright carpet in a jagged semi-circle around her. Every now and then, she would wave her puppet-begloved hand to punctuate crucial elements in the tale. Some parents were hanging around, standing attentively behind the group, ready to intervene if their child should blatantly misbehave. Another woman was settled in a giant armchair away from the group, reading to two young children in her lap. I recognized the same three people from the airplane two weeks previously. This time the woman seemed happy and relaxed. I waved at her, smiling, attracting her attention. She looked at me, smiling back uncertainly. Then a cloud of mistrust veiled her eyes as she drew the children closer to herself. She probably didn't recognize me. Or maybe she did and that was the problem. The little girl stared at me with the same serious air she'd had on the plane. I left them to their story and walked on to the adult section. I was particularly interested in the biology books.

Bourgeon talking about parthenogenesis had revived my curiosity about the subject. I wanted to know if there had been any new developments while I had been lost on my remote island. I perused the shelves, pulling out a few books that looked promising and sat down at one of the crowded massive tables. Much to my disappointment, I found nothing. I went and got another set of books. Nothing again. On the third try, I did find a tome in English that was talking about the huge diversity in the sexuality of organisms. The chapters were arranged in a way as to follow evolution, starting with the most primitive of beings, the amoebas. Fascinated, I took my book to the table. My seat had been taken by a burly gentleman. I didn't even try to explain that he was occupying my place. With my treasure in my hand, I slumped down onto the floor, my back resting on the cool wall. I eagerly started to read.

I learned that amoebas multiply themselves by simple cell division. Therefore, each and every one of the amoebas in existence today carry in themselves a fraction of the original amoeba that started dividing itself millions of years ago. Astounding. I read on to the next chapters, each one equally as fascinating as the other. There were oysters and chickens that start as females and end up as males. There were the ubiquitous male-eating praying mantis and the sperm-selecting insects. I finally got to the chapter on parthenogenesis. Dandelions, snakes, all manner of beings were mentioned, most of which I had already heard of. I also found a passage about the Komodo lizards raised and observed in captivity, the ones that take turns ovulating and batting each other aggressively. Impatient, I flipped on in search of something new to me. By the time I got to the mammals, and then the primates, I had to admit defeat. Of course, no mention was made anywhere of any mammals being able to produce offspring without the help of a male.

My book had been written a few decades previously. I went back to the shelves, looking for a newer edition. I found nothing. Another book attracted my attention, though. It had slid off the shelf and kind of fallen into my hands. Still standing, without looking at the title, I opened it at random. It was describing a very sexy lesbian scene. Nice, and very graphic, but also pornographic. I was curious. And most of all, I had to admit I was compelled to read on until, embarrassed, I snapped the book shut. I looked around me. Nobody had seen me. What a relief. What was this pornographic book doing in a public library anyway? I looked at the title.

No wonder. The book I was holding in my hot little hands was about Bonobo monkeys, formerly called Pygmy Chimpanzees. I had heard about them before. They are an isolated group of monkeys living in the wild forests of the Republic of Congo. They are endangered. They are also, much like many other primates, a matriarchal species. But what differentiates Bonobos from other chimps is that they solve their conflicts, or allay potential ones, with sex. Sometimes same-sex, sometimes with the other gender. They don't seem to consider sexual differentiation an issue. Because of their seemingly tolerant attitudes towards sex—from an anthropomorphic point of view—they have been sometimes misrepresented as some maniacal sex-crazed satyrs. This is not quite the case. Sex, for the average Bonobo, is just another social form of greeting, like a hug. This particular form of socialization seems to work very well for Bonobos. Unlike their cousins, the "regular," more aggressive chimpanzees, Bonobos enjoy a rich, egalitarian, and peaceful communal life. I could only wish we were like them. I wanted to take the book out just to help me visualize a better world. Having no card and still no official address, this was not possible. I promised myself to come back.

In the meantime, I walked over to the closest GLBTQ bookstore I had staked out before on my way home from work. It was a good five blocks away. The sun was shining overhead, casting a happy glow on a colourful crowd that had spilled onto Saint-Laurent Street. It seemed I was the only one who did not have a companion, a child, or even a dog with them. Feeling like a loser, I slipped into the store I had been looking for. The cool air inside distracted me somewhat. I looked around. The first book that caught my attention was a historical study of women who had been born with oversized clitorises. How interesting. I started looking for pictures. There was no time. The employee's gaze was pinned onto my shoulder. Smiling sheepishly, I put the book back. Cold sweat started to slip over me. I stepped gingerly over to another section of the room, one that was away from his stern looks.

The area I had randomly chosen was crammed with books about inter-sexuality. Fascinated, I flipped through a myriad of pages, activating my speed-reading skills learned in CEGEP. I hadn't forgotten how. Luckily for me, the clerk was engaged in an involved telephone conversation. I read on and on at breakneck speed.

Intersexuality, formerly called hermaphroditism or even monstrosity (sic), is a biological occurrence when a human baby is born with what has been more recently called "ambiguous genitalia." I didn't know much else about the subject except for the basic notion that the newborn seems to exhibit genitalia from both sexes at once or in some rare cases, no visible genital apparatus at all. I also knew that throughout history some cultures revered their intersexed members. Unfortunately, it seemed to me that too many cultures were not so positive or tolerant. Especially "Western" communities.

There is a myriad of variations on the theme, and the rate of occurrence of each condition varies with the condition itself. Modern medicine, with its stubborn insistence of classifying what they don't understand, has identified seventeen or eighteen categories of intersex conditions. I was very curious to find out more on the subject. Hearing that my clerk was still busy talking on the phone, I read on.

An interesting new bit of information for me was the reversal in the way modern medicine seemed to be responding to intersex children recently. Traditionally, the parents of intersex children would have been advised to "choose" a gender for their child at birth. Then with the addition of hormones and surgery, the child would be made to conform to the chosen gender as soon as possible. But that was all changing. The medical establishment was finally recognizing the rights of parents, and especially that of children, to let things be and not intervene until adolescence or even never. Society would just have to adapt to the fact that there were not necessarily only two distinct genders in existence.

I got very excited at the prospect of our society becoming more tolerant. And especially that we might have more variations on the sexual theme start-ing with the present generation, when intersex people will start having their own families. Contrary to the old-school medical establishment's "discover-ies," some intersex people are indeed fertile. Actually, it's turning out that, in too many cases, intersexed people had only become sterile as a result of their bodies having been tampered with in the first place. As we are accepting intersex people in our midst without intervention and allow their contribution to the gene pool, our future as human animals is very exciting indeed! I was elated. We, as a society, were getting one thrilling step closer towards my Utopia!

I got interrupted by my clerk. He had finished his telephone call and had come looking for me. He made it clear that I was expected to either buy a book (or books) or leave. My browsing time had obviously expired. I obediently put my books back on the shelf. My meagre budget would not have permitted me such extravagant purchases, plus I was embarrassed to admit that I was too shy to buy any of them anyway. Despite the air-conditioning, a film of sweat had burst out on my forehead, palms, behind my knees, and in my armpits. Flustered, I pushed past my clerk and walked out into the dusty, anonymous heat of the street. I promised myself to be back one day soon, when I felt more self-confident or had more money. I never stopped waiting.

CHAPTER 12

The day after my very educational forays into the world of new publications on sexuality, I had decided to let myself sleep in again. No visits from a welfare worker loomed on the horizon. I was ahead of myself at work. The idea had been to let my dreams reveal a plan of action for me, so that I could make use of all the new information I had been privy to. It was time, I felt, to take the bull by the horns and to help make my world a better one. Unfortunately, the night had not brought me counsel, none that I could remember at least. All I knew as I woke up around ten that morning was that it was a Sunday, and I felt good. I tried to lounge and bide my time, but the beautiful, cloudless blue sky beckoned me outside. After an expedited breakfast of leftovers, I decided to go to the mountain. I was going to watch my thoughts, maybe even find a place to sit and visualize my multi-sexed world peace. I knew there would be lots of people in the park, including families, so I could dress appropriately for the weather without running a chance of being followed and pestered by some sex-crazed maniac.

Charlotte had a beautiful, discreetly sequinned, and elaborately embroidered, short, white Indian cotton dress I had been eying for a while, promising myself to wear it on a special occasion. Which was that particular Sunday. I slipped it on without a bra or panties. The soft cotton felt good on my bare skin. Too good to be followed by a maniac. I reminded myself that they would only harass me on my bad, insecure days. In my experience at least.

I didn't want to ruin my look by carrying food or a water-bottle in a backpack. Instead I hid a few five-dollar bills in the dress's hem and secured it with a safety pin. Slipping on my hippie sandals, I sauntered into the picture, being careful not to shut the door on the first landing so that it wouldn't lock. Once I got to the angel on Park Avenue, I knew I had arrived at the right place. Contrary to how I had felt on the previous day, seeing all the happy people around me did not make me feel lonely at all. Now, with my new knowledge about alternate sexualities, I knew we all already lived in a better world. And most importantly, I belonged in this new world. I loved everyone and everybody.

The *tam-tam* was already running in full swing. A crowd of happy people were dancing and squirming to the primal beat of African drums. I joined them and let myself sway, then shake, swoon, and stomp into a trance. One with the crowd, at ease with the world. Ecstatic. I had arrived home.

I danced and danced for hours. I only stopped when the drumming had ceased and when the last musicians were packing up their gear amidst the feathers, ribbons, and garbage. My entire body still vibrating, I walked back home to Charlotte's, nostrils filled with pheromones, my heart swelled with love.

On the way, I grabbed myself an ice-cold orange soda from the corner store. It was a bit of a forbidden fruit, but this time, I thought the occasion called for it. Besides, Bourgeon drank it too. That made it cool. I climbed the stairs up to Charlotte's apartment, and still wearing her dress, I shook my sandals off and propped up all the pillows I could find on her bed. With a sigh of contentment, I reclined onto Charlotte's sacrosanct love-nest, my drink in hand. The light cotton curtains were gently swaying in the cool, soft late-afternoon breeze. My world was perfect.

Just as I was going to take a first swig of my bright orange drink, there was a knock on the door. Not a doorbell ring from the first landing, as a stranger might have done, but a medium-soft knock right at Charlotte's apartment door, all the way up on the second floor, a mere few feet away from my sanctum. Whomever it was must have been familiar, at least to Charlotte. Familiar enough to know where the creaky parts of the stairway were and sneaky enough not to step on them. I hesitated. Despite the love I was feeling towards everybody, I was no fool. Maybe this was no friend of ours. Maybe I had been followed all the way from the mountain by some maniac after all. A very light-footed one, for sure. I cautiously got up.

Like a hound, I sniffed the air in the antechamber. Of course, I could not actually smell anything. But somehow, maybe from sensing a patient quietness behind the door, I was put at ease. It was almost as if I could actually get a whiff of a friendly presence. Taking a full breath in, bracing myself a little, I opened the door. My long-time friend Stéphane was standing there.

I had not seen Stéphane since my crazy Egg-House days. Because of Julie, I had not kept in touch from our island with any of my old friends. Well, except for Charlotte. I did not know her in the Biblical sense anyway. I was definitely not encouraged to mention any of the men, not even the mostly gay ones, to Julie. Kent whom I had seen recently and who had brought me up-to-date with the lives and deaths of some of our old friends, had not mentioned Stéphane at all. Actually, Kent had never really known Stéphane as he was not a very significant member of our promiscuous group. Being a strict heterosexual and not so pretty, Stéphane offered little interest for the majority of players within our gang. One could say that he represented, in that particular hierarchy anyway, more of a "sneaky gene." But what I—and some other women I knew—had found out from giving this seemingly innocuous specimen of a man half a chance is that Stéphane was a fabulous lover. Deliciously, excruciatingly and insatiably so. I for one had found out this fortunate fact first hand. Live.

As I have already mentioned, Stéphane was not a pretty face by conventional standards. It was almost as if nature, in its whimsical way, had gently gathered his short, hooked nose and his pink chin, complete with its scant stubble of thin hairs, towards each other and left them there. Even the two cat-like lines in between his eyebrows, painted by nature on his otherwise smooth forehead, seemed to point like minuscule arrows down towards the puckering. Had Stéphane been a dandelion or a dahlia, he would have fared better. The green sepals surrounding the colourful, amassed petals of his face could have one day parted with the warm sun's rays, allowing them to splay out into their true beauty. In Stéphane's case, unfortunately, this unfolding never happened.

Stéphane was understandably quite self-conscious of his appearance. To top it all off, he was quite short too, like at most five-foot-two on his tallest day. Maybe it was precisely because of those facts that he had become such a good lover of women. Or maybe he simply loved women and figured out a way to let them know. Unabashedly, unapologetically, Toulouse-Lautrec style. Stéphane was not a seducer. Had he been taller and better-looking, he might have let his successes rise from his penis to his head and thought of himself as God's gift to sisterhood. But Stéphane did not let his conquests go to his head, ever. Well not to the head that was on top of his neck anyway. Even though his penis was not even of memorable proportions, Stéphane knew how to use it and especially when. Actually, he was gentleman enough to have learned all the subtle, complex arts of finding the way to a woman's heart instead of just heading directly to the target of her steaming pussy. One could even say that he was a champion of non-invasive sex. Actually, he would have made a great lesbian lover. Without the slightest trace of hesitation, I let him in.

I don't know what possessed me. Other than plain and simple desire for release maybe. I didn't particularly want Stéphane. I didn't even know if he had come to Charlotte's door looking for her or for me. I asked him. He said he had seen me earlier, dancing at the tam-tam. He had followed me all the way to the apartment. Great. But that didn't take away the fact that he was a man after all. I didn't even know if he had gotten wind of the fact that I had become a lesbian. Immediately, Julie's beautiful body appeared in front of my eyes. Her scent invaded my nostrils. I felt an excruciating ache in my womb. Julie. Maybe all I wanted was revenge on her. But then, I didn't need to go as far as "doing," or get "done by," a man. That would have been a double insult as far as Julie was concerned.

But actually, Julie had nothing to do with this man standing in front of me, smiling. Sweeping Julie's painful memory aside with an impatient wave of my hand, I took full responsibility for my lewdness. I let Stéphane slide my white delicately sequinned dress off and wrap me in the careless shroud of his charm. Just like that.

He was as amazing as I had expected him to be. And more. In the last decade since I saw him, he must have amassed a few new manoeuvres under his belt. I let my guards down. I relaxed. Completely. Like in the best yoga session I could ever hope to have. I gave him full rein over my body. He stepped up to the plate. He took me, slowly, attentively, at once gently and firmly, he rode me as if I were a thoroughbred mare all the way to absolute, unabashed bliss via a complex maze of dark tunnels, swaying tree tops, slippery rivers, and lush, fertile valleys. Then he let me bask for what felt like forever in the Amrita-sprinkled Nirvana of our making. Thank you, Stéphane.

I told him he was beautiful. He got mad and told me he knew he wasn't and never to call him so. I asked him to marry me. Laughing, he said I always asked him that afterwards. Internally, I called myself a fool and pledged that, if I was ever going to come back for more with Stéphane, I would never, ever ask him to marry me, ever again.

I should have known better anyway. Stéphane was a lot of things but one thing he was not was marriageable material. Asking for commitment of any kind, even pinning him down to a time for a simple walk in the park, was akin to expecting a cornered scorpion not to sting you. Stéphane was simply non-committal. This trait was not a sign of meanness on his part, nor conceit. He was just a true free spirit. If he hadn't also been a Virgo, i.e. supposedly practical and a hard worker, he could have made a living as a poet, or better still, a gigolo. Troll-like for sure, but inescapably good.

Stéphane had always been known as having a steady woman somewhere, an older woman. He had often used the familiar line of married men looking for an affair, that he was unhappy with her. Why he had kept her around, I had no idea. The only possible reason I could think of is that her mere presence would have deterred other offers of marriage such as mine, which I am sure would have been showered upon his balding head like spring rain from a big fat cloud of contented females. Or maybe the girlfriend in question never existed at all, and Stéphane only kept her myth going so that he could continue to be free to love. At any rate, nobody I knew had ever seen said girlfriend. Stéphane once told me she had a teenage daughter. Hearing that coming from his own delicious, soft lips had made me quite uneasy at the time.

That Sunday, still softened, still quivering from my orgasms and wanting for more, I suddenly kicked my impromptu lover out. I had opened up an insatiable, complex thirst I didn't know what to do with. We could easily have been going on for the next three days and nights or more. I could tell we were both willing. But why? And then what? It was like trying to explain infinity or eternity. If one being—or two, in this case—get to the end of the universe, then what happens? Is there more infinity after that? And if not, if Infinity ends, then it's not infinity. I put my foot down. I asked him to leave before I made a fool of myself, before I melted into an opaque pool of Amrita just to fizzle into nothingness.

Stéphane didn't protest. He didn't state the obvious, which was that he knew I wanted more. So, so much more. As a painfully endearing lopsided grin split his face in two, exposing that sharp, mischievously crooked tooth of his, he swiftly pulled his short-legged jeans on, popped the snap under his soft, downy little belly, and covered his pale unsalted-butter-coloured chest, smooth as the dunes of PEI, with his white Italian-cotton shirt. He slipped on his sandals and walked out of my life. For what I thought would be forever. All I was left with in the still-vibrating room was my idiotic desire for more, my all-consuming addiction to an ever-evanescent pleasure. My shame. I tried to quench my thirst with my orange soda. It was lukewarm. It made me feel nauseated.

✯ ✯ ✯

By the following day, a mid-July Monday morning, my oxytocin-fuelled compulsion had already worn off. I was still hoping for a Utopic world, but in the meantime, I had to make an honest living. Also, there was my nagging feeling of guilt for having cheated on Julie a little with Bourgeon and a lot with Stéphane. I could have gotten off on a tangent about my gender preference, *à savoir* if maybe I had turned "bi." But really, I had no use for such labels. As far as I was concerned, I was still very, very interested in women. Stéphane had just been a weird, almost extra-terrestrial hiatus, an unlikely tropical island in a sea of horniness. I thought it was unlikely I would ever see him again. I was wrong.

Meanwhile, it was about nine a.m. I decided to put a little more effort into trying to track down my girlfriend, whether she was already my ex or not. I had to know. Allan was my last chance. Maybe he was still working at the same company he had been with seven years previously. I found his number in Charlotte's phone book. That immediately made me wonder about the nature of their relationship. I called the number. A receptionist answered. She informed me that Allan was indeed still employed at that office, but that she was not expecting him until eleven o'clock. Eleven! He must have climbed the corporate ladder to a comfortable rung in order to be able to let himself sleep in. On a Monday morning!

I reminded myself that I could have slept in also. Having a part-time job and living in voluntary simplicity offered me the same luxury. For a brief moment, I even considered going back to bed. But what would I do? Play with myself? Have breakfast in bed? This last option sounded the most alluring, but I had no idea where I would order my meal from. Charlotte's apartment was no hotel. There was no room service. Otherwise there could have been pizza, Chinese food, or roast chicken. Even if those restaurants did deliveries at this relatively early hour, somehow, I knew the food would not cut the cake. I walked out to the kitchen despite the fact that I knew the fridge would be empty. The only possibility of anything edible might have been the lonely apple on the table. I thought of Lizette and Suzy, the two Bonobo monkeys I had read about, sharing the coveted food after sex. A green wave of envy crept into my nose like too much Wasabi. I left the apple on the table as some sort of reminder of the possibility of a better world.

After an invigorating shower, wearing the first thing that fell under my hands from Charlotte's wardrobe, I propelled myself onto the street. The sidewalk was empty. There was not even the scent of my pretty welfare worker floating anywhere around. I walked on and on, hungry, looking for a place to have breakfast. Much to my disappointment, the corner café was closed. There was no other suitable establishment in my *quartier*. By the time I found one, I was already downtown.

The place was seedy and dark, one of those round-the-clock coffee shops frequented by taxi drivers after their night shift. The coffee was predictably weak but surprisingly good. It was almost as if, had it been any stronger, its mediocrity would have just shown up more. I ordered some rye toast. After five minutes, the waitress brought me a huge, steaming pile. It was dripping with real butter as indicated by the rich smell and was accompanied with an over-spilling basket of more butter, peanut butter, and assorted jams and marmalade. The generous pile of food she had placed in front of me was so huge as to make me wonder if I had lost some weight and the waitress had taken pity on me. She looked motherly enough to have wanted to fatten me up a little.

Thanks to the odours around me, my toasts tasted like fried eggs, bacon, and smoked meat. I started chewing half-heartedly, a little nauseous. To distract myself, I looked around. It seemed I was the only person who was actually eating anything that morning. The rest of the patrons, obviously regulars, puffy-eyed and limp-lipped, were slowly slurping their coffee as they threw the occasional glance at the ancient and crooked TV that was offering some soap opera in a language I couldn't place.

Nobody was talking, even though it was obvious they would know each other from having spent every morning in each other's solitary company for years. Being alone and quiet myself, I fit right in. Even the waitress had affectionately called me "*chère*" (dear) as she refilled my coffee cup. I chewed obediently on my stack of rye bread until it was almost all done.

The only reason I did not take the entire contents of my butter and jam basket with me was that I hadn't thought of bringing my backpack. Charlotte's dress had no pockets. I consoled myself with the reminder that the treats had been manufactured by some mean capitalist company anyway and that there would be too much sugar—white death—in them all, including the peanut butter. The entire basket, now threatening, loomed untouched on the table. I wrapped the few remaining slices of uneaten, greasy but otherwise unadorned bread in a napkin and hid them in my hand.

I paid my bill with my free hand, left a generous tip for my motherly waitress, and walked out into the dusty street, promising myself to come back. I didn't want to make it a habit, having enough of them already, but it would be good to give myself a treat every now and then.

By the time I got to the office, it was nearly eleven-o' clock. Everybody in the reading-room was grumpily quiet, as was appropriate for a Monday morning. I tried to match the mood by pasting on a bored expression on my face as if the work could not possibly distract me from the hangover from a much more exciting weekend. And what a weekend I'd had! Starting from Shabbat on Friday, then poutine and *confidences* with Bourgeon, then there had been my discoveries at the library and at the bookstore, followed by dancing myself into a trance at the foot of the angel. And then, of course, there had been my tryst with Stéphane. At the thought of him, I couldn't help my lips from stretching into a wide smile. Somehow my shame had already dissipated, leaving only pure love in my heart.

The other workers looked at me, disgusted. They couldn't possibly know about my weekend, but I guessed that it had been better than theirs, this time. All this communication happened in complete silence. I jumped up and got myself a cup of delicious, organic, fair-trade, shade-grown coffee. I offered my co-workers some too, but was met with a muffled cluster of discontented grunts. I took that for a "No, thanks."

I took my coffee to the telephone in the hall and dialed Allan's office number. This time he was there.

Allan was one of those people whom I would call lucky. He was also beautiful but almost in a caricatured kind of way. His particular brand of good looks was more intriguing than classic. He would charm, without really trying or even knowing it, the very few people he let into his ethereal field. Contrary to some Hollywood-style beauty that attracts everybody's attention the minute they enter a room, Allan would direct his energy from his own centre somewhere halfway between his head and his heart in the other direction, away from himself, and towards a single person of his choice. Then he would wrap the person in an intimate aura, warm but non-invasive, like a compliment from a vegetarian spider, if such things existed. His gentleness coupled with his sharp intelligence reminded me of a crystal hand in a satin glove. Julie had told me that Allan had been voted most likely to succeed from Westmount High School, hands down, with no serious competition. From then on, she said, he had simply continued his climb towards a higher and higher success, whatever he undertook, from relationships to art, or sports, or to his career. All that with a breezy, unpretentious ease.

Distracted as I was by his achievements, I didn't get the feeling I knew him at all. I asked innocently on the phone how his weekend had been. As a matter of fact, he mentioned that he had just come back from a solo show in an Ottawa gallery. I didn't know said gallery, being perennially somewhat out of the fashionable art-loop, but I guessed by the gallery's name that it must have been a prestigious one.

Upon Allan's suggestion, we agreed to continue our conversation the next day over brunch. The venue would be a new fancy resto downtown. And expensive, no doubt. My voluntary simplicity would have to take a back seat for the occasion. I could only hope that Allan would be gentleman enough to pick up the tab.

✷ ✷ ✷

The Tuesday I was supposed to meet Allan, I felt empty inside. All I wanted was news of Julie. Even if I would find out we were done. That way, once Damocles' sword had dropped, I would at least know what foot to stand on. Or learn that I had no foot at all. I felt I was negotiating a slippery slope indeed.

Then seeing Allan waiting for me, smiling, in front of the resto shook me out of my insecurity. He was affable and distinguished. And distant. Luckily for me, he informed me right away that lunch was on him. This was mostly a vegetarian resto, he reassured me, with only a few seafood specialties. He hoped I wouldn't mind. "Oh no," said I. "I could get into seafood!" And really, I could. Maybe it would bring Julie back to me somehow. We were directed towards a quiet corner away from the deliberately subdued bucolic *gloussements* of the crowds of other guests.

I sat down, or rather, I let myself fall, conforming to the best of my ability to the sophisticated ambiance all around me. My borrowed demeanour didn't quite work, and I felt as frumpy as ever. The restaurant had been obviously designed for maximum comfort and ease. The soft, dark, genuine leather covering the chairs, the sophisticatedly sober colour of the walls, even the rounded edges of the perfectly balanced utensil-handles, all had been planned. But all that ingenuity of design was unfortunately of no use to me. Whomever had drafted the interior of the resto must have had in mind someone of the size of the average man. The seat, as comfortable as it might have been for someone else, was much too high for me. My toes, even if I stretched them way down like a *rat d'Opéra*, barely touched the thick Persian carpet beneath us. I could have sat in my habitual cross-legged position except that the armrests were in the way, squishing my bony knees. Plus, my short skirt would have embarrassingly ridden up my splayed thighs. The table, the edge of which arrived at my nipple-level, seemed set for a feast worthy of Kings. The gargantuan dimensions of the utensils as well as the wide, squarish plates that could easily accommodate a lumberjack-size sterling steak with all the trimmings, the thick half-litre goblets, all completed the royal effect. I felt like some tiny blind mouse lost in a land of well-meaning but gently mocking, selfish giants.

I let my feet dangle, fully aware that my calves would swell like waterballoons. I found refuge behind my giant menu. The object in question was a leather-bound affair, a shade darker than the armchairs, as if it had been made of 80 percent dark chocolate. On offer that day were the most impressive of dishes bearing evocative names promising delightfully sinful epicurean pleasures. I closed my eyes and pointed my index finger into the middle of my menu. Without even looking at what fortune had chosen for me, I turned my menu towards the waiter, my finger still stuck onto my random choice. Allan was watching me, smiling. I smiled back, a bit sheepish. I didn't care much about the food. All that I was interested in was hearing about Julie.

By the time my Lobster Thermidor triumphantly appeared, our conversation still hadn't touched the only subject I was really interested in. I had no choice but to dig into my food. I hadn't eaten lobster since my brief prosperous period with Rémi at the manic beginnings of our relationship. We were not even in lobster season. But then, fuelled by the exquisite aroma of ocean that was filling my nostrils, I forgot everything. I allowed myself to shamelessly indulge in the luxurious food splayed out in front of me. Lobster Thermidor was probably the most expensive dish on the menu. Fortunately, Allan had ordered the same thing. The crust of our marine creatures' tails had been split in two, revealing their delicious, *gratiné* contents to our gaping mouths. We consumed, each in his own private cloud of pleasure, our exquisite dishes, punctuated intermittently with almost inaudible sniffles of satisfaction and the odd comment about the exceptional taste of our respective lobsters.

When we got to coffee, I decided to try and get back to my favourite subject. Allan's responses to my easy, direct questions were vague and dry. He kept turning the conversation annoyingly towards his own life, his numerous romantic interests, including Luis, his latest Latin lover, but also Adam, the enigmatic co-worker from my office. I had no idea where Allan would have known Adam from. I doubted very much that it would have been through business ventures. But what did I know? And frankly, I didn't much care about whatever they did or didn't do together.

Then Allan seemed to take an interest in my life. It was as if he was afraid of having said too much already or that he thought he might spill the beans about Julie inadvertently. Did that mean he'd seen her recently? I couldn't tell. Meanwhile, I deliberately didn't offer him much of any interest about me. There was little to declare anyway. There was my new job, true, but how much can one talk about reading newspapers? The conversation was starting to sag.

In order to save the lunch from taking an embarrassed route, I asked Allan about his parents. Maybe by talking about his family, our conversation would extend towards his sister too. No such luck. Allan included stories about aunts, uncles, and cousins, even a dog they'd had for a while, but there was no mention about Julie at all. Actually, the way Allan avoided the subject of

Julie was starting to get suspicious. I concluded that she must indeed be in Montréal. Just as I had thought. They must have already met, maybe even more than once. Allan was just being irritatingly secretive.

Our visit had arrived to its boring conclusion. As soon as politeness allowed, I pretended I was supposed to be somewhere else soon. I didn't even accept Allan's generous offer of dessert. Not only was I stuffed but I needed to breathe as well. After he paid the bill, which, I am sure, would have been exorbitant, we got up, left by the back door, and hugged in the alleyway, tent-style, with lots of space at crotch-level like heterosexuals. Then we parted, each going our own way, me back to work and him I don't know where, but it did look like he was going to take the afternoon off. I wanted to follow him. I held myself back. If I was going to work myself up to another meeting with him, I'd have to behave.

CHAPTER 13

A few days after my lunch with Allan, an envelope arrived in Charlotte's mailbox. Surprisingly, it was addressed to me. There was no return address and the postal stamp was illegible. I ripped the envelope open, impatiently, almost tearing the contents at the same time. Inside, an old-fashioned sepia-toned postcard showed a man and a woman dressed in *fin-de-siècle* garb. The décor looked like the photo had been taken in a studio, complete with painted rural backdrop augmented by some obviously fake flowers and rocks. The woman was sitting gingerly on one of the papier-mâché boulders, looking coy, as a mustachioed man in a black frock coat and bow tie was leaning towards her, wearing a lecherous smile. The caption at the bottom of the card read :

> *Le cœur de la femme est heureux*
> *Quand lui parle son amoureux*

(The heart of a woman is happy when her lover to her speaks)

I looked at the picture again, this time more carefully. The man bore Charlotte's face, and the woman, of course, was Josie. The picture must have been taken recently in one of those made-for-tourists studios with the addition of period costumes. They could easily have been represented as Tarzan and Jane, or Jessie James and female consort, whomever he or she might have been. I turned the card around.

The hand-written message on the back, scrawled in Charlotte's child-like handwriting, said:

Still on our honeymoon. All is fabulous. Don't you worry your pretty head about us. Then we won't worry about you either.

I hope you are still in the apartment. If so, don't hesitate to help yourself to any and all food around. Including the beer.

Charlotte and Josie

That was all. No mention of a possible return date. I was relieved to have gotten permission to drink the beers. They had been gone for quite a while anyway, but this way I felt less guilty for having drunk them. And I wouldn't need to feel obliged to buy replacements.

If the note was meant to be reassuring, it didn't do its job. It only left me confused.

Charlotte did not come back in July nor in August. The city seemed lighter somehow, especially on the weekends with families and friends hitting the countryside. I supposed there would have been quite the influx of tourists around somewhere, but they would have stayed away from the residential areas.

Remarkably, it seemed that, generally speaking, city life suited me. Assiduously working my twenty to twenty-five hours a week could even have allowed me a busy social life. Once they got used to my eccentricities, my co-workers started—hesitantly at first, then more and more enthusiastically—to pile on their offers of going out with them for beers or dancing or whatever after work. I felt liked. Wanted, even. But at the risk of showing a hostility I did not feel towards them, I tried to decline their offers with as much polite-ness as I could come up with, without coming across as rude. I just didn't feel social; that's all. I even recruited my ally Kent's help in trying to explain that I was a bit of an introvert. And especially that I was not interested in trying any one of them in the sack.

My co-workers eventually gave up on me. Except for the occasional tease about my cloistered habits, they seemed to accept what must have seemed to them a monastic lifestyle. I wasn't exactly behaving as a nun, but I did pick up the spiritual component of my life. Yoga came back into my daily activities. A typical day for me would look like this: Get up around seven thirty, wash up, practice yoga for an hour or so, followed by a hearty breakfast, walk to work. Work, walk home while picking up beer and groceries, make, then eat dinner, do dishes, read, or just sit and do nothing. Asleep between eleven and eleven thirty. On weekends, with a green garbage-bag full of dirty laundry on my back, I would join the lively armies mostly made up of couples at the local laundromat. I would take myself out for specialty coffee while my laundry spun and watch others read their *New York Times*. Later I might go to the library or the GLBTQ bookstore and hope to be left alone to read for free. All my research on alternate sexualities was slowly making me feel like an expert on the subject. Some weekend evenings, I would walk over to the nearest *cinéma répertoire* and watch some indie foreign film. I seriously considered learning a new language.

It was a quiet but good life. I wanted for nothing, really. As if to prove that I needed no one, fate didn't place any of my loose-ended or would-be relationships on my path. I didn't see Julie, or Bourgeon, or Charlotte, or even Sonia anywhere I went, all summer long. The very olfactory trail of Sonia's seemed to have vanished from my street. Maybe she had taken the summer off. I couldn't blame her. Who wouldn't want, if they could, to leave behind all the dust, noise, and garbage that seemed to get worse during the summer months? I was beginning to enjoy city living, true. But I wouldn't have refused an offer of charging up my batteries in some pristine setting.

Having nothing to report, I seemed to have lost the urge to write or draw. I thought that if I saw the quiet little girl from the airport again at the library, I would give her all my fancy colouring pencils. That is, if her mother would allow her to accept them. Sadly, I never did see the little family again.

☆ ☆ ☆

I arrived on a certain Tuesday morning in September at work as per usual. The atmosphere in our reading room was unusually quiet. We were only two persons sitting around the imposing table: Helga, my supervisor, and of course, me. For lack of witnesses, I could easily have started flirting with her. I was feeling mischievous. Judging from the way she smiled kindly, with that look of hers that she seemed to reserve only for me, it was possible she was thinking along the same lines.

Then just as I was testing some witty opening lines in my mind, Julie's face appeared in front of me. What was she doing there? My happy mood vanished in an instant. I felt used. I was due some explanations, or at least some communication. Anything would have done. That's when I made up my mind. I would give her an ultimatum. Taking my destiny in my own hands, I would start a new life. Julie would get the rest of the fall to get in touch with me and tell me where we stood or if we even stood at all. Then if I still hadn't heard from her, the waiting, the wondering, would stop. Forever. My deadline would be a generous one: December 31st. If I hadn't heard from Julie by the last day of the year, the waiting would expire like even the best cheese.

I felt myself start to glow. Helga's smile got brighter too. She must have had absolutely no clue as to what was brewing in my feverish brain, but she must have sensed something was up. In retrospect, it's obvious that my end-of-the year ultimatum would have been useless. In my innocence, I had thought I was mistress of my own destiny. How silly I was. How clueless.

It makes me wonder. Had I known on that Tuesday about my personal expiration date, would I have arranged my life otherwise? Would I have returned to Genus Island in an attempt to escape my destiny? And had I gone, would I still have died on November 29th or thereabouts? Was that date inscribed somewhere as being my exit date? In other words, would death have come and got me wherever I was? I still don't have any answers to these questions. All I can hope for is that this story of mine might inspire whoever is still living on the Earth to simply appreciate their good fortune while it lasts.

On that particular Tuesday in September, completely ignorant of my near future and thinking I had taken destiny into my own hands, I did feel almost happy. I thought I had solved my dilemma over Julie. Starting January 1, 2002, I would be free. In the meantime, I would still enjoy my life, as simple and delightful as it was. I got myself a perfect cup of coffee. It might not have been the best choice. The caffeine gave me crazy heart palpitations. I tried to focus my scattered gaze on the work at hand.

Just at that moment, Kent rushed into the reading room. His eyes were wild. Audibly hyperventilating, he leaned on the table as if to prevent himself from falling. After a huge audible gulp, he tried, unsuccessfully, to clear his throat. Still panting, he gestured for Helga and me to follow him. Which we did. Obediently. Obviously, something very serious had just happened. Kent led us all the way into the sacrosanct lair of our big boss, Madame Isabelle.

The door was already open as we got there. This was a very unusual occurrence, as our boss was habitually shrouded in a majestic, almost imperial kind of mystery. Very few people, and certainly not us mere readers, had actually seen her. At first, I had been very curious about her, especially since Kent had told me on my first encounter with him that she was, in his opinion, a lesbian. And a closeted one to boot. Madame Isabelle became in my eyes some sort of challenge, someone to meet for starters and maybe even help out of her heterosexual misfiling. It's not that we lesbians are predators lurking in the shadows, waiting for an innocent waif to seduce and claim as our own. First of all, Dame Isabelle was no waif. What she was, though, if I believed my good friend Kent, was simply someone who might be fun to do. Except that on that day, my timing would have been absolutely wrong.

The woman in front of our bewildered eyes seemed completely dejected. Broken. I assumed from her reputation and the remains of carefully applied makeup that she would usually hold herself high. But this person slumped on a leather chair, one shoe off her nyloned foot, hair dishevelled, mascara running down her cheeks, biting one hand, seemed to have gone beyond the dictates of dignity. She was actually embarrassing to witness. Madame Isabelle acknowledged our arrival by lifting her trembling free hand and pointing at the TV screen along one of the side walls.

At first, I didn't understand what we were supposed to be looking at. The image was so unbelievable, so absurd, that my brain couldn't cope with the information. Then as I was beginning to make sense of what was in front of my eyes, my jaw dropped in shock. I didn't know if I was going to scream, throw up, or follow the big boss's example and quietly whimper. I watched, powerless, as the World Trade Centre in New York crumbled, one tower after the other, over and over. Then I saw, horrified, terrified people scrambling for shelter from the explosion through a dense fog of grey dust, accompanied with the voice-over of a bewildered amateur cinematographer. Then the towers again. There might have been people jumping. Again and again, in a hallucinating, perversely demented loop. Yelps, squeals, bellowing, then an eerie silence. Absolute chaos. Then the screams. Again.

After hours or minutes, I don't know which, a sharp pain brutally yanked me out of my shock. I threw a glance at my hand, the source of the pain. The fingers on my right hand were imprisoned in my supervisor's, as in a tight vice. Carefully, I loosened her grasp. She didn't seem to notice. She still had her eyes riveted on the TV screen, just like Kent's. My fingers and the back of my hand were death-white. I started to feel faint. I had to leave the room. Forgetting to sign out on the time-sheet, I stumbled out of the office and onto the street.

The coffee was churning away in my stomach, lost in a sea of hydrochloric acid. I felt too weak to walk home, so I decided to take the *Métro* and the bus. This was not easy, as I had to make a lot of toilet-stops. The journey home ended up being interminable. Up until that day, I had not realized how awkward it is to find a toilet without having to consume as well. On our island, we just squatted and that was that. But here, getting home with all the pit-stops ended up costing me the price of two orange sodas, a bottle of sparkling mineral water, and a beer.

Had someone asked me at that time if I was feeling lucky to be alive, I would have thrown murderous glances at them. I know now that I was indeed very lucky. I could have been one of the people who showed up at work as usual at the World Trade Centre in New York. I could have been in Somalia or anywhere else where there was a war going on. Instead, I was alive. My biggest source of concern was not knowing where my girlfriend had disappeared to and why.

It took me a whole week to regain my appetite for life. Even after that week, I still had those awful images coming up to haunt my soul, unexpectedly.

✶ ✶ ✶

The horrendous events of September 11th seemed to bring out a wave of goodwill in people. As the firefighters were helping to sort out the debris, many, many other citizens stepped up to the plate, ready to offer assistance of any kind, be it food, time, or even free yoga classes. All this wave of goodwill was not lost on our little eclectic group at the office. Everybody was especially kind to others. The teasing and bantering stopped as if by magic, leaving space for a mutually respectful *camaraderie*. But the biggest change in behaviour in the office came from Madame Isabelle herself. She took to dropping by often into our reading room. Any excuse was good enough for her visits. She would offer words of encouragement, ask us about the coffee, or enquire if our ergonomic chairs were adequate. Fancy chocolates or doughnuts would greet us on our table first thing in the morning. Paper hand-towels got replaced by Egyptian cotton ones to be thrown in a basket after a single use and laundered. The biggest surprise came when Madame Isabelle invited us all out for drinks. The event was to take place in a few days, on the very first Friday after the towers fell.

We were suitably shocked and also delighted at the prospect of strengthening our co-workers' bond. We would be improving boss-employee relations while distracting ourselves from the fate of our less fortunate colleagues in New York. Mme Isabelle invested a lot of care in the preparations for her little party. Our participation was welcome as well. We were promptly handed out a short list of bars to choose from. We had two days to come to a consensus. Then we were asked to dress up for the occasion. There was going to be a theme: island living. As it turned out, that Friday's party was to be one in a series of four, ascending into a whirlwind crescendo until another special event. The event would be that of Adam moving to a remote island in October. "Move to what?" I said, my curiosity piqued. I was told to ask him. And ask I did the next time I ran into him in at the coffee-fountain:

"Hey, Adam! I hear you're moving to an island? Are you going somewhere exotic? Tropical? Taking a sabbatical?"

"Remote, yes. Exotic ... not really. Actually, I'm going to this island in the Salish Sea, in BC. It's called Genius... no wait. Genus Island—"

"What!? That's my island!!!" I yelled out, at once shocked and delighted at the coincidence.

"You have an island!?"

"Well, I don't actually own it ... although it kind of owns me still. I lived there for seven years. The place has a way of growing on you."

"What a coincidence! I'm actually going there to work. Mme Isabelle is sending me on a working holiday of sorts. She has some land there. She's never been, and there were some people caretaking it and now they're—"

"They're gone, right!? Sounds like those 'some people' might be my girlfriend Julie and me!!"

Wow. I couldn't believe it. Mme Isabelle! We only knew her as I. Côté. That's whom we addressed all our progress reports to, via a postal box. So, could it be 'I' for Isabelle, maybe? I'd never made the connection until now. How could I? But I still didn't know the family name of our boss. *Mme Isa... Is it even possible?* So, I asked, "Wait a minute, Adam! Do you know Mme Isabelle's surname?"

"Well, yes... It's Côté..." He looked at me like I was a moron.

Shocked would have been a mild word to describe how I felt. I was vacillating between being furious at Mme Isabelle for not identifying herself to me as my old landlady and wanting to hug her. Then I started wondering. Was my boss really the same Mme I. Côté whose land Julie and I had been living on, the one we had been sending letters to over the course of seven years?

I knew ours was not the only special caretaking situation on the island. There was at least half a dozen or more as the island was getting quietly gentrified. Some of the properties were actually pretty fancy. One even had a swimming pool, the only one on the island. Maybe Adam was going to one of those expensive places. He seemed a bit too fastidious to put up with such simple living as Julie and I had fashioned for ourselves... I had to find out. I ran to Mme Isabelle's office door only to find it closed. My patience would be tested for the whole rest of that day.

The next time Mme Isa came to our reading room, I asked if I could see her in private. She smiled and agreed to see me right away. I followed her to her office, where she invited me to sit. She closed the door. I spoke first.

"This is a bit embarrassing. I just learned your name, Madame Isabelle—"

"Côté. Yes, it's Côté. My full name is Isabelle Nathalie Côté."

"But but ... so it's ... it was ... y-y-you? Are ... did you...?"

"Yes, I am. And yes, I know. Crazy, isn't it!? But really, I only made the connection myself a few weeks ago, as I was talking to your friend Kent. I don't deal with personnel. Nor the payroll of course. You realize this is too big a coincidence for me to have imagined it in my wildest dreams."

Beaming, as if at a big fat joke, this was Madame Isabelle at her most relaxed state that I had seen her in, yet. She chuckled and extended her hand. I raised my own limp fingers towards her. Hesitantly. She touched them very lightly, as if suddenly afraid of some contamination. I took her reluctance as a sign that she had already retracted into her professional shell. I lowered my gaze, afraid of what I would find in her eyes. There was a long silence. Then she continued, politely, business-like.

"Pleased to meet you, Claire. And thank you for looking after the property all those years. I'm happy you seem to have settled well into urban living now. It must have been such a shock for you at first. I've never been to Genus Island, as you know. But judging from your letters, it's a pretty amazing place. Are you here with Julie?"

I didn't know what to answer. It would have been very embarrassing to admit to my boss that I had no idea where my girlfriend had disappeared to, nor if we were even together or not.

"Julie and I needed a break." It was all I could come up with on the spot. "That's kind of why we left..." I left the details out, like whether the break would have been from each other or simply from island living.

Mme Isa continued. "You left without a forwarding address! I was so worried for you!" She was back to being human again, but I was suspicious.

"So sorry, Madame Isabelle. At the time, I had no idea, frankly, exactly what I was going to do once I left the island. I was confused. I came to Montréal because it's the one place I am familiar with. Outside Genus Island, that is. I have friends here. Like Kent, as you know. And then he actually landed me this job..."

"Well, I am happy you ended up working for me. From your detailed accounts in all the letters I received from you over the years, I assumed you were a very capable and responsible person."

Actually, it was Julie who had been so assiduous in her communication. Even with a tinge of guilt, I didn't dare set Mme Isa right.

She continued, unaware of my slight *malaise*. "Seems like I was right. Now that I've met you, I can tell." She was smiling.

I smiled back, sheepish.

"Thanks again for looking after my property!" she said. "From the sound of it, so well! And now, what are your plans? Are you going to stay here? Any ideas if you are ever going back to Genus Island?"

There was no mention of (or further questions about) Julie. My boss must have figured out that it was a touchy subject. Still she went on, innocently driving the knife deeper in the wound:

"You know, Adam will be staying in the house. It just occurs to me that, despite the fact that it technically belongs to me, I never asked you if it was okay. But then, there was the contract ... and since you left—and so suddenly too—it would be, as you should know, null and void. You didn't even let me know where you were going..."

Oh yes, the contract. I remembered there had been one. Somewhere. But really, I had no idea where it was or even what it said. Maybe I had never known. Julie was the one who took care of such things. I had just let her. Besides, my vow of simplicity plus my proletarian, hippie-like background left me with no interest whatsoever for legal documents. Maybe I should have paid more attention. But what difference would it have made to where

I was at? I could hear Madame Isa's voice in the background. I had to make a superwoman effort to pay attention.

"By the way, did you leave anything personal or anything of value in the house?"

Yes, our love-letters and erotic lesbian videos, is what I wanted to say. Instead, I tried to sound nonchalant.

"I've packed everything away. The house is ready to go. It's a good little house. I figured that someone was going to move in sooner or later. Otherwise, the neighbours, the women of the Naiad commune, they would drop by every now and then I'm sure. I told them they can harvest from our garden. I've already asked them to look after the animals..."

True, I did ask them in my note. But I didn't wait around for their answer. Oh well. I was sure they would figure things out and take care of business. That's just the kind of women they were.

"Remember the Naiads? Julie and I mentioned them a few times in our letters..."

"Yes, yes," she said absentmindedly.

Mme Isa seemed to be getting a touch impatient. Maybe our interview was concluded. Or maybe the mention of the lesbian commune was making her uncomfortable.

"The Naiad women are very kind," I added. "However, they do not admit men onto their property except for one day a year. I think, if I remember correctly, this year the magic day will be on the Super Moon in October. I forget the date, being out of touch from it all. Maybe Adam can visit them then, whenever it is. Or I could write to the women and let them know Adam is coming..."

"Adam, oh yes, Adam..." she said, as if she had just remembered him. But there was something else. As if she wanted to tell me something, but changed her mind. Then the moment flittered away. She continued, as if Adam's gender would not be a problem as far as the Naiads are concerned. "Oh you know, Adam can take care of himself. He is very fluid." I had no idea how to interpret her choice of adjective to describe her favourite employee. Unless she was referring to his androgyny. Who knows? Adam could very well succeed in charming the Girlz. He seems to have charmed everybody else around here, including myself.

I continued, "Then the Naiads might show him around on your property. Or maybe you could write them yourself... I have their address. It's easy. Genus is a small island, as you know. You just send your letter to Naiad commune, Genus Island..."

"Thanks, Claire. Maybe it would be better if you contacted them yourself. They know you better than me. It seems to me..."

She was definitely reticent when it came to contacting the Naiad women. Just at that moment, her cell rang. Saved by the bell. Our interview was done. I just had time to slip in my agreement before she actually turned her back to me: "Okay, then. I will. Contact them, I mean."

I was unsure if Madame Isa heard me or not. Quietly, I walked out and closed the door.

★ ★ ★

On Friday September 21st, everybody in our office met at a bar downtown. We had all come to a consensus on a Polynesian establishment. This was despite the fact that Adam's destination would be a Canadian island and not an exotic one. But the island theme was on, and we were bent on living it up with a frenzy augmented by our fears fuelled by the September 11 events. I wore the only Hawaiian shirt I owned. The edges of the collar were a bit frayed, but it was vintage. From the sixties, I think. Madame Isabelle gave us each the choice between some caps and straw hats to complete the effect. Someone brought helium balloons with the inscription "Bon Voyage" on one, "You lucky duck" on another. There were lots with pineapples and palm trees.

The TVs were on, all still displaying news reports on Ground Zero. Kent walked up to the barmaid and kindly asked her to change the channel. Not finding one that did not display the news, she turned the TVs off. We all spread around an entire section of the bar and ordered the most exotic of cocktails. All except for Kent and Adam. I noted this fact and decided to keep my own drinking to one, maybe two, or at most three drinks so that I would not get too drunk to keep an eye on them. The reason I gave to myself for my indiscretion was my protective feelings towards my friend. I didn't want to see him get his heart broken.

I was sitting in a booth with Adam on one side and Kent facing us. Madame Isabelle positioned herself at the head of the main table. This way she could keep a proprietary eye on her crowd. Helga occupied the seat to her right and some strange man—a client maybe, or a lover—on her left. The rest of the employees from our office surrounded her with their jolly, noisy chatter.

There was another person in the room. She was off towards the back of the bar, near the washrooms, and not part of our group. Well, not really. Something about her was vaguely familiar, but I couldn't quite place her. Most of the people in our group seemed to be simply ignoring her, but I couldn't. And neither did Adam. I noticed that he also kept throwing interested glances her way. As far as I was concerned, it was this woman's unusual colouring that kept drawing his and my attention towards her. She was blue. Blue of her long, long hair, blue of her wispy clothes, blue throughout. Even her face seemed blue. Maybe it was just the reflection from her clothes, but blue it definitely appeared to me in the dim light surrounding her. It was almost like she was some sort of genie who had just emerged from her lamp with the light coming from inside her somehow.

Kent, Adam, and I were making up the quiet corner. I noticed that Kent seemed to have accepted the fact that Adam was not interested in him for a potential romance. The atmosphere that wrapped us was more like what you would expect in an abbey. Calm. Benevolent. Serene. I could almost hear Gregorian chants filling our bubble. None of us were small-talkers by nature anyways. And this establishment was not exactly conducive to meaningful exchanges. We were happy to just be. Fortunately—and this might have been because of the new unspoken rule of kindness that had prevailed at the office recently—nobody teased us for being so monastic.

Meanwhile, the occupants of the big table were getting quite boisterous. People were openly flirting with each other. I couldn't help but wonder, again, who had tried whom in the Biblical sense and who remained to be tried. I was sure that eventually everybody would have slept with everybody else. It was that kind of a crowd. Well, maybe not Madame Isabelle. She was the big boss. And Helga, of course. She was, at that table, the token lesbian in a sea of breeders. There might have been a slight, very slight possibility that Helga might once have tried her luck with her boss. Then again, I thought not. Madame Isabelle was too big a fish. And as Kent had warned me, there was the fact that she thought she was heterosexual.

Just then Madame Isabelle herself stood up with all her commanding presence. It was quite obvious that she was already a bit drunk by the way she was slightly swaying, her eyes sparkling with extra fluids. I thought she would offer a toast to us all or to Adam. Or maybe she was simply headed for the washroom. Instead, to my great dismay, she started lurching towards our quiet booth. A wavy smile floated on her heavily-lipsticked, almost drooling lips. I could smell trouble. Paying no attention to Kent or me, she extended her long blood-red nails past me towards Adam in a gesture that might have been intended to be friendly. From my vantage point, her hands seemed like rapacious claws. I snuck up closer to Adam in a futile attempt to protect him. Meanwhile, he seemed oblivious to being the centre of attention of his boss. He was lost in some *rêverie*. Maybe because he smelled impending trouble, Kent got up and abandoned us. I felt a touch betrayed.

Mme Isabelle was not the kind of woman who would accept a rebuttal, especially from one who was obviously her current favourite employee. She leaned further past me, pushing her perfectly-made-up face all the way to Adam's nearest ear, as if she was going to give it a little love-bite. Adam immediately turned a shade of red matching our boss's lips and nail polish. I thought of "accidentally" pulling on Madame Isabelle's sleeve. She would have been easy to take down, tipsy as she was. Some stupid remnant of respect for human dignity prevented me from embarrassing my boss. But something had to be done. Adam's eyes were starting to roll like a panicked horse's. I wished Kent had stayed. He was usually the most diplomatic of us all. Maybe he had simply gone to the washroom or out for a smoke. I thought of getting up too and disrupting the bizarre trio we formed. But then I would have completely abandoned Adam to our Boss's mercy.

Just then, salvation came. The blue girl, who could not have helped but notice the embarrassing scene, appeared at our booth. Holding a blue rose, she inserted her delicate azure-gloved hand into the crimson bubble that Madame Isa had wrapped around herself and her victim. Immediately, Madame Isa retracted like a slug that had been sprinkled with salt.

Instantly saving face, she exclaimed, "Oh, what a beautiful flower!" sliding a twenty-dollar bill into the blue girl's hand and waving her away like a pesky fly.

Blue Girl did not go away with the twenty-dollar bill. She let the money drop onto the table. Then she handed the rose, the colour reminiscent of a Moroccan blue man's garments, to a bewildered Adam. Then she waited patiently, her eyes locked on him until Madame Isabelle, uncharacteristically defeated, slid away. Then still keeping her gaze on her chosen, Blue Girl sat

down on the bench facing him in the place left vacant by Kent. They spontaneously wrapped themselves in a private aura, leaving me no other choice but
to disappear. I went outside where I found Kent. Smoking. I didn't smoke
cigarettes, but I decided to keep him company.

By the time Kent and I came back into the bar, Adam and the blue girl
were gone. They had completely vanished. We did not see them for the rest
of the night. Kent and I concluded they must have left by the back door. Or
maybe the washroom window for all we knew. All that remained from their
presence was the twenty-dollar bill, one indigo-blue rose petal, and a note
that I picked up from the seat where Adam had been sitting. I knew I was
being indiscreet, but I read it anyway. This is what the note said:

> You and I are made of the same fabric.
>
> We find each other at last. Soul-sisters. Twin stars in the
> Infinite Sky.
>
> When you've had enough solitude, come and see me.
>
> I await.
>
> Signed: The Blue Girl

As happy as I was for Adam, I was also jealous. And most importantly,
some deep-seated maternal, protective feeling had come up in me for him
from who knows where. I had never felt that way towards any human before.
Not even Kent. Not to that extent anyway. I was unsure where the feeling
had come from and especially why. Adam was not a close friend. I barely
knew him. Still, something in him made me want to wrap him in my arms
and try to protect him from some unknown danger.

Adam was in someone else's arms now. By the way I had witnessed their
eyes lock, it was obvious to me that they had found each other. That's when
I realized there was something vaguely peculiar about them both and that
it must have been this same peculiarity that had united them and set them
apart from the rest of us. Maybe it was the mention of "soul-sisters" in the
note. Why sisters? How odd. Mystery. All that I could do was to wish them
all the happiness they could endure. I could only hope that the blue girl

would follow Adam to beautiful, wonderful, magical Genus Island. And mostly that they would be as happy as I thought Julie and I had been there. I left the money on the table and took the note to be recycled.

✯　✯　✯

On the following Monday morning, everybody (including Helga) was in jolly spirits. All except me. I realized I had missed out on the bonding part yet again. The gap between myself and the rest of the employees was widening by the minute. This psychological space left me with a lot of time on my hands as I sat listening to the banter around me, distractedly scanning the articles at the same time. I tried to figure out who had ended up with whom on the weekend. Judging from their complicity, they could all have ended up in an orgy as far as I knew. Even Helga? I looked up at her and smiled in a way I thought might be questioning without necessarily prying. Whether she understood my complex feelings or not, she didn't let on either way. She simply smiled back at me with a mischievous look. Giving up, embarrassed, I immersed myself deeper into the article I had been scanning over and over, unable to categorize it. With nothing else to win or lose regarding my monastic status, I might as well get busy.

Who knows? Madame Isabelle might even give me a raise for my assiduity. That is, if she had even been made aware of it. As kind and concerned for our comfort as she had become to us readers and analysts in the last ten days, our big boss seemed completely oblivious to the amount of work, or not, that was being done around her. Somehow there were always generous piles of information on our computers at the end of the day. That was the entire purpose of the exercise, the copying and pasting and the fodder they constituted for our analysts. They all justified our already generous bi-monthly cheques. The rest was, well—as an unfaithful spouse might say—just sex.

Kent did not show up at our reading room that entire week. Neither did Adam. It left me wondering if they had even shown up at the office at all or if they were simply avoiding the pheromone-permeated atmosphere in our room. But what about the blue girl? Didn't Adam disappear with her? Was Kent, once rejected, licking his wounds somewhere? I was left with too many questions hanging in the air. Maybe I should have stayed away as well. But I kept working. I had to admit, albeit reluctantly, that I needed the money.

Kent. I loved my friend Kent. I suspected that he did not repeat with anyone else the error that he and I had made all those years ago when we tried to have sex together as friends. The two of us had not gotten together since I had come back to Montréal. He was often busy or out-of-town with his work and play. But we knew the other would be there anytime we needed an attentive ear or a laugh. However, I did notice that my friend had grown a shade distant recently. It wasn't only since last Friday's office party. It had started even before that. He seemed to be taking more and more space from me, from us. It was almost as if he were on a different timeline than the rest of us. As if he was running some sort of a personal, frenzied race against time.

I had no idea that my own days were numbered. Had I known, I might have started running too. All I thought I needed at the time was a companion, someone I could count on to hang around so that I could stop the nagging ache in my belly. It could have been Julie, Charlotte, Bourgeon, or someone new. Maybe even Sonia. Sonia. Beautiful, smart, delicious Sonia. I hoped she would be thinking of me, oh … just a tiny bit sometimes. I asked whomever might have been listening—be they the Goddess or the imps living in the forest—to give me another chance and send her my way. Please.

Little did I know, as I was daydreaming alone in a roomful of conspiring co-workers, feeling sorry for myself, that even I was going to get another run at love. It was to happen soon. Very soon, actually.

CHAPTER 14

Since I was still only working part-time at the marketing research office, I decided to get a second job. The brilliant idea came to me to offer my body to the art cause. I could be a live model. All that was required was for me to take my clothes off and sit or stand, or improvise a very, very slow dance. Easy enough. I loved to dance. All those years on Genus Island had also made me casual about taking my clothes off. Plus, I had already worked my naked way through art school. It seemed a long time ago, but I believed I could still carry it off.

I started by leaving my application at the Arts Department of Concordia University. Fortunately, being the main art school in Montréal at the time, they had some sort of umbrella office for all the colleges and schools of the city. That way, I only needed to submit a single application instead of one for each school. The salary would be minimal, but I didn't care. The work would be a welcome diversion from reading newspapers. It would inspire me to keep in good shape. It would also round up my income to a less Spartan level. I was ready. Who knows? Maybe I could even revoke my vow of simplicity.

One of these days, I thought, Charlotte would be back from her extended honeymoon, and I would need an apartment of my own. She had been gone for over two months. She was bound to return in the fall, or for sure by winter, with or without Josie. Whatever mysterious source of income she seemed to have an endless supply of, she was bound to get bored, away from her vast and eclectic circle of urban friends. That is if she had gone away somewhere rural. Who knows? She might have gone to Paris instead, or Reykjavik. All I did know is that I sensed, somehow, that she would be back soon.

Just as if the universe had been reading my questioning mind, I received two phone calls on the same day. One was an alluring offer of a sublet. The call did not come from Charlotte, however, as I had anticipated. Double bonus. It was from Sonia.

I had not received any news from my beautiful welfare worker since the unfortunate kimono affair. Except for a few erotic dreams sprinkled throughout my solitary feverish nights, and my sudden recent longing on the previous day, I had barely thought of her at all. The phone hadn't ever rung with her crystalline voice. I thought I had to admit to a complete defeat. And there she was calling me.

As I muttered a bewildered hello, my voice must have sounded quite funny, because she asked me twice if she had the right number. Once we established that I was indeed the right person, she proceeded to ask me if I was still looking for an apartment or at least a sublet. She sounded very excited. I was hoping it might have been because of me, although I doubted it.

"I am going away to Europe for two months. From the first of October to the first of December, actually. Do you like cats? I hope you're not allergic. I have two. They are very nice cats. They won't be any trouble at all! And then there's some houseplants. African violets and such. Do you know about African violets? They don't like to get any water on their leaves. This would not be a real sublet. More like a caretaking. There would be no rent for you to pay. I will pay all my utility bills, too. All you would have to do is make sure you don't burn the place down." She chuckled. "What do you say?"

She spoke to me in French, for which I was thankful. It sounded so pretty coming from her delicious lips that I almost licked the receiver.

"*Euh...*"

"Are you in?"

"Ahem... Can I think about it? If you come back in December, it might be a bit difficult to find a place then—"

"I understand. But still, you'd have over two months to look for a place. Starting now. Or..." She hesitated a bit. "We can work something out when the time comes, if we need to..."

"*We?*" *I love it when you say "we!" And what do you mean, "we can work something out!?"* I wanted to shout all this, but of course did not. *Do you mean there's a possibility we could actually LIVE together when you come back?* Of course, I made no comment at all.

I somehow womanaged to hide my hopefulness and blurted out, tangled up in my own make-believe, *"Bein c'est juste que...* It's just that I really would like to sleep on it or something. Can I call you back in, say, a day or so?"

Sleep on it? Who am I kidding? How can I sleep until this deal is closed?

"Okay, d'abord." She sounded disappointed. Good. One point for me. "Fine. I'll be expecting your call."

Then Sonia actually gave me her personal—not her office—phone number and address. We hung up in unison. Point number three. We were synchronized.

From Sonia's address, it looked like she might live only a block or so from Charlotte's apartment. That explained the sweet scent my nose had caught a couple of months before. I suspected I was going to be wrapped in its charm again. Soon. I swooned, then I did a little gig and *tralala'd* all up and down Charlotte's corridor and around her kitchen. I cracked open a ritualistic beer. Sonia would now have to wonder for a while, maybe even languish a tiny bit ... and it was all because of me. How long I was going to make her wait, I wasn't sure. It was important that I play my cards right. If I called her back right away, I would sound too eager. Desperate, even. But if I waited for more than two days, she might think I didn't care. She might offer her place to someone else. After much deliberation, I decided that eighteen hours would be the perfect amount of time.

The phone rang a second time. It was Concordia University, offering me my first assignment. My modelling was to be for a Drawing 101 class the very next day at 5:30 p.m. That was exactly the time I was going to call Sonia. Confused, I decided to try and sleep on it all and make my mind up on the best time to contact my beautiful woman the next morning. Of course, I hardly slept at all. Again.

The next day, I spent a long time on my morning yoga practice. I must have gone through all the *asanas* I could remember and even invented some new ones, as if I could magically snap into shape from a single session. But I went on folding, twisting, extending, and easing through my body until I felt like a rubber ball. I wasn't preparing so much for the drawing class as I was for Sonia. It's a bit strange, but I was so focussed on getting into shape, on preparing, that I sort of forgot to decide on an alternate time when I was going to call her. Instead, I got ready for my office work with the intention of scanning and copying and pasting for a few hours before I grabbed a light dinner and walked over to the drawing class. I piled layer upon layer of loose clothing on my body but wore no underwear. That way, I would not have any elastic marks come evening. My co-workers in the reading room might wonder for an instant about my weird fashion statement. But they would probably soon shrug it off and add my *accoutrement* to the long list of my bizarre habits. On my way out of the apartment, I stuffed my backpack with a stick of non-aluminium deodorant, a bag of trail mix, and Josie's kimono.

The four hours or so that I spent in the reading room went by without any major incident. I got a glimpse of Kent, so I knew he was alive, but he didn't come in and say hello. He looked so preoccupied that I made no attempts to talk to him. Of our group of readers, only Helga had shown up. She didn't look very friendly either, to the point where I wondered if I had missed some memo stating that some new awful disaster had happened. Again. I drowned myself in my work. Time seemed to be crawling at a snail's pace. Maybe I was a little bit nervous about my modelling assignment after all. But it wasn't really about taking my clothes off in front of strangers. That thought didn't seem to bother me. It was something else, like the idea of impending disaster waiting for me, like a fisherman's net.

✮ ✮ ✮

I arrived at the drawing class early. Despite the fact that we were at the beginning of the fall session, the podium where I was supposed to expose myself was already smeared all over with some charcoal and conté marks. To pass the time, I cleaned my work-space with a rag that was hanging around in a corner of the room. The cloth itself was so dirty that it was unclear to me if I was making things worse or not. Some students started trickling in, looking tired. They were all younger than me. Too bad they did not seem to appreciate the great privilege they had in being able to devote some time to what might be considered as a leisurely activity. I assumed that their education had been paid for by their well-to-do parents. None of the youngsters seemed to already have half a day's work in their body like I had.

The teacher came in. He informed me of what was expected of me. A few "gesture" poses, gradually extending into longer ones, up to a half hour, one or two of those depending on the time remaining. "And no Yoga!" he added sternly. Then he glanced around the room as if looking for someone. Apparently not finding him or her, he disappeared without any sign of recognition of his students' presence in the room. They seemed happy with his lack of direction anyway, not to say complete absence, and soon settled into a slightly bored half-studious concentration. All you could hear in the classroom was the scratching of their pencils and sticks on the manila or newsprint paper and the odd pointillist statement delivered in staccato form. I closed my eyes. It felt as if I was surrounded by a litter of panda cubs munching their way through a bamboo grove.

After my improvised little dance of one, two, and then ten-minute non-yoga poses, I arranged my body in what I thought would be an interesting shape. I half-twisted myself so that I would be like a live sculpture, offering something appealing to each and all of the dozen or so students scattered all around me.

Whomever was supposed to be in charge of the heating didn't do their job. There I was, naked like an earthworm, nipples erect, fingers and toes rendered blue by the cold air of that rainy September evening, shaken by a slight tremor. To make things worse, I had locked myself for a good twenty-eight, long remaining minutes in a pose of my choice, true, but that turned out to be too complicated. I clenched my jaw. Despite my extreme discomfort, I was determined to hang on until coffee break.

Then everything changed. The door flung open, creating an additional icy draft that clawed at the goose-pimples on my already frozen skin with a virtual horse-hair brush. I must have offered the dismal spectacle of a freshly plucked chicken. I opened my eyes.

There she was. Late. Announcing her arrival with a *frou-frou* of brightly-coloured cyclone, she spontaneously opened her black leather satchel, letting a half-ream of Manila paper scatter on the dirty floor. Without any words of apology for having disturbed the studious atmosphere, she gracefully picked the papers up one by one and pinned them all with calculated care, and with a giant black metal clip, onto the only remaining wooden plank that seemed to have been awaiting her arrival. I was fascinated. Seemingly oblivious to me or anyone else in the room, she opened a brand-new-looking pencil case, revealing an impressive assortment of pencils all lined up and perfectly sharpened. She was close enough that I could count them: thirteen in all. I assumed, taking their numbers onto consideration, that the pencils would range from 5H to 8B.

Sonia—because it was her, of course—set herself to the task at hand, namely to reproduce without flinching my bare shape on paper. She lifted her eyes. And that's when she recognized me. I could tell. There was a little start, a shiver of her shoulders, then a glimmer in her eyes, the suggestion of a beginning smile. Then nothing. She retreated into a cool stance, cooler than the surrounding air. I almost hoped that maybe I had been wrong, that maybe there was a speck of a chance that she did not recognize me in my Eve's costume. But then again, there had been the embarrassing kimono sequence on that fated home visit of hers in July. She had already seen me in my barest state. Surely, she would have known it was me trying to hide behind my goose-bumped nakedness. I couldn't decide if this double exposure would have been to my advantage or not. All that was left for me was to admire her professionalism once again and hope at the same time that simple professionalism it was, and not total indifference towards me.

To my great horror, I started feeling my heart pumping harder. Blood rushed towards my face and extremities. It is true that this flush of vital fluids could have been a welcome change, given how cold I had been feeling. Instead, it was unwelcome at that particular time because it was too visible. My ears started burning as if they were red-hot coals. Big fat drops of sweat dripped from my underarms, falling on the podium with what sounded to my alarmed hot ears like raindrops on a tin roof.

And then just as I thought I had reached a paroxysm of embarrassment, there came something worse. My only desperate hope would have been— and I thank the Goddess—that Sonia probably did not, could not, have noticed what was happening. Indeed, my labia, major and minor, had started prickling in the most imperious way, much like the annoying wake-up bugle sound in a summer camp. I tried to shift my body in the most imperceptible way, trying to rub my thighs together to alleviate the intense itch without attracting everyone's attention. Especially Sonia's. All that I womanaged to do was enhance the itching by paying so much attention to it.

I tried to distract myself by breathing deeply and slowly. My exhalations gradually got longer and longer, followed by sucking in huge volumes of cold air, saturated as it was with ink and charcoal, as if each intake would be my last. Then I would collapse my chest again, still decorated with erect nipples floating like buoys. All this was performed in waves of increasing magnitude. If the students' drawings were accurate, they would have had to show my chest as in a cartoon, highlighting my trembling nipples with those parallel curves that are supposed to indicate action. I don't know how I survived the remaining twenty-four minutes or so. All I could guess at was that there must have been a Goddess for pitiful girls like me after all. By some miracle, I was able to hold my excruciating pose without losing my base configuration. I survived the torture. But only to be subjected to more of it later.

Once the interminable session came to a coffee-break, I put my layers back on. I was deliberately ignoring the unspoken rule that I mostly guessed at, of models being required not to dress and undress in front of the students. But why anyway? So that they would be less human? At any rate, I was far from being preoccupied with the rules, spoken or not, even if they had been carved in stone. I was in survival mode. Still panting from the effort of moving after a forced stillness, my ears still burning from embarrassment, shivering like a Chihuahua caught outside in a Canadian winter, I somehow womanaged to find myself in the cafeteria.

I had been so preoccupied with making my exit as swift as possible that I had not noticed what Sonia was up to. She must have put down her pencils and followed me all the way to my precarious refuge. There she was, sitting beside my form that I had slumped on a red plastic chair in a corner of the almost deserted cafeteria. I was still shivering. The first thing Sonia did was to adjust the clothes around my neck, including tucking in all my tags, one by one. She executed this gesture simply, with just a little tender mockery. Sonia did not miss any further opportunities for grooming. She smoothed my hair which, judging from the direction of her caresses must have stuck up like two horns. My dresses and skirts must have somehow been sagging at the waist, revealing the beginnings of the crack of my bum that would have appeared yellowish under the fluorescent light. She fixed it all to what seemed like her own satisfaction. Then she looked me up and down, smiling with a disconcerting familiarity. To fill the silence that was growing at an alarming rate, she started talking about this and that as if we had been long-time friends. Her chattering suited me since I had been rendered completely speechless by her presence. My brain was empty.

After thanking me for having disrobed myself for the art cause, she complimented me on my flexibility and general skill at holding a relatively long, complicated pose. She had, she said, signed up for a month of this drawing class at the last minute. She was not looking for credits, just a way of unleashing some well-needed creativity. According to her, it was also a very opportune coincidence that I happened to be the model that day, since she had another friend who was also interested in caretaking her apartment and she needed to know.

Now there were two people who would be waiting for my answer. Just to add a certain weight, not to say urgency, to her own request, Sonia mentioned with a charming smile that, in her opinion, I would be the best candidate for occupying her apartment. Especially, she said, since I seemed to need it more than her friend did.

Sonia's comment about my seeming neediness disappointed me. I couldn't help but wonder what it was in my behaviour that would have triggered her poor opinion of me. I thought of asking her, but realized it would be better if I remained quiet.

The coffee-break was over. We had to return to class. Me on my dirty podium, Sonia and the other students at their easels. For a brief moment, I considered executing a striptease of sorts in front of everyone, just as a joke. But then, I was unsure of the students' sense of humour. Of course, I guessed that Sonia would chuckle at my improvised performance. But then again, I did not know her enough to trust her not to think me weird. I settled myself as comfortably as I could, closed my eyes, and tried to keep warm for the remaining hour by daydreaming about Sonia and me lounging on a tropical island paradise.

My movie did not last long enough. The subject of the apartment came up in my mind and collapsed my idyllic musings, suddenly, like a power failure. After that I had no other choice but to try and figure out the best tactic to keep Sonia interested in me. My only hope of regaining a semblance of dignity in the rental situation would have been to give her just enough of a clue to my interest in her offer without actually committing myself.

After class, once I was dressed in all my layers and felt that my blue lips had returned to a more natural salmon hue, I informed Sonia that I would call her at work the very next morning. I thought it would make me look more important if she knew I still had something else to settle beforehand. I was also hoping to have her wonder about me for one more night. I doubt that this would have been the case. She had the upper hand in the situation, having two choices of a tenant. It was more likely me who would end up with yet another feverish, nightmarish night. And that's exactly what happened.

Around seven the next morning, I was brutally woken up by a telephone ring. I had just finally dozed off after my gruelling night. Grumpily, I picked up her vintage receiver and croaked a hoarse hello. It was Charlotte. This was an unusual time for her to be calling as she was renowned for her love of sleeping in. I figured that she must be upset, or else be calling from somewhere a few time-zones away. Despite the fact that we hadn't actually seen each other for years, she jumped right into her reason for calling me without even saying hi.

"Where were you last night?" she almost yelled. "I tried to call you several times!"

"Sorry, I was working." Why was I sorry?

"So late? Are you moonlighting?" She had one of her sarcastic intonations.

"I was actually at—"

"Anyway, I will be back in town. Soon. Josie and I are so over. I am still in Ste-Agathe, but will be coming home. Sorry, I don't think that I will be in the mood to have a visitor." She had the questionable courtesy to add, "Even one as charming as yourself. It's just that I would want my apartment back. By October first. Maybe you could leave me your new coordinates so that we could catch up? Later. Whenever that would be. I'm a bit confused these days. All I know is that I need my space."

"So sorry about Josie," I said. "I completely understand that you will need your space. Don't worry about me." (Not that she seemed to be concerned.) "I will figure something out. I have a few days, after all. I will be out of here by the time you get back. No problem. And yes, I'd like for us to catch up with our news. Eventually. No rush. I'll call you when I'm settled. Elsewhere."

The subtleties of arranging my own living situation were obviously lost on my friend. Distracted, she said, *Bon*. Got to go. Lousy long-distance plan. Good luck."

She hung up, leaving me baffled. We were exactly five days before October first. It was just my luck that Sonia's offer was on the table. It was going to be either her apartment or the YWCA. What a choice! I had better call Sonia before she gave up on me. Then, once settled at her place, I could call Charlotte. I knew my friend well enough to trust that she would be over her heartbreak in no time. I would forgive her for having given me such short notice and in such a rude way. Besides, it was her apartment. Charlotte would never apologize anyway. And now I had a better offer.

As far as Sonia was concerned, I had no choice but to admit that she had probably figured out that I was hopelessly infatuated with her. The way she looked at me, amused, how she led me on, it would have been obvious to the most clueless of people. Maybe Sonia would give me a chance. I had to find out. I called her immediately at work, not even wanting to wait until she got home. Our brief conversation was businesslike and to the point. We agreed to meet at her apartment on the following Friday, September the 28th, at five. That would have been three short days later. Those very same three days turned out to be extremely long. It was not only because of my being anxious but also because of all the unexpected events that also happened in that relatively short time-span.

CHAPTER 15

It all started with a letter in Charlotte's mailbox. The address had been more drawn than written, in an awkward, childlike hand, with what looked like white correcting ink. The fire-engine red envelope, decorated with several iridescent rainbows, was addressed to Charlotte. However, it looked too intriguing for me to pass over. I opened it without the slightest remorse at my indiscretion.

Inside there was a single small card. It had been hand-drawn graffiti-style and was an invitation to a party, a masked ball, in a loft on Villeneuve Street. According to the stamp, the card had been sent more than a month previously. I deduced that the delay in the delivery must have been because the postal employees had a hard time deciphering the address. The party would be on that same night, September 25th, as on a Tuesday. A weekday. A workday. And then, why not? The card also made it clear that all genders would be welcome. I would then qualify. Without any hesitation, I decided to go. Having no mask at hand, I thought I would pick up something appropriate downtown, on my way up to the party from work.

I had a modelling session early that evening, so once again I piled on a silk slip, some full skirts, and a long dress from Charlotte's closet and layered a wide t-shirt and two sweaters on top. Thus *accoutrée*, I walked to the office. Once there I peeled off the uppermost layers and hid them under my chair. My co-workers, engaged in a lively discussion, totally ignored me. As I listened, I found out to my great surprise that three people from the office had also received an invitation to the same masked ball: my lesbian supervisor Helga, my gay friend Kent, and the beautiful, enigmatic and androgynous Adam.

Helga declared that she would not go, since her girlfriend was not invited. She preferred to stay home and cocoon. This was the first time I'd heard of any girlfriend. *Good for her,* I thought. Adam was momentarily not available for comment. Kent did not commit himself. I guessed that whether he was going or not would largely be influenced by Adam's decision. I couldn't help but wonder if the blue girl would be there too.

The remainder of our day went by with my witnessing the usual bantering from my co-workers, their throwing of bouncy-balls made from all the elastic bands in the room, their staple-gun fights, and the sporadic scanning of the odd article sometimes accompanied by corresponding discussions about some of the most controversial or funny issues. All that sprinkled with delicious cookies and organic fair-traded, shade-grown coffee, chocolate truffles, and other delicacies, all compliments of Madame Isabelle. Some employees claimed that they had to spend an extra hour at the gym just to get rid of the calories accumulated at work. Oblivious to most of the goodies and of participating in the talk, I worked on.

One article in particular attracted my attention. Ignoring the "don't read, just scan" rule, I allowed myself the luxury of reading the entire five paragraphs of the article. It was talking about a rare blood disorder, an enzyme deficiency actually, called Porphyria. The symptoms of this disease are peculiar. For one thing, it makes people sensitive to daylight. Also, if you collect the urine of a person who has Porphyria and expose it to sunlight, it will turn purple. Another peculiarity of the disease is that the symptoms are made worse by eating garlic. Some people with a certain kind of Porphyria also have brown teeth that fluoresce in UV light. The article went on to say that, because of all the symptoms of that disease, Porphyria may have been the origin of many vampire stories.

I simply had to share the article with my co-workers. I was very careful not to divulge my own Transylvanian heritage, as I knew it would give them more fodder for future teasing. The group liked my story. Their response got so lively and loud that Kent poked his nose in, possibly looking for well-needed comic relief. Once he found out what the hilarity was about, he threw me a meaningful wink. He knew my little genealogical secret. Thankfully, he didn't turn me into the clutches of the laughing hyenas.

On my part—and I had no real reason for this—the article and related vampire stories made me think of Adam. It wasn't, fortunately, the blood-sucking part. Something, rather, about his pale complexion, his androgyny, and even his subdued, almost ghost-like nature presented a very intriguing character indeed. He would look perfect in a black velvet cape lined with crimson satin, his black hair parted in the middle and pomaded to a hard lustre. Then I felt bad for having classified him with the vampires. The time had come, I resolved, for us to get better acquainted. That is, if he would let me. *Nothing like the present moment,* I thought. After all, he would be staying at our house on Genus. I got up and wandered around the office looking for him. All the doors were closed except for Madame Isabelle's. She looked up, smiled, and asked me if everything was okay. I said yes and slunk back to my scanning for the next few hours.

Once my short day at the office was done, I wandered into a small Greek café downtown for an early-dinner salad. It was cold in the place. The salad was frigid and the owner had been skimpy with the feta cheese. I had ordered the wrong thing, but it was too late to ask for anything else. The only good thing about my salad is that it did not fill me up. I needed my belly to be as flat as possible for my following assignment.

The class was Painting 314. I was relieved to notice that Sonia was not attending this one. As happy as I would have been to bathe in her angelic aura, I was not ready to bask in it with all the abandon that her presence would require.

The professor of this class, a sort of antediluvian lizard-like character long past retirement age, reminded everybody of his claim to have come from Paris. Judging from the way he dressed, the accentuated curve of his spine, and the astonishing number of lines on his face, he might even have rubbed shoulders with the great ones, the likes of Picasso and Dali. Unfortunately, except for the mention of his Parisian origins, he chose not to divulge much else about his past. Too bad. I would have loved to hear some of his stories.

Having obviously been formed from the Old School, he seemed lost in the relatively *minable* present. When I got the call for this assignment, I had been warned that this particular professor had a tendency to ask for long poses, sometimes the whole length of a three-hour class. I didn't think I would mind that as long as I was allowed to recline. Yes, they informed me,

I could do whatever I wanted. I could even go to sleep. For three and a half hours, with two fifteen-minute breaks.

To my great surprise, the professor provided me with not one but two inflatable cushions to lay under me on the dirty podium. They were the kind with a hole in them, designed for people suffering from hemorrhoids. Ignoring my own obvious questions that came up regarding whether they had been used before and to what ends, I diligently set myself to the task of blowing the first one up to the great amusement of the students. One of the budding artists, seemingly the most compassionate one, having taken pity on me, kindly offered to help me with the second cushion. I took a quick look at him. My gaydar detected him as a homosexual. As embarrassing as it is to admit my own ignorance and unnecessary prejudice, I have to confess that I declined his offer, being paranoid of the possibility of somehow (by osmosis?) catching AIDS. How crass of me. But that's exactly what I did. I declined his offer as graciously as I could. I went on blowing one cushion after the other until my trachea burned.

After setting my two insufficiently inflated pillows on the podium, I draped a shawl on them, then lay my already freezing body on the improvised nest. This time I chose a comfortable pose. I closed my eyes and sent myself onto my virtual beach. There were no perverts on this beach, no coconut-scented, sun-screened families, no mosquitoes nor pests of any sort. Not even Sonia or any other luscious but troubling woman. I had my perfect beach all to myself.

Someone had set an alarm. It rang irritatingly after an hour, chasing me out of my *rêverie* and into my cold body. My teeth were softly rattling. Any attempt at movement, even the tiniest one, would send shivers down my limbs. The gay student sprung up, came over, and with a quiet voice, asked me to please stay still for one more minute. Maybe he wanted to capture a few last lines before the break, I thought. Instead of returning to his easel, he produced a small piece of white chalk from some hidden pocket like a magician without a *bâton*. He proceeded to draw, carefully and with his left hand, the contours of my anatomy on the podium and on the shawl draped over the cushions. Then seemingly satisfied with his work, he excused himself for the delay and offered a helping hand to get me up.

Surprised but thankful, since I was quite stiff, I accepted. His gesture was so gallant, it made me feel like some sort of Grande Dame. Smiling, I looked up at his eyes. They were a beautiful medium-light blue, almost turquoise, the colour of robin's eggs but translucent and clear. Lost in his kind gaze, I reached for my kimono behind me and put it on, transfixed. I had found another soulmate. Just like that, as magically and simply as that. With Kent and maybe Sonia, it would make three. For the time being, I didn't know what to do with this gift of kinship that had just presented itself. There was really nothing else for me to do than let the universal love sink into the soft chambers of my heart.

While I had been lost in my musings, my new friend had gently broken our gaze and disappeared. He promptly returned with two steaming cups of mint tea. He offered me one with his left hand. I accepted the hot beverage gratefully, without the slightest trace of paranoia this time.

He was obviously left-handed. This detail reminded me of something I had heard somewhere a long time ago, maybe from one of the Naiads. It was about the correlation between left-handedness and homosexuality. According to whomever had told me the story, it seemed that an unusually high per-centage—and I don't remember the exact figure, just that it was surprisingly high—of male gay people, and an even higher percentage, maybe even as high as 40 percent of lesbians, are left-handed. Or was it that 40 percent of left-handed women were lesbians? Either way, it was an interesting bit of trivia but not particularly useful in this scenario. I thought of asking him if he had heard of the same phenomenon. Oblivious to my thoughts, he had taken me by the hand and brought me in front of his easel. The image on the small canvas represented a smaller, unmistakeable but quite flattering version of me. Somehow, he had managed to capture my very soul. I blushed.

My new friend shook my hand and introduced himself. His name was David. After that, he went right into telling me the basics of his personal story. His parents had disinherited him because he was gay. They would have liked to make a lawyer out of him and marry him off to the perfect woman of their own choice, or at least someone they would approve of and who would give them the best descendants. A grand-daughter for beauty, a grandson for posterity. David, free from their archaic psychological shackles, decided to pursue his real passion, which was art. He was living in voluntary simplicity. He was happy. To pay his bills, he worked at night as a waiter in a popular gay bar in the village. I wondered how he and my other soulmate Kent would get along.

The other students were trickling back in, clutching junk food and diet soft drinks in their paws. I realized I hadn't gone to the bathroom during the break. There was no time now. I'd just have to pinch my own meatus for another hour. I tried as best as I could to fit into the white chalk marks. The problem was that the lines had followed my contours but gave no clue as to what was supposed to happen with the bulk of my body. I needed help. The students complied. With the help of their paintings and their verbal suggestions, we all managed to more or less reconstruct the pose. Then we sank into the dusty and slightly stinky sounds of paintbrushes on canvas with the occasional clinking of metal on the rims of jars of progressively murkier water. The alarm sounded for the second break. Some of the students seemingly engrossed in their painting were continuing to work through it. I threw my kimono on and fled to the bathroom. When I came back, David was nowhere to be seen. Having nothing else to do, I lay down on my nest before the end of break and went back to my idyllic beach. This time, I did not need the markers. My body remembered.

The professor only came back into class close to the very end, a mere ten minutes or so before the third ring of the alarm clock. He came right up to me. Close. Too close, as only a myopic person would allow themselves to do. His breath stank of alcohol and pipe tobacco. I squirmed, which reminded me how much I really needed to pee. Again. It was as if the cold atmosphere had wanted to squeeze all extra fluids out of me. Harrumphing and snorting, he turned his back to me then shuffled towards a few of the students' easels, scattering a few encouraging comments all around as if he were feeding ducks. Then as soon as the final alarm rang, the students put their things away in a flurry, ignoring everyone else including the bewildered professor. I threw as many of my clothes on as I could in the least amount of time and ran out of the room towards the washrooms.

When I came back, my new friend David was still in the room. He might have been waiting for me. I was happy to see him as I realized I had not been ready to let him go. He told me he was going to a party and was wondering if I was interested in accompanying him. It turned out it was the same party that Charlotte had received the invitation to and that I was going to crash. What an amazing coincidence. But then again, if he really was my soulmate, it would make perfect sense that we were destined to spend more time together. I told him I didn't have a proper costume and had planned on picking something up on my way. Laughing, he said he had been thinking along similar lines for himself. *"C'est toujours meilleur à deux."*

We headed for the sex-shops all along Ste-Catherine and Saint-Laurent Streets. Despite the abundant choices, I couldn't find anything that suited my mood. Actually, I wasn't quite sure what my mood was. I felt a bit tired, carrying a full day in my body. I was hungry too. I let David pick for me. He chose a thin moustache and an aubergine *lamé* bodysuit. I wasn't sure about the bodysuit, but I bought it anyway on David's enthusiastic insistence:

"Here, you can put this on once we're there," he said, pinning the bodysuit on my shoulders to check for size. "The legs are a bit long... You can always roll them up. All these skirts will have to go. The jacket is good. Keep the jacket."

However, I stopped at the rubber set of male genitalia. David feigned understanding my reticence, but he couldn't help exhaling with a sigh that might have meant "Too bad. What a shame, though."

David had style. I had to admire him for that. He also had no problem finding accessories for himself. There was a pair of thigh-high vinyl boots, some oversized *tigré* sunglasses, a sequinned purse and a feather boa, all in hues of bubble-gum pink and magenta. He was squealing with excited pleasure. I offered him Josie's fire-red Kimono. He would look absolutely outrageous. Better than me, of course. That's what I hate the most about going anywhere in drag. The queens get all the fun of dressing up.

Remembering the party was originally supposed to be a masked ball, we added two black velvet eye-masks. David's had pink fluff around the eyes; mine was plain. I had no idea how he would negotiate the wearing of both the tigré sunglasses and the mask. He had my full confidence that he would figure it out.

We arrived at the party around ten thirty. It was obviously much too early. An army of young and short beings of indeterminate gender, looking more like extraterrestrial elves than people, were climbing up and down some elaborate scaffolding. They were weaving a network of Mylar strips into a sort of giant spider web. The floor was littered with balloons and other unidentifiable light objects. Then someone must have pulled on an invisible cable, because the balloons and everything rose from the floor into the air, all the way up to the twenty-foot ceiling. I was amazed. It was almost like I rose into the air too. David slid a card in my hand and disappeared behind a beatific ear-to-ear smile like a Cheshire cat. I noticed he was missing a canine tooth. I found myself quite alone on the floor, which had been rendered shiny by a smattering of scattered sequins.

Hunger gripped my belly. There was a table along one wall of the vast hall with some small objects on it. I made my way towards it, hoping for food. At first, I was disappointed to find what I thought were miniature art objects instead of edibles. But then I got taken in, fascinated by the intricate detail of the pieces. They had been exquisitely fashioned to make reference to human or animal body parts, what detail I was unsure of, but with a marked preference for genitalia-like forms. The *objets d'art* were not necessarily exact replicas but more like exaggerated renditions of an exquisitely sensual nature. I thought I recognized a few clitorises, or were they miniature penises? There were bums, balls—hairy or not—swollen vagina-like openings, a few rows of tiny breasts, and lips.

"Go ahead, don't be shy. Have one. Or two. Have as many as you want," said a contralto voice behind me.

I turned around, startled. A friendly-looking smiling character handed me an enormous square black plate with a small selection of objects on it. The being's skin was white, tinted a subtle lavender hue, probably from the skillful application of makeup. The surreal violet of the eyes could have been the result of blue contacts that an albino might wear over their red pupils. The person was so tall and smooth that I felt like some sort of troglodyte. I gulped.

"You mean that these creations are actually edible?"

No answer, just the plate pushed closer to my nose. It smelled like the ocean.

I looked more carefully. Oh yes, there was a giant prawn slit down the middle with a little orange pearl—possibly a single sturgeon egg—nestled in the fold. And then there was a scallop sliced in half crosswise, into which two plump sections of peeled mandarin had been inserted on each side, and a single black peppercorn glued on top, and an oversized but squat spear of asparagus wrapped at its base with a calamari tentacle then punched into an unpeeled kiwi scrotum. I was skeptical. Besides, I don't eat animals.

The person holding the plate seemed to be patiently waiting for me to get over myself and graciously accept the offering. Meanwhile, the violet eyes had taken me in. Looking at me from behind enormous Elton John-style, iridescent royal-blue frames, empty of lenses, I felt myself wrapped in their enchantment, forgetting my manners and the fact I was vegetarian and staring. Not being able to stop myself from gaping, I checked out the rest of the costume, trying to affix a gender to its intriguing wearer. There was a starched collar and black leather bow tie around the neck, hiding the presence or absence of an Adam's apple, loose chartreuse netting on the chest, and from the waist down, tight shorts also made of black leather. Aha. Now we were getting somewhere. The diminutive pants revealed a characteristic bulge that made me conclude temporarily that the person inside them would be male. But then, there had been the breasts, tiny like a pre-pubescent nymphet's but unmistakeably feminine, adorning the chest under the fishnet. Then there was the graceful curve of a waistline also. I was confused.

I finally had to stop staring and accept the plateful of food. Relieved of a burden in more ways than one, the character swiftly spun on stiletto heels towards the set of flapping half-doors leading back to the kitchen. Just before the person's disappearance, I noted that the buttocks were firm and high like a guy's. I thought of the stone chimeras guarding the entrance to the Belvedere Palace in Vienna.

Oh well. By then I was too hungry to care. I stuffed my mouth with the contents of my plate. Seafood was not really meat, I reasoned. Mother Ocean herself was offering her bounty. It would have been rude to refuse. Her sweet, pungent scent filled my nostrils and brought me back to Genus Island.

When I went back for more, at first I only chose the food that I thought I recognized: Vulvas made out of giant prawns cleaved to reveal a nest of fish roe; clusters of Nori-wrapped miniature scallops encircled with calamari tentacles; clitorises shaped from the entire intact flesh of crab-claws held together with delicately sliced green onion leaves; giant octopus suckers that didn't have anything done to them to make them look like anuses with a touch of hemorrhoids. Feeling insatiable, I continued stuffing more and more delicacies, including those of a progressively unknown nature, into my mouth. At some point, I stopped to see if anyone was watching. No one seemed to pay any attention to me, so I went on filling my belly. After I was quite full, I went back for more. Just as in fairy tales, the table seemed to replenish itself by magic. Once I felt I couldn't possibly take another bite, I chose four more pieces of my favourite morsels and put them on my plate. They were the crab-claw-clitorises. I sat down on the scintillating floor in a quiet corner of the room, took a deep breath, and then licked my edible clitorises one by one before I introduced them to my gaping mouth. I said a sort of prayer for each morsel, a dedication to each of my current love-interests: One for Sonia, one for Bourgeon, and one—albeit slightly reluctantly, I noticed—for Julie. And while I was at it, I added Charlotte as well.

I was still the only person in the room who was not working towards preparing for the party. It was time for me to give back for all the goodies I had ingested. The kitchen doors had now been propped open, letting a bright light spill out. I walked in. The first person I saw was David. The apron he was wearing was already smeared with something violet-black, like so many bruises. Maybe it was octopus ink. David waved to me in a slightly distracted but friendly way and then returned to his task of piping some pink rosettes around a giant hermaphroditic-looking confection. I felt that my presence was neither necessary nor wanted. I'd just have to come back later. Leaving the buzzing kitchen, I picked up my backpack, crossed the loft, passing by the busy extraterrestrial elves, and ejected myself into the night.

★ ★ ★

When I came back two hours later, shivering, the party was in full swing. The piles of skirts and assorted tops I had thrown on that morning weighed heavily on my body and made me feel out of place. I disappeared into the washroom and stripped down to the silk slip. Despite my faith in David's good taste in clothes, I still couldn't get myself to don the aubergine bodysuit. Besides, my belly would be too big and unattractive after all the food I had ingested. The slip, a half-size too big for me, would be loose enough to slide over any unsightly bulges. After I stuffed all my superfluous clothes in my backpack, I donned the eye-mask. I was ready to face the music.

A happy, colourful crowd of adults were squirming on the floor to the rousing sounds of the music, bouncing like so many rubber toys. I realized I had forgotten to don the mustache. But then again, it would only have worked with the bodysuit and jacket. Fortunately, nobody seemed to care about what I or anybody else was wearing or not anyway. Some people, including obvious women, had already taken their tops off and kept their masks on. It was a very pretty but slightly odd sight because of the masks.

Inspired, I joined the crowd, exuding smells of sweat but also vanilla, cinnamon, patchouli, and mystery. I longed for Sonia.

I closed my eyes, only opening them intermittently just to locate myself. Flashes of light would penetrate my consciousness like strobes. Sometimes I would see what might have been a man disguised as what might be a woman or vice versa. But more often than not, the image that would present itself to my retina would not belong to any particular gender. I quickly adjusted to simply accepting whatever fascinating shapes or colours presented themselves.

Except for the vision of a middle-aged woman—relatively boring in the sea of visual excitement. Her image seemed to be recurring with increasing frequency until I realized she was trying to dance with me. She might have been a housewife, the kind who would be taking evening adult-education classes to keep herself young and interesting after her kids had flown the coop. I had seen many women like her when I attended art school myself for a short time. Their crazed frenzy, their determination to catch up on some elusive lost time, had contributed to my resolve never to have kids.

Perhaps giving up on me, she closed her eyes. I decided to let my compassion take over. I gave her all my attention. I started this by taking an inventory of her, just to see who I was working with. The first details that I was made aware of were her clothes, of a calculated chic that suited the décor in a sober, unobtrusive way. Probably expensive garb it was, the kind that would be so by chance, without insisting on their price, but rather worn with feigned nonchalance. Her mask was black velvet just like mine. It was the only inexpensive part of her attire. Even so, she somehow womanaged to make it look pricey.

I was finding it hard to keep in touch with my compassion, but I was determined to persist.

Her ears caught my gaze. Almost as exquisite as I remembered Sonia's to be, they were adorned with perfectly round, identical pink pearls. *How dare she borrow one of Sonia's attributes?* I thought. I decided on the spot that the ears did not look good on this woman. Still not finding anything to like, I considered her attitude. She was dancing with a grace seasoned with experience, with the kind of self-assurance of one who is familiar with dance from ballet to tango but also with abandon, as if no one was watching, as per the saying. One thing in her favour. Another positive element was that she did not seem to bear that frenzy, that *rage de vivre,* I was expecting to see in a person of her age and class.

I let myself be touched by her energy. What I found was someone gentle and well-meaning, almost vulnerable. Her lips were slightly parted. I could guess more than see from behind her mask that her eyelids were still softly shut like butterfly wings. The shiny waves of hair framing a perfectly oval face were cleverly tinted but cut in an ever so slightly old-fashioned style. She was gently bobbing like a small buoy in the sea of dancers. Then she opened her eyes and noticed I was looking at her. I felt my cheeks and nose fill with blood. I let it happen, thinking I would make things worse by trying to stop the flood. She peeled her mask off.

Her eyes were of a blue that I could qualify as excessive, almost acidic. My opinion of her that had started to veer towards a positive slant changed instantly because of this detail. I felt ill at ease. Her smell, which I hadn't really noticed until then, started to repel me as well. The figure that she composed seemed old-fashioned and straight. But somehow, my gallantry took over once again. I accepted the message of her body language. I started to really dance with her instead of just looking. I squirmed for the length of a few songs with her, twirling her by the hand as called for by the music, keeping eye contact until I felt we had danced enough for me to be able to politely take my leave. Which I did, bowing deeply in a theatrical gesture I thought she would like.

She offered her name, Nicole, as she bade me *"Adieu" wit*h a wave that reminded me of the Queen of England's. Still in control of my revulsion, I took her hand and landed a kiss on it, light as a dragonfly. I did not reveal my own name nor anyone else's. The chemistry was sadly lacking between us. She seemed like one of those women who might have wanted to try her luck with another woman, either to fill the void left by a distracted husband or to prove to herself that she is not—heaven forbid—gay herself.

Either way, I could not offer her whatever she might have wanted. My agenda was full enough as it was with uncertainties, lusting, and confusion. With an apologetic smile, as if I had something more important to attend to, I turned my back to her.

Just then, as if destiny had wanted to throw a wrench in the spinning wheels of my romantic situation, I caught sight of Bourgeon. There she was, dancing a few meters before me, smiling and carefree, surrounded with friends her own age. Her little metal skull just like mine was bobbing along on its chain around her neck in response to her genteel steps. I immediately wanted to join the cheerful clan. However, this time I would be the older woman. And that I could not bear. Hoping that Bourgeon didn't see me, I left the group to their joyful dancing and sauntered back towards the food table, seeking a precarious comfort by caressing my own little metal skull.

Adam was standing there, gazing at all the offerings splayed out on the long table. He didn't see me, occupied as he appeared to be with admiring the elaborate morsels in front of him. I stayed back so that I could scan him properly. Even from my side-view, he seemed to be wrapped in some sort of sacred aura. There he was, peacefully glowing, wrapped in translucent tints, floating on a metaphysical cloud like those pictures of people appearing in a multicoloured sky and emitting rainbow colours corresponding to each of their chakras. He was wearing a royal blue velvet vest over a *velours* bodysuit of the same hue but a shade darker. The titanium white satin of his collar and cuffs and his knee-high white leather boots added a studied contrast to the dark velvet. His androgyny, his other-worldly presence, seemed even more accentuated here than at the office. At the same time, he fit in perfectly with the party's all-gender theme. He brazenly wore no mask.

But what intrigued me the most was his chest. Just like that other person who had offered me a plate of food when I first arrived at the party, Adam also had those pre-pubescent promises of breasts peeking out from the open front of his vest. I couldn't help but lower my gaze. And yes, oh surprise, Adam had a matching little belly. Like a Renaissance Madonna. If I didn't know better, I would have said he was in the beginnings of a first trimester of pregnancy. But unlike the first person I had seen, here there was no male genitalia to be guessed at. Not even a tiny penis inside his snug-fitting tights. No amount of tucking could possibly have offered the smooth crotch I found myself rudely staring at. There was no doubt about it. Adam was unmistakeably a girl. I looked at his hands. Tiny like a girl's. I wondered if Kent had seen Adam yet. If he did, he would be very, very disappointed. Maybe he had seen Adam and ran. Maybe that was why I couldn't find my friend anywhere.

Then a girl dressed all in blue approached Adam. I recognized her as the person he had disappeared with a week and a half previously at our office party on Saint-Denis Street. She wasn't wearing a mask either, but what she was also wearing were a nymphet's breasts. I remember thinking that they seemed to be in fashion at that party. I felt old once again and out of place. *Banal.* And try as I might, I couldn't quite make out what was happening at this blue girl's crotch level, as she was wearing a short and tight leather miniskirt. Besides, I wasn't sure I would have been ready for whatever I might have found even if I had been successful at seeing something, anything, recognizable.

Meanwhile the blue girl had walked into Adam's aura. They ignored me and merged, forming a puff of pink-violet cloud around themselves. I left them to their unmasked bliss. One thing was certain: It would be much easier for "Adam" to communicate with the Naiads once "he" arrived on Genus Island. All "he" would have to do is show up in all his small-breasted glory. "He" would have to be careful about the belly, though, if indeed there was a pregnancy case to deal with. If it had been me, I would have played the parthenogenesis card, the one the Naiads would so much want to believe.

Bourgeon's mother got away with it. At any rate, I wasn't going to get involved. Although the whole situation simply left me utterly confused, I was also curiously neutral about Adam's gender situation. In a way, I was more concerned about the ambiguity of my feelings about Adam staying at Julie's and my homestead. I was mostly hoping he wouldn't find our love letters. The *vidéos* he could watch to his heart content as far as I was concerned. The garden? It was completely out of my hands.

✗ ✗ ✗

Somebody came up close behind me. I turned around. There was Bourgeon, smiling in that half-enigmatic, half-inviting way of hers. Inviting to what? As per our last conversation, she was self-avowedly asexual. I looked at her divinely delicate throat encircled by the chain bearing the articulated skull. My fingers travelled towards the area of my own thymus gland. Yes, my matching skull was still there. Taking this commonality as a good sign, I let her wrap her slender fingers around my right wrist. She led me back into the happy horde of dancers. I must admit, I was just a shade reluctant as I had also been eyeing another one of those shrimp-vulva concoctions. Mesmerized, I followed.

Bourgeon with her spontaneous, almost juvenile grace soon inspired me to dance with abandon. I surprised myself with executing moves that I didn't even know I had in my *répertoire*. In the middle of the second song we had been dancing to, she came closer to me and encircled her frail arms around my sweaty, thick-feeling neck. Unable to resist this invitation for gallantry, I slid my hands around her slender waist. I held on with a sensuous firmness. Gently, not possessively, I drew her closer. She took her mask off. I let mine drop to the floor.

She was wearing a little frog-green, desperately thin silk dress, sumptuous in its simplicity. If she was wearing panties, I couldn't feel any traces of them. In contrast, the silk slip I was wearing suddenly felt thick and coarse. Its colour, milkmaid pink, would also have been uncool.

The heat of her lithe body made my sweaty hands tremble. Her breath, as sylphlike as the rest of her, made me think of moss and other moist, cool forest greenery with just a spicy hint of alcohol. My nostrils got lost in her thick mane, which she wore short with renegade locks that occasionally fell over her sparkling brown eyes. I could feel her nipples almost at the same level as mine, despite the fact that she was shorter than me. There they were, her little nubbins and mine slightly larger, all dancing close to each other, having a grand time until hers seemed to be actually searching for mine. I felt an all-too familiar lance of pain slice through my lower belly.

Utterly distraught, I gently retracted my hands. My arms sadly dangling at my sides, I half-heartedly let the space grow between us. Once the song we had been dancing to was finished, I told her I needed some air. She said she could use some too. After we each grabbed our jackets, she followed me on the swirly metal staircase towards the roof. As we ascended, the entire staircase vibrated with each of our steps like one of those huge Japanese drums, sounding to my paranoid ears like it was foreboding gloom.

Once we arrived on the roof, I was somewhat relieved to notice that we were alone. Nobody would disturb or distract us. From what? I could only hope to be able to behave appropriately towards her.

The freshness of the September night, as well as Bourgeon's sparkly presence, made me shiver. My little elf, for her part, seemed animated by some interior glowing embers that, coupled with her wood-creature's appearance, presented a show all to itself. I stopped to wonder how a person so tiny could exude a puff of energy as vast as the immensity of the canopy over our heads.

As if we had gotten in touch with some supernatural presence, we tilted our suddenly pious gazes in unison towards the few stars that were bright enough to show through the pollution of the city. Overwhelmed, hanging on for dear life so as not to take off into astral journeys, we kept ourselves down-to-earth by starting to identify some of the barely visible classical constellations that we each knew: The Big Dipper, Cassiopeia, Orion's belt. As it often happens in that kind of activity, we could not quite agree on the location of the North Star.

And that's when, as I was still stretching my neck searching for the elusive star, my eyelids scrunched into miniature accordions, she took my hands in hers, still moist and warm from dancing. She brought her face close to mine. She kissed me. Softly. My knees buckled under me. I answered the call of her lips, then of her perfect tongue. We started swaying then, dancing slowly this time, her movements sinking into my very soul. Alone, together under the star-scattered sky.

I have no idea how long we danced like that, entwined. All that I knew—and this by the light of some telepathy that came from the very fact of our proximity, and dare I say, perfect attraction towards each other—is that I had to resist. Yes, despite my desperate hunger and with all the strength of my will, I held back. I stopped the movement of my hands, starved by desire, from travelling all over her excruciatingly inviting body. I could feel my lips, the ones at the juncture of thighs, swelling as well as my little pearl that felt gigantic. From its impervious clamouring, she demanded all my attention without any trace of ambiguity.

I was so intoxicated I completely ignored my telepathic message, and still kissing her, gently drew her loins closer to mine. Our pubis touched, separated only by two thin layers of silk, sharing the same incandescent heat. I almost unperceptively cleaved my thighs so that I could contain her better, to align our energies. That's when she seemed to suddenly wake up from a dream. She pushed me away. Gently but firmly. Horrified, as I was melting with apologies, I heard our voices, which seemed to come from somewhere other than our throats:

"Oh, I'm so sorry," she blurted out, "but ... I felt you were excited ... and I ... before you try to go too far..."

"But ... but Bourgeon, I thought that..."

"I thought I already told you that—"

I interrupted her with a wary gesture. I could simply not bear to hear her tell me again that she had no desire for me nor anyone. I would almost have preferred if she had told me I was not her type. That, at least, I would have understood. It was ignoble and unfair that a person as intelligent, as sensuous, as attractive as she would call herself asexual. I had listened attentively to her story that night we had *poutine* together. Contrary to the counsellors who had told her that her asexuality was due to a certain childhood trauma, I chose to believe her. Or, more correctly, I felt her. Her tiny person reminded me more of an elf or a mermaid from children's stories. Or even as some sort of juvenile angel eternally animated with a mischievous ... but asexual energy. I started shivering more than ever. My teeth were actually rattling.

With difficulty, I said, "*Je suis tellement désolée* ... I am so, so sorry, Bourgeon. You might be free from the claws of desire, but je *ne suis pas faite de bois* ... I am not made of wood." (Although from the sensation in my crotch, I could have sworn to the contrary.)

But already she had flown, as light as the nocturnal breeze that was shaking my whole body like a maple tree in November. I went back down the noisy metal stairs. There she was, dancing with her friends. She threw me a smile, as if nothing had happened. I returned her smile, feeling mine tinted with regret and embarrassment. I turned slightly from her, not enough to appear hostile by completely turning my back but just enough to be able to calm the violent undertow that was still agitating my entire body like a top-loading washing machine. I tried a few dance steps, eyelids lowered.

Just as I was starting to feel calmer, my antennae picked up the strangely familiar warmth of a body that was getting closer behind me. The presence would soon penetrate my bubble. I did not turn around. I could feel a soft silky cloth covering my eyes, then my temples, then being tied behind my head. Someone had blindfolded me.

My first reaction would have been to rip the cloth off and turn around to see who had made such an invasive gesture. But instead, I let my arms dangle by my side. It was just that kind of a party. Everything was fair game. I would cooperate. I would abandon myself. Continuing to dance, swaying to the perfect music, now free of any shyness that an exterior gaze would have caused, like a child thinking you can't see her because she can't see you, I twirled, jumped, shook myself. All this over not more than two square feet of floor, I figured, and without bumping into anybody.

I could still feel the familiar presence near me, almost like a protector. The person came closer until they seemed to merge their energy with mine. They were able to match their moves to mine perfectly with no delays, as if they could anticipate each of the movements I was going to make before I even knew myself. As if moved by telepathy. Then I realized to my great disappointment that I was dancing with a man. The sureness of his movements, a sort of brusqueness all the way to his musky smell was unmistakable. I couldn't understand why I was feeling so strangely relaxed in his presence.

It had been a long time since I had danced with a person of the opposite sex. There had been Stéphane of course. But that was sex, not dancing. This partner seemed somehow to have known, or at least guessed, at my ambivalence. He did not breathe down my neck, nor did he make any attempt to grind his swelled crotch into mine. On the contrary. Except for a few touches, an elbow maybe, or a shoulder that reminded me he was still there, his presence was as non-invasive as the soft air around us.

I could not shake the growing sensation that, somehow, I knew this person intimately. But who could it be? Stéphane maybe? No, it wasn't him. It couldn't be. For one thing, he was decidedly straight. He wouldn't have gotten an invitation to this kind of party. And then the smell was not his. Not at all. Whereas Stéphane was more of a forest, this guy's scent, underneath the musk, reminded me also of something oceanic. Not fishy like women are said to be. It was more like I would imagine a salty old sailor would smell, minus the pipe tobacco. Adam? I hardly knew him. Besides, he had just revealed his feminine nature that night. Kent? Too tall. Allan? Also too tall. Then who on earth? I had completely run out of ideas from my meagre répertoire of men I knew. Of course, all I would have to do was take off my blindfold. But that would have been cheating. I was starting to feel a kind of perverse pleasure in bathing in the ambiguity of a presence both familiar and mysterious. Any trace of caution that might have come up, given that I was dancing with a man, all my apprehensions melted away in the heat of the moment. We danced for hours or minutes, I don't know. I was getting really good at ignoring time, especially when I was enjoying myself. Eventually, the images of possible candidates gradually ceased to present themselves on the blank screen of my memory.

All was well until my moving hands accidentally touched what I assumed to be his midriff. Without thinking, I let my hands slide down from what would have been his ribcage towards his hips. *Quelle surprise!* As my hands gathered at the waist and followed the contours of the body, I was stunned to discover them widening into the girth of healthy, broad hips. My dance partner was molded into the perfect hourglass-shape of a woman! Feeling that he had been discovered, my partner stiffened instantaneously. Then nothing. He must have stepped back. The warmth of the body was suddenly missing from the clutch of my hands. But it was too late. My touch had already recognized the shape of the curves for having travelled them, sometimes slowly, or wet-ly, saltily, in a hot desert or in the pelting rain, sometimes with an imperious but always tender desire, hundreds of times. But never weary.

I tore off my blindfold in a single impatient gesture. The person I had been dancing with in such perfect unison had already turned their back and was pushing their way through the crowd, leaving me with only a few flashes of light to record onto my retina. But I knew who it was. It had to be. But how?

I continued to fix the bright whiteness of the jagged-edged T-shirt appearing and reappearing, further and further away amidst the dancers like a racoon's tail. The sleeves and the neckband had been roughly cut, as if in a hurry and with badly sharpened scissors. The air of the fugitive, the gait, were screaming: generic butch. But an inescapable detail had revealed the person's identity. Inexorably. In the rush of flight, the T-shirt had slipped from the left shoulder. I caught a glimpse of the evidence in a last flash just before it completely got lost from my sight. There it was, floating like a shattered mast in a storm, the jagged missing-tooth-smile of a rotten old pervert, her signature, her medal for bravery: the famous golden yellow scar.

I cried out, "JULIE!!"

Obviously, she was not going to turn around. My long-lost love, my lifetime companion, my *numéro une* of seven blissful years had already disappeared through the wave of dancers who had spontaneously, and in complicity, cleaved, then closed in behind her, much like the Red Sea must have done after Abraham and his clan got away from the Romans. Or was it Moses and the Egyptians?

Furious, I tried to push my way through the happy ocean of bodies who seemed to be turning against me in common accord. Eventually, after much elbowing and swerving, I found myself out on the dark cold street. It had rained, one of those impromptu storms typical of Montréal. The pavement as well as the parked cars sparkled to make any cross-dresser jealous. A small multicoloured group of obviously drunk people were weaving down the street, laughing and talking loudly, almost yelling. Julie had completely vanished.

Enraged and ashamed in some way, I went back into the party. I walked directly to the bar. I ordered a gin and tonic. Julie's favourite. Then another and another. Thanks to some occasional bulimic binges in my careless youth—and I might be able to thank my hybrid vigor for this—I knew my body to be capable of supporting alcohol better than a sailor on leave. I generally did not take advantage of my genetic asset. I rarely got drunk. Especially after I had started hanging out with Julie.

This time I was determined to sink into total oblivion. The first drink had gotten me instantly fuzzy. After that, I hovered on a sort of plateau of intoxication that seemed to stretch into infinity. In that way, any alcohol I consumed past the first drink would have been a waste of time and money. Someone else's money. The drinks as well as the food were free as birds. I flew with it all.

Just as the barman was refusing to serve me yet another drink, Nicole, the housewife I had briefly danced with, slipped in beside me. Peeling me off the counter, she whispered, *"Allons fumer un joint sur le toit."*

"Fumer ... quoi?" said I from a hazy cloud. She was too old for smoking pot.

"T'en veux?" (You want some?)

Two fat resin-stained joints floated in front of my crossed eyes. *Oh yes. I must be seeing double. I am properly drunk. At least I am not blind.*

"Oké!" I hiccupped simply and probably too loud.

Neither my jacket nor the borrowed kimono I had lent David were anywhere in sight. Having anticipated this problem, Nicole handed me a pashmina shawl, or was it cashmere? I wasn't quite sure what it was made of, just that it was green, soft, and smelled like her. Contrary to how I had felt about her and her scent previously, this time the shawl seemed comforting to me. I accepted her offering, and clutching the cloth in my sweaty hands, followed Nicole like a sleepwalker back up the metal stairway spiralling all the way to the sky. I was caught in a strange déjà-vu.

Once we were on the roof, I slumped onto the nearest ledge. She let herself slide gracefully beside me. Neither of us seemed to mind the wetness of the *garnotte* under our bums. My companion gently pried her shawl from my clutches and wrapped my shoulders with it tenderly, like a mother. I felt pitiful. She ignited the joint with a lighter that had a miniature image of a palm-studded beach on it. I could tell this was not her first time. That she smoked, that is. As for any attempts at seduction, I wasn't sure anymore. The sky had cleared again. Fortunately, Nicole did not attempt to identify any of the stars from the infinity above our heads. We just sat and smoked in some pious silence that seemed perfectly suited to the occasion, as if in a ritual.

She did not try to kiss me. This fact surprised me somewhat, but at the same time, I felt relieved. Once our ritual came to its natural conclusion, we got up in unison, our bums damp and dotted with a few pieces of gravel. Laughing, we brushed each other's behinds like two long-time girlfriends. We went back into the hot furnace of dancers. In my advanced state of drunkenness, I felt I was in a medieval representation of Hell in the style of Hieronymus Bosch.

I had always been curious what it would be like to walk into those kinds of pictures and participate in the macabre, bucolic scenes. This time I just felt out of place. One glance at Nicole, as I handed her shawl back, told me she must have shared my uneasiness. The music was too loud, the lights too bright. The sight and the smell of the food made me feel nauseous. I looked for my things. There was my jacket hovering in a corner, dusty. My backpack was nearby. The kimono, however, had vanished. I figured I could always retrieve it the next day. Or if anybody liked it enough to take it, they must have needed it, according to my logic back from my shoplifting days. I might have to buy another one for Josie. While I was at it, I might buy one for myself too. Some other time. All I knew was that I didn't want to waste any more time in the inferno. I had to get out. Without looking back, I ejected myself onto the street, slinging my backpack on one shoulder. Nicole was there at the entrance with my kimono in hand. She must have been watching me for a while for her to know about the details of this accessory, even up to whom I had lent it to. But at the time, lost in my personal drunken vapour, I was totally oblivious to her attentiveness.

A voice coming through my personal fog was speaking to me:

"*Je te dépose quelque part?*"

I was being offered a lift. I realized I could have said any place. Not wanting to go back to Charlotte's just to be alone once again, I searched my empty brain for some exotic alternative. I wanted to take some sort of revenge on Julie, or Bourgeon, or even Sonia. On all of them, whomever they were or might have been. Anything to get me out of my *ennui*, my loneliness. I heard a weak voice murmuring through my own throat:

"*Chez toi.*"

(Your place.)

CHAPTER 16

I had no idea what Nicole's real address might have been. The place where I woke up after the party was, according to her, not hers. She had taken me to an apartment in the Mile End not far from Charlotte's place. Even in my drunken stupor, I had recognized the *quartier*. But not the apartment where I was. Nicole had explained to me, smiling in that already familiar and disarming smile of hers, that she was married to a man. That is why she had accepted her friend's offer of a place for the weekend to "have some space to think." Based on that fact, I figured she would have been typical of many other women of her age and social class.

Nicole's assumed emotional state was not the only thing that was familiar to me in that apartment. Yes, there were the cats, the kind that can make a comfortable home out of anywhere they grace with their presence. But it was more than that. It was the particular smell of the place. That *effluve*—that fragrance at once light and tenacious that was not Nicole's. I couldn't quite place it. Where did I smell it before? All I knew was that the scent had provoked a strong sensation in my guts, a mix of shyness and excitement.

All would be revealed to me later. But at the time, upon arriving at said apartment, I had other, more urgent preoccupations such as trying to save face and show Nicole a good time. Like a good little lesbian. Never mind that I was in an advanced state of intoxication and that Nicole would have been only my second woman lover, ever. Well, on a one-on-one basis anyway, without counting the orgies I had been privy to what seemed like centuries ago. They didn't count, having been anonymous for the most part. This was, I thought, my big chance to show this woman the ropes. A heavy responsibility at the best of times.

I don't quite remember how we got to the place. I have a vague recollection of Nicole gently leading me to her car that was parked a street or two or three away. The fresh air did not sober me up as much as I had hoped. The simple task of putting one foot before the other seemed impossible. I needed her guidance and the support of her firm hold on my elbow. There was just enough lucidity left in my consciousness for me to realize that, despite the super joint we had smoked together, Nicole was coping much better than I. This fact would be a great asset, I concluded, especially since she would be the one driving. I let myself be led to a fire-red Toyota. Nicole gallantly opened the door for me, and I did my best to get in as gracefully as I possibly could. Once seated and eventually buckled in after many failed tries, I closed my eyes. My fuzzy head started spinning. The car took off without a lurch, gently, much as I might have been expecting given what I knew so far about Nicole's temperament.

The trip to the apartment seemed interminable. I remember stopping at a *Dépanneur* or a pharmacy, I'm not sure which, nor did I ever figure out what Nicole needed to get so late at night. I was starting to be afraid that I could not stay awake and alert long enough to step up to my self-assigned role of champion tribadist. I assumed that Nicole was a neophyte as far as lesbianism was concerned. I could easily have been her very first idyll. The feeling of responsibility at this perspective, along with all the alcohol coursing through my veins, weighed on my heart like a stone.

Once in the apartment, Nicole lit a series of soft lamps and candles in a sequence that even in my comatose state I could recognize as discreet. Then she fitted me in the most comfortable soft velvet chair. Two cats padded in. One of them landed immediately in my lap and started purring. Joan Armatrading wafted through the air at a respectable volume, given the lateness of the night.

After a few songs, a steaming cup of mint tea appeared on the coffee-table in front of me, filling my nostrils with hot freshness. I heard in a fuzzy dream:

"Tiens, prends cela. Ça va t'éviter la gueule de bois demain matin." (It will fix your hangover tomorrow.)

Obedient, I took both white pills that Nicole had pressed into my palm. I was just lucid enough to notice that she had put them in my left hand. How could she have known I was left-handed?

I doubt I would have been able to talk to her about the alleged correlation between handedness and sexual preference. I think I did ask her if she was a nurse and maybe she smiled and said no but that she was a mother and that it was the same kind of thing. I do remember that her face looked beautiful, like that of an angel. There she was, looking at me, half-amused, half-concerned, appearing and re-appearing in my intermittent vision like when you are on a carousel and you have to wait to go the whole way around before you see the only person you know. I was trying hard to keep myself from passing out. Then somehow, probably with the help of my invigorating *tisane*, I womanaged to rise up from my chair. The cat that was on my lap fell to the floor with an embarrassingly loud thud. I must have forgotten it was there and had gotten up too suddenly.

From my new vantage point, Nicole's lips were a mere ten centimeters away. Carefully, so as not to topple over, I leaned towards her and planted as soft a kiss on them as I could come up with. She responded, but very faintly. I failed to feel her. Alarmed, I took her face in my hands and pushed a thick, hot tongue into her mouth. It was too much. She recoiled like a salt-sprinkled slug.

"*Laisse-moi faire.*" She was taking over. I let her.

I would like to say that we had an incomparable night of loving. However, I am not so sure we did. Some intermittent out of focus images do come back to me, such as my attempts at classic moves with me on top. What I remember the most is our hysterical peals of laughter, probably because we could not quite match our apparatus. There was also the shimmering of her magnificent silky hair and how it somehow seemed instrumental in my feeling of being thrown in the air like an inflatable doll. There were other things too, other moves, other attempts. There must have been. I forget. They all left me with impressions more than actual memories.

All that I do know is that whatever happened on that night, it went on until dawn. Thanks to the pills—probably aspirin—I felt no headache at all come morning. There was no remorse, either, in my heart. Actually, based on our shared playful mood and a certain aura of complicity that seemed to pervade us, I concluded we must have had a good time. Of a common accord, we went out for breakfast at a popular local joint. We were ravenous. Another good sign. Despite the fact that I had thought we were both vegetarians—give or take the odd fish or two—we devoured our three eggs each, bacon, and home fries like lumberjacks. Maybe we were just relieved to have come out of our clandestine affair relatively unscathed.

In any case, I felt no shame. There was almost no remorse at all in my heart for having cheated on everyone I was interested in. I also ignored the pangs of guilt about having ingested three crisp strips of pork. But still, despite my resolve to see our night as something that just had to happen and that it was good, I did not feel confident enough to give her my real name. I was quite sure that I had womanaged to keep my identity secret throughout our entire wild night. Nicole didn't give me her coordinates either. I didn't quite know what to do with this blatant omission on our part, just that it must probably have been the best strategy for both of us. I could only imagine Nicole later, writing in her journal on the following night, telling her own version of her forays, lyricizing it all into a Sapphic initiation. On my part, I felt a perverse pleasure in knowing I had taken revenge on Julie. This was, I admit, not very charitable on my part. But it was true.

In our haste to go out for breakfast, I didn't really take notice of the address of our borrowed apartment. All I knew is that the area and the street were familiar for being near Charlotte's. I could easily orient myself. If I had taken note of the address of the apartment where Nicole and I had just had our night of love, I would have been a whole lot less self-assured.

✮ ✮ ✮

September 27, 2001. *Bon.* This was my situation, two days after the party: My girlfriend who was probably actually my ex was behaving like a male and didn't want to talk to me; then the only female friend I could have confided in, Charlotte, had been gone for the longest time with a cross-dresser only to come back with a broken heart; also my best gay friend Kent was too busy with his own affairs, plus I was in lust with a girl too young for me who called herself asexual; and then I kept meeting another one, a welfare worker who seemed to only want to play (that is if she was even interested at all); and to top it all off, I had just spent a night with a woman who was old enough to be my mother ... not to mention I had eaten pig. I had put myself into a real mess.

According to my habit when faced with a complicated situation, I took refuge in my spirituality. Forgiveness, especially for myself, would be the only viable alternative. This strategy would work best, I decided, if I took a few days off. I would fast. I would stay away from parties and other distractions, from work, even from books. I would meditate all day as if I were in an ashram.

It was a good idea. My resolve didn't last long. A mere day, actually. All that I could womanage after that was to abstain from junk food and take a few more days off work. I used up my free time cleaning Charlotte's apartment and sorting through my meagre belongings in anticipation for my imminent stay at Sonia's.

Julie and whatever had happened to her was also on my mind. A lot. My attempts at meditation had only worsened my wondering about her. It was like that story where the guru says that in order to achieve peace of mind one cannot think of monkeys. Then, of course, one can only think of monkeys. They hang from the trees. They invade your inner eyeballs. They cackle in your ears and tickle your hair follicles. Hundreds, thousands of them. I decided to talk to the only person who could help me get rid of my monkeys and shed a light on my mystery. He would be my last chance at solving the riddle. I absolutely had to contact Julie's brother Allan. Again. This time I had to play my cards right. There had to be bait. I called him at work. He was in.

"Hi, Allan! How are you?"

"Good, good. How can I help you?"

"..."

His question rendered me speechless. Instead of interpreting it as a simple willingness on Allan's part to practice *seva*, or selfless service, I felt irritated. I felt I had been put in the category of the needy, the ones who can't keep their own lives together. Complete honesty (getting to the point) would be the best strategy in my diminished state. Taking a huge breath, I jumped in.

"*Euh* ... You're my girlfriend's brother. I hardly know you. But Julie is in Montréal. That, I know. It's about all that I know, actually. And that she won't talk to me. I have no idea why. She has often talked about you while

259

we were on Genus. She called you her best friend. Surely she must have contacted you?"

"..."

Why was he silent? Did Julie already make him promise not to tell me anything? I had better jump in and make him an offer he couldn't refuse.

"Okay. Here's the deal. I know Julie enough to be sure she has talked to you at least once. As for me, I have no idea if we are still together or not. It's not fair. The only way to make it fair is for one of you to tell me what's going on. Since she refuses to talk to me, you're my only chance. I want to make a deal with you."

"Go on. I am intrigued." I could hear him smile. Guardedly.

"I can arrange a date for you with a very charming, smart, and interesting guy. He's a long-time friend of mine. His name is Kent. I know you two will get along like a house on fire. In exchange, you let me know if, according to Julie, she and I are still together."

"Well..."

"Is she just taking a break or...? That's all I want to know. Honest. It's only fair, isn't it?"

I was beginning to sound frantic. I took a deep breath. *No whining,* I reminded myself. I might still have a modicum of a chance.

"It's an unusual proposition you're offering me."

"It's a simple deal. I'm aware that this offer of a date for you with my friend has nothing to do with my relationship with Julie. But it's all I can come up with. I just need to know. And believe me, you will not be disappointed with your date. I am not asking you to give out any secrets that Julie may have confided in you. All I need to know is if we are together or not. Simple. Maybe you can persuade her to contact me or leave me a note or something. Anything. Just so that I know where we stand."

"Let me think about it..."

My heart was beating hard. Holding my breath, I gave him space. I had spoken. The ball was in his court. A full electrified minute must have gone by before he answered.

"Okay. Deal."

"Oh, thank you!! I will contact my friend and arrange a meeting. How about if we make it informal? Let's go for lunch somewhere!"

"Sounds good. How about that smoked meat place on Saint-Laurent?"

Whew. I had him. I'd have to revoke my aversion to meat, but who cared? Maybe I was destined to become a carnivore once again. The way my life was unfolding, nothing would surprise me.

"Smoked meat it is! Thanks, Allan. You're great. I'll talk to Kent, and I'll call you. Soon."

"Bye, Claire!"

Now all that remained was for me to convince my friend Kent. I pronounced my retreat over and flew out of the apartment, grabbed a couple of bagels at the bakery, and munching all the way, half-ran, half-panted to work. I got there in record time but with a sore stomach. I made my way to the coffee fountain with the intention of drowning my bagels with extra liquid and maybe aid a faulty digestion. Luckily, Kent was at the drinking trough. He was quite alone. This was my perfect opportunity to jump right into the business at hand.

"Hi, Kent! Guess what!? I know this really swell guy. He's a long-time friend of mine. Just like you." I lied about my relationship with Allan but it took what it took. "This may sound off the wall and forward on my part, but I was just talking with him, and ... and I had this thought. I think you have a lot in common. It would be a waste if you two never got to meet." All this was said at a mile a minute, my eyes popping out like some kind of a maniac's.

Kent just looked at me like I had landed from another planet. Trying to calm down, I continued. "I know this is out of the blue. It's just that you're great; he's great... I like you both. And you'd really like each other. I'm sure."

"Out of the blue for sure..." He was smiling. A good sign. "But why? And why now?"

"Oh, just because ... never mind why! What do you say? I've talked to him about you, and he says he's interested!" I repressed an urge to be jumping up and down for emphasis.

"You what!?"

"A person has to start somewhere. How about we have lunch? The three of us. Like friends. Nothing fancy. No commitment. Just friends having a good time."

"Looks like you already have it figured out?" Still smiling. Still good.

"Well, actually I don't. It's just that I thought—"

"You got me curious about this guy. By the way, what's his name?"

"Allan. His name is Allan. He's a broker. But he's very nice. He's also a fine artist..."

Should I divulge that he also happens to be my girlfriend's brother? Probably not. Kent might get suspicious. Better to stay on the safe side.

"So, what do you say? If you're interested, let's do it soon. How does today sound?"

"Wow. You're eager. What's in it for you?"

"Oh," I lied, "just getting two fine young gentlemen such as yourselves to meet."

If Kent suspected that I had a stake in the affair, he didn't let on.

"Okay. I'm in. Why not!? I must say, you got me curious."

Jubilant, I called Allan back right away. As it turned out, he was free for us three to have a date on that same day. We were to meet at one thirty in front of the most popular smoked meat place on Saint-Laurent. I had a few hours to get over my aversion to meat. The bacon with Nicole had been a dream. This thing here was real. The stakes were high for me, but I was determined to make the best of the opportunity I had arranged for myself. At least I had no chance of being seen by someone like Bourgeon at this temple to the king of beef.

Kent had a meeting at another office that morning, so I started out towards the restaurant alone. I took my time. Once I got there, I was no longer on my own. A long line of jolly people was snaking along on the sidewalk, waiting to get in. Their various accents from Paris, southern France, England, Australia, and other places on the planet that I did not recognize clued me in on the fact that this particular establishment must have been featured in many tourist guides. The patrons might all have been inspired by the good late-September weather—our famous "Indian summer." Kent and Allan were nowhere in sight. Maybe they had both gotten cold feet. And then they both arrived at the same time. We all laughed at this serendipity. It got our meeting off to an auspicious start.

Kent and Allan didn't seem to mind the fact that we were in for a long wait. They jumped on the opportunity of having extra time to get to know each other, right there in the lineup. They seemed just as delighted with each other as I had led them to believe. I was proud of myself. Until I remembered why I had orchestrated this meeting. The two men seemed completely oblivious to my presence. I figured it was best I let them get acquainted for the time being. I would have to put my own questions about Julie on the back burner.

Once we were seated and our orders given, I tried, with the patience of a spider and the determination of couch-grass, to introduce my own subject of concern into the conversation. Every now and then, whenever there was a rare break in the chatter, I would make a seemingly inoffensive general comment such as one on the subject of gays' and lesbians' faithfulness in relationships. Then I would graduate to asking my friends what they thought the difference was between transsexuals, transgendered, and cross-dressers. They looked at me briefly with disbelieving eyes, meaning, perhaps, *"If you don't know, we're not going to be the ones telling you. This is too embarrassing."*

All my comments had to be inserted while they were gulping their toasted rye bread stuffed with obscenely purple-pink slices of dead cows and mouthfuls of coleslaw. All their replies to me were brief, as if they wanted to get them out of the way so that they could return to their real interest, which was, of course, themselves and each other. And their food.

Having returned to my vegetarian commitment, I had omitted the meat from my own meal. Also, in accordance with a spirit of vegetarianism, I refrained from making any comments about the appearance of my pickled gherkin, the dimensions of which, I had noticed, was much inferior to that of my two male friends. They, on the other hand, seemed completely oblivious to this flagrant example of sexism that had put them at an advantage. Especially since they also had huge piles of smoked meat at their disposal and I did not have any. There they were, devouring their own phallic symbols with an enthusiasm augmented by their privilege, a given sense of propriety. I could have left them then and there to share their feast without me, and it wouldn't have made any difference. The pervading smell of dead flesh got even worse. I knew I only had a few minutes left before I would start heaving.

Luckily, this is when Kent got up to go to the toilet. As soon as he was out of sight and without letting me utter a single word, Allan finally spoke to me. He started by thanking me for having introduced him to such an interesting person as Kent was. Then he droned on and on, describing at length my friend's most charming attributes and how impressed he himself had been. I could hardly contain my impatience. Finally, as Kent was already coming back from the latrines, Allan acknowledged that it was time for him to hold up his end of the deal. He swiftly leaned towards me. His gaze intense, he whispered quickly and in a single sentence:

"His name is Julian, *Julien* in French; yes, he's a man now; he doesn't want to see you nor for me to talk about him to you in any way, so this conversation between us didn't happen; do you understand?"

Conversation? What conversation? He didn't even wait for my reaction. Turning a radiantly smiling face towards Kent, Allan said no more to me. My heart and throat tightened. A crowd of questions immediately spilled into my brain. I couldn't stop any of them, so I let them flow, bewildered. Then, once all possible questions had gone through my being like an invading army, an emptiness pervaded except for a long trail of tracks in the mud lining my soul.

We were about to be ushered out of the café, since the boys had finished eating. Nobody seemed to care that most of my own plate of toast, coleslaw and small gherkin lay virtually untouched. Stunned into a comatose trance, I didn't even notice that the two new acquaintances must have paid my bill. I followed them out into the street like a ghost. They both kissed me on both cheeks and turned their back in tandem, their steps already synchronized. Two peas in a pod. Seeing them like that made my own loneliness slice through my guts with searing pain. I stood on the sidewalk, alone in the crowd closing in on me for what must have been a long, long time. More confused, angry, hurt, and numb than I had ever been my entire life except for when my mother had died.

My new secret had killed everything I knew, everything I cared for, all the way down to my will to live. This time there wouldn't even be my friends from Egg House to distract me from the agonizing pain of loss. I had no idea where I should go or what to do. All I knew is that I couldn't go back to work and lock myself in. Besides, it was a beautiful day. *How dare it be so sunny?* I remember thinking. I started to wander. I ended up, dazed, in front of the public baths. Mechanically, I consulted the notice board where I had left a message for Julie. The thought of her as Julie, my woman, my love of seven years, brought an avalanche of tears to my eyes. Hoping against hope. Since my message had disappeared a few weeks previously though, I thought I might still have a glimmer of a chance that it had been Julie—oh damn, Julien—who had intercepted it and that I would find a reply.

I pretended to be surprised that there was no note for me, blinking through my tears. Then, oh horror, I found myself hoping that Bourgeon would magically appear like the pixie that she really was. As if she would have caught a telepathic message from me. Was it going to be that easy to let go of Julie? Just move on? I was well aware that Bourgeon could never be a replacement for my lost girlfriend. But friendship would have been what I really needed. Youth, freshness, and a carefree attitude would be most welcome. I didn't even feel the need to talk about Julien to my new potential friend. It was as if Julie had never existed.

Maybe Julie never did really exist. Maybe that's how this Julien, this stranger, had always felt too. The peeing while standing, Julie's dislike of her own femininity, it all made sense then in a bizarre kind of way. Julien could just wander around, I thought, with his new, "liberated" giant clitoris and a set of fake hairy balls flopping between his thighs for all I cared. After all, half the world's population walks around like that. What difference would one more person make?

After all those months, weeks, days, and agonizing minutes spent in uncertainty, I realized my new information had finally left me curiously indifferent. Numb. It was suddenly that easy. Julie was as good as dead to me. I had, in all that time of wondering, gone through all the stages of mourning. I could finally move on with my life. As I reached for my sleeve to wipe my nose, I noticed my tears had already dried.

✯　✯　✯

The next day, a glorious Friday September 28th around 6:00 p.m., I left work with a slip of paper in my hand. It had Sonia's address on it. I already guessed from her scent-trail that she lived in the same *quartier* as Charlotte. But nothing could have prepared me for the shock that was to come. First of all, the building corresponding to the address on my small piece of paper was strangely familiar. Three stories, it was just one of the hundreds of buildings, all similar, that lined up in a row on Esplanade Street near the *Collège Français*. Nothing remarkable in itself, really, except for an extra dose of familiarity, a nagging sensation of *déjà-vu* more profound than what my simple wanderings throughout the area might have caused. True, this street was also on my favourite itinerary to downtown. But there was something else. I knew the building itself. Somehow, I had the feeling I actually knew it intimately. But how? Perplexed, I climbed the stairs to the second floor and turned the old-fashioned bell handle.

Sonia opened the door, smiling, so beautiful, *si radieuse*. She invited me in. And that is when, no further than in her entrance hall, I understood where my feeling of familiarity had come from. My heart shrank by a few sizes. I had to grasp the doorknob with two hands, three if I had had that many, to prevent myself from running out of there like a banshee. I recognized the apartment. The same filtered light, the cats, and of course, Sonia's scent. I had not, could not have, placed the smell that other night because I was not expecting it. And I was filthy drunk and stoned out of my skull. And now the delicious whiff was filling my nostrils, implacable and enchanting.

This apartment was—Oh horror! —the same one I had just spent a sleepless night in with Nicole a mere few days previously.

Cold sweat drained out of my armpits into the palms of my hands and through the soles of my feet. It kept on coming, pouring out of me in torrents for the entire forty-four minutes—according to the giant clock in the living-room—of delicious torture verging on ecstasy, like the best of orgasms, that I spent in the company of this incomparable angel-goddess. If she noticed my *malaise,* she didn't let on. She stayed cool throughout like a blade of grass in springtime. Maybe she thought my torment was simply caused by the Pavlovian effect she had on me. In that, she was right, but *"Oh yes, Sonia, there was so much more!"* Sonia's discretion was making the situation, awkward enough for me as it was, worse by a thousand-fold.

Sonia invited me to sit in her comfortable velvet chaise, the same one that I had hovered on, drunk and stoned out of my mind three days previously. I could almost still smell myself there. Hopefully Nicole would have opened the windows of the apartment after our famous night. She must have. I sniffed around as discreetly as I could. This time, only my gentle hostess' sublime scent could be detected floating around, wrapping us in its delicate shroud.

We talked about the apartment of course, but also of this and that as one would expect in a quite ordinary scene. For my part, I was dense with confusion. I was vacillating between talking to her as if I would with a potential friend using the familiar *tu* or of keeping our conversation on a professional level as in a welfare worker and client interaction with *vous.* I ended up talking with the semblance of a computer-generated voice. That way I could also avoid the tell-tale pronouns whenever I could. Meanwhile, my brain was spinning on a completely different track. That of sheer panic.

Sometimes I felt obligated to reveal my idyll with Nicole. Then I would think better of it. I had no idea if Nicole had told Sonia the tale of our strange night together. Really, there didn't seem to have been a reason for her to have done this. Our night had probably been nothing to brag about, but it might not have been bad enough to warrant a confession of sorts. Also, Nicole could not have known that her friend Sonia knew me. I felt I could safely assume that either the story had not been told or at least that my identity would be protected. After all, I was quite sure I did not reveal my true name on that wild night of debauchery. I could therefore, theoretically, be free to embrace Sonia in my barely hesitant arms. I could disclose my unabashed attraction towards her. I could take her there, and there, on her thick Chinese embossed rug, and on her sofa, in the kitchen, under a mass of bubbles in her claw-footed bathtub, and in a myriad of other equally creative places.

I wanted to get down on my knees in front of her and tell her she was the only one in the whole world whom I really craved. And if she ever did find out about my single night of trespassing, I would be ready to lie to her—me who only lies to the government, specifically to welfare—by saying that it was Nicole who had seduced me, that I never desired her, that I was sorry, that... that ... that...

I never uttered any of these things. During all this time, as I was utterly impotent in stopping the words that were escaping from my mouth in answer to her questions, Sonia was skillfully extricating all kinds of information about my private life. Applying her professional listening skills to perfection, she followed my diarrhea of words with patient attentiveness as I witnessed the emergence of a person—the real me—who was totally different from the image I was trying to project: sophisticated, worldly, and successful. This other person, namely me, unable to stop the flow of her words, bared her very essence like Niagara Falls. And the four-country-wide Iguaçu falls. Hypnotized, I could hear my voice telling all sorts of details about my whole life from its sad beginnings up to that moment. There were just a few pertinent omissions. Those would have to have been about my relationships.

It was only with an incredible force of will that I was able to save myself, but barely, from spilling the beans about my tryst with Nicole. I talked about my childhood, my mother, my non-existent father, then Genus Island, the

Naiads, even Ralph the wonder-pig and Sam the cat. The garden, of course, and how I strived for simplicity, a light carbon imprint, and how all of it had not been enough to save our planet. To my great astonishment, Sonia seemed surprisingly aware of the existence of Genus Island and the women's commune on it. Immersed as I was in the quagmire of my own stories, I forgot to ask her how she knew about them. I brought up a few names, Calypso, Diane... There I drew a blank. She must have known about the commune only from hearsay and not actually from having been there, I concluded.

Still in a trance, emboldened by the fact that we had, in a way, my island in common, I threw into the pile of names some of my Montréal friends and acquaintances, most of whom I yet had to catch up with: Charlotte, Rémi, Kent, Allan. I even divulged the little I knew about Josie. Anything, anybody, just to make me look more sociable than I actually was. By some amazing *tour de force,* I womanaged to minimize my relationship with my ex-girlfriend. And most importantly, I completely omitted the part of her metamorphosis from woman to man. Bourgeon escaped any mention as well. Barely. A faint voice of intuition whispered to me that it would be better not to bring in any love-interests, be they real or imagined, from the past, present, or future. I obeyed.

As much as I was not quite ready to come out to Sonia, and consequently to disclose that I would have been the ideal candidate to fall irremediably in love with her, I also wanted to appear free to her eyes just in case I might kindle her interest in me. Incidentally, I also covered my past sexual relationships with men with an opaque veil. Even the ones I had thought I had loved well. My brief marriage with George suffered the worst from this omission. It was as if he had never existed at all. Rémi and Stéphane appeared as mere friends.

Nothing in Sonia's apartment nor in her demeanour gave me any clues as to her interest, or lack of, in lesbian relationships in general or in me in particular. At least I suspected her to be pro-women with her books and her music collection, which I was able to scan hastily during the few gaps in our conversation. Any signs of lesbianism, be they books, music, DVDs, or even toys, she would have hidden somewhere else. Her bedroom maybe. If she even had them at all. As much as I was burning to go into her room to find out, I had to restrain myself. There would be plenty of time for going through with a fine-toothed comb once I had the run of the place.

In the meantime, I had to accept her coquettish, flirting attitude as possibly a simple generic attitude with her and not to interpret it as necessarily being proof of a personal interest in me. Coming from anybody other than Sonia, her demeanour would have completely deflated my ardour towards her. I am not a great fan of flirting. A direct approach, honesty, has always gotten my support. But in Sonia, the very attributes I would normally run away from seemed as naturally seductive as the pulse of the little blue vein on her exquisitely slender neck. I had to hold myself back, by gripping the arms of my chair with all ten fingers, to prevent myself from biting her.

As if she were willing to give me a few seconds of reprieve from the delicious torture of her presence, Sonia excused herself and disappeared into the kitchen. She came back with a steaming pot of tea. The odour, calming in a vaguely medicinal kind of way, instantly brought me back to my night with Nicole. Did Sonia only have a single kind of tea or did I inspire women to try and cure an at once mysterious and obvious affliction in me? I don't think I was stupid enough to ask my question out loud.

Meanwhile, the cats had made themselves comfortable on our respective laps. The neutered male on me, the female—possibly spayed too—on the sofa with her. They were called Farinelli and Sappho. The first one, according to Sonia, was named after the famous Italian castrato from the eighteenth century.

"This Farinelli," she said, pointing to the purring mass of black hair curled up on my lap, "never did sing, either before his operation or after." She smiled softly. "But he didn't meow either. Still doesn't. He kind of found his own voice, which is like a short grunt, if you're lucky. He only does it if he really likes you."

Much like Sonia's possible sexual orientation, the situation of the female cat was left unclear. All I knew was that she was named after a Greek poetess, famous for her avowed lesbianism. So, there might have been a glimmer of hope for me right there.

Meanwhile, I was sipping my medicinal tea, trying to let myself nestle as nonchalantly as I could in the soft chair, the most comfortable one in the world. The only problem was that said chair was shamefully reminding me of my tryst with Nicole, and my infidelity vis-à-vis beautiful, exquisite, love-of-my-life Sonia, a few days before. Driven by some perverse desire tinted with masochism, I found myself trying to stretch my visit as far as I could, ignoring my other instinct to fly out of there and put an abrupt end to my torment. I tried to encourage Sonia to talk about herself. It was obvious she would remain a discreet mystery to me. Our conversation slowly and naturally came to a pause. To an innocent bystander, we may have offered the image of serenity as might happen between two friends having afternoon tea. However, the same innocent bystander would have totally missed the low-level tremor sputtering in me like an old-fashioned generator running out of gas.

Finally, as all things good or bad come to an end, Sonia gently pried me away from my attempts at presenting a prematurely domestic scene.

"*Alors, l'affaire est conclue.* So, it's a done deal," she declared.

Before I even had time to remember what the deal was, she handed me a few pages, hand-written with round, carefully formed letters.

"Here are some instructions about the apartment. Nothing fancy or unusual, but you might find them useful. I left you a local phone number of a friend of mine, in case you need anything else," she articulated in her lilting French. Farinelli looked up at me and made a strange squawking sound. Sonia looked at him tenderly, dragging some of her look up to me as she said, with an added smile, "He seems to like you. It's as if he recognizes you somehow."

I had scored a point. I also felt extremely lucky that my previous meeting with the cat would remain our little secret. Sonia continued, unaware of the uncomfortable scene we had just avoided. "Oh, and my friend is going to drive me to the airport on October first. We will meet for lunch before she takes me. Why don't you come for lunch too, and you'll get to meet her, and I give you the keys then?"

Lunch with Sonia. Wow. But who was this friend of hers? Could it be Nicole? Surely, she must have more than one friend ... but Nicole was the very same friend who had stayed at Sonia's apartment that famous time I spent the night with her. I bet she was the one. I could simply check the name on the papers Sonia still had in her hands. But I was too scared. If it was Nicole, I might not be able to hide my reaction. There was no way I was going to take that chance. I would just have to miss lunch. *But how? By telling Sonia I don't eat lunch? Or that I don't eat at all?*

While I was looking for a way out of this precarious situation, Sonia was smiling at me with a benevolently soft gaze as one would look at a stray dog missing a leg. Mortified, I blurted out, "I think I'll ... *c'est-à-dire que...* It's just that I won't be able to do lunch with you on October first."

There. I've said it. Now what?

Sonia seemed a bit taken aback. She sighed. Just a little sigh, nothing deep or too annoyed. Still, I felt like I'd hurt her feelings.

"*Oké d'abord.* I will leave the keys in an envelope in the mailbox then."

I felt as relieved as I felt stupid. We had possibly just evaded a very awkward lunch. But what was the most difficult thing for me was to hide my disappointment at missing an opportunity of seeing Sonia again in a friend-like context, even if I would have had to share her with Nicole or anyone else. I knew I did not have much of a choice. Sonia seemed to already have invested her trust in me. Missing lunch would be the price to pay for not betraying that trust. If she only knew! But maybe she wouldn't care that her friend and I had a roll in the hay? Once. And I was too drunk and stoned to remember anything. I did not know Sonia enough (Yet?) to take the chance of telling her (What?) and facing the consequences.

By some unexpected miracle, I was able to shake my misgivings away with a simple shrug of my shoulders. I gave Sonia my best smile. She smiled back. We didn't shake hands. This came as a relief as it kept our interaction on a friendly level instead of being business-like. A kiss would have been quite welcome though. Even if it had been planted instead of on the lips, on each other's cheeks. Twice, French-style. But no kisses of any kind happened.

Only once Sonia's door closed behind me did I wonder, once again, if Nicole might have talked about me. But I hadn't given her my name, or at least I was quite sure I had not. Or did I? An annoying uncertainty started chewing at my heart. And then, catching me at that moment of weakness, Julie(n) drifted back into my consciousness. Drat!

We had to talk. I knew that. How or when, I had no clue. All I did know was that our relationship would not be completely over until we came to some sort of agreement. A closure. She (yes, "she" … the old Julie) owed me, for the sake of those seven years. Then and only then, after our coming to terms, maybe our last meeting ever, could I lose her to the clan of the opposite sex.

I had been more right than I even realized, a few months before, when I thought that (s)he would not hesitate to undergo surgery to make a change for herself. At the time, I was thinking maybe a nose job. But from that to having her breasts removed and maybe a penis sewn on … to getting a beard growing … all that made me very, very uncomfortable. I knew I was being unfair, unkind, and selfish. But no amount of guilt or self-sermon could chase my *malaise* away.

✫   ✫   ✫

Still in shock from my meeting with Sonia, and for lack of having anything else to do, feeling restless, I walked back to Charlotte's apartment to pack my bags. It was quite premature, especially since I only had very few possessions. I was simply hoping that doing something mindless would shake the sadness and confusion gnawing at my heart like a rapacious monster. With tears softly running from my puffy eyes, I stuffed my clothes and few personal items in my backpack, the same I had arrived with in Montréal a mere three months previously. As I licked the salt off my lips, I congratulated myself on my own frugality for having resisted the call to indulge in shopping. I would miss having access to Charlotte's wardrobe though. After I had hand-washed all of her clothes that I had worn, I reluctantly put them back in her closet, hoping she wouldn't notice I had borrowed them.

The next three days were spent with me living out of my famous bag as if I were a transient. I valiantly put myself to the task of cleaning Charlotte's apartment. Eventually it shone as if a swarm of fairy-tale good witches had gone through. The fridge proudly boasted a six-pack of imported beers, and even, as a sort of proletarian manifesto, a few of my kind of brew too. With any traces of decaying vegetables erased, the crisper compartment was ready for the new mascots Charlotte was unfailingly bound to re-introduce.

All dry goods were tidily put away in hermetically sealed tins and jars to the great despair, I was sure, of the cockroaches. Not a speck of dust hung on, not even behind the bed or under the table, not even under the claw-footed bathtub. A new tube of toothpaste, not my favourite brand but apparently that of the Josie/Charlotte tandem, rested on the rim of the bathroom sink. Even the hardwood floor, creaking and sagging in its middle from a century of use, shone like the inside of some weird golden tunnel with the kitchen and its houseplants, its comfortable chair, and yes, the promise of wonderful meals as a reward at its end. After I was done, I did not dare touch anything for fear of soiling the miracle I had just created. There was nothing left to report in my notebook. A chapter of my life had just closed. All that remained was the wait, the long silent anticipation until a new door would open.

272

On the night of September 30, 2001, the day before Sonia's departure and Charlotte's supposed arrival, I declared myself officially homeless. I could maybe have invited myself to Kent's. But something, maybe a misplaced pride, prevented me from asking him for shelter even for a single night. Maybe he had a guest for all I knew. I could not face the possibility of the humiliation of being bumped for a lover of his. So that is how, according to my travel theme, I donned my backpack and took the bus from Park Avenue all the way down to the bottom of the hill and descended into the bowels of the *Métro*.

My plan had been to settle myself on one of the long wooden benches of *la Gare Centrale*. I could imagine I was in heaven. Any departure towards an exciting destination, any family reunion, any kisses between lovers or friends would take on a festive air. And I would be witness to it all. In a way by my mere presence, my proximity, I would belong—albeit for a fleeting few minutes—to a community of travellers. We would all be equal.

Unfortunately, I was informed around eleven-thirty that the *Gare* would be closed for the night for security reasons. I was left to spend the rest of my sleepless night wandering the streets.

Tired, sad and sore, I ventured into an all-night dive. That's where I finally had the courage to take out the set of hand-written instructions Sonia had given me. She was right. There was nothing special to them at first glance. There were notes mostly about the cats and the plants, with a special mention not to let any water touch the leaves of her African Violets as it would kill them almost instantly. My knowledge about houseplants was quite limited but even I had heard about the "no watering the AVs' leaves" rule. I was thus quite confident I would be a good caretaker. Sonia's handwriting—a fragment of her soul, really—was dainty and at once playful and tidy, just like her, and floated before my sleep-deprived eyes. I longed for her. Desperately. Now I would have to wait two long months. My mind wandered into a Never-Neverland of her and me getting to know each other, the food we would eat, and the conversations we would have...

And then, written in a hastier hand (like an afterthought), came the post scriptum:

If you need anything that is not on this note, feel free to call my friend Nicole at (a phone number I no longer recall).

Nicole?! Could this have been the same one I had gotten to know in a biblical sense? Chances would be yes. After all, it was a Nicole who took me to Sonia's apartment that famous night. One who knew the place. *Unless she used a fake name at the time...*

Who was I kidding? She was obviously the honest type. I could only hope there would be no need to call her. I was relieved that at least I'd had the presence of mind to skip lunch with the two of them.

✮ ✮ ✮

As the pale light of October first started to assault my puffy eyes, with my breath rancid, my backpack curiously heavy on my tired shoulders but still insisting on the travel theme, I dragged my carcass back to the toilets at the *Gare Centrale*. The water I splashed on my face, sticky with dust, smelled saturated with chlorine and the usual concoction of suspect chemicals. Still trying to be ecological, I dried myself as best as I could on the sleeve of my sweater.

I found a public telephone and called work, explaining that I was going to take an extra day off to move. It was still early. I was hoping to be able to simply leave a message without having to talk to a human. No such luck. Our receptionist answered in that sexy-almost-slutty-but-just-professional-enough voice of hers. Maybe she had been requested to show up at work early, anticipating an important call from overseas. Her voice showed a marked disappointment at recognizing mine. As she seemed to have better things to do than to listen to my message, let alone to pass it on to Helga, it was doubtful that my immediate boss would ever hear what I was up to that morning. *Oh well, what's a few hours here or there,* I thought. We made up our own hours anyway. As long as the work was done by the end of the month, everyone was happy.

A coffee kiosk was just opening its wrought-iron gates. I splurged in a super-octane brew and a croissant that was, according to a proud notice board, made with real butter. While I was waiting for the caffeine to kick in, I observed the few people milling about at this early hour. Everyone, from the last of the cleaners to the first commuters, seemed tired, closed, and rushed. I was no longer in paradise. At best, I was in a kind of purgatory, an eternal limbo of waiting. And then the caffeine kicked in. I felt swept up, in tune with all the rush around me. My backpack, miraculously light, seemed to float on my shoulders, lifting me up like angel wings. Maybe I had landed in some kind of new paradise after all. One with the urgency of an urban mission.

It was still too early to show up at Sonia's. They hadn't even had their famous lunch yet. I flew towards the Mont-Royal. After climbing all one hundred twenty-nine (or so) steps to the *chalet* at the top, I went in and crossed the great cool hall. Each one of my steps, despite my efforts to pass unnoticed, echoed all the way past the dark rafters up into the frescoes painted on the ceiling like some local Christian and Aboriginal version of the Sistine Chapel. Somewhat overwhelmed, I descended towards the toilets.

The odour in the washrooms hadn't changed since my most tender childhood. It brought me back to grade school, complete with the nuns warning us against the unmentionable dangers we risked in such public places. Yes, there were the lesbians of course, waiting to lure you into one of the cabinets to kiss you and make you engage in unnatural acts. But worse even than them, there were the *"maniaques."* This word would translate as "maniacs," but really, these men were so, so much viler. They would be lurking in corners, bushes, and yes, especially in public washrooms, always hungry, just waiting to pounce on you, and like vampires, contaminating your virgin soul and turning you into awful monsters just like them.

There were many of these *maniaques* all over the city, from the crumbling demolition sites of Verdun to the goosefoot-invaded desolate pastures on the Mont-Royal, through the deserted downtown alleys and just around the corner in the bowels of the Métro. Their number was so great that, if you were to round them up, they would make up a whole army. But in their natural state, they were solitary beings, these predators, like wolves exiled from their clan. Sometimes—we were warned—there might be one hiding behind each door of the public washroom's stalls. That's why you always had to check, before you were caught with your pants down, that your door would close properly. Only a properly closed door would temporarily protect you from them. Barely. The warning did not deal with the fact that most of the latches in public washrooms were either broken of nonexistent.

An ancestral, at once shameful and scary kind of nausea descended on me. And yet as far as I could remember, apart from having been hounded, tracked, stalked, and occasionally had my breast or keychain grabbed, I had not actually been abused by maniacs or anyone else. Just scared. It was more as if the dysfunctional shame, the abuse of the girls of my generation and those that came before, would have found refuge here like ghosts chased from wherever they might have come from. Against my will, images streamed in front of my bewildered eyes of all the times when, as a pre-pubescent child, then an adolescent and a young adult, I had escaped (just) from a long line-up of these maniacs just by sheer luck or a well-placed derogatory comment. Or by running away as fast as I could. One of them had even followed me all the way to the apartment I shared with Rémi. I did not see him coming. He had been right there at the door, blocking my way.

That day I had just come back from the laundromat, sweaty, braless, wearing my baggiest and weirdest dress to camouflage a pre-menstrual belly. All my good clean skinny clothes were in the huge black plastic bag I held in my right hand. In my other hand was the key. I opened the door, put the bag inside on the floor. When I turned around to retrieve my key and close the door, there he was. Tall, greasy, stinky. Beastly. Reaching for me with his fat fingers like rotting sausages, the bloatedness of which would have matched my belly.

I don't know how I got away, but I did. All I remember is being inside the vestibule, leaning against the closed door with my set of keys clutched in my fingers. When I let go of the keys, there were big red indents on my fingers and superficial scratches on the back of my hands, but no blood. The Tweety keychain that Rémi had given me had been ripped off.

I had won the battle but not the war. Even though I had escaped, even though I was safe in my body, in my soul I felt only shame. Did I encourage this person to follow me home because I was not wearing a bra? Was it my smell, the promise of blood that attracted him like a wild beast, or both?

I still had to show up at work that day. I was the sole breadwinner of our little trio comprised of my out-of-work boyfriend, our cat Minuit, and me. Disgusted, I took a shower in the hopes of washing off the demons. Then, despite the sweltering heat, I piled on some of Rémi's baggiest clean shirts and t-shirts and turtleneck sweater until there was only my head sticking out unadorned. To make things even safer, I threw a hooded rain poncho on top of everything else.

The temperature must have been over 30° C that day. I arrived at work covered with sweat. My face was puffy and red. I peeled off most of my boyfriend's clothes down to a single short-sleeved Def Leppard t-shirt. My co-workers didn't miss a chance at teasing me, suggesting I should take a shower if I was going to start jogging to the office. Despite my protests and my telling them what happened, they kept up their bantering until I yelled, crying, for them to stop. The silence that ensued only made me feel more embarrassment and shame.

After those memories, I could not get myself to use the bathrooms at the Mont-Royal Chalet. A well-dressed woman bearing a vague resemblance to Sonia came into the washroom. That's when, jolted back to the present, I noticed I was trembling all over. I slunk into the closest cabinet and peed all my disgust and fear out. It must have been one of my longest pees ever.

The woman must have had a very full bladder too. She and I emerged at the same time. Maybe she had also been exorcising some of her own demons. I wanted so badly to share my *maniaque* stories with her, the fear, the disgust, the shame. I was aching to find some kinship with her. But she was not Sonia. Instinct told me sternly that it was not the time nor place, let alone the right person to be trying to make contact with. *She might think me a weirdo.* I tried to smile. I was right. She looked at me with a touch of fear in her eyes. She was out of there in a flash, flying like the hummingbird she must have been without even drying the tips of her wings.

I splashed water on my face from one of the single-spouted taps lined up like hardened inch-worms just waiting for the magic wand to get them out of their imprisonment. The temperature of the water, however, was perfect. Whichever civil-servant's job it had been to set the degrees of hot and cold had done a good job. The debit was stingy, though. I had to press on the handle many times to get myself clean to my satisfaction. My fingers some-what shrivelled from too much chlorine, I emerged from the gloomy depths, my heart lighter. As a good Canadian, I treated myself to a double cone of maple-walnut ice cream at the kiosk that had just opened. Then, sitting on the wide stairs outside, I revelled in the unctuous matter, letting its sweet weight settle in my stomach. Through a puffy line of orange and gold treetops, the city could be felt through the soles of my feet with its busy drum-roll.

When I moved into Sonia's, it was only around two in the afternoon, but I was drowsy because the effects of my caffeine had long worn off. The apartment was already curiously and painfully empty of her lovely presence. Even her characteristic scent had mysteriously vanished. Depositing my worn backpack on her sofa, the one she had sat on the last day I saw her, I tried to scan the room through her eyes. Nothing unusual. I got up to check the houseplants throughout the place. Farinelli and Sappho, a little shy at first, were now following me everywhere. A quick glance to their respective bowls with their names on them revealed that they probably hadn't eaten since their mistress left. How could I blame them? I could only hope they would not go on a hunger strike for the entire length of my stay.

My own cat, Sam, had been as loyal as they. As independent as he was, whenever Julie and I were gone for a few days, he did not touch any food we left him as a back-up in case the hunt was sparse. He would apparently lose all interest in hunting also. Allowing himself to indulge in an anorexia corresponding to the number of days we were gone, he would appear a few days after our return (to make us wonder if he had died, maybe, or to punish us?), skinny, his hair dull, and indifferent. Then he would finally break his fast, but only after we gave him lots of attention and our heartfelt apologies. Only then would he go back to hunting.

How was he faring? I wondered. I tried to send him a telepathic message to let himself be adored by the Naiads. Surely, he would have realized by now that Julie and I were not coming back. He would have allowed his own survival instincts to kick in. He would have gone hunting again. Surely.

"Sam, mon bel, un de mes deux seuls vrais amis, avec toi et Ralph. Laisse-toi gâter, que la chasse soit bonne, profite de la vie du mieux que tu peux ! La vie est courte, tu sais..."

I told him that he and Ralph were my only true friends. I told him to let himself be spoiled by the Naiads, hoped that the hunting would be good, and that he enjoy life to its fullest, since it is so short.

There was no answer from the cosmos, only the weird non-meowing from Farinelli at my feet. Unless he was channelling Sam. I bent down to caress him. Both he and Sappho ran away.

Contrary to the cats, I felt hungry as a wolf. My voracity had little to do with the ingestion of calories required to keep a body alive. I was hungry for *her*. Driven by a burst of energy at once bizarre and frenzied, I watched myself open her fridge, her cupboards and her pantry, searching for anything I could stuff my face with.

Like a fury, I made a pile of all the foodstuffs I could find that were passably edible on the spot without cooking. I ate it all in record time: an entire (thankfully small) bag of nacho corn chips, which I tore open with my teeth and that I ingurgitated with an insipid-looking home-made dip followed by an entire jar of (commercial, thankfully) *salsa piquante*; the remains of an expensive tin full of nuts without a single peanut; two apples (one half-ripe, another past its prime); two trays of organic brown-rice crackers (one with sesame seeds and the other one laced with Nori seaweed); a can of unsweetened whole corn; a tin of smoked oysters; a small jar of marinated artichoke hearts; about twenty mixed olives; all of a small bagful of Thompson raisins; leftover Chinese take-out maybe passed its due date; and five sweet cocktail gherkins, which I usually detest.

I only stopped short of the anchovies. Over the mass of half-chewed food in my distended stomach, I poured the contents of a small bottle of Veuve Cliquot that I had found lying on its side behind a box of organic buttermilk pancake mix.

Either Sonia had forgotten the champagne or she had hidden it with the intention of drinking it alone or with someone other than me. I was past caring. Once I had finished drinking the expensive alcohol, I resumed my bulimia with three squares of baklava topped with what remained of a barely touched small tub of cherry-and-chocolate-nib ice cream.

I had finally consumed anything readily edible except for the anchovies. All that over the course of three hours. A nausea at once caused by the gargantuan amounts I had *empiffrée* (stuffed) myself with and by my guilt at having burglarized Sonia's food supplies took me over like a tsunami. All I could do was promise myself that I would replace it all.

This did not happen. If reincarnation exists, I will probably have to set my karma right on that matter. I might come back as a perennially starved person doomed to stuff myself until I burst. Maybe, on the contrary, I would be too skinny for not having enough to eat. I don't know. Or maybe I just don't know *yet*.

Meanwhile, on that day when the time came to go to bed, I simply couldn't get myself to settle into Sonia's bed. And yet I had already spent a night of love there with someone other than the woman I craved. It was as if this time I lacked the necessary dignity, as if I had lost it to guilt. However, I allowed myself to use the Mennonite-style wool quilt that was hovering on the bed. I spent my first (my second, really) night as well as the next six sleeping on Sonia's *divan*. Stuffed to the gills without being satiated, I fell asleep on that night in a heavy slumber full of bizarre dreams that I did not quite remember the next day except for a residual unease.

On the seventh day, a Sunday, it was only after a beeswax candle-lit ritual bath and anointing myself with lavender, vanilla, white Musk, and who knows what else from a collection of small vials on Sonia's bathroom shelf, clean as a new penny and shaved even, did I dare drag the Mennonite quilt all the way back to the bedroom.

Everything was harmonized in pastel blue, magenta, and silver. A reproduction of a faux-rococo painting of an angel hovered on the wall, looking over whomever would be sleeping in the vast bed. She would protect the sleeper with her at once transparent and strong outstretched wings. As I threw the quilt over the bed, I thanked the guardian angel. I would need all the help and protection I could get. Protection from what or whom? I would have to admit it might be mostly from myself, in this haven of peace.

I caressed lightly, with trembling fingers, the perfectly soft pillows. Feeling strangely virginal, I slid a hesitant hand between the silky satin sheets. It was like caressing her soft skin. Then I let myself slip with a voluptuous pleasure tinted with reverential, almost religious fear between the soft sheets. I finally fell asleep, one cat on either side of my feet. We slept the slumber of those who have no cares in the world. The next day, I felt all strange, as if I were still dreaming. I walked to work on a cloud. Everybody remarked on how good I looked. Kent asked me if I was in love. If he only knew!

That night, boldened, I decided to call Charlotte from Sonia's phone. True, my friend had warned me not to call her first, before she was ready. But I was feeling strong, invincible, actually. And besides, I hadn't given her Sonia's telephone number. Charlotte did not answer of course. Josie's name had already been deleted from the message on her answering machine. Too bad. Josie intrigued me. I knew very little, if anything, about cross-dressers. I didn't even know what the currently correct name might be to call Josie. Still, I would have been very interested in getting to know her if only in the name of political correctness. Too bad, but it looked like I had missed my chance. I left Sonia's phone number and address on Charlotte's machine, anticipating the time when she would be ready to contact me. Whenever that would be. I hoped it would be soon. I missed her.

As the days passed at Sonia's, I was getting progressively bolder. I allowed myself to start searching the apartment, pretending a cleaning spree. I went slowly, meticulously. There was no rush. The kitchen was the first room to submit to my scrutiny. Everything was neatly in place: the latest in appliances and gadgets, the extensive fresh-looking selection of herbs and spices, health-food cookbooks, expensive-looking cat-litter and minuscule, equally expensive-looking tins of cat food. Nothing seemed to be missing from a healthy lifestyle for human and animals.

An almost manic cleanliness reigned everywhere, especially in the kitchen. I had been scared to use her stove and had refrained from cooking for fear of disturbing the cleanliness. Even the cleaning tools—broom, mop, buckets, rags—all was spotless and fresh, like the reputation of the *Sainte Vierge*.

Then came the living room. I knew already from my first visit with Sonia at her apartment that the shelves carried an excellent selection of music from female singers, as well as choice classical pieces. Somehow, the harp had until now missed my scrutiny. There it was, sitting quietly in the corner of the living room, waiting, it seemed, to be noticed. Curiously, this was the first time I saw it, as if it had magically just appeared. I have always loved harp music. Personally, I didn't know anyone who played the harp. I let out a giant sigh—a sigh tinted with a melancholy entangled with desire for Her, the beautiful, the angelic, the incomparable Sonia. I didn't touch the harp for fear of trespassing some secret boundary. I was doomed to resume my search for her essence elsewhere.

The bathroom was next. To my great disappointment, there was nothing there that even remotely enlightened me on her intimate sanitary habits. No interesting or hazardous drugs hovered in her medicine cabinet or on her shelves. Of course, if she had any, she would have taken them with her. Besides, she didn't seem the type to indulge in such pharmacopeia. Sonia, the princess of wholesome, healthy balanced living. Her apparent healthy habits were the attributes I was most comfortable with.

I lost myself in a dream. There she was in my Genus-island flower garden, *céleste*, wearing a transparent shirt, her nimble digits caressing the chords of her harp as I was expertly milking the goats, which were as beatified by her music as per their relief to be delivered of their sweet white burden. Sonia would easily and gracefully fill the void left by Julie. Oh sorry. Julien. *Bweurk!* My beautiful idyllic image fell to pieces.

Meanwhile, I got back to my surveillance work at Sonia's. It was time, finally, to go through her sacrosanct bedroom with a fine-toothed comb.

Despite the fact that I had been sleeping in her big bed for a few days at least, I had only actually spent my nights there, not touching anything but the bed and whatever was on it. I had even abstained from lighting a candle for fear of awakening the disrespectfully lusty genie in me.

The time had finally come to explore Sonia's sanctum. Starting with the closet, I flung the mirrored doors open. It was quite full without being over-stuffed. All the clothes seemed of quality without being necessarily expensive. Lots of cotton, silk (fine or raw), some vintage. No cashmere. This fact reassured me, given the awful treatment the goats are subjected to. Most of the clothes' colour scheme matched that of the bedroom, in fresh hues ranging from blue to turquoise via salmon pinks, and magenta, seasoned with lavender. *A bit weird to match one's clothes to the colours of one's wall*, I thought, *but then again, Sonia can get away with anything*. As if to save her from being excessively coordinated, a few surprising colours—canary yellow, parrot green, fire-engine red even—and one flowery, almost garish dress also stuck out from amidst the matching sets. A few evening dresses completed the collection. There was the obligatory little black dress with a touch of lace, a few sequinned numbers. On the side shelves, I found a pile of sweaters, most of them soft and many hand-knit, possibly from hand-spun wool of darker colours, wine red, bottle green, aubergine, multi-coloured...

Sonia was slightly taller than me, which was not unusual as most people were, but she was more delicate-boned than Charlotte. As much as I would have liked to get into the skin of the woman I currently lusted after, I avoided trying on any of the clothes for fear of bursting them at the seams. However, I unashamedly buried my face in one of her silk shawls hanging from a wooden hanger. It did not carry her scent. Maybe she hadn't worn it for a while. Disappointed, I put it back, but askew. I tried to fix my clumsiness but the cloth kept slipping through my fingers like an eel. I put it back as well as I could and closed the door. For my penance at my clumsiness, I let a few days pass by before I resumed my search.

One rainy afternoon with nothing to do, I allowed myself to take a glimpse under the bed. There was almost no dust, and only a very few cat-hairs there. I extricated a flattened black plastic bag. Inside I found a few posters. One of them was called "Sisters," from a photographer named Anne Cunningham. I loved that photo. As it happened, I had a copy as well on Genus. I had received it as a gift. I forget from whom. Curiously, Julie had never let me pin it on our wall. She had thought it too controversial. The women's bodies on the poster, she said, were too conventionally thin and young. Plus, their faces didn't show. Julie stated that the image, as beautifully evocative as it might have been, would be harmful for the feminist cause, as it was showing women in a stereotypical and impersonal way because of the fact that they were thin and headless.

I thought it was funny that Sonia and I were harbouring the same photo under our beds. I couldn't help but wonder if she kept hers hidden for the same reasons as Julie had in preventing me from posting my own. Maybe Sonia was more like me than I thought. Maybe she had a Julie hidden somewhere too. I hoped not.

The single drawer of her night table, on the right side of the bed, didn't have a Bible in it but a book by the Buddhist monk Pema Chödrön. One more thing Sonia and I had in common. True, I had only started to read one of the monk's books, and it had been a long time ago, but I did remember liking her. I made a mental note to myself to read this book and memorize some passages so I could quote them to Sonia when she came back.

If Sonia kept a journal, she must have taken it with her. Too bad. I would have loved to commit the indiscretion of sneaking a peek at it. In the drawer of the left-side table, I found a flat box of paper tissue and an astonishing array of calming herbal supplements, the likes of Hops, Valerian, Passiflora and a mix of Camomile and other plants I did not recognize. Madame suffers from insomnia? Wherever she went, she was obviously planning on catching up on her sleep without any help from her herbs. Unless she simply forgot to take them.

There were no traces whatsoever to be found of Sonia having any kind of sex-life. No condoms, lube, or even massage oil. Unless, of course, she took whatever it might have been with her. To use with whom?

Or maybe she was asexual like Bourgeon. I suddenly felt vulgar for being so preoccupied with the matter. *Never mind,* I said to myself. *Sonia is way beyond your reach anyway, even if she were interested in relationships.* Whereas my ship was more of a rowboat or a kayak at best, hers would have been a hundred-foot schooner.

Then my groping hands found something else. I could feel it at the very back of her dresser on the left. The heart side. The object was stuffed so far back that I had to pull the drawer quite far out, to the point that its contents almost spilled onto the floor. The object in question was a small frame. And in the frame, a photograph of a little girl about four or five years old. I don't know much about kids, so I could only guess at her age. But what I did know for sure was that she looked like a younger Sonia. Same curls, same sparkle in the eyes, same cute little nose. Could Sonia have a little daughter? The thought melted my heart. Of course, it also ruined my fantasy of having Sonia all to myself one day. But that thought was just that: a fantasy. I turned the frame around. All it said was, "*Ariane à Lanoraie, le 4 août 2001.*" So, the picture was recent. I immediately changed my dreams of what life with Sonia would look like to include this beautiful little being.

The knowledge of Sonia having a little girl in her life made me want to try harder to be good. I didn't quite know how a prospective parent should behave, so I started with trying to at least eat better. I put myself on a balanced *régime*. I ate well and just enough, mostly raw. I had made a list, before I completely forgot, of all the food I had eaten on my first day with the intention of replacing it someday. I promised myself, once the provisions replenished, to hide it all away from temptation. I abstained from masturbating. I tried to read, in addition to Pema Chödrön, at least one chapter a day from the many learned and/or feminist books that stuffed Sonia's shelves. I even curbed my beer-consumption mostly to weekends, and then to only one per weekend day. I practiced yoga for at least an hour (well, sort of) every day. After purchasing organic shampoo, so as not to use Sonia's, I washed my hair every three or four days on average. Dancing was the most fun. Often, I would put some world-beat CD on and squirm for a minimum of twenty minutes at a time, twirling an imaginary Sonia (and now, a delighted Ariane too) around in *ochos, pirouettes,* and jive, with the cats weaving between our feet.

My determination to show a changed, fit, improved Claire to Sonia on her return carried me through my occasional moments of doubt and laziness. Maybe she would show some interest in me … oh… just a little bit. Little did I know that all I would achieve was being in excellent shape when I died.

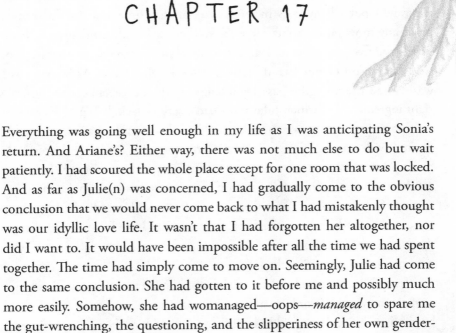

CHAPTER 17

Everything was going well enough in my life as I was anticipating Sonia's return. And Ariane's? Either way, there was not much else to do but wait patiently. I had scoured the whole place except for one room that was locked. And as far as Julie(n) was concerned, I had gradually come to the obvious conclusion that we would never come back to what I had mistakenly thought was our idyllic love life. It wasn't that I had forgotten her altogether, nor did I want to. It would have been impossible after all the time we had spent together. The time had simply come to move on. Seemingly, Julie had come to the same conclusion. She had gotten to it before me and possibly much more easily. Somehow, she had womanaged—oops—*managed* to spare me the gut-wrenching, the questioning, and the slipperiness of her own gender-reversal. Part of me admired her for having let go of me, of us, so easily. But then again, this would have been understandable since she had been the one initiating the change. And now that the wheels of transformation were put in motion, liberated from the thread of uncertainly as to where we stood, our last remaining *fil conducteur*, our connecting thread, I was free as a bird.

I know that many girlfriends of female-to-male persons say they love the person and not the gender. Yes, I had loved the magnificent person that Julie had been. I will always love her. I didn't know this new Julien. One day, I thought I would get to know and maybe love him as well. And as Julien was seemingly not ready to come into contact with me, I found myself not ready to get to know him either. I had enough on my own plate anyway with trying to figure out my own life.

The time had come to take the reins into my own hands. As much as I was reluctant to admit it, I had been riper than I thought to leave our relationship and take a break from our life on Genus Island—for a while, at least. Maybe I would go back to the island one day. But if I ever did go back, my life would have to be completely different. Would I move in with the Naiads? Or live alone somewhere in a cabin in the woods? I was floating in limbo.

Yes, limbo. Funny, that's just like me here in this non-space-non-time. Anyway, I put all my eggs in one basket at that time and decided not to make any moves until Sonia came back. Then, if I could convince her I was worth the trouble, we would do a *bout de chemin ensemble* in Montréal, or who knows, on Genus Island or Bora Bora for all I knew. As insecure as I was, I knew my strengths: passably intelligent, kind, excellent cook (given the right ingredients, of which Julie and I had a serious lack, living as we were in voluntary simplicity on a remote island), and also recently shaved, reasonably fit, and with squeaky clean hair. My infatuation with Sonia would certainly make me a considerate, attentive lover, sensitive and sensuous. What more would a woman, even one as beautiful as Sonia, want? I could show her around. She seemed to know Genus Island a little. I could take her to my secret spots, and not just the ones on my body. I could introduce her to the Naiads, but only once our relationship was secure lest she run off with someone more interesting than me...

Meanwhile, I was still in Montréal. I would need to renew my friendships or make new ones, if only to appear more interesting to Sonia. Kent would be my first choice. We could have dinner. I invited him the very next time we met at the coffee-fountain.

Kent and I shared a very similar sense of justice. Maybe this had to do with the fact that he was a Libra. With me as an Aries, we completed each other just like biblical husband and wife are supposed to do. For example, we naturally, without even trying, ended up sharing the limelight in our con-versations, never interrupting, taking equal time even if we were passionate about sharing a particular story. When we used to go out to a *resto*, we always split the bill in half, regardless of who ate or drank what, since we had shared the same experience. Unless one of us had announced they were taking the other one out, in which case the other would reciprocate some other time. We never counted but somehow always seemed to come out equal. I imag-ined that, had we been compatible sexually, we would have also been fair with our orgasms. At first sight, all this might appear artificial, contrived, but it worked well for us. It was this sense of fairness that had probably kept our friendship intact over the years, despite seven years of physical separation. It was time to reconnect our lives, soulmates that we were.

Kent, as I remembered from our Egg-House days, loved good food. He also showed a keen discernment when it came to wine. I could never measure up to the bar, but I could always count on his diplomacy in not making fun of me for my lack of culture. We could plan our menu and go shopping together. We would make a whole day of it just like in the old days. I hadn't spent much time with him since I had come back to Montréal. It was time for us to set things right.

We met at the Marché Jean-Talon early Saturday morning. We planned our menu according to the fruits and vegetables in season. Aubergines, squash, and late tomatoes. Then after having consumed a poutine each, we walked all the way back to the Main for protein for our dinner. Prawns, frozen crab, and Atlantic salmon, with a selection of cheeses for dessert, French-style, fresh figs and persimmon. We brought everything back to Sonia's apartment, then went out again looking for the best baklava. We found it at one of the many Greek bakeries on Park Avenue.

On our way back to Sonia's apartment, we stopped at another bakery to pick up a baguette and a few other ingredients necessary for our feast. Kent insisted on choosing the wine. Obviously, I gave him *carte blanche*. I got the Tequila and Cointreau for our apéros. The Tequila was Mexican, of course. Cheap but still the best.

It was still early afternoon. We made two different marinades and placed the prawns and fish in each of them. After prepping as much as we could, we put everything in the fridge and went for a leisurely stroll on Mont-Royal. Kent had returned to the wonderful friend I had known before. The professional young man I had initially been disappointed to find at the office had vanished altogether. In no time, we were laughing, reminiscing about some of the funniest highlights from our Egg-House days and some more recent funny incidents that had happened at the office.

However, as the evening progressed, a certain melancholy seemed to be throwing a shadow on our reunion. The silences between our sentences gradually lengthened until they became almost awkward. Maybe my friend had had his heart prematurely broken by Allan? No, it wasn't that. I was sure of it. I had seen him go through enough breakups in the past to know he was more resilient than to let himself be so sad just for a failed potential relationship, especially one so new.

I also noticed he drank very little, despite the fact that the wine was excellent. That was a sure sign he was not suffering from a broken heart, as per his habit, he would have been drowning his sorrows in alcohol. Something was off. To be fair, I tried to slow down my own drinking. It turned out to be difficult with the wine being so exceptionally good. I decided to break the silence that was almost turning to ice. I tipped the two-thirds-full bottle towards his glass. He stopped me gently but firmly. This irritated me.

"But what on earth is going on, Kent!? Is the wine not good enough for you?" I blurted out.

Kent's delicate face split into a sad, almost apologetic smile. I barely recognized him. He didn't reply. Instead, he softly tipped the bottle towards my own glass, suggesting I drink as much as I wanted. I obeyed but was ill at ease. The scene had spoiled my drinking pleasure.

By the time we got to dessert, there was still half a bottle of wine left. The wine was too dry for dessert. Even I knew that. So, saving it could not have been the reason that Kent had stopped drinking. There was the bottle hovering on the table, looking larger than life, proof of the malaise we had shrouded ourselves in. Something was seriously wrong. To make things worse, there were those long silences that neither of us bothered to break. Luckily, though, neither of us attempted to indulge in small talk. We were well beyond such pretense.

I had eaten too much too fast. Tension was preventing my stomach from digesting all that food. I suggested we go for a walk instead of watching the foreign movie we had so carefully chosen. Kent agreed. He seemed relieved.

The October weather was incredibly soft, like a caress. As we walked side by side, the silence between us slowly turned into a fraternal complicity. I knew Kent would speak soon but not before he was ready. It was only when we got to Duluth Street that he stopped and turned towards me.

"Can you keep a secret?" Of course I would. He knew I would. I nodded, solemn.

Then he continued. "This is awkward ... but ... I know you. I trust you. I just need for you to promise you won't tell. Anyone."

This was getting too serious. I started to shiver despite the unseasonably balmy evening air.

"Okay, I promise. Trust me." I felt dishonest, as if I was sure to betray him.

Kent took a deep breath. "This is so difficult. I can't find the words..."

I took his hands in mine and gazed deep into his eyes, as softly as I could.

After another huge, audible breath, he said what he had to say: "I have ... I am ... I am HIV positive."

Our eyes simultaneously filled with tears. I was speechless. There was nothing to say. True, we were in 2001. Modern medicine had come to the rescue since the eighties, when the disease had first been identified. Being HIV positive was no longer a death sentence. There was a much better chance of survival for people dealing with the disease, and their quality of life had greatly improved. But there would still be the cocktail of megavitamins to take, the constant vigilance not to pass it on, blood-tests to check on T-cells... It was all overwhelming.

To go back to Sonia's and watch our movie would have been pointless. Still holding his hands, I got up on tiptoe and kissed him on the cheek. I whispered in his ear that I loved him more than anyone else in the whole world, that he was my best friend ever, my spiritual brother, my soulmate. That I would be there for him. Always.

I wished with all my heart that I could turn back time. I wished I had been more present in his life. Maybe I could have prevented him from the reckless act of passion that had changed his fate in a few miserable seconds of bliss.

We hugged slowly and long. We parted ways. Wherever he was going, I could not follow. His personal dark fate had already swallowed him in its private, inevitable embrace. I was excluded. He didn't turn back.

The following Monday, whenever I saw Kent, he tried to pretend that nothing had happened. It must have been hard for him to keep up appearances as I had always known him as being honest and direct. For my part, I felt limp as a wet rag. Every time I would see him, I would have to use my superwoman powers not to melt into a tearful heap.

Once we ran into each other in the corridor. There was no one else around. He slipped into my reluctant ears an almost inaudible murmur: "Maybe it would be better if we didn't see each other outside the office."

The sharp pain through my guts cut me in half. Although I could understand intellectually how he might think this separation to be necessary, I was hemorrhaging inside. He had left me no choice but to acquiesce. It was his call, not mine.

During the following days, weeks, I worked on trying to convince myself that my friend would recover, that the megavitamin cocktails he would have started taking would delay his *dégénérescence*.

I could not possibly have known he would outlive me.

✽ ✽ ✽

A mere few days after my sad date with Kent, feeling insanely lonely, I decided it was high time I try and track down my psychic gaze-tickling friend Rémi. Maybe he could cheer me up. The telephone book in Sonia's kitchen offered seven R. Lauzons. One less than the receptionist's at the Bains Schubert. A bargain. I tried the one that said R. M. Lauzon, as Rémi's middle name was Mario. Bingo. We recognized each other's voices right away. Rémi seemed to find it totally natural to get a call from me out of the blue. Well, after all, he was psychic. Not a single trace of reproach at my having abandoned him to the attendants at the mental hospital seemed to interfere with his enthusiasm at finally hearing from me.

As we chatted away like old friends who had just seen each other the day before, my residual remorse melted away. He was doing well. Strategically switching his keen interests from TV shows to that of computers, he had turned his hobby into something more useful. Eventually he had carved himself a position as audio-visual technician at a local CEGEP. Just to make sure that everything was indeed all right, I hazarded to ask him about his health.

"You mean my mental health?" he said with an audible smile. "Oh yes, *J'me suis calmé depuis le temps.* I've calmed down, since."

"*Mais écoute ben ça.* I am married now. Actually, you know her. Or more like you've known her once … intimately." His tone suddenly got mischievous. His smile must have turned into an ear-to-ear grin.

I didn't get it. Images from my short list of women I had tried to have sex with in my crazy stoned life rolled in front of my eyes like an old-fashioned 8mm *vidéo*. The reel was very brief. And scratchy. Just a few people piled on top of each other, someone more competent luring a woman away from me,

290

a stranger's tongue in my ears ... other than that, not much. Except maybe people I had always wanted to do, like Charlotte, but she didn't count as we never consummated my attraction towards her.

"*Euh, c'est-à-dire que...*"

"*Mais rappelle-toi! C'est elle qui m'en a parlé.* Don't you remember? She told me about you!"

"*Ben voyons...*" I was still not getting it.

After letting me languish for several minutes, he revealed a name. He was almost laughing by then: "Suzanne. *Tu te souviens, maintenant?*"

"*Euh...non...*"

Then he volunteered a man's name: "*Et Gilles, alors, ça te dit quelque chose? Un ménage à trois un après-midi de septembre chez toi?*"

There it was. A place. Context. Time reference. Everything fell in a shambled heap of haphazard recognition. Hazy images of a warm early fall afternoon. The bedroom thick with blue hashish smoke. Three people. Two pairs of breasts, one penis bent sideways like a frequent masturbator's. A strictly right-handed one, apparently. Shocks of blonde hair and fuzzy flashes of golden sunbeams popping in and out like *siffleux* (groundhogs) through the thick powder-blue air. Pale skins. Theirs, not mine, as I've always been the outdoorsy type. Faces blurred on the movie-screen of a myopic person who lost their glasses in the fog. Maybe it had been triggered by some bad genetic memory. My wildly beating heart had turned me into a scared crow. In that hazy room, head spinning, I had fallen into the throes of a major panic attack.

Of the sexual act itself, if act there had been, nothing. I have no recollection what or whose orifice the crooked penis might have disappeared into. All that remained in my consciousness from that particular event was the terror of feeling like my heart was going to split out of my chest and fly away, turning me into an over-wound drumming bear toy with wings and a sardonic smile.

I might have passed out. In the next scene, I am lying on my bed. Utterly alone. The only thing that eventually calmed me down that day was my crazy cat Minuit, the schitzo feline that would otherwise routinely be climbing the walls, rebounding like a screen-saver all over whichever room she happened to be in. Yet there she was, sitting on my chest right on top of my heart. Still as a marble sphinx. For once in her life, she had calmed down just long enough to eventually get my own heart back to a more normal pace. How did she know it was the perfect thing to do? Then off she went again, sharpening her claws halfway up the curtains, ready for mischief, never to settle again.

Rémi was patiently waiting for the lightbulb of my memory to turn on. I figured I might still have a chance in getting out of this one with a minimum of embarrassment. I tried to pretend lamely at amnesia.

"Bon, puisque tu le dis...Tu es sûr qu'on a couché ensemble ?" (Are you sure we did this thing?) I didn't dare ask how Suzanne had said that it had been. That's if we had done the deed at all.

Rémi, rich from his wife's account of the events, seemed to have gained a better rendition of the story than what I remembered. Maybe to save me from embarrassment, he discreetly dropped the subject. Our conversation continued as if nothing had happened. We could have talked about the price of gas or about the weather and it wouldn't have made any difference. There was no room for awkwardness. Be here now. Dear Rémi. I really wanted to meet his wife. I knew she would be a very special person.

Rémi and I did, however, catch up on the whereabouts of people we both knew, namely his brother Jacques. He did manage to steal some of the bulbs off the cross on Mont-Royal before the city made it impossible. Then there was their baby sister Carole and also Laure, Rémi's ex before me. A cluster of friends. No other surprises. Save an alcohol problem here and there and some minor health issues, everybody seemed to be doing fine enough. I didn't tell Rémi about Julie(n).

We promised to meet in person. Soon. He offered to get me one of those long-life bulbs from his brother next time we met. Jacques and I had always hit it off. I was touched by Rémi's offer.

Something in me told me that this meeting would never take place. Our lives, our interests, were too different. Without the guilt that had kept me tied to Rémi in some way, I felt like we had nothing to tell each other anymore. Plus, now that he was married, it would have been inappropriate for him to tickle me with his famous gaze. Disappointed, I bid him goodbye, and we hung up.

Our conversation had lasted a mere twenty minutes at most. It was only once I had nestled the receiver in Sonia's vintage telephone cradle that I remembered my drawing, the one with the bird-women in the lobby of the Place Ville-Marie. I had a funny feeling that it was Rémi who had "borrowed" it from the student show all those years ago. Too bad. I would have liked to see it once again. *Oh well*, I thought. *He can have it.* And "now," floating in this limbo sort of place I am in, it is of no use to me anyway.

I don't know if Rémi would have eventually found out about my death. It would be unlikely. The news of my death wouldn't change much for him anyway, even if he had eventually heard of my demise. All I knew at that time after our conversation was that I had lost one more friend from my past. There was really no one else left for me in Montréal.

Maybe this was a good thing, I led myself to believe. I was finally free. Free of a past that had become too heavy, free as a bird that had just taken its first flight out of the nest. Ready to soar into the blue skies of new promise, I stepped outside. The October weather was superb. Since I was a detailed person, I chose the kind of bird I was going to be. I picked the swallow. Shaking my shoulders and my bum, oblivious to the fact that I was standing on the sidewalk, I unfurled my wings, still moist from useless tears. I opened my virtual forked tail in a roguish V-shape. Yes, we were in October and not in early summer, but that is exactly where my metaphor ended. Busy as I was flying, I almost succeeded in ignoring such insignificant detail as time.

Animated by some sort of juvenile-animal energy, I flew all the way to the *Marché Jean-Talon*. I bought a big bagful of red, red Mackintosh apples and a Blue Hubbard squash. It was truly blue. I love Montréal in the fall. One can really feel the seasons rolling in despite the fact that one is in a city.

Still faithful to my bird-metaphor, I let my heart soar all the way up into the bright-coloured maples that flanked the long sidewalk ahead of me. My feet hardly touched the ground despite the heaviness of the produce in my backpack. I flew through Little Italy, genuinely happy for the first time in months, maybe years. Decades.

When I got home to Sonia's, I felt an irrepressible urge to share my immense joy. There was no one around. The image of the Girlz back on Genus Island came into my mind. Giddy from my ecstatic day, that very same evening, I wrote them a letter:

Hello all you lovely Naiads!

Well, here I am in Montréal! I don't even remember if I told you in my note back in June that it's where I would be. To tell you the truth, I wasn't quite sure myself where I would end up, or if, once

I ended up here or somewhere else, if I was going to stay and for how long.

And here we have it. I am where I am and it's the perfect place for me. I had forgotten how beautiful Québec can be in the fall! I've missed this explosion of colours and didn't even know it.

Do you remember my—our—friend Charlotte? She came out to Genus for a visit, once... Well, anyway, it turns out that she has just stepped out of a relationship with a trans-woman named Josie! Or maybe they are (is) merely a cross dresser... Anyway, maybe there's hope for Charlotte if you know what I mean!! It would be kind of cool if she were warming up to be a lesbian. Who knows? Anyway, that relationship, as all the other ones I've seen Charlotte go through, didn't last more than a few summer months. Too bad. I kind of liked Josie and would have loved to get to know them. Josie is gone now. Who knows where. Charlotte went away too. And now she's back. Haven't seen her yet. Just talked to her on the phone. She seems to need time to lick her wounds.

As for me, well, I think I'm in love. What am I saying!? I AM in LOVE. Yess! Her name is Sonia. She is absolutely superb. I can only use superlatives when I am talking about her. Unfortunately, she is gone for a few months. I am caretaking her apartment, looking after her cats, and watering her plants. But she's coming home soon.

I have not one, but two jobs. One needs that to survive around here. But I don't mind; it keeps me busy until Sonia comes home. One job is reading newspapers! Can you believe it? It's for a marketing research company. Otherwise I take my clothes off for the sake of Art. Yes, I'm a nude model at Concordia University and a few colleges around town. Taking my clothes off, as you may remember about me, is the easy part. The harder part is staying still. And not shivering, as those places seem to have a small budget for heating. I can't imagine what winter will be like!

I'm eating well, mostly organic, and keeping myself in good shape. For me and especially for Sonia. She's not coming back until December first, so meanwhile, there's lots of space here if you want to get off your rock and come visit for a while. Once your harvest is in, of course, and the garden is put to bed. I know it's a big job, but you must be almost done! By the way, I hope you're getting a decent feast out of my garden too!

Yes, I miss you all. Really, really miss you. Winters can be long on Genus. I'll show you a good time here!! Fun is what Montrealers know how to do. And they do it well, and often.

Lots of Hugs all around,

Claire

Ps. Hope Ralph and Sam are doing well. Give them a hug for me, too.

The letter, in its bragging way, would have been written more for me than the Naiads. I was really craving some company. Why not them!? Of course, I omitted any mention of Julie(n). The Girlz would be smart enough to have figured out by then that we were no longer an item. There would be no need to get lost in all the gory details. And maybe they had known all along that we were doomed, maybe even from the start. They might not have guessed about the sex change. I wasn't going to be the one telling them, for sure.

As for Sonia, I was fully aware that I was trying to lead my friends to believe that the relationship was more advanced, and especially more reciprocated than it really was. Oh well, said I, maybe if I can convince my friends I can *amadouer* Sonia too. Let's be positive. The whole idea of "creating one's destiny by imagining it right" hadn't worked for me. Yet. Not in that situation anyway. That fact didn't keep me from trying, though, eternal optimist that I was. Or should I say naïve?

In my letter to the Naiads, I didn't ask them about Adam. As confused as I was about their gender identity, and despite the cute little breast-looking knobbies I had glimpsed on their chest, they would still, as far as I knew and generally speaking, be considered a "he" on account of, if nothing else, the name. Therefore, the Naiads would have little to do with him. *Too bad,* really, I thought, since he seemed to be a very interesting kind of character. The blue girl too, but I knew even less about her.

After reading and re-reading my letter countless times, I finally deemed it good enough to send. True, it contained a few exaggerations, but I womanaged to convince myself they were simple affirmations. I was sure of a brand-new life ahead of me. The Naiads would be the first ones to witness it.

In my excitement to send my letter off, I didn't notice I had forgotten to give them Sonia's address.

✭ ✭ ✭

So, Calypso, Minerva, and Diane drove across the continent in their dilapidated truck. After two flat tires and a lost tailpipe, they finally spilled out at Sonia's door in Montréal. It was already mid-November. They said they had been worried about me but more importantly they were smart. They had found Charlotte's address in their archives, tracked her down, and with her help, figured out where I was staying.

"And oh," they said, "by the way, she sends her love. And apparently, you got a small package from the airport. She was wondering if she should open it for you."

As for all of us getting together, she was quoted as having said, "Let's do lunch. Or something."

Or something. Right. How disappointing to see that Charlotte did not show more enthusiasm to see me. I figured the package would be the knife I had had confiscated at the airport. It seemed that was so long ago. It would have taken them over four months to figure things out and put my innocent little penknife in the mail. I remembered the troglodyte at the counter. I sent him a virtual hug. As for Charlotte, maybe once I got over my grudge, I could give her a call. After all, she was just being herself. But in the meantime, I was going to be busy with my Naiad friends. As much as I was happy to see them, I was embarrassed to be found alone in Sonia's apartment. My unease magically melted as soon as Calypso extricated a few bottles of home-made blackberry wine, the first one of which she uncorked with a smart little pop.

We caught up with the news from Genus. It turned out that Minerva had almost run off with one of the nomads. The only thing that prevented that disaster from happening was the fact that said nomad ran off herself with another nomad. The new pair went off to the Michigan Wymmin's festival, leaving Minerva behind. After a week or so spent in seclusion in the Moon lodge, a very contrite Minerva came out, a few kilos thinner, radiant, ready to resume her loving relationship with Calypso. Seeing them together in Montréal, it was obvious to me that they had mended whatever parts of their hearts needed fixing.

And yes, Ralph the Pig had let himself be adopted. Sam was a bit more reluctant and only showed up occasionally at the Naiad's door. But he seemed to enjoy having gone wild and looked healthy. I sighed in relief. The chickens were fine as chickens are wont to be. They had been very reliable egg-layers. They still were.

Of all the presents the three Naiads had brought, the Cinderella pumpkin was my favourite. It came from Julie's and my garden. It had been fed with our own compost. The earth had been dug with our own hands and anointed with our very personal juices. It was made from Julie and me. I still could not bring myself to talk about her. As if they had known intuitively to be discreet, the Naiads did not bring the subject up. It was as if we all knew we would talk about it when the time came, which was not yet.

I had to admit that the Girlz' arrival lightened up my dull life as a breath of fresh air. Their laughter filled Sonia's apartment with a wholesomeness that I had almost forgotten. Stealthily, slowly, I had alienated myself in an urban lifestyle without even noticing it.

Calypso and Minerva, as the designated couple, ended up occupying Sonia's bed. I was a bit uneasy about this, especially the night we all got quite drunk and the lovers crashed out more than they fell asleep on what I considered to be a sacrosanct place. I did not dare complain and let them be, promising myself to thoroughly sage the place once they were gone.

One day, still avoiding any mention of Julie, I asked the Girlz about Adam. They looked at each other knowingly, then Minerva and Calypso fixed their gaze on Diane. She had obviously been appointed as messenger.

"Adam!? Adam who!??" she said, indignantly. "You know our policies about men. Or did you forget already?"

Embarrassed but still determined to carry my idea to some sort of a conclusion, I went on.

"Well, there's this person ... a bit androgynous, true. *("He even has breasts",* I wanted to say, but didn't). His name is Adam. Very kind and gentle. He's a co-worker at the marketing research place where I work. Turns out by some weird coincidence that my—*our*—boss is Madame Isabelle, the woman who owns the land I lived on with ... Julie."

This was the first time I had mentioned my ex-girlfriend's name. I hesitated, wondering if the Naiads would start asking about her. They didn't.

"Yes, yes, I remember you talking about the owner of your place," Diane continued. "You had yourselves a nice little situation. Anyway, she was your landlady and now she's your boss!? Wow. Now that is one big fat giant coincidence."

"Yes, well. There's this guy..."

"Not interested, really."

"Oh, come on. He's staying in my house! Well my old house, you know. The one Julie and I built on Madame Isabelle's land."

"Who is Madame Isabelle?"

"My old landlady and new boss!!" *Why are they being so weird?* I did not want to digress from my focus. A bit frustrated, I continued, "Adam. He is supposed to be staying in my ... our old house. Probably with this woman. You must have noticed her. She's all blue. At least she was, before she ... they ... left Montréal?"

Silence. All three women looked at each other as if to say, *"Should we tell her she's totally mentally ill?"* and *"Who's going to tell her?"*

Diane the Warrioress spoke once again.

"Ahem... We don't know of any Adam. There is a blue-coloured person next door in your old house. But this person is a man. No mistake. And there is also a woman. The two are a het couple. Definitely. Het. His partner is Ève. Ève is a woman. No doubt about that. How do we know? Because she's pregnant. She's due next May. Actually."

"WHAT? How could that be!?" I was absolutely flabbergasted.

Then I started to piece together the little that I knew about the two unusual characters. Their androgyny, the fact that they seemed to have some mysterious thing in common... I couldn't make any sense of it at all.

Minerva took pity on me. She led me out of my utter confusion. After a quick glance at the two others, seeking and then getting slight nods of approval, she started her story:

"Well, actually Ève and Claude—the Blue person—are what is called intersex. It is a relatively rare phenomenon. You might know about it. You have always been interested in 'other' sexualities. I remember that. Anyway, they are both intersex. Ève, if I can say it this way, is more female, and Claude is more male. They came to Genus to start themselves a new life. Much to their delight, they discovered they are compatible. As in fertile. So, Ève got pregnant. A real miracle. Intersex people were thought to be infertile for the longest time. But now 'they,' as in the medical establishment, have discovered that many more intersex people can have children than they had originally thought. Fascinating, isn't it?"

Calypso continued. "it was the medical interventions that intersex people were subjected to, albeit with the best of intentions, in the desire to make them 'normal' that was, in too many cases, making them sterile." She said this nonchalantly, examining her dirty nails as if they were more interesting to her than the astounding story they had just told me.

I slowly closed my gaping jaw. Amazing. I had read about intersex people, true, but never in my wildest dreams would I have thought I would meet one—or two—in the flesh. I wished I had gotten to know Adam/Ève better. "Aren't you all totally flabbergasted?" I blurted out.

All three of them took a collective deep breath.

"It's just that now we might have to kind of revise the rules," said Diane. "Or not. Because, despite their particular biology, it doesn't take away from the fact that Ève and Claude are actually, technically, a heterosexual couple. He has a penis. She has a uterus. They are pregnant. End of story."

I couldn't believe my ears. How could they possibly not be interested in such a rare phenomenon?

As if she had been reading my mind, Diane said:

"And they don't want to be considered a phenomenon, a curiosity, either. They only told us about themselves because ... I don't know ... maybe because they felt they had to tell someone? We asked them if it was okay to tell you. They said yes. As a matter of fact, they said your boss—we didn't know her name then—your Madame Isabelle knows too. She knew it from the beginning. It was she who offered them your place. She didn't seem to think you would come back. Maybe she was hoping we would take them in or something. Maybe. Frankly, we have no idea what she was thinking. It's none of our business anyway."

Yes, the house—Julie's and mine—was actually Madame Isabelle's, as per our contract. Julie and I had had our chance. Now it was someone else's turn. With a bit of a disappointment at having been dislodged so easily, I said, "She did tell me Adam would be living there..."

My voice trailed off. The subject of Adam and the blue person had distracted me from the fact that they were actually staying at my—our—house. But then with the Naiads by my side, the old feelings were resurfacing like a badly concealed murder victim. True, Mme Isa was probably right about me not going back to Genus Island. Our contract, whatever it had been, was null by then. She said so herself. But something about it all didn't seem fair. Anguish, remorse, and frustration gnawed at my heart. How dare Mme Isabelle dismiss seven years of my life with a simple wave of her hand? Just like that? Julie and I had built the house, installed the outhouse, the garden. What about the animals? I hoped that Ralph would shun the new arrivals. I couldn't stand the thought he might be friends with the newcomers. But then again, I remembered that our animals had been adopted by the Naiads anyway. Now I was angry at our past neighbours too. I wasn't sure why, but I was. It seemed like everyone from Julie to Mme Isa, to Adam/Ève and Claude, to Charlotte, Kent, and now the Naiads ... all had betrayed me in some way.

I wanted to chase my old neighbours out of Sonia's apartment. I wanted them and everybody out of my life. Forever. How could they let this betrayal happen? They would all have to go. All of them. However, I still had to show up at work. I would just have to avoid Mme Isabelle Côté. I would have to let go of any hope of my boss and I ever being friends. Not that it would have been a possibility anyway. I would just show up, work, and leave. And collect my cheque. Easy.

I wouldn't shun Sonia, of course. Or Bourgeon. They were my future. Maybe. They were my only hope. I went for a walk. Alone.

I must have walked for hours. Then slowly, with the rain helping not so much by washing off my grudges but more because I had not dressed properly and was getting cold and soaked, I forced myself to realize how unfair I was being. Life is just that, life. Adam/Ève and blue-person Claude had probably had their share of prejudice throughout their whole life. Who was I to judge? "We are one," my favourite song in times of doubt came up again. I turned around. By the time I flew back up into my three friends' arms, drenched but grinning like a madwoman, I was singing at the top of my lungs. After they got over an initial surprise, their own good humour soon took over. Before long, we were passing a huge doobie around, a guitar appeared from somewhere, and with spoons gleaned from the kitchen drawers, we were making music and being friends again.

Our happiness lasted about a week. At first, I was really proud to show off my city to my friends. I took them to the angel on Avenue du Parc, told them about the summer tam-tam, I took them to Saint-Laurent Street to shop for exotic imported food and to rue Mont-Royal for cool clothes. We went to the famous poutinerie where I had not-shared one with Bourgeon, and to the gay village.

When all was said and done, one dark evening we just stared at each other. In those five short months since I left Genus, I had changed and they had not. With their long unkempt hair, body odours, and an almost preachy kind of attitude regarding where our society was headed, they seemed provincial to me. Out of place. Like the bright green tree-frogs that, once their pond dries up for summer, have to hide in the grey mud just to survive.

I felt criticized. Despite my having kept up my recycling practices and my faithfulness to my vow of simplicity, in their opinion, I was leading a sinful life. I had let myself be absorbed by the tentacles of the big city. There I was, living with a flush toilet, using disposable tissues with plastic in it, drinking bad water, breathing bad air, and contributing to it all with my acquiescence. And reading newspapers for a job!! Discouraged, I didn't dare argue.

It came to be one day, once the novelty of urban excitement wore off, that there was nothing else to say. I was welcome to come back home whenever I wanted. I could move in and be one of them. All I had to do was to say yes. In the meantime, they were headed home before the weather got much worse. Those mountain passes could be treacherous. Or maybe they would do a loop through the States and avoid the snow. What a brilliant idea. Lost in the planning of their return home, they completely ignored me. I got up. They looked as if they had just noticed me. Oh. Did I want to come?

For a short minute, I was tempted. As if he had felt my dilemma, Farinelli jumped on my lap with that funny squeak of his. I looked at my friends as realistically as I could. Calypso and Minerva were in a relationship. Diane … I've always been a bit scared of her. In my mind, I went through the ten other women from the Naiads that had been left behind. Maybe it was the particular mood I was in, but none of them excited me.

I smiled and told my friends I would stay. For Sonia—not like they believed my story anyway—for... just because. I almost said I still wanted to talk to Julie—oops Julien—but thought better of it. We had womanaged to avoid the subject for a week. I wasn't going to break that particular silence.

By the time the Girlz left, I was almost relieved. I was sure they were happy to go too. Their fluttering colourful skirts and shawls like that of a gang of old-fashioned gypsies is the last image I have of them. I did and still do wish them well. I cannot help but wonder how long it would have taken them to realize I am no more. I can only wonder. Had I known what sad fate was waiting for me in Montréal, I would have run away with them. Hands down. Maybe I could have escaped my destiny, if such a thing exists. I can only wonder about that too.

CHAPTER 18

On November 29, 2001, nine days after the Girlz left and the day I died, I woke up early. A feeling that something big, something very important was going to happen came over me. With a trepidation I hadn't felt for a long time, I jumped out of bed. I cranked Sonia's old-fashioned thermostat up to 72° Fahrenheit. I don't know how much that would have made in Celsius, but I guessed from where the number was on the dial that it was going to be hot and expensive. Promising myself it was going to be a single occurrence, I thought I might offer some money to Sonia when she came back, to pay for my extravagance. She would be sure to shrug it off anyway. That's the kind of woman I knew her to be. Then I remembered my shopping list of all the food I had devoured on my first day. There were only two days left for me to replenish the larder, and I hadn't even started. Confident that the shopping would get done in time, I found the list and put it in my wallet.

Sonia had a very nice little espresso maker. I splurged on a double Americano, half caffeinated, half-decaf. My personal favourite. There was a third of a *filone* bread on the counter. After cutting it in two lengthwise and opening it like a book, I topped the soft middle with slices of *Brie triple-crème* and smeared it all with big dollops of fig jam. Sonia did not have a microwave oven. Another thing we had in common. I lay the two sides of my open-face sandwich on the little tray of the toaster oven and grilled it to perfection.

A copy of *Le Devoir* newspaper had already been delivered to Sonia's door by Louisa, who lived with her daughter Marie-Reine, coincidentally in Charlotte's building. Louisa was not the crazy one across the landing. She lived one floor below Charlotte's. She was a single mom. Every day except Sundays, Louisa would deliver the paper in the neighbourhood before she went to work as a waitress for lunch and dinner at a popular deli downtown. She was a hard worker, more than I had ever been, even on Genus. Leafing through the small paper, looking for the classifieds, I wished her well.

Actually, it was more than that. I wanted to be friends with her. I started to hope she would be able to make space for friendship. She was so busy. Maybe I could lighten her load and help her look after her daughter, for example. Maybe her daughter would play with Sonia's little Ariane. We would all form a neat little extended family. But other than a vague feeling of sympathy towards Louisa and seven-year-old Marie-Reine, I knew very little of them. Still, I felt I would do anything just to have her—or most anyone for that matter—as a friend. I resolved to contact them.

Meanwhile, as I was planning the next stage of my new life, my initial feeling of excitement at the prospect of a new day completely evaporated. It got replaced by a deep feeling of desperation, coming from seemingly nowhere. A rapidly rising loneliness tore at my ribcage as my heart ached, begging to be let free. I crumpled the newspaper I still had in my hands and dropped my heavy head on the kitchen table, tears streaming from my eyes. I tried to calm down. Then with limbs that seemed to be made of lead, I got up and put on some music from Sonia's collection. It took the whole length of a Chopin recital to finally soothe me.

I had to take action. Failing to materialize an instant friend, I could at least look for an apartment. I did not want for Sonia to offer me shelter just because she felt sorry for me. I would need my own place, one where I could invite people, anyone I wanted. Sonia would have to be the first guest. She could easily fill my lonely nights. Inevitably, I got lost on a Sonia-tangent. She did offer me a place to stay. Maybe it was not entirely out of pity. Maybe she would not share her bed, I thought—well, not right away, at least—but there was that one locked room. I could easily make it mine. Was that the room she was going to offer me? But what about Ariane? Was she even her daughter? A niece, perhaps? There were no toys or even girl's clothes anywhere in the apartment. Why? I was so utterly confused.

As I was witnessing the two hemispheres of my brain fighting out their arguments, I remembered that I hadn't kept up my yoga practice. The last time I had unfurled a mat was before the Girlz came. Of course, there had been no space while they were visiting. And once they were gone, I had already taken up the bad habit of eating my breakfast pretty much as soon as I got up. Then by the time I remembered to keep up my practice, my belly would be too full. Those forward bends and inversions would have been murder.

On that particular day, despite the fact that I'd had my breakfast, I fetched Sonia's yoga mat, rolled up her pink and blue beveled Chinese rug, pushed the coffee-table aside, and got to work. I would get myself in shape for me and especially for Sonia.

After picking a CD with the most appropriate-looking picture, I did four Sun Salutations to the music, alternating sides with my initiating foot. Then, animated by some rebellious spirit, I moved away from any classic asanas. Twirling, jumping, pirouetting, I let my body go wherever it wanted to. The result, I hoped, would be some sort of ritualistic Tantra-inspired dance that I dedicated to the woman of my dreams.

Gradually, the knots that had piled up in my entire body started to release. I still could not execute any digestion-disturbing moves, but as long as I remained upright, I could dance some more, all the way to ecstasy like a dervish. I almost got there. Inspired, out of breath, I left the room as it was with the rug rolled up and the coffee-table pushed to the side, the yoga mat in the middle of the floor. On the next day and the one following, until Sonia came home, I would do some yoga first thing in the morning.

The CD had ended. I shut the perfect sound system off and sat down on the mat with the intention of closing my session with meditation. After three minutes or so I gave up. The new exciting day was calling me with images of all the great things I was going to do until Sonia came home.

In preparation, I washed my hair with my organic shampoo as per my new habit. I wore my favourite clothes of the moment: a retro, sky-blue pair of jeans with rhinestones on the pockets, a white silk shirt, and under them a brand-new black lace bra and matching panties that I had just bought for very special occasions. The time had come. This was going to be a very special day. I could tell. A pink sweater knitted by my mother out of thick wool completed my outfit. I felt so good I didn't even look into the mirror for fear of ruining my mood, in case the image I saw wouldn't match how appealing I felt. As a last touch of *coquetterie,* I slipped my stick of Kohl in my bag for later.

As if I knew somehow that I wasn't coming back I checked on the plants, watering can in hand. They were fine, as I had just watered them yesterday, but in my haste, I spilled some droplets on one of the African violet's leaves. I tried to mop up the mess but only ended up smearing the water in between the hairs. It seemed okay for the moment. I could only hope it would still be okay by the time Sonia came home.

Then I dusted most of the surfaces I could find, including the books and CDs, a job that I usually tried to avoid. The cats got extra food.

Finally, satisfied with my work, I donned my rain poncho, twirling it like a magician's cape, and crowned myself with a handmade virgin-wool tuque that the Girlz had brought me from Genus. I recognized the wool. It had come from their sheep. It still had their characteristic earthy animal smell. The Girlz had also gifted me with matching socks, which I didn't wear that day, as they were too thick to fit in my boots. Once I was duly attired, I sauntered down the flight of stairs and landed on the street. It was still littered with fallen maple leaves and became my personal yellow brick road on the way to the Land of Oz.

As I left the path to cross Avenue du Parc on my way downtown, I stopped for a moment to look at the angel pointing towards the eastern sky. Massive and silent, she seemed that day to be waiting for something, someone. To mask the vague uneasiness that I was suddenly feeling, I told myself she was waiting for her winter repose, for the blanket of snow that would cover her until the next year's summer craziness.

For some reason that seemed strange to me—and not knowing, of course, the fate that was waiting for me later that day—images from my past, near and far, started appearing in front of my eyes like a movie. Faces of people I knew, Rémi, Kent, Charlotte, and all the others, even Adam and the blue girl, Julie (of course) but not Julien, the Naiads. All of them. Sonia, Sonia, Sonia ... my mother...

I remember thinking it odd that I would see these images. There is, of course, the saying that most people see their entire lives in front of their eyes just a few moments before their death. It might have been exactly what was happening to me. But me not having any clue what was in store for me that day, I did not understand what was happening. I had no choice but to observe the images until they eventually faded of their own accord, much to my relief.

By the time I arrived at the office, I was feeling chatty and light-hearted again. Concentration was difficult. I had the giggles. By some curious twist of fate, everybody had shown up and seemed to be feeling good, even Mme Isabelle, who popped her head into the reading room wondering what all the jocularity was about. Even Kent, my seemingly lost friend, had apparently let go of his principles and given me a big smile and a hug. He invited me out for coffee. Hearing that, everybody else wanted to come too. Except for Mme Isa, who had to "mind the fort" as she put it, with a wan smile. I was secretly happy she declined. Some resentments have a way of showing up unexpectedly.

Our friendly little group walked to a popular café nearby. Despite the reality of the November weather, a Juney, last-day-of-school feeling seemed to pervade. We joked around about skipping school just like teenagers. Even the people who hadn't talked to each other for months seemed to be friends again. I assumed they had gotten over their bad sexual relationships with each other, judging by their bragging.

We all bathed in an atmosphere of conviviality, of reconciliation, of a hint of nostalgia. A lot of love. I spoke little. I was observing. I was mostly listening. Happy to be alive, happy for everything. I had finally found some new friends. I belonged. Sonia would come back in a few days. I was free from Julien. And from Julie too, since she no longer existed.

Our brunch stretched on until after three in the afternoon. A few people returned to work. Kent was one of them. It was the end of the month, and the firm was having her "period," as the end-of-the-month rush was usually called. The others such as myself who didn't have a report to write up took the rest of the day off.

I separated from the happy group and started to wander. Wandering was, by the way, one of my favourite (if rare) pastimes. For that activity to unfurl to perfection, one had to be tuned in. To what, I didn't exactly know. All I did know was that true wandering was not an everyday occurrence. You couldn't make it happen. It had to come to you. Then when it came, the feeling of belonging, of communion with one's environment, with the universe, would kick in. Everything would fall into place. Strangers would smile, the traffic would part to let you get across the street, you might even win something. Kind of like the best of orgasms or a super-cool acid trip but a thousand-fold better because you were lucid. Completely.

I was feeling lucky, like I was riding the crest of a wave on top of an ocean of infinite possibilities. My solar plexus was humming. And yes, proof that I was tuned in, complete strangers were actually smiling at me and I would return their smile. All the streetlights at each intersection I wanted to cross were green. Even the grey sky intermittently opened up, revealing its true brilliant blue beyond.

My steps took me to *le Vieux Montréal*. For a short minute, I was disappointed. It was dinnertime by then, as my stomach didn't fail to remind me, but all the *restos* around would be very expensive. I could blow a week's wages on a lavish dinner, but I would feel like a loser for splurging all by myself. I would save the fancy dinner for Sonia. She was worth two week's wages, plus champagne. Meanwhile, I brazenly took my fate in my own hands and walked to Chinatown, hoping to find the best soup, or to resume my perfect wandering, for the perfect soup to find me. On my way, I bought a lottery ticket. Just in case.

Dark had already settled into the evening sky. The neon light of a tiny resto beckoned me through the late November drizzly fog. I remembered this place from my distant past. It was very popular for a while, because some local celebrities had recommended it. Hard to find, as you could only access it through an alley, it reminded me of one of those story-book places that only the pure of heart or the lucky can find. And I did. I entered without hesitation. Inside, happy, noisy clusters of people were already crowded around a smattering of round tables, chowing down on huge aromatic dishes under the steamy greenish-yellow light of blinking overhead neon. Being the only one alone, I crouched in the corner near the washrooms at a table just vacated by one of the employees.

As I was studying the greasy, worn menu, I noticed two shapes, one dark and the other one light, in my peripheral vision. The dark shape, almost diabolic, appeared more like a shadow than a real person. The other light one seemed almost ethereal, like an angel in comparison. They both sat down at my small table, right in front of me. I lowered my menu.

My face split in two with the biggest grin I've had for a long time. The dark devil in front of me was my friend Mike. I hadn't seen him since he took me to the cemetery, oh it must have been a dozen years before. On that day, a beautiful sunny May afternoon, as he casually suggested we go for a stroll through the cemetery, he also confided in me that he only took his favourite people there. I didn't believe him as we had just met. I do remember having been flattered, in an odd sort of way. It was also the day we saw the transvestite digging up a grave, which was just as odd. For Mike, always on the lookout for the bizarre, it would have been an everyday occurrence.

Obviously on that day in November in the restaurant, I did not see anything odd about the fact that I was meeting a devilish friend I had gone to the cemetery with ten years previously. Who knows? Maybe for those who might be looking for signs, he could really have been my Angel of Death, sent to me by the cosmos to guide me to the other side. But I could not possibly have any clue about any of that.

The other person, the light one, was no other than Stéphane. He looked like some kind of elf-angel that night. And to me, totally oblivious to the fate that was awaiting me, all I saw were two interesting, albeit a bit unusual companions to have dinner with. I was delighted.

Oh yes, I remembered. Mike and Stéphane knew each other. I couldn't help but wonder if Mike had heard of my one-afternoon stand with Stéphane. I didn't care, really. It had all seemed like a dream. As far as dreams go, they do not repeat themselves, not exactly. Stéphane, according to his nature, stayed quiet throughout the meal and left all the talking to Mike. Every now and then, he would throw me a knowing glance which I did my best to ignore.

And an interesting talk it was. Mike, as I remembered, always had some very unusual stories to tell. I suspected that he would exaggerate, maybe even lie a little for the sake of whichever tale he happened to pull out of his vast répertoire. But I didn't mind as he could spin quite a good yarn. He hadn't changed. Except for a few white hairs scattered throughout his mass of curly black hair, he was the same devil I had known, and I told him so. He returned my comment by complimenting me on how radiant I looked and how I hadn't changed either. I didn't believe him, but again, I unashamedly accepted the compliment. I felt very comfortable in my two friends' presence. In my naiveté, I thanked Dame Fate for having sent them my way to crown my perfect day.

We ordered a giant bowl of seafood wonton soup with three bowls. It was so good I completely forgot that I don't like sharing food. We even fed each other some choice morsels with our chopsticks, which practice I have heard is considered rude in many Asian cultures. If that is true, we must have broken the rules several times that night with the opulence of dish after dish that followed: BBQ duck, Ma Po Tofu, and Buddha's Delight with its seven kinds of mushrooms.

When we finally got our fortune cookies, I got a promise of a long prosperous life. I kept it and put it in my wallet, alongside the lottery ticket and my shopping list. I made a mental note to myself to share the loot with my friends if I won. Mike's cookie predicted that he was going to meet a long-lost true friend. We laughed in recognition. Stéphane got some wise words from Confucius. I forget what they were.

Then, our meal eaten, I walked with my friends to the Saint-Laurent Métro to bid them what I thought to be a temporary good-bye. As I stood there on the street, watching them through the heavy glass doors as they made their way towards the escalators, I saw a bizarre vision flash in front of my bewildered eyes. It seemed that Stéphane had suddenly grown wings—or was it someone else from some other mysterious realm? This being, whomever it was, instead of going down and disappearing like a normal person intending to take the *Métro* should have, seemed to be ascending through some pale mist, up to who knows where. Meanwhile, to my great astonishment, Mike, or a semblance of him, had miraculously sprouted shiny bat-like wings. This second being made their way down into the bowels of the Métro until they disappeared.

I blinked. The vision had vanished. Had it really happened or had I made it up in a strange foreboding vision? I didn't know, then. I still don't know. All that I remember is that I found myself staring through the heavy glass doors at the dark emptiness of the escalators for what seemed like an eternity. Maybe I was, actually, gazing at eternity.

Some irresistible force drew me backwards. Was it fear or fate? I still don't know. All that I know for sure is that I found myself stepping off the sidewalk and crossing the street backwards, with my gaze still turned towards the empty *bouche de Métro*. Apart from the fact that I don't remember if I looked both ways for the possibility of traffic, it would have been, really, a banal movement on an ordinary day. Except that, in this case, this day was not so ordinary for me. Why did Claire cross the road? To get away from a bizarre vision? But it was long gone. All had returned to normal. There was no threat to me or to any one else who might have dared find themselves in the drizzly fog on that November night.

There was no need for me to go to the other side of the street. Sonia's place, albeit quite a few blocks further up the street, was on the Métro side. I would have had to cross the street again to get home. I didn't even like this other side of Saint-Laurent where I found myself. I never walked on it. It was darker even in the daytime, and there were fewer shops, and the ones there were less interesting. All the good stuff happened on the other side, the side I had retreated from. So again, why did I unexpectedly cross the street? The answer to that, much like the one involving the proverbial chicken, is open to interpretation. To get to the other side? What other side? And why? So I could meet my fate? I don't know the answer to that. All I do know is that I crossed the shiny pavement. Backwards and without looking. Luckily, there was no traffic. None at all. Seemingly that was not the time or place I was to meet my demise. Yet. One other major coincidence had yet to happen.

Fuelled by the energy of what I thought to be my perfect day, I trundled on up the silent hill past the rows of dark buildings that, even if I had not known what fate was awaiting me, have always appeared gloomy to me. I continued to put one foot ahead of the other slowly, like a stubborn donkey, trying to save my breath, all the way up to Sherbrooke Street towards a livelier scene, then safely home to Sonia's. Once there I was going to treat myself to a well-deserved steaming cup of sweet hot chocolate.

Just before I reached the St-Laurent and Sherbrooke Street intersection at the top of the hill, and as I was about to pass the massive *Salle de Spectacles* on the opposite side of the street, I saw a familiar silhouette briskly approaching the front door. My heart stopped for a second. The figure was that of Julien. This time I knew it without a shadow of a doubt. Judging by how magical my day had been unfolding, I was not surprised in the least at seeing him.

My soul jumped out of my body towards him. The time had come. We absolutely needed to talk. I had to tell him something, anything. Tell him that I knew: that I loved him anyway. That I loved him, pure and simple. Maybe we could be friends. Maybe we could do this transition thing together. I could gradually, with time and little by little, get used to her being him.... I would witness the unfolding of the chrysalis into a beautiful butterfly, colourful, self-confident, and most of all, free...

Julien had grabbed the handle of the massive door. Soon he would be swallowed by the building. Ensconced as I was in the shadows on the opposite side of the street from him, I was quite sure he hadn't seen me yet. I felt the urge to yell his name as I have always known it: *"Julie!!"*

No, that wouldn't work. I had to use his new name or he would ignore my cries. Out of breath from having just climbed the big hill, I tried to clear my throat to yell his new name: Julien

I did not call him. I couldn't. I knew it wouldn't work. As I knew this new him, he would just run away from me. Again. I had to get closer, so he could not get away so easily this time. I was shaking like a leaf.

Meanwhile, I could see in my left peripheral vision that the light at the Sherbrooke and St-Laurent intersection had just changed to green. My main gaze was still fixed on Julien. He was standing in the doorway, light streaming out from around him like a halo. Mesmerized, I took my left foot off the sidewalk and stepped down onto the street. The driver of the black truck coming on my right must have been completely busy with trying to make the hill. Maybe he was driving a standard and wanted to catch the light so that he would not have to make a hill start. Or maybe he was simply tired and was rushing home. At any rate, he must have been pressing the gas to the floor. As far as I was concerned, he appeared out of nowhere. For him, I must have appeared out of nowhere too.

What can I say? It was a drizzly, foggy November night. There was no traffic on Sherbrooke. The driver obviously did not see me. I certainly did not see him. By the time I heard him come near, he had already hit me. I died on the spot. I didn't suffer.

I was so busy dying that I didn't have time to notice if Julien was even aware of what was happening. Nevertheless, he was, in some strange sort of way, instrumental in my premature death. I do not hold any grudges. How can I? You see, I was, and still am, open to the idea that we are all voluntary players in the game called life. There might be as much of a possibility that we each create our own reality than the other way around. We have free choice. Or do we only think we have?

Paradoxically, there might also be some universal laws over which we have no control. We could call those forces "destiny." Those forces that pair up with the Laws of Nature like velocity and gravity and the plethora of natural phenomena like earthquakes and Ice Ages or the theory that we are falling into the sun. It could be simply that my turn was up. The luck of the draw. The way the cookie crumbles.

Some might argue that I still had my life before me. For my part, I say that I mostly avoided getting old.

✷   ✷   ✷

Contrary to popular belief, it seems to me that the dead have no extra-sensory powers. This residual of an "I," this leftover "me," certainly doesn't have any. I have no idea what happened to my body. My memories of my life are just a distant, progressively fading movie.

I can only assume that, other than the truck driver and the medical attendants who must have certified my death, it would have been Sonia who might have been the first from my friends and acquaintances to find out what happened to me. Upon her arrival home, she might have thought I had disappeared for a few days so that she could settle back into her place. But she knew undoubtedly that I was madly infatuated with her. Surely, I would come back if only to see her one last time and to get my stuff out. Especially since there was no note.

She would have found the yoga mat laid out, her Chinese carpet rolled up, the coffee-table pushed to the side, and a crumpled newspaper lying on the kitchen floor. My personal belongings would be scattered around the place. Some of her non-perishable food would still be missing. She might even notice the disappearance of the Veuve Cliquot champagne. The cats might look upset. The African violet might be dead. The heat might have turned the apartment into a tropical mess.

I hope Sonia is not mad at me. And more importantly, I hope she will miss me (oh, just a little bit) when she eventually learns that I died. Maybe she was the one who ended up identifying my body at the morgue. Her training as a social worker would have kicked in. She would have been smart enough to have figured out to look for me in hospitals, then at the morgue.

If indeed she did identify me, I can only hope my body did not disgust her too much. Even being dead, one can still retain a modicum of pride, no?

It is highly possible that Sonia would have only mentioned the professional side of her relationship with me, if she ever talked to the police. I can only hope she will not get into trouble for harbouring me for a few months. As for her lack of response to my evident crush on her, I hold no grudges. Sure, I would have liked to occupy a more important place in her life, but that's just the way it went. In a way, I cannot but understand. At least we avoided breaking my heart, which was bound to happen. Of all the people I am curious about what will happen to, Sonia is the first one. Julien in this case will have to content himself with being my *numéro deux*.

Then there would be the people at the office. Since I had finished my work for November, they would not be expecting to see me for a few days, a week at most. We kept our own hours. I could have bought myself a computer and worked at home, due to bad weather. Except for my supervisor Helga, no one would really notice I didn't show up until maybe the end of December, when the articles were due for the reports. I wonder how Kent would feel about my death once he heard about it. He might be a bit sad. But then again, he had his own battles to fight.

I don't even know if Charlotte would have gotten wind of my demise. Or the Naiads. Or even Julien. Not knowing any of these facts is of no consequence anyway.

Soon, any events relating to me from that era will have completely faded away. Already, earthly persons and events seem insignificant, minuscule compared to the vastness of the universe. If reincarnation exists, if our destinies are intertwined, I might see Sonia again and some of the others. Will I recognize her or any of them? Maybe I could get another chance with Sonia. Maybe. Who knows? Maybe Julien and I would get another round.

Or I could be other than human. I could be a lily. I could be seen at the Jean-Talon market next summer. Sonia or Julien or even Bourgeon would find me so beautiful they would have to buy me and take me home. And then there I would be, filling the room with my heady perfume every day at dusk. For a while.

Or … (oh horror!) … I could come back as a slug in my old garden on Genus, according to my karma for having killed so many.

What I suspect, however, is that I might not remember this past life, the one about this person called Claire. Or I might only have dim memories like some vague *déjà-vus*. Now that my story is told, it is nothing but one story amongst billions of others.

EPILOGUE

Excerpt from Julien's journal:

Saturday, November 30, 2001

The show last night was great. Kid Koala. Claire would have liked it. Speaking of whom, some really bizarre thing happened as I came back out of the cabaret. I found Claire's wallet. Yes, as strange as it might seem, there it was. Lying by the side of the pavement. I almost passed it by. It was the God's eye on it, that Indian symbol on it, that caught my attention. I recognized it right away. It was kind of staring at me actually.

So, to get back to Claire's wallet. The insides of it I mean. There was not much in it other than Claire's BC medical card—that's how I knew for sure, right off the bat, that the wallet was hers—then a laminated four-leaf clover she found in our garden and had immortalized for good luck. There was some small change plus a fortune from a Chinese cookie. It said, "You will have a long and prosperous life." I can understand why she kept the tiny piece of paper. She was a bit superstitious like that. There was also a bizarre grocery list. Not the kind of things she would eat. Or used to eat anyway. I figure she's changed her diet.

And then check this out: There was also a lottery ticket. I know it's not really my business, but I checked the number in this morning's

315

paper. Wow. She's won $80,000! Not quite the big one but still. Nothing to turn your nose up at. Wow again. And Wowzers. She hasn't even signed the ticket yet. But I know the money is hers. The fortune-cookie was right.

I also know Claire well enough to know that she'll share. That's the kind of person she is. She won't share food with you. But otherwise, she's very generous. And fair. After all, I'm the one who found her wallet. So anyway, I bet she will help me out with my transition. A gift from fate if one was to believe in such things. Now all I have to do is track her down...

☆　☆　☆

CPSIA information can be obtained
at www.ICGtesting.com
Printed in the USA
LVHW110136190422
716593LV00018B/610/J

9 781525 596025